JEANETTE WINTERSON

Written on the Body

Jeanette Winterson was born in Lancashire in 1959, grew up in Lancashire, and now lives in London. *Oranges Are Not the Only Fruit* won the Whitbread Award for best first novel; her adaptation of *Oranges* for BBC television has won her prizes around the world, including a British Academy of Film and Television Arts award for best drama. Her novel *The Passion* won the John Llewellyn Rhys Memorial Prize. When *Sexing the Cherry* was published in 1989, Jeanette Winterson received the E. M. Forster Award from the American Academy and Institute of Arts and Letters. Her most recent work is *The World and Other Places,* a collection of short stories.

Written on the Body

Jeanette Winterson

VINTAGE INTERNATIONAL
Vintage Books
A Division of Random House, Inc.
New York

FIRST VINTAGE INTERNATIONAL EDITION, FEBRUARY 1994

Copyright © 1992 *by Great Moments Ltd*

All rights reserved under International and Pan-American Copyright
Conventions Published in the United States by Vintage Books, a division
of Random House, Inc , New York Originally published in hardcover in
Great Britain by Jonathan Cape, London, in 1992 First published in the
United States by Alfred A Knopf, Inc , New York, in 1993

Library of Congress Cataloging-in-Publication Data
Winterson, Jeanette, 1959–
Written on the body/Jeanette Winterson —1st Vintage international ed
p   cm
ISBN 0-679-74447-9
1 Married women—England—Fiction I Title
[PR6073 I558W56 1994]
823'.914—dc20   93-23335
CIP

Author photograph © *Jillian Edelstein*

Manufactured in the United States of America
3579E864

for Peggy Reynolds with love

My thanks are due to Don and Ruth Rendell whose hospitality gave me the space to work. To Philippa Brewster for her editorial inspiration. To all those at Jonathan Cape who have worked so hard to produce this book.

Why is the measure of love loss?

It hasn't rained for three months. The trees are prospecting underground, sending reserves of roots into the dry ground, roots like razors to open any artery water-fat.

The grapes have withered on the vine. What should be plump and firm, resisting the touch to give itself in the mouth, is spongy and blistered. Not this year the pleasure of rolling blue grapes between finger and thumb juicing my palm with musk. Even the wasps avoid the thin brown dribble. Even the wasps this year. It was not always so.

I am thinking of a certain September: Wood pigeon Red Admiral Yellow Harvest Orange Night. You said, 'I love you.' Why is it that the most unoriginal thing we can say to one another is still the thing we long to hear? 'I love you' is always a quotation. You did not say it first and neither did I, yet when you say it and when I say it we speak like savages who have found three words and worship them. I did worship them but now I am alone on a rock hewn out of my own body.

CALIBAN You taught me language and my profit on't is
I know how to curse. The red plague rid you
For learning me your language.

Love demands expression. It will not stay still, stay silent, be good, be modest, be seen and not heard, no. It will break out in tongues of praise, the high note that smashes the glass and spills the liquid. It is no conservationist love. It is a big game hunter and you are the game. A curse on this game. How can you stick at a game when the rules keep changing? I shall call myself Alice and play croquet with the flamingoes. In Wonderland everyone cheats and love is Wonderland isn't it? Love makes the world go round. Love is blind. All you need is love. Nobody ever died of a broken heart. You'll get over it. It'll be different when we're married. Think of the children. Time's a great healer. Still waiting for Mr Right? Miss Right? and maybe all the little Rights?

It's the clichés that cause the trouble. A precise emotion seeks a precise expression. If what I feel is not precise then should I call it love? It is so terrifying, love, that all I can do is shove it under a dump bin of pink cuddly toys and send myself a greetings card saying 'Congratulations on your Engagement'. But I am not engaged I am deeply distracted. I am desperately looking the other way so that love won't see me. I want the diluted version, the sloppy language, the insignificant gestures. The saggy armchair of clichés. It's all right, millions of bottoms have sat here before me. The springs are well worn, the fabric smelly and familiar. I don't have to be frightened, look, my grandma and grandad did it, he in a stiff collar and club tie, she in white muslin straining a little at the life beneath. They did it, my parents did it, now I will do it won't I, arms outstretched, not to hold you, just to keep my balance, sleepwalking to that armchair. How happy we will be. How happy everyone will be. And they all lived happily ever after.

It was a hot August Sunday. I paddled through the shallows of the river where the little fishes dare their belly at the sun. On either side of the river the proper green of the grass had given way to a psychedelic splash-painting of virulent Lycra cycling shorts and Hawaiian shirts made in Taiwan. They were grouped the way families like to group; dad with the paper propped on his overhang, mum sagging over the thermos. Kids thin as seaside rock sticks and seaside rock pink. Mum saw you go in and heaved herself off the stripey fold-out camping stool. 'You should be ashamed of yourself. There's families out here.'

You laughed and waved, your body bright beneath the clear green water, its shape fitting your shape, holding you, faithful to you. You turned on your back and your nipples grazed the surface of the river and the river decorated your hair with beads. You are creamy but for your hair your red hair that flanks you on either side.

'I'll get my husband to see to you. George come here. George come here.'

'Can't you see I'm watching television?' said George without turning round.

You stood up and the water fell from you in silver streams. I didn't think, I waded in and kissed you. You put your arms around my burning back. You said, 'There's nobody here but us.'

I looked up and the banks were empty.

You were careful not to say those words that soon became our private altar. I had said them many times before, dropping them like coins into a wishing well, hoping they would make me come true. I had said them many times before but not to you. I had given them as forget-me-nots to girls who should have known better. I had used them as bullets and barter. I don't like to think of myself as an insincere person but if I say I love you and I don't mean it then what else am I? Will I cherish you, adore you, make way for you, make myself better for you, look at you and always see you, tell you the truth? And if love is not those things then what things?

August. We were arguing. You want love to be like this every day don't you? 92 degrees even in the shade. This intensity, this heat, sun like a disc-saw through your body. Is it because you come from Australia?

You didn't answer, just held my hot hand in your cool fingers and strode on easy in linen and silk. I felt ridiculous. I was wearing a pair of shorts with RECYCLE tattooed across one leg. I remembered vaguely that I had once had a girlfriend who thought it rude to wear shorts in front of public monuments. When we met I tethered my bike at Charing Cross and changed in the toilets before meeting her by Nelson's Column.

'Why bother?' I said. 'He only had one eye.'

'I've got two,' she said and kissed me. Wrong to seal illogic with a kiss but I do it myself all the time.

You didn't answer. Why do human beings need answers? Partly I suppose because without one, almost any one, the question itself soon sounds silly. Try standing in front of a class and asking what is the capital of Canada. The eyes stare back at you, indifferent, hostile, some of them look the other way. You say it again. 'What is the capital of Canada?' While you wait in the silence, absolutely the victim, your own mind doubts itself. What *is* the capital of Canada? Why Ottawa and not Montreal? Montreal is much nicer, they do a better espresso, you have a friend who lives there. Anyway, who cares what the capital is, they'll probably change it next year. Perhaps Gloria will be at the swimming pool tonight. And so on.

Bigger questions, questions with more than one answer, questions without an answer are harder to cope with in silence. Once asked they do not evaporate and leave the mind to its serener musings. Once asked they gain dimension and texture, trip you on the stairs, wake you at night-time. A black hole sucks up its surroundings and even light never escapes. Better then to ask no questions? Better then to be a contented pig than an unhappy Socrates? Since factory farming is tougher on pigs than it is on philosophers I'll take a chance.

We walked back to our rented room and lay on one of the single beds. In rented rooms from Brighton to Bangkok, the bedspread never matches the carpet and the towels are too thin. I put one underneath you to save the sheet. You were bleeding.

We had rented this room, your idea, to try to be together for more than dinner or a night or a cup of tea behind the library. You were still married and although I don't have many scruples I've learned to have some about that blessed state. I used to think of marriage as a plate-glass window just begging for a brick. The self-exhibition, the self-satisfaction, smarminess, tightness, tight-arsedness. The way married couples go out in fours like a pantomime horse, the men walking together at the front, the women trailing a little way behind. The men fetching the gin and tonics from the bar while the women take their handbags to the toilet. It doesn't have to be like that but mostly it is. I've been through a lot of marriages. Not down the aisle but always up the stairs. I began to realise I was hearing the same story every time. It went like this.

Interior. Afternoon.
  A bedroom. Curtains half drawn. Bedclothes thrown back.
A naked woman of a certain age lies on the bed looking at the
ceiling. She wants to say something. She's finding it difficult.
A cassette recorder is playing Ella Fitzgerald, 'Lady Sings the
Blues'.

NAKED WOMAN   I wanted to tell you that I don't usually
do this. I suppose it's called committing
adultery. (*She laughs.*) I've never done it
before. I don't think I could do it again.
With someone else that is. Oh I want to
do it again with you. Over and over
again. (*She rolls on to her stomach.*) I
love my husband you know. I do love
him. He's not like other men. I couldn't
have married him if he was. He's different, we've got a lot in common. We
talk.

Her lover runs a finger over the bare lips of the naked
woman. Lies over her, looks at her. The lover says nothing.

NAKED WOMAN   If I hadn't met you I suppose I *would*
be looking for something. I might have
done a degree at the Open University. I
wasn't thinking of this. I never wanted
to give him a moment's worry. That's
why I can't tell him. Why we must be
careful. I don't want to be cruel and
selfish. You do see that don't you?

Her lover gets up and goes to the toilet. The naked woman
raises herself on her elbow and continues her monologue in the
direction of the en suite bathroom.

NAKED WOMAN   Don't be long darling. (*She pauses.*) I've
               tried to get you out of my head but I
               can't seem to get you out of my flesh.
               I think about your body day and night.
               When I try to read it's you I'm reading.
               When I sit down to eat it's you I'm eat-
               ing. When he touches me I think about
               you. I'm a middle-aged happily married
               woman and all I can see is your face.
               What have you done to me?

Cut to en suite bathroom. The lover is crying. End scene.

It's flattering to believe that you and only you, the
great lover, could have done this. That without you, the
marriage, incomplete though it is, pathetic in many ways,
would have thrived on its meagre diet and if not thrived at
least not shrivelled. It has shrivelled, lies limp and unused,
the shell of a marriage, its inhabitants both fled. People
collect shells though don't they? They spend money on
them and display them on their window ledges. Other
people admire them. I've seen some very famous shells
and blown into the hollows of many more. Where I've
left cracking too severe to mend the owners have simply
turned the bad part to the shade.

See? Even here in this private place my syntax has
fallen prey to the deceit. It was not I who did those
things; cut the knot, jemmied the lock, made off with
goods not mine to take. The door was open. True, she
didn't exactly open it herself. Her butler opened it for her.
His name was Boredom. She said, 'Boredom, fetch me a
plaything.' He said, 'Very good ma'am,' and putting on
his white gloves so that the fingerprints would not show

he tapped at my heart and I thought he said his name was Love.

You think I'm trying to wriggle out of my responsibilities? No, I know what I did and what I was doing at the time. But I didn't walk down the aisle, queue up at the Registry Office and swear to be faithful unto death. I wouldn't dare. I didn't say, 'With this ring I thee wed.' I didn't say, 'With my body I thee worship.' How can you say that to one person and gladly fuck another? Shouldn't you take that vow and break it the way you made it, in the open air?

Odd that marriage, a public display and free to all, gives way to that most secret of liaisons, an adulterous affair.

I had a lover once, her name was Bathsheba. She was a happily married woman. I began to feel as though we were crewing a submarine. We couldn't tell our friends, at least she couldn't tell hers because they were his too. I couldn't tell mine because she asked me not to do so. We sank lower and lower in our love-lined lead-lined coffin. Telling the truth, she said, was a luxury we could not afford and so lying became a virtue, an economy we had to practise. Telling the truth was hurtful and so lying became a good deed. One day I said, 'I'm going to tell him myself.' This was after two years, two years where I thought that she must leave eventually eventually, eventually. The word she used was 'monstrous'. Monstrous to tell him. Monstrous. I thought of Caliban chained to his pitted rock. 'The red plague rid you for learning me your language.'

Later, when I was freed from her world of double meanings and masonic signs I did turn thief. I had never stolen from her, she had spread her wares on a blanket and asked me to choose. (There was a price but in brackets.) When we were over, I wanted my letters back. My copyright she said but her property. She had said the same about my body. Perhaps it was wrong to climb into her lumber-room and take back the last of myself. They were easy to find, stuffed into a large padded bag, bearing the message on an Oxfam label that they were to be returned to me in the event of her death. A nice touch; he would no doubt have read them but then she would not have been there to take the consequences. And would I have read them? Probably. A nice touch.

I took them into the garden and burned them one by one and I thought how easy it is to destroy the past and how difficult to forget it.

Did I say this has happened to me again and again? You will think I have been constantly in and out of married women's lumber-rooms. I have a head for heights it's true, but no stomach for the depths. Strange then to have plumbed so many.

We lay on our bed in the rented room and I fed you plums the colour of bruises. Nature is fecund but fickle. One year she leaves you to starve, the next year she kills you with love. That year the branches were torn beneath the weight, this year they sing in the wind. There are no ripe plums in August. Have I got it wrong, this hesitant chronology? Perhaps I should call it Emma Bovary's eyes or Jane Eyre's dress. I don't know. I'm in another rented room now trying to find the place to go back to where things went wrong. Where I went wrong. You were driving but I was lost in my own navigation.

Nevertheless I will push on. There were plums and I broke them over you.

You said, 'Why do I frighten you?'

Frighten me? Yes you do frighten me. You act as though we will be together for ever. You act as though there is infinite pleasure and time without end. How can I know that? My experience has been that time always ends. In theory you are right, the quantum physicists are right, the romantics and the religious are right. Time without end. In practice we both wear a watch. If I rush at this relationship it's because I fear for it. I fear you have a door I cannot see and that any minute now the door will open and you'll be gone. Then what? Then what as I bang the walls like the Inquisition searching for a saint? Where will I find the secret passage? For me it'll just be the same four walls.

You said, 'I'm going to leave.'

I thought, Yes, of course you are, you're going back to the shell. I'm an idiot. I've done it again and I said I'd never do it again.

You said, 'I told him before we came away. I've told him I won't change my mind even if you change yours.'

This is the wrong script. This is the moment where I'm supposed to be self-righteous and angry. This is the moment where you're supposed to flood with tears and tell me how hard it is to say these things and what can you do and what can you do and will I hate you and yes you know I'll hate you and there are no question marks in this speech because it's a fait accompli.

But you are gazing at me the way God gazed at Adam and I am embarrassed by your look of love and possession and pride. I want to go now and cover myself with fig leaves. It's a sin this not being ready, this not being up to it.

You said, 'I love you and my love for you makes any other life a lie.'

Can this be true, this simple obvious message, or am I like those shipwrecked mariners who seize an empty bottle and eagerly read out what isn't there? And yet you are there, here, sprung like a genie to ten times your natural size, towering over me, holding me in your arms like mountain sides. Your red hair is blazing and you are saying, 'Make three wishes and they shall all come true. Make three hundred and I will honour every one.'

What did we do that night? We must have walked wrapped around each other to a café that was a church and eaten a Greek salad that tasted like a wedding feast. We met a cat who agreed to be best man and our bouquets were Ragged Robin from the side of the canal. We had about two thousand guests, mostly midges and we felt we were old enough to give ourselves away. It would have been good to have lain down there and made love under the moon but the truth is that, outside of the movies and Country and Western songs, the outdoors is an itchy business.

I had a girlfriend once who was addicted to starlit nights. She thought beds belonged in hospitals. Anywhere she could do it that wasn't pre-sprung was sexy. Show her a duvet and she switched on the television. I coped with this on campsites and in canoes, British Rail and Aeroflot. I bought a futon, eventually a gym mat. I had to lay extra-thick carpet on the floor. I took to carrying a tartan rug wherever I went, like a far-out member of the Scottish Nationalist Party. Eventually, back at the doctor's for the fifth time having a thistle removed, he said to me, 'You know, love is a very beautiful thing but there are clinics for people like you.' Now, it's a serious matter to have 'PERVERT' written on your NHS file and some indignities are just a romance too far. We had to say goodbye and although there were some things about her that I missed it was pleasant to walk in the country again without seeing every bush and shrub as a potential assailant.

Louise, in this single bed, between these garish sheets, I will find a map as likely as any treasure hunt. I will explore you and mine you and you will redraw me according to your will. We shall cross one another's boundaries and make ourselves one nation. Scoop me in your hands for I am good soil. Eat of me and let me be sweet.

June. The wettest June on record. We made love every day. We were happy like colts, flagrant like rabbits, dove-innocent in our pursuit of pleasure. Neither of us thought about it and we had no time to discuss it. The time we had we used. Those brief days and briefer hours were small offerings to a god who would not be appeased by burning flesh. We consumed each other and went hungry again. There were patches of relief, moments of tranquillity as still as an artificial lake, but always behind us the roaring tide.

There are people who say that sex isn't important in a relationship. That friendship and getting along are what coast you through the years. No doubt this is a faithful testimony but is it a true one? I had come to this feeling myself. One does after years of playing the Lothario and seeing nothing but an empty bank account and a pile of yellowing love-notes like IOUs. I had done to death the candles and champagne, the roses, the dawn breakfasts, the transatlantic telephone calls and the impulsive plane rides. I had done all of that to escape the cocoa and hot water bottles. And I had done all of that because I thought the fiery furnace must be better than central heating. I suppose I couldn't admit that I was trapped in a cliché every bit as redundant as my parents' roses round the door. I was looking for the perfect coupling; the never-sleep non-stop mighty orgasm. Ecstasy without end. I was deep in the slop-bucket of romance. Sure my bucket was a bit racier than most, I've always had a sports car, but you can't rev your way out of real life. That home girl gonna get you in the end. This is how it happened.

I was in the last spasms of an affair with a Dutch girl called Inge. She was a committed romantic and an anarcha-feminist. This was hard for her because it meant she couldn't blow up beautiful buildings. She knew the Eiffel Tower was a hideous symbol of phallic oppression but when ordered by her commander to detonate the lift so that no-one should unthinkingly scale an erection, her mind filled with young romantics gazing over Paris and opening aerograms that said Je t'aime.

We went to the Louvre to see a Renoir exhibition. Inge wore her guerilla cap and boots in case she should be mistaken for a tourist. She justified her ticket price as 'political research'. 'Look at those nudes,' she said, although I needed no urging. 'Bodies everywhere, naked, abused, exposed. Do you know how much those models were paid? Hardly the price of a baguette. I should rip the canvases from their frames and go to prison crying "Vive la resistance".'

Renoir's nudes are not at all the world's finest nudes, but

even so, when we came to his painting of La Boulangère, Inge wept. She said, 'I hate it because it moves me.' I didn't say that thus are tyrants made, I said, 'It's not the painter, it's the paint. Forget Renoir, hold on to the picture.'

She said, 'Don't you know that Renoir claimed he painted with his penis?'

'Don't worry,' I said. 'He did. When he died they found nothing between his balls but an old brush.'

'You're making it up.'

Am I?

Eventually we resolved Inge's aesthetic crisis by taking her Semtex to a number of carefully chosen urinals. They were all concrete Nissan huts, absolutely ugly and clearly functionaries of the penis. She said I wasn't fit to be an assistant in the fight towards a new matriarchy because I had QUALMS. This was a capital offence. Nevertheless, it wasn't the terrorism that flung us apart, it was the pigeons . . .

My job was to go into the urinals wearing one of Inge's stockings over my head. That in itself might not have attracted much attention, men's toilets are fairly liberal places, but then I had to warn the row of guys that they were in danger of having their balls blown off unless they left at once. A typical occasion would be to find five of them, cocks in hand, staring at the brown-streaked porcelain as though it were the Holy Grail. Why *do* men like doing everything together? I said (quoting Inge), 'This urinal is a symbol of patriarchy and must be destroyed.' Then (in my own voice), 'My girlfriend has just wired up the Semtex, would you mind finishing off?'

What would you do under the circumstances? Wouldn't impending castration followed by certain death be enough to cause a normal man to wipe his dick and run for it? They didn't. Over and over again they didn't, just flicked the drops contemptuously and swapped tips about the racing. I'm a mild-mannered sort but I don't like rudeness. On the job I found it helped to carry a gun.

I pulled it out of the waistband of my RECYCLE shorts (yes I've had them a long time) and pointed the barrel at the nearest dangle. This caused a bit of a stir and one said, 'You a loony or something?' He said that but he zipped his flies and buzzed off. 'Hands up *boys*,' I said. 'No, don't touch it, it'll have to dry in the wind.'

At that moment I heard the opening bars of 'Strangers in the Night'. It was Inge's signal to say we had five minutes ready or not. I motioned my doubting John Thomases through the door and broke into a run. I had to get into the mobile burger-bar Inge used as a hide-out. I threw myself in beside her and looked back from between the bread rolls. It was a beautiful explosion. A splendid explosion, much too good for a load of demi-johns. We were alone on the edge of the world, terrorists fighting the good fight for a fairer society. I thought I loved her and then came the pigeons.

She forbade me to telephone her. She said that telephones were for Receptionists, that is, women without status. I said, fine, I'll write. Wrong, she said. The Postal Service was run by despots who exploited non-union labour. What were we to do? I didn't want to live in Holland. She didn't want to live in London. How could we communicate?

Pigeons, she said.

That is how I came to rent the attic floor of the Pimlico Women's Institute. I don't feel a great deal about the Women's Institute either way, they were the first to campaign against aerosols that contain CFCs and they make a mean Victoria sponge but I don't really care. The point was that their attic faced roughly in the direction of Amsterdam.

I can tell by now that you are wondering whether I can be trusted as a narrator. Why didn't I dump Inge and head for a Singles Bar? The answer is her breasts.

They were not marvellously upright, the kind women wear as epaulettes, as a mark of rank. Neither were they pubescent playboy fantasies. They had done their share of time and begun to submit to gravity's insistence. The flesh was brown, the aureoles browner still, nipples bead black. My gypsy sisters I called them, though not to her. I had idolised them simply and unequivocally, not as a mother substitute nor a womb trauma, but for themselves. Freud didn't always get it right. Sometimes a breast is a breast is a breast.

Half a dozen times I picked up the phone. Six times I put it down again. Probably she wouldn't have answered. She would have had it disconnected but for her mother in Rotterdam. She never did explain how she would know it was her mother and not a Receptionist. How she would know it was a Receptionist and not me. I wanted to talk to her.

The pigeons, Adam, Eve and Kissmequick, couldn't manage Holland. Eve got as far as Folkestone. Adam dropped out and went to live in Trafalgar Square, another victory to Nelson. Kissmequick was scared of heights, a drawback for a bird, but the WI took him in as their mascot and rechristened him Boadicea. If he has not died yet he is still living. I don't know what happened to Inge's birds. They never came to me.

Then I met Jacqueline.

I had to lay a carpet in my new flat so a couple of friends came over to help. They brought Jacqueline. She was the mistress of one of them confidante of both. A sort of household pet. She traded sex and sympathy for £50 to tide her over the weekend and a square meal on Sunday. It was a civilised if brutal arrangement.

I had bought a new flat to start again from a nasty love affair that had given me the clap. Nothing wrong with my organs, this was emotional clap. I had to keep my heart to myself in case I infected somebody. The flat was large and derelict. I hoped I might rebuild it and myself at the same time. The clap-giver was still with her husband in their tasteful house but she'd slipped me £10,000 to help finance my purchase. Give/Lend was how she put it. Blood money was how I put it. She was buying off what conscience she had. I intended never to see her again. Unfortunately she was my dentist.

Jacqueline worked at the Zoo. She worked with small furry things that wouldn't be nice to visitors. Visitors who have paid £5 don't have a lot of patience for small furry things who are frightened and want to hide. It was Jacqueline's job to make everything bright and shiny again. She was good with parents, good with children, good with animals, good with disturbed things of every kind. She was good with me.

When she arrived, smart but not trendy, made-up but not conspicuously, her voice flat, her spectacles clownish, I thought, I have nothing to say to this woman. After Inge, and my brief addictive return to Bathsheba the dentist, I could not foresee pleasure in any woman, especially not one who had been victimised by her hairdresser. I thought, You can make the tea and I'll joke with my old friends about the perils of a broken heart and then you shall all three go home together happy in your good deed while I open a can of lentils and listen to 'Science Now' on the wireless.

Poor me. There's nothing so sweet as wallowing in it is there? Wallowing is sex for depressives. I should remember my grandmother's motto offered to the suffering as pastoral care. Not for her the painful dilemma, the agonised choice, 'Either shit or get off the pot.' That's right. At least I was between turds.

Jacqueline made me a sandwich and asked if I had any washing-up I'd like done. She came the next day and the day after that. She told me all about the problems facing lemurs in the Zoo. She brought her own mop. She worked nine to five Monday to Friday, drove a Mini and got her reading from book clubs. She exhibited no fetishes, foibles, freak-outs or fuck-ups. Above all she was single and she had always been single. No children and no husband.

I considered her. I didn't love her and I didn't want to love her. I didn't desire her and I could not imagine desiring her. These were all points in her favour. I had lately learned that another way of writing FALL IN LOVE is WALK THE PLANK. I was tired of balancing blindfold on a slender beam, one slip and into the unplumbed sea. I wanted the clichés, the armchair. I wanted the broad road and twenty-twenty vision. What's wrong with that? It's called growing up. Maybe most people gloss their comforts with a patina of romance but it soon wears off. They're in it for the long haul; the expanding waistline and the little semi in the suburbs. What's wrong with that? Late-night TV and snoring side by side into the millennium. Till death us do part. Anniversary darling? What's wrong with that?

I considered her. She had no expensive tastes, knew

nothing about wine, never wanted to be taken to the opera and had fallen in love with me. I had no money and no morale. It was a marriage made in heaven.

We agreed that we were good for each other whilst sitting in her Mini eating a Chinese take-away. It was a cloudy night so we couldn't look at the stars and besides, she had to be up for work at half past seven. I don't think we even slept together that night. It was the next night, freezing cold in November and I'd lit the fire. I'd arranged a few flowers because I like to do that anyway but when it came to getting out the tablecloth and finding the good glasses I couldn't be bothered. 'We're not like that,' I told myself. 'What we have is simple and ordinary. That's why I like it. Its worth lies in its neatness. No more sprawling life for me. This is container gardening.'

Over the months that followed my mind healed and I no longer moped and groaned over lost love and impossible choices. I had survived shipwreck and I liked my new island with hot and cold running water and regular visits from the milkman. I became an apostle of ordinariness. I lectured my friends on the virtues of the humdrum, praised the gentle bands of my existence and felt that for the first time I had come to know what everyone told me I would know; that passion is for holidays, not homecoming.

My friends were more circumspect than me. They regarded Jacqueline with a wary approval, regarding me as one might a mental patient who has been behaving for a few months. A few months? More like a year. I was rigorous, hard working and . . . and . . . what was that word beginning with B?

'You're bored,' my friend said.

I protested with all the fervour of a teetotaller caught glancing at the bottle. I was content. I had settled down.

'Still having sex?'

'Not much. It doesn't matter you know. We do now and then. When we both feel like it. We work hard. We don't have a lot of time.'

'Do you look at her and want her? Do you look at her and notice her?'

I lost my temper. Why was my happily settled, happily happy Heidi house coming under fire from a friend who had put up with all my broken hearts without a word of reproach? I struggled in my mind with all kinds of defences. Should I be hurt? Surprised? Should I laugh it off? I wanted to say something cruel to expiate my anger and to justify myself. But it's difficult with old friends; difficult because it's so easy. You know one another as well as lovers do and you have had less to pretend about. I poured myself a drink and shrugged.

'Nothing's perfect.'

The worm in the bud. So what? Most buds do have worms. You spray, you fuss, you hope the hole won't be too big and you pray for sunshine. Just let the flower bloom and no-one will notice the ragged edges. I thought that about me and Jacqueline. I was desperate to tend us. I wanted the relationship to work for not very noble reasons; after all it was my last ditch. No more racing for me. She loved me too, yes she did, in her uncomplicated undemanding way. She never bothered me when I said, 'Don't bother me,' and she didn't cry when I shouted at her. In fact she shouted back. She treated me like a big cat in the Zoo. She was very proud of me.

My friend said, 'Pick on someone your own size.'

And then I met Louise.

If I were painting Louise I'd paint her hair as a swarm

of butterflies. A million Red Admirals in a halo of movement and light. There are plenty of legends about women
turning into trees but are there any about trees turning
into women? Is it odd to say that your lover reminds
you of a tree? Well she does, it's the way her hair fills
with wind and sweeps out around her head. Very often
I expect her to rustle. She doesn't rustle but her flesh has
the moonlit shade of a silver birch. Would I had a hedge
of such saplings naked and unadorned.

At first it didn't matter. We got on well as a threesome. Louise was kind to Jacqueline and never tried to
come between us even as a friend. In any case, why
should she? She was happily married and had been so
for ten years. I had met her husband, a doctor with just
the right bedside manner, he was unremarkable but that
is not a vice.

'She's very beautiful isn't she?' said Jacqueline.

'Who?'

'Louise.'

'Yes, yes, I suppose she is if you like that sort of thing.'

'Do you like that sort of thing?'

'I like Louise yes. You know I do. So do you.'

'Yes.'

She went back to her *World Wildlife* magazine and
I went for a walk.

I was only going for a walk, any old walk, nowhere
special walk, but I found myself outside Louise's front
door. Dear me. What am I doing here? I was going the
other way.

I rang the bell. Louise answered. Her husband Elgin was
in his study playing a computer game called HOSPITAL.
You get to operate on a patient who shouts at you if
you do it wrong.

'Hello Louise. I was passing so I thought I might pop in.'

Pop in. What a ridiculous phrase. What am I, a cuckoo clock?

We went down the hall together. Elgin shot his head out of the study door. 'Hello there. Hello, hello, very nice. Be with you, little problem with the liver, can't seem to find it.'

In the kitchen Louise gave me a drink and a chaste kiss on the cheek. It would have been chaste if she'd taken her lips away at once, but instead she offered the obligatory peck and moved her lips imperceptibly over the spot. It took about twice as long as it should have done, which was still no time at all. Unless it's your cheek. Unless you're already thinking that way and wondering if someone else is thinking that way too. She gave no sign. I gave no sign. We sat and talked and listened to music and I didn't notice the dark or the lateness of the hour or the bottle now empty or my stomach now empty. The phone rang, obscenely loud, we both jumped. Louise answered it in her careful way, listened a moment then passed it over to me. It was Jacqueline. She said, very sad, not reproachful, but sad, 'I wondered where you were. It's nearly midnight. I wondered where you were.'

'I'm sorry. I'll get a cab now. I'll be with you soon.'

I stood up and smiled. 'Can you get me a cab?'

'I'll drive you,' she said. 'It would be nice to see Jacqueline.'

We didn't talk on the way back. The streets were quiet, there was nothing on the road. We pulled up outside my flat and I said thank you and we made an arrangement to meet for tea the following week and then she said, 'I've got tickets for the opera tomorrow night. Elgin can't come. Will you come?'

'We're supposed to be having a night in tomorrow.'
She nodded and I got out. No kiss.

What to do? Should I stay in with Jacqueline and hate it and start the slow motor of hating her? Should I make an excuse and go out? Should I tell the truth and go out? I can't have it all my own way, relationships are about compromise. Give and take. Maybe I don't want to stay in but she wants me to stay in. I should be glad to do that. It will make us stronger and sweeter. These were my thoughts as she slept beside me and if she had any fears she did not reveal them in those night-time hours. I looked at her lying trustfully in the spot where she had lain for so many nights. Could this bed be treacherous?

By morning I was bad tempered and exhausted. Jacqueline, ever cheerful, got into her mini and went to her mother's. At noon she rang to ask me over. Her mother wasn't well and she wanted to spend the night with her.

'Jacqueline,' I said. 'Stay the night. We'll see each other tomorrow.'

I felt reprieved and virtuous. Now I could sit in my own flat by myself and be pragmatic. Sometimes the best company is your own.

During the interval of *The Marriage of Figaro* I realised how often other people looked at Louise. On every side we were battered by sequins, dazed with gold. The women wore their jewellery like medals. A husband here, a divorce there, they were a palimpsest of love-affairs. The chokers, the brooch, the rings, the tiara, the studded watch that couldn't possibly tell the time to anyone without a magnifying glass. The bracelets, the ankle-chains, the veil hung with seed pearls and the earrings that far outnumbered the ears. All these jewels were escorted by amply cut grey suits and dashingly spotted ties. The ties twitched when Louise walked by and the suits pulled themselves in a little. The jewels glinted their own warning at Louise's bare throat. She wore a simple dress of moss green silk, a pair of jade earrings, and a wedding ring. 'Never take your eyes from that ring,' I told myself. 'Whenever you think you are falling remember that ring is molten hot and will burn you through and through.'

'What are you looking at?' said Louise.

'You bloody idiot,' said my friend. 'Another married woman.'

Louise and I were talking about Elgin.

'He was born an Orthodox Jew,' she said. 'He feels put upon and superior at the same time.'

Elgin's mother and father still lived in a 1930s semi in Stamford Hill. They had squatted it during the war and made a deal with the Cockney family who eventually came home to find the locks changed and a sign on the parlour door saying SABBATH. KEEP OUT. That was Friday night 1946. On Saturday night 1946 Arnold and Betty Small came face to face with Esau and Sarah Rosenthal. Money changed hands, or to be more precise, a certain amount of gold, and the Smalls went on to bigger things. The Rosenthals opened a chemist shop and refused to serve any Liberal or Reformed Jews.

'We are God's chosen people,' they said, meaning themselves.

From such humble, arrogant beginnings, Elgin was born. They had intended to call him Samuel but, while she was pregnant, Sarah visited the British Museum and, unmoved by the Mummies, came at last to the glory that was Greece. This need not have affected the destiny of her son but Sarah developed serious complications during her fourteen-hour labour and it seemed that she would die. Sweating and delirious, her head twisting from side to side, she could only repeat over and over again the single word ELGIN. Esau, drawn and down at heel, twisting his prayer shawl beneath his black coat, had a superstitious side. If that were his wife's last word then surely it should mean something, become something. And so the word was made flesh. Samuel became Elgin and Sarah did not die. She lived to produce thousands of gallons of chicken soup and whenever she ladled it into the bowl she said, 'Elgin, Jehovah spared me to serve you.'

And so Elgin grew up thinking that the world ought to serve him and hating the dark counter in his father's little shop and hating being set apart from the other boys but wanting it more than anything.

'You're nothing, you're dust,' said Esau. 'Raise yourself up and be a man.'

Elgin won a scholarship to an Independent school. He was small, narrow-chested, short-sighted and ferociously clever. Unfortunately his religion excluded him from Saturday games and whilst he managed to avoid persecution he courted isolation. He knew he was better than those square-shouldered upright beauty queens whose good looks and easy manners commanded affection and respect. Besides, they were all queer, and Elgin had seen them grappling one another, mouths open, cocks hard. No-one tried to touch him.

He fell in love with Louise when she beat him in single combat at the Debating Society finals. Her school was only a mile away from his and he had to walk past it on the way home. He took to walking past it at just the time when Louise was leaving. He was gentle with her, he tried hard, he didn't show off, he wasn't sarcastic. She had only been in England for a year and it was cold. They were both refugees and they found comfort in each other. Then Elgin went to Cambridge, choosing a college outstanding for its sporting prowess. Louise, arriving a year later, had just begun to suspect him of being a masochist. This was confirmed when he lay on his single bed, legs apart, and begged her to scaffold his penis with bulldog clips.

'I can take it,' he said. 'I'm going to be a doctor.'

Meanwhile, at home in Stamford Hill, Esau and Sarah, locked in prayer through the twenty-four hours of the Sabbath, wondered what would happen to their boy who had fallen into the clutches of a flame-haired temptress.

'She'll ruin him,' said Esau, 'he's doomed. We're all doomed.'

'My boy, my boy,' said Sarah. 'And only five feet seven.'

They didn't attend the wedding held in a Registry Office in Cambridge. How could they when Elgin had arranged it for a Saturday? There was Louise in an ivory silk flapper dress with a silver headband. Her best friend Janet holding a camera and the rings. Elgin's best friend whose name he couldn't remember. Elgin, in a hired morning suit just a size too tight.

'You see,' said Louise, 'I knew he was safe, that I could control him, that I would be the one in charge.'

'And what about him, what did he think?'

'He knew I was beautiful, that I was a prize. He wanted something showy but not vulgar. He wanted to go up to the world and say, "Look what I've got." '

I thought about Elgin. He was very eminent, very dull, very rich. Louise charmed everyone. She brought him attention, contacts, she cooked, she decorated, she was clever and above all she was beautiful. Elgin was awkward and he didn't fit. There was a certain amount of racism in the way he was treated. His colleagues were mostly those young men he had been taught with and inwardly despised. He knew other Jews of course, but in his profession they were all comfortable, cultured, liberal. They weren't Orthodox from Stamford Hill with nothing but a squatted semi between themselves and the gas chamber. Elgin never talked about his past, and gradually, with Louise beside him, it became irrelevant. He too became comfortable and cultivated and liberal. He went to the opera and he bought antiques. He made jokes about Frummers and matzos and even lost his accent. When Louise encouraged him to get in touch with his parents he sent them a Christmas card.

'It's her,' said Esau behind the dark counter. 'A curse on women since the sin of Eve.'

And Sarah, polishing, sorting, mending, serving, felt the curse and lost herself a little more.

'Hello Elgin,' I said as he came into the kitchen in his navy blue corduroys (size M) and his off-duty Viyella shirt (size S). He leaned against the stove and fired a staccato of questions at me. That was his preferred method of conversation; it meant he didn't have to expose himself.

Louise was chopping vegetables. 'Elgin's going away next week,' she said, cutting through his flow as deftly as he would a windpipe.

'That's right, that's right,' he said cheerfully. 'Got a paper to give in Washington. Ever been to Washington?'

Tuesday the twelfth of May 10.40. British Airways flight to Washington cleared for take-off. There's Elgin in Club Class with his glass of champagne and his headphones on listening to Wagner. Bye Bye Elgin.

Tuesday the twelfth of May 1 pm. Knock Knock.
'Who's there?'
'Hello Louise.'
She smiled. 'Just in time for lunch.'

Is food sexy? *Playboy* regularly features stories about asparagus and bananas and leeks and courgettes or being smeared with honey or chocolate chip ice-cream. I once bought some erotic body oil, authentic Pina Colada flavour, and poured it over myself but it made my lover's tongue come out in a rash.

Then there are candle-lit dinners and those leering waistcoated waiters with outsize pepperpots. There are, too, simple picnics on the beach which only work when you're in love because otherwise you couldn't bear the sand in the brie. Context is all, or so I thought, until I started eating with Louise.

When she lifted the soup spoon to her lips how I longed to be that innocent piece of stainless steel. I would gladly have traded the blood in my body for half a pint of vegetable stock. Let me be diced carrot, vermicelli, just so that you will take me in your mouth. I envied the French stick. I watched her break and butter each piece, soak it slowly in her bowl, let it float, grow heavy and fat, sink under the deep red weight and then be resurrected to the glorious pleasure of her teeth.

The potatoes, the celery, the tomatoes, all had been under her hands. When I ate my own soup I strained to taste her skin. She had been here, there must be something of her left. I would find her in the oil and onions, detect her through the garlic. I knew that she spat in the frying pan to determine the readiness of the oil. It's an old trick, every chef does it, or did. And so I knew when I asked her what was in the soup that she had deleted the essential ingredient. I will taste you if only through your cooking.

She split a pear; one of her own pears from the garden. Where she lived had been an orchard once and her particular tree was two hundred and twenty years old. Older than the French Revolution. Old enough to have fed Wordsworth and Napoleon. Who had gone into this garden and plucked the fruit? Did their hearts beat as hard as mine? She offered me half a pear and a piece of Parmesan cheese. Such pears as these have seen the world, that is they have stayed still and the world has seen them. At each bite burst war and passion. History was rolled in the pips and the frog-coloured skin.

She dribbled viscous juices down her chin and before I could help her wiped them away. I eyed the napkin; could I steal it? Already my hand was creeping over the tablecloth like something out of Poe. She touched me and I yelped.

'Did I scratch you?' she said, all concern and remorse.

'No, you electrocuted me.'

She got up and put on the coffee. The English are very good at those gestures.

'Are we going to have an affair?' she said.

She's not English, she's Australian.

'No, no we're not,' I said. 'You're married and I'm with Jacqueline. We're going to be friends.'

She said, 'We're friends already.'

Yes we are and I do like to pass the day with you in serious and inconsequential chatter. I wouldn't mind washing up beside you, dusting beside you, reading the back half of the paper while you read the front. We are friends and I would miss you, do miss you and think of you very often. I don't want to lose this happy space where I have found someone who is smart and easy and who doesn't bother to check her diary when we arrange to meet. All the way home I told myself these things and these things were the solid pavement beneath my feet and the neat clipped hedges and the corner shop and Jacqueline's car. Everything in its place; the lover, the friend, the life, the set. At home the breakfast cups are where we left them and I know, even if I close my eyes, the exact spot of Jacqueline's pyjamas. I used to think that Christ was wrong, impossibly hard, when he said that to imagine committing adultery was just as bad as doing it. But now, standing here in this familiar unviolated space, I have already altered my world and Jacqueline's world for ever. She doesn't know this yet. She doesn't know that there is today a revision of the map. That the territory she thought was hers has been annexed. You never give away your heart; you lend it from time to time. If it were not so how could we take it back without asking?

I welcomed the quiet hours of late afternoon. No-one would disturb me, I could make smoky tea and sit in my usual place and hope that the wisdom of objects would make some difference to me. Here, surrounded by my tables and chairs and books, I would surely see the need to stay in one place. I had been an emotional nomad for too long. Hadn't I come here weak and bruised to put a fence round the space Louise now threatened?

Oh Louise, I'm not telling the truth. You aren't threatening me, I'm threatening myself. My careful well-earned life means nothing. The clock was ticking. I thought, How long before the shouting starts? How long before the tears and accusations and the pain? That specific stone in the stomach pain when you lose something you haven't got round to valuing? Why is the measure of love loss?

This prelude and forethought is not unusual but to admit it is to cut through our one way out; the grand excuse of passion. You had no choice, you were swept away. Forces took you and possessed you and you did it but now that's all in the past, you can't understand etc etc. You want to start again etc etc. Forgive me. In the late twentieth century we still look to ancient daemons to explain our commonest action. Adultery is very common. It has no rarity value and yet at an individual level it is explained away again and again as a UFO. I can't lie to myself in quite that way any more. I always did but not now. I know exactly what's happening and I know too that I am jumping out of this plane of my own free will. No, I don't have a parachute, but worse, neither does Jacqueline. When you go you take one with you.

I cut a slice of fruit bread. If in doubt eat. I can understand why for some people the best social worker is the fridge. My usual confessional is a straight Macallan but not before 5 o'clock. Perhaps that's why I try and have my crises in the evening. Well, here I am at half past four with fruit bread and a cup of tea and instead of taking hold of myself I can only think of taking hold of Louise. It's the food that's doing it. There could not be a more unromantic moment than this and yet the yeasty smell of raisins and rye is exciting me more than any *Playboy* banana. It's only a matter of time. Is it nobler to struggle for a week before flying out the door or should I go and get my toothbrush now? I am drowning in inevitability.

I phoned a friend whose advice was to play the sailor and run a wife in every port. If I told Jacqueline I'd ruin everything and for what? If I told Jacqueline I'd hurt her beyond healing and did I have that right? Probably I had nothing more than dog-fever for two weeks and I could get it out of my system and come home to my kennel.

Good sense. Common sense. Good dog.

What does it say in the tea-leaves? Nothing but a capital L.

When Jacqueline came home I kissed her and said, 'I wish you didn't smell of the Zoo.'

She looked surprised. 'I can't help it. Zoos are smelly places.'

She went immediately to run a bath. I gave her a drink thinking how I disliked her clothes and the way she switched on the radio as soon as she got in.

Grimly I began to prepare our dinner. What would we do this evening? I felt like a bandit who hides a gun in his mouth. If I spoke I would reveal everything. Better not to speak. Eat, smile, make space for Jacqueline. Surely that was right?

The phone rang. I skidded to get it, closing the bedroom door behind me.

It was Louise.

'Come over tomorrow,' she said. 'There's something I want to tell you.'

'Louise, if it's to do with today, I can't . . . you see, I've decided I can't. That is I couldn't because, well what if, you know . . . '

The phone clicked and went dead. I stared at it the way Lauren Bacall does in those films with Humphrey Bogart. What I need now is a car with a running board and a pair of fog lights. I could be with you in ten minutes Louise. The trouble is that all I've got is a Mini belonging to my girlfriend.

We were eating our spaghetti. I thought, As long as I don't say her name I'll be all right. I started a game with myself, counting out on the cynical clock face the extent of my success. What am I? I feel like a kid in the examination room faced with a paper I can't complete. Let the clock go faster. Let me get out of here. At 9 o'clock I told Jacqueline I was exhausted. She reached over and took my hand. I felt nothing. And then there we were in our pyjamas side by side and my lips were sealed and my cheeks must have been swelling out like a gerbil's because my mouth was full of Louise.

I don't have to tell you where I went the next day.

During the night I had a lurid dream about an ex-girlfriend of mine who had been heavily into papier-maché. It had started as a hobby; and who shall object to a few buckets of flour and water and a roll of chicken wire? I'm a liberal and I believe in free expression. I went to her house one day and poking out of the letter-box just at crotch level was the head of a yellow and green serpent. Not a real one but livid enough with a red tongue and silver foil teeth. I hesitated to ring the bell. Hesitated because to reach the bell meant pushing my private parts right into the head of the snake. I held a little dialogue with myself.

ME: Don't be silly. It's a joke.
I: What do you mean it's a joke? It's lethal.

ME: Those teeth aren't real.
I: They don't have to be real to be painful.
ME: What will she think of you if you stand here all night?
I: What does she think of me anyway? What kind of a girl aims a snake at your genitals?
ME: A fun-loving girl.
I: Ha Ha.

The door flew open and Amy stood on the mat. She was wearing a kaftan and a long string of beads. 'It won't hurt you,' she said. 'It's for the postman. He's been bothering me.'

'I don't think it's going to frighten him,' I said. 'It's only a toy snake. It didn't frighten me.'

'You've nothing to be frightened of,' she said. 'It's got a rat-trap in the jaw.' She disappeared inside while I stood hovering on the step holding my bottle of Beaujolais Nouveau. She returned with a leek and shoved it in the snake's mouth. There was a terrible clatter and the bottom half of the leek fell limply on to the mat. 'Bring it in with you will you?' she said. 'We're eating it later.'

I awoke sweating and chilled. Jacqueline slept peacefully beside me, the light was leaking through the old curtains. Muffled in my dressing gown I went into the garden, glad of the wetness sudden beneath my feet. The air was clean with a hint of warmth and the sky had pink clawmarks pulled through it. There was an urban pleasure in knowing that I was the only one breathing the air. The relentless in-out-in-out of millions of lungs depresses me. There are too many of us on this planet and it's beginning to show. My neighbour's blinds were down. What were their dreams and nightmares? How different it would be to see them now, slack in the jaw, bodies open. We might be able to say something truthful to one another instead of the usual rolled-up Goodmornings.

I went to look at my sunflowers, growing steadily, sure that the sun would be there for them, fulfilling themselves in the proper way at the proper time. Very few people ever manage what nature manages without effort and mostly without fail. We don't know who we are or how to function, much less how to bloom. Blind nature. Homo sapiens. Who's kidding whom?

So what am I going to do? I asked Robin on the wall. Robins are very faithful creatures who mate with the same mate year by year. I love the brave red shield on their breast and the determined way they follow the spade in search of worms. There am I doing all the digging and there's little Robin making off with the worm. Homo sapiens. Blind Nature.

I don't feel wise. Why is it that human beings are allowed to grow up without the necessary apparatus to make sound ethical decisions?

The facts of my case are not unusual:

1 I have fallen in love with a woman who is married.

2 She has fallen in love with me.

3 I am committed to someone else.

4 How shall I know whether Louise is what I must do or must avoid?

The church could tell me, my friends have tried to help me, I could take the stoic course and run from temptation or I could put up sail and tack into this gathering wind.

For the first time in my life, I want to do the right

thing more than I want to get my own way. I suppose I owe that to Bathsheba . . .

I remember her visiting my house soon after she had returned from a six-week trip to South Africa. Before she had gone, I had given her an ultimatum: Him or me. Her eyes, which very often filled with tears of self-pity, had reproached me for yet another lover's half-nelson. I forced her to it and of course she made the decision for him. All right. Six weeks. I felt like the girl in the story of Rumpelstiltskin who is given a cellar full of straw to weave into gold by the following morning. All I had ever got from Bathsheba were bales of straw but when she was with me I believed that they were promises carved in precious stone. So I had to face up to the waste and the mess and I worked hard to sweep the chaff away. Then she came in, unrepentant, her memory gone as ever, wondering why I hadn't returned her trunk calls or written poste restante.

'I meant what I said.'

She sat in silence for about fifteen minutes while I glued the legs back on a kitchen chair. Then she asked me if I was seeing anybody else. I said I was, briefly, vaguely, hopefully.

She nodded and turned to go. When she got to the door she said, 'I intended to tell you before we left but I forgot.'

I looked at her, sudden and sharp. I hated that 'we'.

'Yes,' she went on, 'Uriah got NSU from a woman he slept with in New York. He slept with her to punish me of course. But he didn't tell me and the doctor thinks I have it too. I've been taking the antibiotics so it's probably all right. That is, you're probably all right. You ought to check though.'

I came at her with the leg of the chair. I wanted to run it straight across her perfectly made-up face.

'You shit.'

'Don't say that.'

'You told me you weren't having sex with him any more.'

'I thought it was unfair. I didn't want to shatter what little sexual confidence he might have left.'

'I suppose that's why you've never bothered to tell him that he doesn't know how to make you come.'

She didn't answer. She was crying now. It was like blood in the water to me. I circled her.

'How long is it you've been married? The perfect public marriage. Ten years, twelve? And you don't ask him to put his head between your legs because you think he'll find it distasteful. Let's hear it for sexual confidence.'

'Stop it,' she said, pushing me away. 'I have to go home.'

'It must be seven o'clock. That's your home-time isn't it? That's why you used to leave the practice early so that you could get a quick fuck for an hour and a half and then smooth yourself down to say, "Hello darling," and cook dinner.'

'You let me come,' she said.

'Yes, I did, when you were bleeding, when you were sick, again and again I made you come.'

'I didn't mean that. I meant we did it together. You wanted me there.'

'I wanted you everywhere and the pathetic thing is I still do.'

She looked at me. 'Drive me home will you?'

I still remember that night with shame and rage. I didn't

drive her home. I walked with her through the dark lanes to her house hearing the swish of her trenchcoat and the rub of her briefcase against her calf. Like Dirk Bogarde she prided herself on her profile and it was lit to suitable effect under the dull streetlights. I left her where I knew she'd be safe and listened to the click of her heels dying away. After a few seconds they stopped. I was familiar with this; she was checking her hair and her face, dusting me from coat and loins. The gate squeaked and closed metal on metal. They were inside now, four-square, everything shared, even the disease.

As I walked home, breathing deeply, knowing that I was shaking and not knowing how to stop it, I thought, I'm as guilty as her. Hadn't I let it happen, colluded with the deceit and let all my pride be burnt away? I was nothing, a weak piece of shit, I deserved Bathsheba. Self-respect. They're supposed to teach you that in the Army. Perhaps I should enlist. Would it recommend me though, to write Broken Heart under Personal Interests?

At the Clap Clinic the following day, I looked at my fellow sufferers. Shifty Jack-the-lads, fat businessmen in suits cut to hide the bulge. A few women, tarts yes, and other women too. Women with eyes full of pain and fear. What was this place and why had nobody told them? 'Who gave it to you love?' I wanted to say to one middle-aged woman in a floral print. She kept staring at the posters about gonorrhoea and then trying to concentrate on her copy of Country Life. 'Divorce him,' I wanted to say. 'You think this is the first time?' Her name was called and she disappeared into a bleak white room. This place is like the ante-chamber to Judgement Day. A pot of stale Cona coffee, a few scruffy leatherette benches, plastic flowers in a plastic vase and all over the walls, top to bottom, posters for every genital wart and discoloured emission. It's impressive what a few inches of flesh can catch.

Ah, Bathsheba, it's not the same as your elegant surgery is it? There your private patients can have their teeth removed to Vivaldi and enjoy twenty minutes' rest on a reclining sofa. Your flowers are delivered fresh every day and you serve only the most aromatic herbal teas. Against your white coat, their heads on your breast, no-one fears the needle and syringe. I came to you for a crown and you offered me a kingdom. Unfortunately I could only take possession between five and seven, weekdays, and the odd weekend when he was away playing football.

My name was called.

'Have I got it?'

The nurse looked at me the way you do a flat tyre and said, 'No.'

Then she started filling out a form and told me to come back in three months.

'What for?'

'Sexually transmitted diseases are not normally an isolated problem. If your habits are such that you have caught it once it's likely that you will catch it again.' She paused. 'We are creatures of habit.'

'I haven't caught it, any of it.'

She opened the door. 'Three months will be sufficient.'

Sufficient for what? I walked down the corridor past SURGERY and MOTHER AND BABY and OUTPATIENTS THIS WAY. It's a feature of the Clap Clinic that it's situated well out of the way of proper deserving patients. Its labyrinthian cunning means that the user will have to ask at least five times how to get there. Although I lowered my voice, particularly in deference to MOTHER AND BABY, I was returned no such courtesy. 'Venereal Disease? Down the end turn right turn left straight on through the gates past the lift up the stairs down the corridor round the corner, through the swing doors and there you are,' yelled the male nurse, carefully stopping his trolley-load of dirty sheets on my foot . . . 'You did say VENEREAL?'

Yes I did, and I said it again to the junior doctor rakishly swinging his stethoscope at the OUTPATIENTS. 'Clap Clinic? No problem, you're not more than five minutes away by wheelchair.' He pealed with laughter like a posse of ice-cream vans and pointed in the direction of the incinerator chute. 'That's the quickest way. Good luck.'

Maybe it's my face. Maybe I look like a doormat today. I feel like one.

On the way out I bought myself a large bunch of flowers.

'Visiting someone?' said the girl, her voice going up at the corners like a hospital sandwich. She was bored to death, having to be nice, jammed behind the ferns, her right hand dripping with green water.

'Yes, myself. I want to find out how I am.'

She raised her eyebrows and squeaked, 'You all right?'

'I shall be,' I said, throwing her a carnation.

At home, I put the flowers in a vase, changed the sheets and got into bed. 'What did Bathsheba ever give me but a perfect set of teeth?'

'All the better to eat you with,' said the Wolf.

I got a can of spray paint and wrote SELF-RESPECT over the door.

Let Cupid try and get past that one.

Louise was eating breakfast when I arrived. She was wearing a red and green guardsman stripe dressing gown gloriously too large. Her hair was down, warming her neck and shoulders, falling forward on to the table-cloth in wires of light. There was a dangerously electrical quality about Louise. I worried that the steady flame she offered might be fed by a current far more volatile. Superficially she seemed serene, but beneath her control was a crackling power of the kind that makes me nervous when I pass pylons. She was more of a Victorian heroine than a modern woman. A heroine from a Gothic novel, mistress of her house, yet capable of setting fire to it and fleeing in the night with one bag. I always expected her to wear her keys at her waist. She was compressed, stoked down, a volcano dormant but not dead. It did occur to me that if Louise were a volcano then I might be Pompeii.

I didn't go in straight away, I stood lurking outside with my collar turned up, hiding to get a better view. I thought, If she calls the police, it's only what I deserve. But she wouldn't call the police, she'd take her pearl-handled revolver from the glass decanter and shoot me through the heart. At the post-mortem they'll find an enlarged heart and no guts.

The white table-cloth, the brown teapot. The chrome toast-rack and the silver-bladed knives. Ordinary things. Look how she picks them up and puts them down, wipes her hands briskly on the edge of the table-cloth; she wouldn't do that in company. She's finished her egg, I can see the top jagged on the plate, a bit of butter that she pops into her mouth from the end of her knife. Now she's gone for a bath and the kitchen's empty. Silly kitchen without Louise.

It was easy for me to get in, the door was unlocked. I felt like a thief with a bagful of stolen glances. It's odd being in someone else's room when they're not there.

Especially when you love them. Every object carries a different significance. Why did she buy that? What does she especially like? Why does she sit in this chair and not that one? The room becomes a code that you have only a few minutes to crack. When she returns, she will command your attention, and besides it's rude to stare. And yet I want to pull out the drawers and run my fingers under the dusty rims of the pictures. In the waste basket perhaps, in the larder, I will find a clue to you, I will be able to unravel you, pull you between my fingers and stretch out each thread to know the measure of you. The compulsion to steal something is ridiculous, intense. I don't want one of your EPNS spoons, charming though they are, with a tiny Edwardian boot on the handle. Why then have I put it in my pocket? 'Take it out at once,' says the Headmistress who keeps an eye on my conduct. I managed to force it back into the drawer, although for a teaspoon it put up a lot of resistance. I sat down and tried to concentrate myself. Right in my eyeline was the laundry basket. Not the laundry basket . . . please.

I have never been a knicker-sniffer. I don't want to lard my inner pockets with used underwear. I know people who do and I sympathise. It's a dicey business going into a tense boardroom with a large white handkerchief on one side of the suit and a slender pair of knickers on the other. How can you be absolutely sure you remember which is where? I was hypnotised by the laundry basket like an out-of-work snake charmer.

I had just got to my feet when Louise strode through the door, her hair piled up on her head and pinned with a tortoiseshell bar. I could smell the steam on her from the bath and the scent of a rough woody soap. She held out her arms, her face softening with love, I took her two hands to my mouth and kissed each slowly so that I could memorise the shape of her knuckles. I didn't only want Louise's flesh, I wanted her bones, her blood, her tissues, the sinews that bound her together. I would have held her to me though time had stripped away the tones and textures of her skin. I could have held her for a thousand years until the skeleton itself rubbed away to dust. What are you that makes me feel thus? Who are you for whom time has no meaning?

In the heat of her hands I thought, This is the campfire that mocks the sun. This place will warm me, feed me and care for me. I will hold on to this pulse against other rhythms. The world will come and go in the tide of a day but here is her hand with my future in its palm.

She said, 'Come upstairs.'

We climbed one behind the other past the landing on the first floor, the studio on the second, up where the stairs narrowed and the rooms were smaller. It seemed that the house would not end, that the stairs in their twisting shape took us higher and out of the house altogether into an attic in a tower where birds beat against the windows and the sky was an offering. There was a small bed with a patchwork quilt. The floor sheered to one side, one board prised up like a wound. The walls, bumpy and distempered, were breathing. I could feel them moving under my touch. They were damp, slightly. The light, channelled by the thin air, heated the panes of glass too hot to open. We were magnified in this high wild room. You and I could reach the ceiling and the floor and every side of our loving cell. You kissed me and I tasted the relish of your skin.

What then? That you, so recently dressed, lost your clothes in an unconscious pile and I found you wore a petticoat. Louise, your nakedness was too complete for me, who had not learned the extent of your fingers. How could I cover this land? Did Columbus feel like this on sighting the Americas? I had no dreams to possess you but I wanted you to possess me.

It was a long time later that I heard the noise of schoolchildren on their way home. Their voices, high-pitched and eager, carried up past the sedater rooms and came at last, distorted, to our House of Fame. Perhaps we were in the roof of the world, where Chaucer had been with his eagle. Perhaps the rush and press of life ended here, the voices collecting in the rafters, repeating themselves into redundancy. Energy cannot be lost only transformed; where do the words go?

'Louise, I love you.'

Very gently, she put her hand over my mouth and shook her head. 'Don't say that now. Don't say it yet. You might not mean it.'

I was protesting with a stream of superlatives, beginning to sound like an advertising hack. Naturally this model had to be the best the most important, the wonderful even the incomparable. Nouns have no worth these days unless they bank with a couple of Highstreet adjectives. The more I underlined it the hollower it sounded. Louise said nothing and eventually I shut up.

'When I said you might not mean it, I meant it might not be possible for you to mean it.'

'I'm not married.'

'You think that makes you free?'

'It makes me freer.'

'It also makes it easier for you to change your mind. I don't doubt that you would leave Jacqueline. But would you stay with me?'

'I love you.'

'You've loved other people but you still left them.'

'It's not that simple.'

'I don't want to be another scalp on your pole.'

'You started this, Louise.'

'I acknowledged it. We both started it.'

What was all this about? We had made love once. We had known each other as friends for a couple of months and yet she was challenging my suitability as a long-term candidate? I said as much.

'So you admit that I am just a scalp?'

I was angry and bewildered. 'Louise, I don't know what you are. I've turned myself inside out to try and avoid what happened today. You affect me in ways I can't quantify or contain. All I can measure is the effect, and the effect is that I am out of control.'

'So you try and regain control by telling me you love me. That's a territory you know, isn't it? That's romance and courtship and whirlwind.'

'I don't want control.'

'I don't believe you.'

No and you're right not to believe me. If in doubt be sincere. That's a pretty little trick of mine. I got up and reached for my shirt. It was under her petticoat. I picked up the petticoat instead.

'May I have this?'

'Trophy hunting?'

Her eyes were full of tears. I had hurt her. I regretted telling her those stories about my girlfriends. I had wanted to make her laugh and she had laughed at the time. Now I had strewn our path with barbs. She didn't trust me. As a friend I had been amusing. As a lover I was lethal. I could see that. I wouldn't want to have much to do with me. I knelt on the floor and clasped her legs against my chest.

'Tell me what you want and I'll do it.'

She stroked my hair. 'I want you to come to me without a past. Those lines you've learned, forget them. Forget that you've been here before in other bedrooms in other places. Come to me new. Never say you love me until that day when you have proved it.'

'How shall I prove it?'

'I can't tell you what to do.'

The maze. Find your own way through and you shall win your heart's desire. Fail and you will wander for ever in these unforgiving walls. Is that the test? I told you that Louise had more than a notion of the Gothic about her. She seemed determined that I should win her from the tangle of my own past. In her attic room was a print of the Burne-Jones picture titled *Love and the Pilgrim*. An angel in clean garments leads by the hand a traveller footsore and weary. The traveller is in black and her cloak is still caught by the dense thicket of thorns from which they have both emerged. Would Louise lead me so? Did I want to be led? She was right, I hadn't thought about the hugeness of it all. I had some excuse; I was thinking about Jacqueline.

It was raining when I left Louise's house and caught a bus to the Zoo. The bus was full of women and children. Tired busy women placating cross excitable kids. One child had forced her brother's head into his satchel, scattering schoolbooks over the rubber floor, enraging her pretty young mother to the point of murder. Why is none of this work included in the Gross National Product? 'Because we don't know how to quantify it,' say the economists. They should try catching a bus.

I got off at the main entrance to the Animal House. The boy in the booth was bored and alone. He had his feet propped on the turnstile, the wet wind pushing through his window and spatting his micro TV. He didn't look at me as I leaned for shelter against a perspex elephant.

'Zoo's shuttin' in ten,' he said mysteriously. 'No admin after five pm.'

A secretary's dream; 'No admin after five pm.' That amused me for two seconds and then I saw Jacqueline coming towards the gate, her beret pulled against the drizzle. She had a carrier bag full of food, leeks prodding through the sides.

'Nite luv,' said the boy without moving his lips.

She hadn't seen me. I wanted to hide behind the perspex elephant, jump out at her and say, 'Let's go for dinner.'

I am often beset by such romantic follies. I use them as ways out of real situations. Who the hell wants to go for dinner at 5.30 pm? Who wants to have a sexy walk in the rain alongside thousands of home-time commuters, all like you, carrying a shopping bag full of food?

'Stick to it,' I told myself. 'Go on.'

'Jacqueline.' (I sound like someone from the CID.)

She turned up her face, smiles and pleasure, handed me the bag and wrapped herself in the coat. She started walking towards her car, telling me about her day, there was a wallaby that had needed counselling, did I know that the Zoo used them in animal experiments? The Zoo decapitated them alive. It was in the interests of science.

'But not in the interests of wallabies?'

'No,' she said. 'And why should they suffer? You wouldn't chop my head off, would you?'

I looked at her appalled. She was joking but it didn't feel like a joke.

'Let's go and get some coffee and a bit of cake.' I took her arm and we walked away from the carpark towards a homely tea-shoppe that normally served the outflow of the Zoo. It was pleasant when the visitors weren't there and they weren't there on that day. The animals must pray for rain.

'You don't usually pick me up from work,' she said.

'No.'

'Is there something to celebrate?'

'No.'

Condensation ran down the windows. Nothing was clear any more.

'Is it about Louise?'

I nodded, twisting the cake fork between my fingers, pushing my knees against the underside of the dolls' house table. Nothing was in proportion. My voice seemed too loud, Jacqueline too small, the woman serving dough-nuts with mechanical efficiency parked her bosom on the glass counter and threatened to shatter it with mammary power. How she would skittle the chocolate eclairs and with a single plop drown her unwary customers in mock cream. My mother always said I'd come to a sticky end.

'Are you seeing her?' Jacqueline's timid voice.

Irritation from gut to gullet. I wanted to snarl like the dog I am.

'Of course I'm seeing her. I see her face on every hoarding, on the coins in my pocket. I see her when I look at you. I see her when I don't look at you.'

I didn't say any of that, I mumbled something about yes as usual but things had changed. THINGS HAD CHANGED, what an arsehole comment, I had changed things. Things don't change, they're not like the seasons moving on a diurnal round. People change things. There are victims of change but not victims of things. Why do I collude in this mis-use of language? I can't make it easier for Jacqueline however I put it. I can make it a bit easier for me and I suppose that's what I'm doing.

She said, 'I thought you'd changed.'

'I have, that's the problem, isn't it?'

'I thought you'd already changed. You told me you wouldn't do this again. You told me you wanted a different life. It's easy to hurt me.'

What she says is true. I did think I could leave with the morning paper and come home for the 6 o'clock news. I hadn't lied to Jacqueline but it seemed I had been lying to myself.

'I'm not running around again, Jacqueline.'

'What *are* you doing then?'

Good point. Would that I had the overseeing spirit to interpret my actions in plain English. I would like to come to you with all the confidence of a computer programmer, sure that we could find the answers if only we asked the proper questions. Why aren't I going according to plan? How stupid it sounds to say I don't know and shrug and behave like every other idiot who's fallen in love and can't explain it. I've had a lot of practice, I should be able to explain it. The only word I can think of is Louise.

Jacqueline, exposed under tea-shoppe neon, wraps her hands around her cup for comfort but gets burned. She spills into her saucer and, while mopping at it with the inadequate serviette, knocks her cake on to the floor. Silently but with eagle eye, the Bosom bends to clear it up. She's seen it all before, it doesn't interest her except that she wants to close in a quarter of an hour. She retreats behind her counter and switches on the radio.

Jacqueline wiped her glasses.

'What are you going to do?'

'It's for us to decide that. It's a joint decision.'

'You mean we'll talk about it and you'll do what you want anyway.'

'I don't know what I want.'

She nodded and got up to leave. By the time I had found the change to pay our host Jacqueline was somewhere down the street, going for her car I thought.

I ran to catch up with her but when I got to the Zoo carpark it was locked. I caught hold of the diamond-shaped tennis netting and vainly shook the smug padlock. A wet May night, more like February than sweet spring, it should have been soft and light but the light was soaked up by a row of weary streetlamps reflecting the rain. Jacqueline's Mini stood alone in a corner of the bleak paddock. Ridiculous this waste sad time.

I walked across to a small park and sat on a damp bench under a dripping willow. I was wearing baggy shorts which in such weather looked like a recruitment campaign for the Boy Scouts. But I'm not a Boy Scout and never was. I envy them; they know exactly what makes a Good Deed.

Opposite me, the relaxed smart houses built on the park showed yellow at one window, black at another. A figure pulled the curtains, someone opened the front door, I could hear music for a moment. What sane sensible lives. Did those people lie awake at night hiding their hearts while giving their bodies? Did the woman at the window quietly despair as the clock pushed her closer to bed-time? Does she love her husband? Desire him? When he sees his wife unlace herself what does he feel? In a different house is there someone he longs for the way he used to long for her?

At the fairground there used to be a penny slot-machine called 'What the Butler Saw'. You jammed your eyes against a padded viewfinder, put in the coin and at once a troupe of dancing girls started tossing their skirts and winking. Gradually they cast off most of their clothes, but if you wanted the coup de grace you had to get in another coin before the butler's white hand drew a discreet blind. The pleasure of it, apart from the obvious, was depth simulation. It was intended to give the feel of a toff at the music hall, in the best seat of course. You could see rows of velvet seats and a rake of Brylcreemed hair. It was delicious because it was puerile and naughty. I always felt guilty but it was a hot thrill of guilt not the dreadful weight of sin. Those days made me a voyeur, though of a modest kind. I like to pass by bare windows and get a sighting of the life within.

No silent films were shot in colour but the pictures through a window are that. Everything moves in curious clockwork animation. Why is that man throwing up his arms? The girl's hands move soundlessly over the piano. Only half an inch of glass separates me from the silent world where I do not exist. They don't know I'm here but I have begun to be as intimate with them as any member of the family. More so, since as their lips move with goldfish bowl pouts, I am the scriptwriter and I can put words in their mouths. I had a girlfriend once, we used to play that game, going round the posh houses when we were down at heel making up stories about the lamplit well-to-do.

Her name was Catherine, she wanted to be a writer. She said it was good exercise for her imagination to invent little scenarios for the unsuspecting. I don't want to be a writer but I didn't mind carrying her pad. It did occur to me, those dark nights, that movies are a terrible sham. In real life, left to their own devices, especially after 7 o'clock, human beings hardly move at all. Sometimes I panicked and told Catherine we'd have to call the ambulance.

'No-one can sit still for that long,' I said. 'She must be dead. Look at her, rigor mortis has set in, not so much as a squint.'

Then we'd go to an arthouse showing of Chabrol or Renoir and the entire cast spent the whole picture running in and out of bedrooms and shooting at one another and getting divorced. I was exhausted. The French crack on about being an intellectual resource but for a nation of thinkers they do run around a lot. Thinking is supposed to be a sedentary occupation. They pack more action into their arty films than the Americans manage in a dozen Clint Eastwoods. *Jules et Jim* is an action movie.

We were so happy those wet carefree nights. I felt we were like Dr Watson and Sherlock Holmes. I knew my place. And then Catherine said she was leaving. She didn't want to do it but she felt that a writer doesn't make a good companion. 'It's only a matter of time', she said, 'before I become an alcoholic and forget how to cook.'

I suggested we wait and try and ride it out. She shook her head sadly and patted me. 'Get a dog.'

Naturally I was devastated. I enjoyed our wandering nights together, the brief stop at the fish shop, falling into the same bed at dawn.

'Is there anything I can do for you before you go?' I asked.

'Yes,' she said. 'Do you know why Henry Miller said "I write with my prick"?'

'Because he did. When he died they found nothing between his legs but a ball-point pen.'

'You're making it up,' she said.

Am I?

I was sitting on the bench smiling soaked to the skin. I wasn't happy but the power of memory is such that it can lift reality for a time. Or is memory the more real place? I stood up and wrung out the legs of my shorts. It was dark, the park belonged to other people after dark and I didn't belong to them. Best to go home and find Jacqueline.

When I got to my flat the door was locked. I tried to get in but the chain was across the door. I shouted and banged. At last the letter-box flipped open and a note slid out. It said GO AWAY. I found a pen and wrote on the backside. IT'S MY FLAT. As I feared there was no response. For the second time that day I ended up at Louise's.

'We're going to sleep in a different bed tonight,' she said as she filled the bathroom with clouds of steam and incense oils. 'I'm going to warm the room and you're going to lie in the tub and drink this cocoa. All right Christopher Robin?'

Yes, with or without a blue hood. How tender this is and how unlikely. I don't believe any of it. Jacqueline must have known I'd have to come here. Why would she do that? They're not in it together are they, to punish me? Perhaps I've died and this is Judgement Day. Judgement or not I can't go back to Jacqueline. Whatever happens here, and I held out no great hopes, I knew that I'd split myself from her in ways that were too profound to heal. In the park in the rain I had recognised one thing at least; that Louise was the woman I wanted even if I couldn't have her. Jacqueline I had to admit had never been wanted, simply she had had roughly the right shape to fit for a while.

Molecular docking is a serious challenge for bio-chemists. There are many ways to fit molecules together but only a few juxtapositions that bring them close enough to bond. On a molecular level success may mean discovering what synthetic structure, what chemical, will form a union with, say, the protein shape on a tumour cell. If you make this high-risk jigsaw work you may have found a cure for carcinoma. But molecules and the human beings they are a part of exist in a universe of possibility. We touch one another, bond and break, drift away on force-fields we don't understand. Docking here inside Louise may heal a damaged heart, on the other hand it may be an expensively ruinous experiment.

I put on the rough towelling robe Louise had left for me. I hoped it wasn't Elgin's. There used to be a scam in the undertaking trade whereby any man sent to the Chapel of Rest in a good suit of clothes had the lot tried on by the embalmer and his boys while he, the deceased, was made ready for the grave. Whoever the clothes best fitted put a shilling on them; that is, the shilling went in the Poor Box and the clothes went off the dead man's back. Obviously he was allowed to wear them while ritual viewing took place but as soon as it was time for the lid to be screwed down, one of the lads whipped them off and covered the unfortunate in a cheap winding sheet. If I was going to stab Elgin in the back I didn't want to do it in his dressing gown.

'That's mine,' said Louise as I came upstairs. 'Don't worry.'

'How did you know?'

'Do you remember when you and I were caught in that terrible shower on the way to your flat? Jacqueline insisted that I undress and she gave me her dressing gown to wear. It was very kind but I longed to be in yours. It was your smell I was after.'

'Wasn't I in mine?'

'Yes. All the more tempting.'

She had lit a fire in the room with the bed she'd called a Lady's Occasional. Most people don't have open fires any more; Louise had no central heating. She said that Elgin complained every winter although it was she not he who bought the fuel and stoked the blaze.

'He doesn't really want to live like this,' she said, meaning the austere grandeur of their marital home. 'He'd be much happier in a 1930s mock Tudor with underfloor hot air.'

'Then why does he do it?'

'It brings him huge originality value.'

'Do you like it?'

'I made it.' She paused. 'The only thing Elgin's ever put into this house is money.'

'You despise him, don't you?'

'No, I don't despise him. I'm disappointed in him.'

Elgin had been a brilliant medical trainee. He had worked hard and learned well. He had been innovative and concerned. During his early hospital years, when Louise had supported him financially and paid all the bills that accumulated round their modest life together, Elgin had been determined to qualify and work in the Third World. He scorned what he called 'the consultancy trail', where able young men of a certain background put in their minimum share of hospital slog and were promoted up the ladder to easier and better things. There was a fast-track in medicine. Very few women were on it, it was the recognised route of the career doctor.

'So what happened?'

'Elgin's mother got cancer.'

In Stamford Hill Sarah felt sick. She had always got up at five o'clock, prayed and lit the candles, gone to work preparing the day's food and ironing Esau's white shirts. She wore a headscarf in those early hours, only placing her long black wig a few moments before her husband came downstairs at seven. They ate breakfast and together got into their ancient car and drove the three miles to the shop. Sarah mopped the floor and dusted the counter while Esau put his white coat over his prayer shawl and shifted the cardboard boxes in the back room. It cannot truly be said that they opened their shop at nine, rather they unlocked the door. Sarah sold toothbrushes and lozenges. Esau made up paper packets of medicine. They had done so for fifty years.

The shop was unchanged. The mahogany counter and glass cabinets had been where they were since before the war, since before Esau and Sarah bought a sixty-year lease to carry them into old age. On one side of them, the cobbler had become a grocery store had become a delicatessen had become a Kosher Kebab House. On the other side, the take-in laundry had become a dry cleaners. It was still run by the children of their friends the Shiffys.

'Your boy,' said Shiffy to Esau. 'He's a doctor, I saw him in the paper. He could bring a nice practice here. You could expand.'

'I'm seventy-two,' said Esau.

'So you're seventy-two? Think of Abraham, think of Isaac, think of Methuselah. Nine hundred and sixty-nine. That's the time to worry about your age.'

'He's married a shiksa.'

'We all make mistakes. Look at Adam.'

Esau didn't tell Shiffy that he never heard from Elgin any more. He never expected to hear from him again. Two weeks later when Sarah was in hospital unable to speak for the pain, Esau dialled Elgin's number on his Bakelite sit-up-and-beg telephone. They had never bothered to get a later model. God's children had no need of progress.

Elgin came at once and spoke to the doctor before he met his father at the bedside. The doctor said there was no hope. Sarah had cancer of the bone and would not live. The doctor said she must have been in pain for years. Slowly crumbling, dust to dust.

'Does my father know?'

'In a way.' The doctor was busy and had to get on. He gave his notes to Elgin and left him at a desk under a lamp with a blown bulb.

Sarah died. Elgin went to the funeral then took his father back to the shop. Esau fumbled with the keys and opened the heavy door. The glass panel still had the gold lettering that had once announced the signs of Esau's success. The upper arc had said ROSENTHAL and the lower, CHEMIST. Time and the weather had beat upon the sign and although it still declared ROSENTHAL, underneath it now read HE MIST.

Elgin, close behind his father, was sick to the stomach at the smell. It was the smell of his childhood, formaldehyde and peppermint. It was the smell of his homework behind the counter. The long nights waiting for his parents to take him home. Sometimes he fell asleep in his grey socks and shorts, his head on a table of logarithms, then Esau would scoop him up and carry him to the car. He remembered his father's tenderness only through the net of dreams and half-wakefulness. Esau was hard on the boy but when he saw him head down on the table, his thin legs loose against the chair, he loved him and whispered in his ear about the lily of the valley and the Promised Land.

All this cut at Elgin as he watched his father slowly hang his black coat on the peg and shrug his arms into his chemist's uniform. He seemed to take comfort from this regular act, didn't look at Elgin but got out his order book and sat muttering over it. After a while Elgin coughed and said he had to go. His father nodded, wouldn't speak.

'Is there anything I can do for you?' asked Elgin not wanting an answer.

'Can you tell me why your mother died?'

Elgin cleared his throat a second time. He was desperate.

'Father, mother was old, she didn't have the strength to get better.'

Esau rocked his head up and down up and down. 'It was God's will. The Lord giveth and the Lord taketh away. How many times have I said that today?' There was another long silence. Elgin coughed.

'I have to be getting on.'

Esau shuffled back round the counter and dug in a large discoloured jar.

He gave his son a brown paper bag full of lozenges.

'You have a cough my boy. Take these.'

Elgin stuffed the bag in his overcoat pocket and left. He walked as hard as he could away from the Jewish quarter and when he reached a main road he hailed a cab. Before he climbed in he dumped the bag in a bus-stop bin. It was the last time he saw his father.

It's true that when Elgin began, he didn't realise that his obsessional study of carcinoma would bring more substantial benefits to himself than to any of his patients. He used computer simulations to mimic the effects of rapidly multiplying rogue cells. He saw gene therapy as the likeliest way out for a body besieged by itself. It was very sexy medicine. Gene therapy is the frontier world where names and fortunes can be made. Elgin was wooed by an American pharmaceutical company who got him off the shop floor and into a lab. He'd never liked hospitals anyway.

'Elgin', said Louise, 'can no longer wrap a Band-Aid round a cut finger but he can tell you everything there is to know about cancer. Everything except what causes it and how to cure it.'

'That's a bit cynical isn't it?' I said.

'Elgin doesn't care about people. He never sees any people. He hasn't been on a terminal care ward for ten years. He sits in a multi-million pound laboratory in Switzerland for half the year and stares at a computer. He wants to make the big discovery. Get the Nobel prize.'

'There's nothing wrong with ambition.'

She laughed. 'There's a lot wrong with Elgin.'

I wondered if I could live up to Louise.

We lay down together and I followed the bow of her lips with my finger. She had a fine straight nose, severe and demanding.

Her mouth contradicted her nose, not because it wasn't serious, but because it was sensual. It was full, lascivious in its depth, with a touch of cruelty. The nose and the mouth working together produced an odd effect of ascetic sexuality. There was discernment as well as desire in the picture. She was a Roman Cardinal, chaste, but for the perfect choirboy.

Louise's tastes had no place in the late twentieth century where sex is about revealing not concealing. She enjoyed the titillation of suggestion. Her pleasure was in slow certain arousal, a game between equals who might not always choose to be equals. She was not a D.H. Lawrence type; no-one could take Louise with animal inevitability.

It was necessary to engage her whole person. Her mind, her heart, her soul and her body could only be present as two sets of twins. She would not be divided from herself. She preferred celibacy to tupping.

Elgin and Louise no longer made love. She took the spunk out of him now and again but she refused to have him inside her. Elgin accepted this was part of their deal and Louise knew he used prostitutes. His proclivities would have made that inevitable even in a more traditional marriage. His present hobby was to fly up to Scotland and be sunk in a bath of porridge while a couple of Celtic geishas rubber-gloved his prick.

'He wouldn't want to be naked in front of strangers,' said Louise. 'I'm the only person, apart from his mother, who's seen him undressed.'

'Why do you stay with him?'

'He used to be a good friend, that's before he started working all the time. I'd have been happy enough to stay with him and live my own life, except that something happened.'

'What?'

'I saw you in the park. It was a long time before we met.'

I wanted to question her. My heart was beating too fast and I felt both enervated and exhausted, the way I do when I drink without eating. Whatever Louise had to say I wouldn't have been able to cope with it. I lay on my back and watched the shadows from the fire. There was an ornamental palm in the room, its leaves reflected to a grotesque outsize. This was no tame domestic space.

In the hours that followed, waking and sleeping with a light fever that bore on me out of passion and distress, it seemed as if the small room was full of ghosts. There were figures at the window gazing out through the muslin curtains, talking to one another in low voices. A man stood warming himself by the low grate. There was no furniture apart from the bed and the bed was levitating. We were surrounded by hands and faces shifting and connecting, now looming into focus vaporous and large, now disappearing like the bubbles children blow.

The figures assumed shapes I recognised; Inge, Catherine, Bathsheba, Jacqueline. Others of whom Louise knew nothing. They came too close, put their fingers in my mouth, in my nostrils, drew back the hoods of my eyes. They accused me of lies and betrayal. I opened my mouth to speak but I had no tongue only a gutted space. I must have cried out then because I was in Louise's arms and she was bending over me, fingers on my forehead, soothing me, whispering to me. 'I will never let you go.'

How to get back into my flat? I telephoned the Zoo the following morning and asked to speak to Jacqueline. They said she hadn't come in to work. I had a mild temperature and only a pair of shorts at my disposal but I thought it best to try and settle matters with her as soon as I could. No way out but through.

Louise lent me her car. When I got to my flat the curtains were still drawn but the chain was off the door. Cautiously I pushed it open. I half expected Jacqueline to fly at me with the mincer. I stood in the hall and called her name. There was no answer. Strictly speaking Jacqueline didn't live with me. She had her own room in a shared house. She kept certain things in my flat and as far as I could see they were gone. No coat behind the door. No hat or gloves shoved in the hall stand. I tried the bedroom.

It was wrecked. Whatever Jacqueline had done the previous night she hadn't had time to sleep. The room looked like a chicken shed. There were feathers everywhere. The pillows had been ripped, the duvet gutted and emptied. She had torn the drawers from their chests and tipped the contents about like any good burglar. I stood too stunned to make much of it, I bent and picked up a T-shirt then dropped it again. I would have to use it as a duster since she'd cut a hole in the middle. I backed out into the sitting room. That was better, no feathers, nothing broken, simply everything was gone. The table, the chairs, the stereo, the vases and pictures, the glasses, bottles, mirrors and lamps. It was blissfully zen. She had left a bunch of flowers in the middle of the floor. Presumably she couldn't fit them into her car. Her car. Her car was locked up like an accessory after the fact. How had she got away with my things?

I went to pee. It seemed like a sensible move providing that the toilet was still there. It was but she had taken the toilet seat. The bathroom looked like it had been the target of a depraved and sadistic plumber. The taps were twisted on their sides, there was a monkey wrench skewed under the hot water pipe where someone had done their best to disconnect me. The walls were covered in heavy felt-tip pen. It was Jacqueline's handwriting. There was a long list of her attributes over the bath. A longer list of my disabilities over the sink. Pasted like an acid-house frieze around the ceiling was Jacqueline's name over and over again. Jacqueline colliding with Jacqueline. An endless cloning of Jacquelines in black ink. I went and peed in the coffee pot. She didn't like coffee. Staring blearily back at the bathroom door I saw it had SHIT daubed across it. The word and the matter. That explained the smell.

The worm in the bud. That's right, most buds do have worms but what about the ones that turn? I thought Jacqueline would have crept away as quietly as she had crept in.

The wise old hands who advocate a sensible route, not too much passion, not too much sex, plenty of greens and an early night, don't recognise this as a possible ending. In their world good manners and good sense prevail. They don't imagine that to choose sensibly is to set a time-bomb under yourself. They don't imagine you are ripe for the cutting, waiting for your chance at life. They don't think of the wreckage an exploding life will cause. It's not in their rule book even though it happens again and again. Settle down, feet under the table. She's a nice girl, he's a nice boy. It's the clichés that cause the trouble.

I lay down on the hard wooden floor of my new zen sitting room and contemplated a spider throwing a web. Blind nature. Homo sapiens. Unlike Robert the Bruce I had no ingenious revelations only a huge sadness. I'm not the kind who can replace love with convenience or passion with pick-ups. I don't want slippers at home and dancing shoes in a little bed-sit round the block. That's how it's done isn't it? Package up your life with supermarket efficiency, don't mix the heart with the liver.

I've never been the slippers; never been the one to sit at home and desperately believe in another late office meeting. I haven't gone to bed by myself at eleven, pretending to be asleep, ears pricked like a guard dog for the car in the drive. I haven't stretched out my hand to check the clock and felt the cold weight of those lost hours ticking in my stomach.

Plenty of times I've been the dancing shoes and how

those women have wanted to play. Friday night, a week-end conference. Yes, in my flat. Off with the business suit, legs apart, pulling me down on them, a pause for champagne and English cheese. And while we're doing that somebody is looking out of the window watching the weather change. Watching the clock, watching the phone, she said she'd ring after her last session. She does ring. She lifts herself off me and dials the number resting the receiver against her breast. She's wet with sex and sweat. 'Hello darling, yes fine, it's raining outside.'

Turn down the lights. This is outside of time. The edge of a black hole where we can go neither forward nor back. Physicists are speculating on what might happen if we could lodge ourselves on the crater sides of such a hole. It seems that due to the peculiarities of the event horizon we could watch history pass and never become history ourselves. We would be trapped eternally observing with no-one to tell. Perhaps that's where God is, then God will understand the conditions of infidelity.

Don't move. We can't move, caught like lobster in a restaurant aquarium. These are the confines of our life together, this room, this bed. This is the voluptuous exile freely chosen. We daren't eat out, who knows whom we may meet? We must buy food in advance with the canni-ness of a Russian peasant. We must store it unto the day, chilled in the fridge, baked in the oven. Temperatures of hot and cold, fire and ice, the extremes under which we live.

We don't take drugs, we're drugged out on danger, where to meet, when to speak, what happens when we see each other publicly. We think no-one has noticed but there are always faces at the curtain, eyes on the road. There's nothing to whisper about so they whisper about us.

Turn up the music. We're dancing together tightly sealed like a pair of 50s homosexuals. If anyone knocks at the door we won't answer. If I have to answer we'll say she's my accountant. We can't hear anything but the music smooth as a tube lubricating us round the floor. I've been waiting for her all week. All week has been a regime of clocks and calendars. I thought she might telephone on Thursday to say that she couldn't come, that sometimes happens even though we're only together one weekend in five and those stolen after-office hours.

She arches her body like a cat on a stretch. She nuzzles her cunt into my face like a filly at the gate. She smells of the sea. She smells of rockpools when I was a child. She keeps a starfish in there. I crouch down to taste the salt, to run my fingers around the rim. She opens and shuts like a sea anemone. She's refilled each day with fresh tides of longing.

The sun won't stay behind the blind. The room is flooded with light that makes sine waves on the carpet. The carpet that looked so respectable in the showroom has a harem red to it now. I was told it was burgundy.

She lies against the light resting her back on a rod of light. The light breaks colours under her eyelids. She wants the light to penetrate her, breaking open the dull colds of her soul where nothing has warmed her for more summers than she can count. Her husband lies over her like a tarpaulin. He wades into her as though she were a bog. She loves him and he loves her. They're still married aren't they?

On Sunday, when she's gone, I can open the curtains, wind my watch and clear the dishes stacked round the bed. I can make my supper from the left-overs and think about her at home for Sunday dinner, listening to the gentle ticking of the clock and the sound of busy hands running her a bath. Her husband will feel sorry for her, bags under her eyes, worn out. Poor baby, she hardly got any sleep. Tuck her up in her own sheets, that's nice. I can take our soiled ones to the launderette.

Such things lead the heart-sore to the Jacquelines of this world but the Jacquelines of this world lead to such things. Is there no other way? Is happiness always a compromise?

I used to read women's magazines when I visited the dentist. They fascinate me with their arcane world of sex tips and man-traps. I am informed by the thin glossy pages that the way to tell if your husband is having an affair is to check his underpants and cologne. The magazines insist that when a man finds a mistress he will want to cover his prick more regally than of old. He will want to cover his tracks with a new aftershave. No doubt the magazines know best. There's Mr Right furtively locking the bathroom door to try on his brand new six-pack of boxer shorts (size L). His faithful greying Y-fronts lie discarded on the floor. The bathroom mirror is fixed to give him a good view of his face but to get at the important thing he will have to balance on the edge of the bath and hold on to the shower rail. That's better, now all he can see is an ad from a men's magazine, fine lawn cotton pouched round a firm torso. He jumps down, satisfied, and splashes on a bucket load of Hommage Homme. Mrs Right won't notice, she's cooking a curry.

If Mrs Right is having an affair it will be harder to spot, so the magazines say, and they know best. She won't buy new clothes, in fact, she's likely to dress down so that her husband will believe her when she says she's going to an evening class in mediaeval lute music. Unless she has a career, it will be very difficult for her to get away with it regularly except in the afternoons. Is that why so many women are choosing careers? Is that why Kinsey found that so many prefer sex in the afternoon?

I had a girlfriend once who could only achieve orgasm between the hours of two and five o'clock. She worked in the Botanical Gardens in Oxford where she bred rubber plants. It was tricky work trying to satisfy her, when at any moment a fee-paying visitor with the proper ticket of admission might require advice about *Ficus elastica*. Nevertheless, passion propelled me and I visited her in the depths of winter, muffled from head to foot, stamping rushes of snow from my boots like a character from *Anna Karenina*.

I've always been fond of Vronsky but I don't believe in living out literature. Judith was deeply sunk in Conrad. She sat amongst the rubber plants reading *Heart of Darkness*. The most erotic thing I might have said to her was, 'Mistah Kurtz – he dead.' The Soviets, I am told, suffer extremely from having to wear wrappings of fur when outside, only to shed down to their knickers when inside. This was my problem. Judith lived in a perpetual hot-house world of shorts and T-shirts. I had to carry my skimpy garments with me or risk a dash through the cold aided only by a duffle-coat. One quiet afternoon after sex on the wood chippings beneath a trailing vine, we had a tiff and she locked me out of the greenhouse. I ran from window to window banging vainly at the panes. It was snowing and I was wearing only my Mickey Mouse one-piece.
'If you don't let me in I'll die.'
'Die then.'
I decided I was too young to freeze to death. I ran

through the streets back to my lodgings with as much insouciance as I could muster. An old-age pensioner gave me 50p for rag week and I wasn't arrested. We should be thankful for small mercies. I rang Judith to tell her it was all off and would she return my things?

'I've burnt them,' she said.

Perhaps I'm not meant to have any worldly goods. Perhaps they are blocking my spiritual progress and my higher self continually chooses situations where I will be free of material burdens. It's a comforting thought, slightly better than being a sucker . . . Judith's bottom. I treasure it.

Into the heart of my childish vanities, Louise's face, Louise's words, 'I will never let you go.' This is what I have been afraid of, what I've avoided through so many shaky liaisons. I'm addicted to the first six months. It's the midnight calls, the bursts of energy, the beloved as battery for all those fading cells. I told myself after the last whipping with Bathsheba that I wouldn't do any of it again. I did suspect that I might like being whipped, if so, I had at least to learn to wear an extra overcoat. Jacqueline was an overcoat. She muffled my senses. With her I forgot about feeling and wallowed in contentment. Contentment is a feeling you say? Are you sure it's not an absence of feeling? I liken it to that particular numbness one gets after a visit to the dentist. Not in pain nor out of it, slightly drugged. Contentment is the positive side of resignation. It has its appeal but it's no good wearing an overcoat and furry slippers and heavy gloves when what the body really wants is to be naked.

I never used to think about my previous girlfriends until I took up with Jacqueline. I never had the time.

With Jacqueline I settled into a parody of the sporting colonel, the tweedy cove with a line-up of trophies and a dozen reminiscences about each. I have caught myself fancying a glass of sherry and a little mental dalliance with Inge, Catherine, Bathsheba, Judith, Estelle . . . Estelle, I haven't thought about Estelle for years. She had a scrap metal business. No, no, no! I don't want to go backwards in time like a sci-fi thriller. What is it to me that Estelle had a clapped-out Rolls-Royce with a pneumatic back seat? I can still smell the leather.

Louise's face. Under her fierce gaze my past is burned away. The beloved as nitric acid. Am I hoping for a saviour in Louise? An almighty scouring of deed and misdeed, leaving the slab clean and white. In Japan they do a nice virgin substitute with the white of an egg. For twenty-four hours at least, you can have a new hymen. In Europe we have always preferred a half lemon. Not only does it act as a crude pessary, it also makes it very difficult for the most persistent of men to drop anchor in what may seem the most pliant of women. Tightness passes for newness; the man believes his little bride has satisfyingly sealed depths. He can look forward to plunging her inch by inch.

Cheating is easy. There's no swank to infidelity. To borrow against the trust someone has placed in you costs nothing at first. You get away with it, you take a little more and a little more until there is no more to draw on. Oddly, your hands should be full with all that taking but when you open them there's nothing there.

When I say 'I will be true to you' I am drawing a quiet space beyond the reach of other desires. No-one can legislate love; it cannot be given orders or cajoled into service. Love belongs to itself, deaf to pleading and unmoved by violence. Love is not something you can negotiate. Love is the one thing stronger than desire and the only proper reason to resist temptation. There are those who say that temptation can be barricaded beyond the door. The ones who think that stray desires can be driven out of the heart like the moneychangers from the temple. Maybe they can, if you patrol your weak points day and night, don't look don't smell, don't dream. The most reliable Securicor, church sanctioned and state approved, is marriage. Swear you'll cleave only unto him or her and magically that's what will happen. Adultery is as much about disillusionment as it is about sex. The charm didn't work. You paid all that money, ate the cake and it didn't work. It's not *your* fault is it?

Marriage is the flimsiest weapon against desire. You may as well take a pop-gun to a python. A friend of mine, a banker and a very rich man who had travelled the world, told me he was getting married. I was surprised because I knew that for years he had been obsessed with a dancer who for wild and proper reasons of her own wouldn't commit. Finally he had lost patience and chosen a pleasant steady girl who ran a riding school. I saw him at his flat the weekend before his wedding. He told me how serious he was about marriage, how he had read the wedding service and found it beautiful. Within its confines he sensed happiness. Just then the doorbell rang and he took receipt of a van-load of white lilies. He was arranging them enthusiastically and telling me his theories on love, when the doorbell rang again and he took receipt of a crate of Veuve Clicquot and a huge tin of caviare. He had the table set and I noticed how often he looked at his watch.

'After we're married,' he said, 'I can't imagine wanting another woman.' The doorbell rang a third time. It was the dancer. She had come for the weekend. 'I'm not married yet,' he said.

When I say 'I will be true to you' I must mean it in spite of the formalities, instead of the formalities. If I commit adultery in my heart then I have lost you a little. The bright vision of your face will blur. I may not notice this once or twice, I may pride myself on having enjoyed those fleshy excursions in the most cerebral way. Yet I will have blunted that sharp flint that sparks between us, our desire for one another above all else.

King Kong. The huge gorilla is at the top of the Empire State Building holding Fay Wray in the palm of his hand. A bevy of aircraft have been sent to wound the monster but he brushes them away as you would a fly. In the grip of desire a two-seater bi-plane with MARRIED on the side will hardly scratch the beast. You'll still lie awake at night twisting your wedding ring round and round.

With Louise I want to do something different. I want the holiday and the homecoming together. She is the edge and the excitement for me but I have to believe it beyond six months. My circadian clock, which puts me to sleep at night and wakes me up in the morning in a regular twenty-four-hour fashion, has a larger arc that seems set at twenty-four weeks. I can override it, I've managed that, but I can't stop it going off. With Bathsheba, my longest love at three years, the faithful ticker was cheated. She was so little there that while she occupied a fair stretch of time, she filled my days hardly at all. That may have been her secret. If she had lain with me and eaten with me and washed scrubbed and bathed with me, maybe I'd have been off in six months, or at least itching. I think she knew that.

So what affects the circadian clock? What interrupts it, slows it, speeds it? These questions occupy an obscure branch of science called chronobiology. Interest in the clock is growing because as we live more and more artificially, we'd like to con nature into altering her patterns for us. Night-workers and frequent fliers are absolutely the victims of their stubborn circadian clocks. Hormones are deep in the picture, so are social factors and environmental ones. Emerging from this melée, bit by bit, is light. The amount of light to which we are exposed crucially affects our clock. Light. Sun like a disc-saw through the body. Shall I submit myself sundial-wise beneath Louise's direct gaze? It's a risk; human beings go mad without a little shade, but how to break the habit of a lifetime else?

Louise took my face between her hands. I felt her long fingers tapering the sides of my head, her thumbs under my jawbone. She drew me to her, kissing me gently, her tongue inside my lower lip. I put my arms around her, not sure whether I was a lover or a child. I wanted her to hide me beneath her skirts against all menace. Sharp points of desire were still there but there was too a sleepy safe rest like being in a boat I had as a child. She rocked me against her, sea-calm, sea under a clear sky, a glass-bottomed boat and nothing to fear.

'The wind's getting up,' she said.

Louise let me sail in you over these spirited waves. I have the hope of a saint in a coracle. What made them set out in years before the year 1000 with nothing between themselves and the sea but pieces of leather and lath? What made them certain of another place uncharted and unseen? I can see them now, eating black bread and honeycomb, sheltering from the rain under an animal hide. Their bodies are weathered but their souls are transparent. The sea is a means not an end. They trust it in spite of the signs.

The earliest pilgrims shared a cathedral for a heart. They were the temple not made with hands. The Eklasia of God. The song that carried them over the waves was the hymn that rung the rafters. Their throats were bare for God. Look at them now, heads thrown back, mouths open, alone but for the gulls that dip the prow. Against the too salt sea and the inhospitable sky, their voices made a screen of praise.

Love it was that drove them forth. Love that brought them home again. Love hardened their hands against the oar and heated their sinews against the rain. The journeys they made were beyond common sense; who leaves the hearth for the open sea? especially without a compass, especially in winter, especially alone. What you risk reveals what you value. In the presence of love, hearth and quest become one.

Louise, I would gladly fire the past for you, go and not look back. I have been reckless before, never counting the cost, oblivious to the cost. Now, I've done the sums ahead. I know what it will mean to redeem myself from the accumulations of a lifetime. I know and I don't care. You set before me a space uncluttered by association. It might be a void or it might be a release. Certainly I want to take the risk. I want to take the risk because the life I have stored up is going mouldy.

She kissed me and in her kiss lay the complexity of passion. Lover and child, virgin and roué. Had I ever been kissed before? I was as shy as an unbroken colt. I had Mercutio's swagger. This was the woman I had made love with yesterday, her taste was fresh on my mouth, but would she stay? I quivered like a schoolgirl.

'You're shaking,' she said.

'I must be cold.'

'Let me warm you.'

We lay down on my floor, our backs to the day. I needed no more light than was in her touch, her fingers brushing my skin, bringing up the nerve ends. Eyes closed I began a voyage down her spine, the cobbled road of hers that brought me to a cleft and a damp valley then a deep pit to drown in. What other places are there in the world than those discovered on a lover's body?

We were quiet together after we had made love. We watched the afternoon sun fall across the garden, the long shadows of early evening making patterns on the white wall. I was holding Louise's hand, conscious of it, but sensing too that a further intimacy might begin, the recognition of another person that is deeper than consciousness, lodged in the body more than held in the mind. I didn't understand that sensing, I wondered if it might be bogus, I'd never known it myself although I'd seen it in a couple who'd been together for a very long time. Time had not diminished their love. They seemed to have become one another without losing their very individual selves. Only once had I seen it and I envied it. The odd thing about Louise, being with Louise, was déjà vu. I couldn't know her well and yet I did know her well. Not facts and figures, I was endlessly curious about her life, rather a particular trust. That afternoon, it seemed to me I had always been here with Louise, we were familiar.

'I've spoken to Elgin,' she said. 'I told him what you are to me. I told him we'd been to bed together.'

'What did he say?'

'He asked which bed.'

'Which bed?'

'Our marital bed, as I suppose he'd call it, was made by him when we were living on my money in a tiny house. He was training, I was teaching, he made the bed in the evenings . . . It's very uncomfortable. I told him we'd used my bed. The Lady's Occasional . . . He was calmer then.'

I could understand how Elgin felt about his bed. Bathsheba had always insisted that we use their marital bed. I had to sleep on his side. It was the violation of innocence I objected to, a bed should be a safe place. It's not safe if you can't turn your back before it's occupied again. I air my scruples now but it didn't stop me at the time. I do despise myself for that.

'I told Elgin I had to be able to see you, to be free to come and go with you. I told him I wouldn't lie and that I didn't want him to lie to me . . . He asked me if I was going to leave him and I said I honestly didn't know.'

She turned to me her face serious and disturbed. 'I honestly don't know. Do you want me to leave him?'

I swallowed and struggled hard for the answer. The answer in my throat coming straight from my heart was 'Yes. Pack now.' I couldn't say that, I made my answer from my head.

'Shall we see how we go?'

Louise's face betrayed her for a second only but I knew that she too had wanted me to say yes. I tried to help us both.

'We could decide in three months. That would be fairer wouldn't it? To Elgin, to you?'

'What about you?'

I shrugged. 'I've done with Jacqueline. I'm here for you if you want me.'

She said, 'I want to offer you more than infidelity.'

I looked into her lovely face and I thought, I'm not ready for this. My boots are still muddy from the time before. I said, 'Yesterday you were angry with me, you accused me of trophy hunting and you told me not to declare my love to you until I had declared it to myself. You were right. Give me time to do the work I must do. Don't make it easy for me. I want to be sure. I want you to be sure.'

She nodded. 'When I saw you two years ago I thought you were the most beautiful creature male or female I had ever seen.'

Two years ago, what was she talking about?

'I saw you in the park, you were walking by yourself, you were talking to yourself. I followed you for about an hour and then I went home. I never imagined to see you again. You were a game in my head.'

'Do you often follow people in the park?'

She laughed. 'Never before and only once since. The second time I saw you. You were in the British Library.'

'Translating?'

'Yes. I noted your seat number and I asked the desk clerk if he knew your name. When I had your name I found your address and that is why six months ago you found a drenched distressed creature in the road beyond your door.'

'You told me you had had your bag stolen.'

'Yes.'

'You asked me if I could let you dry off and phone your husband.'

'Yes.'

'None of that was real?'

'I had to speak to you. It was the only thing I could think of. Not very clever. And then I met Jacqueline and I thought I must stop and I thought about Elgin and tried to stop. I lured myself into believing that we could be friends, if I was your friend that would be enough. We made good friends, didn't we?'

I dwelt on that day when I had found Louise in the rain. She looked like Puck sprung from the mist. Her hair was shining with bright drops of rain, the rain ran down her breasts, their outline clear through her wet muslin dress.

'It was Emma, Lady Hamilton, who gave me the idea,' said Louise, stealing my thoughts. 'She used to wet her dress before she went out. It was very provocative but it worked on Nelson.'

Not Nelson again.

Yes, that day. I saw her from my bedroom window and rushed out. It was an act of kindness on my part but a very delightful one. It was I who had telephoned her the following day. She very kindly invited me to lunch. All that I could follow, what I couldn't follow was the spring of her motive. I don't lack self-confidence but I'm not beautiful, that is a word reserved for very few people, people such as Louise herself. I told her this.

'You can't see what I can see.' She stroked my face. 'You are a pool of clear water where the light plays.'

There was a hammering at the door. We both jumped.

'It must be Jacqueline,' said Louise. 'I thought she'd be back when it got dark.'

'She's not a vampire.'

The hammering stopped then a key was inserted carefully into the lock. Had Jacqueline been checking to see if anyone was home? I heard her come in and go into the bedroom. Then she opened the sitting room door. She saw Louise and burst into tears.

'Jacqueline, why did you steal my stuff?'

'I hate you.'

I tried to persuade her to sit down and have a drink but as soon as she'd taken the glass she threw it at Louise. It missed and shattered on the wall behind. She leapt across the room and took one of the sharpest largest pieces and made for Louise's face. I grabbed Jacqueline's wrist and twisted it back against her arm. She cried out and dropped the glass.

'Out,' I said, still holding her. 'Give me the keys and get out.' It was as if I'd never cared for her at all. I wanted to wipe her away. I wanted to blot out her blazing stupid face. She didn't deserve this, in a corner of my mind I knew it was my weakness not hers that had brought us to this shameful day. I should have smoothed things down, parried, instead I slapped her across the face and tore my keys from her pocket.

'That was for the bathroom,' I said as she felt her bleeding mouth. Jacqueline stumbled towards the door and spat in my face. I took her by the collar and frog-marched her to her car. She skidded away without her lights on.

I stood watching her go, hands limp at my sides. I groaned and sat on the low wall beside my flat. The air was cool and calming. Why had I hit her? I'd always prided myself on being the superior partner, the intelligent sensitive one who rated good manners and practised them. Now I'd shown myself to be a cheap thug in a scrap.

She'd angered me and I'd responded by thumping her. How many times does that turn up in the courts? How many times have I curled my lip at other people's violence? I put my head in my hands and cried. This ugliness was my doing. Another failed relationship, another hurt human being. When was I going to stop? I pulled my knuckles along the rough brick. There's always an excuse, a good reason for behaving as we do. I couldn't think of a good reason.

'All right,' I said to myself. 'This is your last chance. If you're worth anything show it now. Be worth Louise.'

I went back inside. Louise was sitting very still looking at the glass between her hands as though it were a crystal ball.

'Forgive me,' I said.

'You didn't hit me.' She turned to me, her full lips in a long straight line. 'If you ever do hit me I shall leave you.'

My stomach contracted. I wanted to defend myself but I couldn't start to say anything. I didn't trust my voice.

Louise got up and went to the bathroom. I didn't warn her. I heard her open the door and draw in her breath sudden and sharp. She came back and held out her hand. We spent the rest of the night cleaning.

The interesting thing about a knot is its formal complexity. Even the simplest pedigree knot, the trefoil, with its three roughly symmetrical lobes, has mathematical as well as artistic beauty. For the religious, King Solomon's knot is said to embody the essence of all knowledge. For carpet makers and cloth weavers all over the world, the challenge of the knot lies in the rules of its surprises. Knots can change but they must be well-behaved. An informal knot is a messy knot.

Louise and I were held by a single loop of love. The cord passing round our bodies had no sharp twists or sinister turns. Our wrists were not tied and there was no noose about our necks. In Italy in the fourteenth and fifteenth centuries a favourite sport was to fasten two fighters together with a strong rope and let them beat each other to death. Often it was death because the loser couldn't back off and the victor rarely spared him. The victor kept the rope and tied a knot in it. He had only to swing it through the streets to terrify money from passers-by.

I don't want to be your sport nor you to be mine. I don't want to punch you for the pleasure of it, tangling the clear lines that bind us, forcing you to your knees, dragging you up again. The public face of a life in chaos. I want the hoop around our hearts to be a guide not a terror. I don't want to pull you tighter than you can bear. I don't want the lines to slacken either, the thread paying out over the side, enough rope to hang ourselves.

I was sitting in the library writing this to Louise, looking at a facsimile of an illuminated manuscript, the first letter a huge L. The L woven into shapes of birds and angels that slid between the pen lines. The letter was a maze. On the outside, at the top of the L, stood a pilgrim in hat and habit. At the heart of the letter, which had been formed to make a rectangle out of the double of itself, was the Lamb of God. How would the pilgrim try through the maze, the maze so simple to angels and birds? I tried to fathom the path for a long time but I was caught at dead ends by beaming serpents. I gave up and shut the book, forgetting that the first word had been Love.

In the weeks that followed Louise and I were together as much as we could be. She was careful with Elgin, I was careful with both of them. The carefulness was wearing us out.

One night, after a seafood lasagne and a bottle of champagne we made love so vigorously that the Lady's Occasional was driven across the floor by the turbine of our lust. We began by the window and ended by the door. It's well-known that molluscs are aphrodisiac, Casanova ate his mussels raw before pleasuring a lady but then he also believed in the stimulating powers of hot chocolate.

Articulacy of fingers, the language of the deaf and dumb, signing on the body body longing. Who taught you to write in blood on my back? Who taught you to use your hands as branding irons? You have scored your name into my shoulders, referenced me with your mark. The pads of your fingers have become printing blocks, you tap a message on to my skin, tap meaning into my body. Your morse code interferes with my heart beat. I had a steady heart before I met you, I relied upon it, it had seen active service and grown strong. Now you alter its pace with your own rhythm, you play upon me, drumming me taut.

Written on the body is a secret code only visible in certain lights; the accumulations of a lifetime gather there. In places the palimpsest is so heavily worked that the letters feel like braille. I like to keep my body rolled up away from prying eyes. Never unfold too much, tell the whole story. I didn't know that Louise would have reading hands. She has translated me into her own book.

We tried to be quiet for Elgin's sake. He had arranged to be out but Louise thought he was at home. In silence and in darkness we loved each other and as I traced her bones with my palm I wondered what time would do to skin that was so new to me. Could I ever feel any less for this body? Why does ardour pass? Time that withers you will wither me. We will fall like ripe fruit and roll down the grass together. Dear friend, let me lie beside you watching the clouds until the earth covers us and we are gone.

Elgin was at breakfast the following morning. This was a shock. He was as pale as his shirt. Louise slid into her place at the foot of the long table. I took up a neutral position about half way. I buttered a slice of toast and bit. The noise vibrated the table. Elgin winced.

'Do you have to make so much noise?'

'Sorry Elgin,' I said, spattering the cloth with crumbs.

Louise passed me the teapot and smiled.

'What are you so happy about?' said Elgin. 'You didn't get any sleep either.'

'You told me you were away until today,' said Louise quietly.

'I came home. It's my house. I paid for it.'

'It's our house and I told you we'd be here last night.'

'I might as well have slept in a brothel.'

'I thought that's what you were doing,' said Louise.

Elgin got up and threw his napkin on the table. 'I'm exhausted but I'm going to work. Lives depend on my work and because of you I shall not be at my best today. You might think of yourself as a murderer.'

'I might but I shan't,' said Louise.

We heard Elgin clatter his mountain bike out of the hall. Through the basement window I saw him strap on his pink helmet. He liked cycling, he thought it was good for his heart.

Louise was lost in thought. I drank two cups of tea, washed up and was thinking of going home when she put her arms around me from behind and rested her chin on my shoulder.

'This isn't working,' she said.

She asked me to wait three days and promised to send me a message after that time. I nodded, dog-dumb, and went back to my corner. I was hopelessly in love with Louise and very scared. I spent the three days trying again to rationalise us, to make a harbour in the raging sea where I could bob about and admire the view. There was no view, only Louise's face. I thought of her as intense and beyond common sense. I never knew what she would do next. I was still loading on to her all my terror. I still wanted her to be the leader of our expedition. Why did I find it hard to accept that we were equally sunk? Sunk in each other? Destiny is a worrying concept. I don't want to be fated, I want to choose. But perhaps Louise had to be chosen. If the choice is as crude as Louise or not Louise then there is no choice.

I sat in the library on the first day trying to work on my translations but jotting on the blotter the line of my true enquiry. I was sick to the gut with fear. The heavy fear of not seeing her again. I wouldn't break my word. I wouldn't go to the phone. I scanned the row of industrious heads. Dark, blonde, grey, bald, wig. A long way round was a bright red flame. I knew it wasn't Louise but I couldn't take my eyes off the colour. It soothed me the way any bear will soothe a child not at home. It wasn't mine but it was like mine. If I made my eyes into narrow slits the red took up the whole room. The dome was lit with red. I felt like a seed in a pomegranate. Some say that the pomegranate was the real apple of Eve, fruit of the womb, I would eat my way into perdition to taste you.

'I love her what can I do?'

The gentleman in the knitted waistcoat opposite looked up and frowned. I had broken the rule and spoken out loud. Worse, I had spoken to myself. I gathered my books and rushed from the room, past the suspicious gaze of the guards and out down the steps built through the massive columns of the British Museum. I started to walk home, convincing myself that I would never hear from Louise again. She would go to Switzerland with Elgin and have a baby. A year ago Louise had given up her job at Elgin's request so that they could start a family. She had miscarried once and had no wish to do it again. She told me she was firm about no baby. Did I believe her? She had given the one reason I believe. She said, 'It might look like Elgin.'

Reason. I was caught in a Piranesi nightmare. The logical paths the proper steps led nowhere. My mind took me up tortuous staircases that opened into doors that opened into nothing. I knew my problem was partly old war wounds playing up. Put in a situation that smelt anything like the one with Bathsheba and I hit out. Bathsheba had always been asking for time to make definite decisions only to come back with a list of compromises. Louise, I knew, wouldn't make compromises. She would vanish.

Ten years of marriage is a lot of marriage. I can't be relied upon to describe Elgin properly. More importantly I'd never met the other Elgin, the one she'd married. No-one whom Louise had loved could be worthless, if I believed that I'd have to accept that I might be worthless too. At least I had never pressured her to leave. It would be her own decision.

I had a boyfriend once called Crazy Frank. He had been brought up by midgets although he himself was over six feet tall. He loved his adopted parents and used to carry them one on each shoulder. I met him doing exactly that at a Toulouse-Lautrec exhibition in Paris. We went to a bar and then on to another bar and got very drunk and while we were in a shot bed in a cheap pension he told me about his passion for miniatures.

'You'd be perfect if you were smaller,' he said.

I asked him if he took his parents everywhere with him and he said that he did. They didn't need much room and they helped him to make friends. He explained that he was very shy.

Frank had the body of a bull, an image he intensified by wearing great gold hoops through his nipples. Unfortunately he had joined the hoops with a chain of heavy gold links. The effect should have been deeply butch but in fact it looked rather like the handle of a Chanel shopping bag.

He didn't want to settle down. His ambition was to find a hole in every port. He wasn't fussy about the precise location. Frank believed that love had been invented to fool people. His theory was sex and friendship. 'Don't people always behave better towards their friends than their lovers?' He warned me never to fall in love, although his words came too late because I had already fallen for him. He was the perfect vagabond, swag bag in one hand, waving with the other. He never stayed anywhere long, he was only in Paris for two months. I begged him to come back to England with me but he laughed and said England was for married couples. 'I have to be free,' he said.

'But you take your parents wherever you go.'

Frank left for Italy and I came home to England. I was torn with grief for two whole days and then

I thought, A man and his midgets. Was that what I wanted? A man whose chest jewellery rattled when he walked?

It was years ago but I still blush. Sex can feel like love or maybe it's guilt that makes me call sex love. I've been through so much I should know just what it is I'm doing with Louise. I should be a grown-up by now. Why do I feel like a convent virgin?

The second day of my ordeal I took a pair of handcuffs to the library with me and locked myself to my seat. I gave the key to the gentleman in the knitted waistcoat and asked him to let me free at five o'clock. I told him I had a deadline, that if I didn't finish my translation a Soviet writer might fail to find asylum in Great Britain. He took the key and said nothing but I noticed he'd disappeared from his place after about an hour.

I worked on, the concentrated silence of the library giving me some release from thoughts of Louise. Why is the mind incapable of deciding its own subject matter? Why when we desperately want to think of one thing do we invariably think of another? The overriding arch of Louise had distracted me from all other constructs. I like mental games, I find it easy to work and I work quickly. In the past whatever my situation I have been able to find peace in work. Now that facility had deserted me. I was a street yob who had to be kept locked up.

Whenever the word Louise came into my mind I replaced it with a brick wall. After a few hours of this my mind was nothing but brick walls. Worse, my left hand was swelling up, I don't think it was getting enough blood being strapped to the chair leg. There was no sign of the gentleman. I signalled to a guard and whispered my problem. He returned with a fellow guard and together they picked up my chair and carried me sedan style down the British Library Reading Room. It is a tribute to the scholarly temperament that nobody looked up.

In the supervisor's office I tried to explain.

'You a Communist?' he said.

'No I'm a floating voter.'

He had me cut loose and charged me for Wilful Damage To Reading Room Chair. I tried to make him amend that to 'accidental damage' but he wouldn't. Then he filed his report very solemnly and told me I'd have to hand over my ticket.

'I can't hand over my ticket. It's my livelihood.'

'Should a thought a that before you handcuffed yourself to Library Property.'

I gave him my ticket and got an appeal form. Could I fall any lower?

The answer was yes. I spent the whole night prowling outside Louise's house like a private dick. I watched the lights going off at some windows, on at others. Was she in his bed? What did that have to do with me? I ran a schizophrenic dialogue with myself through the hours of darkness and into the small hours, so called because the heart shrivels up to the size of a pea and there is no hope left in it.

By morning I was home shivering and wretched. I welcomed the shivering since I hoped it might portend a fever. If I were delirious for a few days her leaving me might hurt less. With luck I might even die. 'Men have died from time to time and worms have eaten them, but not for love.' Shakespeare was wrong, I was living proof of that.

'You ought to be dead proof,' I said to myself. 'If you're living proof he was right.'

I sat down to make a will leaving everything to Louise. Was I in sound mind and body? I took my temperature. No. I peered at my head in the mirror. No. Better go to bed close the curtains and get out the gin bottle.

That was how Louise found me at 6 o'clock on the evening of the third day. She'd been telephoning since noon but I had been too sodden to notice.

'They've taken my ticket away,' I said when I saw her. I burst into tears and lay blubbering in her arms. There was nothing she could do except give me a bath and a sleeping draught. In my sinking haze I heard her say, 'I will never let you go.'

No-one knows what forces draw two people together. There are plenty of theories; astrology, chemistry, mutual need, biological drive. Magazines and manuals worldwide will tell you how to pick the perfect partner. Dating agencies stress the science of their approach although having a computer does not make one a scientist. The old music of romance is played out in modern digital ways. Why leave yourself to chance when you could leave yourself to science? Shortly the pseudo-lab coat approach of dating by details will make way for a genuine experiment whose results, however unusual, will remain controllable. Or so they say. (See splitting the atom, gene therapy, in vitro fertilisation, cross hormone cultures, even the humble cathode ray for similar statements.) Never mind. Virtual Reality is on its way.

At present to enter a virtual world you would have to put on a crude-looking diving helmet of the kind people used to wear in the 1940s and a special glove rather like a heavy gardening gauntlet. Thus equipped you would be inside a 360° television set with a three-dimensional programme, three-dimensional sound, and solid objects that you could pick up and move around. No longer would you be watching a film from a fixed perspective, this is a film-set you can explore, even alter if you don't like it. As far as your senses can tell you are in a real world. The fact that you are in a diving helmet wearing a gardening glove won't matter.

In a little while, the equipment will be replaced by a room that you can walk into like any other. Except that it will be an intelligent space. The room will be a wall-to-wall virtual world of your choosing. If you like, you may live in a computer-created world all day and all night. You will be able to try out a Virtual life with a Virtual lover. You can go into your Virtual house and do Virtual housework, add a baby or two, even find out if you'd rather be gay. Or single. Or straight. Why hesitate when you could simulate?

And sex? Certainly. Teledildonics is the word. You will be able to plug in your telepresence to the billion-bundle network of fibre optics criss-crossing the world and join your partner in Virtuality. Your real selves will be wearing body suits made up of thousands of tiny tactile detectors per square inch. Courtesy of the fibreoptic network these will receive and transmit touch. The Virtual epidermis will be as sensitive as your own outer layer of skin.

For myself, unreconstructed as I am, I'd rather hold you in my arms and walk through the damp of a real English meadow in real English rain. I'd rather travel across the world to have you with me than lie at home dialling your telepresence. The scientists say I can choose but how much choice have I over their other inventions? My life is not my own, shortly I shall have to haggle over my reality. Luddite? No, I don't want to smash the machines but neither do I want the machines to smash me.

August. The street like a hotplate cooking us. Louise had brought me to Oxford to get away from Elgin. She didn't tell me what had happened in the previous three days, she kept her secret like a war-time agent. She was smiling, calm, the perfect undercover girl. I didn't trust her. I believed she was about to break it off with me, that she had made it up with Elgin and begged this Roman holiday as a way out with a frisson of regret. My chest was full of stones.

We walked, swam in the river, read back to back as lovers do. Talked all the time about everything except ourselves. We were in a Virtual world where the only taboo was real life. But in a true Virtual world I could have gently picked up Elgin and dropped him for ever from the frame. I saw him from the corner of my eye waiting waiting. Elgin squatted over life until it moved.

We were in our rented room, the windows wide open against the heat. Outside, the dense noises of summer; shouts from the street, a click of a croquet ball, laughter, sudden and incomplete and above us Mozart on a tinkly piano. A dog, woof woof woof, chasing the lawn mower. I had my head on your belly and I could hear your lunch on its way to your bowels.

You said, 'I'm going to leave.'

I thought, Yes, of course you are, you're going back to the shell.

You said, 'I'm going to leave him because my love for you makes any other life a lie.'

I've hidden those words in the lining of my coat. I take them out like a jewel thief when no-one's watching. They haven't faded. Nothing about you has faded. You are still the colour of my blood. You are my blood. When I look in the mirror it's not my own face I see. Your body is twice. Once you once me. Can I be sure which is which?

We went home to my flat and you brought nothing from your other life but the clothes you stood up in. Elgin had insisted that you take nothing until the divorce settlement had been agreed. You had asked him to divorce you for Adultery and he had insisted it was to be Unreasonable Behaviour.

'It will help him to save face,' you said. 'Adultery is for cuckolds. Unreasonable Behaviour is for martyrs. A mad wife is better than a bad wife. What will he tell his friends?'

I don't know what he told his friends but I know what he told me. Louise and I had been living together in great happiness for nearly five months. It was Christmas time and we had decorated the flat with garlands of holly and ivy woven from the woods. We had very little money; I had not been translating as much as I should have been and Louise could not resume work until the new year. She'd found a job teaching Art History. Nothing mattered to us. We were insultingly happy. We sang and played and walked for miles looking at buildings and watching people. A treasure had fallen into our hands and the treasure was each other.

Those days have a crystalline clearness to me now. Whichever way I hold them up to the light they refract a different colour. Louise in her blue dress gathering fir cones in the skirt. Louise against the purple sky looking like a Pre-Raphaelite heroine. The young green of our life and the last yellow roses in November. The colours blur and I can only see her face. Then I hear her voice crisp and white. 'I will never let you go.'

It was Christmas Eve and Louise went to visit her mother who had always hated Elgin until Louise told her she was divorcing him. Louise hoped that the season of goodwill might work in her favour and so when the stars were hard and bright she wrapped her mane around her and set off. I waved, smiling, how fine she would look on the Steppes of Russia.

As I was about to close the door, a shadow came towards me. It was Elgin. I didn't want to invite him in but he was menacing in an unlikely jovial way. My neck prickled like an animal's. I thought for Louise's sake I must get it over with.

I gave him a drink and he talked aimlessly until I could bear it no longer. I asked him what he wanted. Was it about the divorce? 'In a way,' he said smiling. 'I think there's something you should know. Something Louise won't have told you.'

'Louise tells me everything,' I said coldly. 'As I do her.'

'Very touching,' he said watching the ice in his Scotch. 'Then you won't be surprised to hear she's got cancer?'

Two hundred miles from the surface of the earth there is no gravity. The laws of motion are suspended. You could turn somersaults slowly slowly, weight into weightlessness, nowhere to fall. As you lay on your back paddling in space you might notice your feet had fled your head. You are stretching slowly slowly, getting longer, your joints are slipping away from their usual places. There is no connection between your shoulder and your arm. You will break up bone by bone, fractured from who you are, you are drifting away now, the centre cannot hold.

Where am I? There is nothing here I recognise. This isn't the world I know, the little ship I've trimmed and rigged. What is this slow-motion space, my arm moving up and down up and down like a parody of Mussolini? Who is this man with the revolving eyes, his mouth opening like a gas chamber, his words acrid, vile, in my throat and nostrils? The room stinks. The air is bad. He's poisoning me and I can't get away. My feet don't obey me. Where is the familiar ballast of my life? I am fighting helplessly without hope. I grapple but my body slithers away. I want to brace myself against something solid but there's nothing solid here.

The facts Elgin. The facts.
   Leukaemia.
   Since when?
   About two years.
   She's not ill.
   Not yet.
   What kind of leukaemia?
   Chronic lymphocytic leukaemia.
   She looks well.
   The patient may have no symptoms for some time.
   She's well.
   I took a blood count after her first miscarriage.
   Her first?
   She was badly anaemic.
   I don't understand.
   It's rare.
   She's not ill.
   Her lymph nodes are now enlarged.

Will she die?
They're rubbery but painless.
Will she die?
Her spleen isn't enlarged at all. That's good.
Will she die?
She has too many white T-cells.
Will she die?
That depends.
On what?
On you.
You mean I can look after her?
I mean I can.

Elgin left and I sat under the Christmas tree watching the swinging angels and the barleysugar candles. His plan was simple: if Louise came back to him he would give her the care money can't buy. She would go with him to Switzerland and have access to the very latest medico-technology. As a patient, no matter how rich, she would not be able to do that. As Elgin's wife she would.

Cancer treatment is brutal and toxic. Louise would normally be treated with steroids, massive doses to induce remission. When her spleen started to enlarge she might have splenic irridation or even a splenectomy. By then she would be badly anaemic, suffering from deep bruising and bleeding, tired and in pain most of the time. She would be constipated. She would be vomiting and nauseous. Eventually chemotherapy would contribute to failure of her bone marrow. She would be very thin, my beautiful girl, thin and weary and lost. There is no cure for chronic lymphocytic leukaemia.

Louise came home her face shining with frost. There was a

deep glow in her cheeks, her lips were icy when she kissed me. She pushed her frozen hands under my shirt and held them against my back like two branding irons. She was chattering about the cold and the stars and how clear the sky was and the moon hung in an icicle from the roof of the world.

I didn't want to cry, I wanted to talk to her calmly and gently. But I did cry, fast hot tears falling on to her cold skin, scalding her with my misery. Unhappiness is selfish, grief is selfish. For whom are the tears? Perhaps it can be no other way.

'Elgin's been here,' I said. 'He told me you have cancer of the blood.'

'It's not serious.' She said this quickly. What did she expect me to do?

'Cancer's not serious?'

'I'm asymptomatic.'

'Why didn't you tell me? Couldn't you have told me?'

'It's not serious.'

There is a silence between us for the first time. I want to be angry with her now. I was pent-up with rage.

'I was waiting for the results. I've had some more tests done. I haven't got the results yet.'

'Elgin has, he says you don't want to know.'

'I don't trust Elgin. I'm having a second opinion.'

I was staring at her, my fists clenched so that I could dig my nails into my palms. When I looked at her I saw Elgin's square spectacled face. Not Louise's curved lips but his triumphant mouth.

'Shall I tell you about it?' she said.

In the hours of the night until the sky turned blue-black,

then pearl grey, until the weak winter sun broke on us, we lay in one another's arms wrapped in a travel rug and she told me what she feared and I told her my fears. She would not go back to Elgin, of that she was adamant. She knew a great deal about the disease and I would learn. We would face it together. Brave words and comfort to us both who needed comfort in the small cold room that compassed our life that night. We were setting out with nothing and Louise was ill. She was confident that any costs could be met from her settlement. I was not so sure but too tired and too relieved to go further that night. To reach one another again had been far enough.

The following day when Louise had gone out I went to see Elgin. He seemed to be expecting me. We went into his study. He had a new game on his computer screen. This one was called LABORATORY. A good scientist (played by the operator) and a mad scientist (played by the computer) fight it out to create the world's first transgenic tomato. Implanted with human genes the tomato will make itself into a sandwich, sauce or pizza topping with up to three additional ingredients. But is it ethical?

'Like a game?' he said.

'I've come about Louise.'

He had her test results spread out on a table. The prognosis was about 100 months. He pointed out to me that whilst it was easy for Louise to be careless about her condition as long as she felt fit and well, that would change when she began to lose her strength.

'But why treat her as an invalid before she is an invalid?'

'If we treat her now there is a chance that the disease might be halted. Who knows?' He shrugged and smiled and jangled a few keys on his terminal. The tomato leered.

'Don't you know?'

'Cancer is an unpredictable condition. It is the body turning upon itself. We don't understand that yet. We know what happens but not why it happens or how to stop it.'

'Then you have nothing to offer Louise.'

'Except her life.'

'She won't come back to you.'

'Aren't you both a bit old for the romantic dream?'

'I love Louise.'

'Then save her.'

Elgin sat down at his screen. He considered our interview to be over. 'The trouble is', he said, 'that if I choose the wrong gene I shall get squirted with tomato sauce. You do see my problem.'

Dear Louise,

I love you more than life itself. I have not known a happier time than with you. I did not know this much happiness was possible. Can love have texture? It is palpable to me, the feeling between us, I weigh it in my hands the way I weigh your head in my hands. I hold on to love as a climber does a rope. I knew our path would be steep but I did not foresee the sheer rock face we have come to. We could ascend it, I know that, but it would be you who took the strain.

I'm going away tonight, I don't know where, all I know is I won't come back. You don't have to leave the flat; I have made arrangements there. You are safe in my home but not in my arms. If I stay it will be you who goes, in pain, without help. Our love was not meant to cost you your life. I can't bear that. If it could be my life I would gladly give it. You came to me in the clothes you stood up in, that was enough. No more Louise. No more giving. You have given me everything already.

Please go with Elgin. He has promised to tell me how you are. I shall think of you every day, many times a day. Your hand prints are all over my body. Your flesh is my flesh. You deciphered me and now I am plain to read. The message is a simple one; my love for you. I want you to live. Forgive my mistakes. Forgive me.

I packed and took a train to Yorkshire. I covered my tracks so that Louise could not find me. I took my work and some money that I had, the money left over from paying the mortgage for a year, money enough for a couple of months. I found a tiny cottage and a P.O. Box for my publishers and a friend who had committed to help me. I took a job in a fancy wine bar. A supper bar designed for the nouveau refugees who thought that fish and chips were too working class. We served pommes frites with Dover sole that had never seen a cliff. We served prawns so deeply packed in ice that we sometimes dropped them in a drink by mistake. 'It's a new fashion Sir, Scotch on the rocks à la prawn.' After that everybody wanted one.

My job was to unload coolers of Frascati on to fashionably tiny tables and take the supper order. We offered Mediterranean Special (fish and chips), Pavarotti Special (pizza and chips), Olde Englysshe Special (sausage and chips) and Lovers Special (spare ribs for two with chips and aromatic vinegar). There was an à la carte menu but nobody could find it. All night the handsomely studded green baize door to the kitchens swung back and forth offering a brief glimpse of two busy chefs in hats like steeples.

'Chuck us another pizza Kev.'

'She wants sweetcorn extra.'

'Well give us the tin opener then.'

The ceaseless pinging from the banks of microwaves stacked like a NASA terminal was largely drowned out by the hypnotic thud of the bass speakers in the bar. No-one ever asked how their food was cooked and, had they, they would have been reassured by a postcard of the kitchens signed compliments of the chef. They were not our kitchens but they might have been. The bread was so white it shone.

I bought a bicycle to cover the twenty miles that separated the bar from my rented hovel. I wanted to be too exhausted to think. Still every turn of the wheel was Louise.

My cottage had a table, two chairs, a peg-rug and a bed with a winded mattress. If I needed heat I chopped wood and lit a fire. The cottage had been long abandoned. No-one wanted to live in it and no-one else would have been stupid enough to rent it. There was no telephone and the bath sat in the middle of a semi-partitioned room. The draught wheezed in through a badly boarded up window. The floor creaked like a Hammer horror set. It was dirty, depressing and ideal. The people who owned it thought I was a fool. I am a fool.

There was a greasy armchair by the fire, armchair shrunken inside its loose covers like an old man in a heyday suit. Let me sit in it and never have to get up. I want to rot here, slowly sinking into the faded pattern, invisible against the dead roses. If you could see through the filthy windows you'd see just the back of my head bulging over the line of the chair. You'd see my hair, sparse and thinning, greying, gone. Death's head in the chair, the rose chair in the stagnant garden. What is the point of movement when movement indicates life and life indicates hope? I have neither life nor hope. Better then to fall in with the crumbling wainscot, to settle with the dust and be drawn up into someone's nostrils. Daily we breathe the dead.

What are the characteristics of living things? At school, in biology I was told the following: Excretion, growth, irritability, locomotion, nutrition, reproduction and respiration. This does not seem like a very lively list to me. If that's all there is to being a living thing I may as well be dead. What of that other characteristic prevalent in human living things, the longing to be loved? No, it doesn't come under the heading Reproduction. I have no desire to reproduce but I still seek out love. Reproduction. Over-polished Queen Anne style dining-room suite reduced to clear. Genuine wood. Is that what I want? The model family, two plus two in an easy home assembly kit. I don't want a model, I want the full-scale original. I don't want to reproduce, I want to make something entirely new. Fighting words but the fight's gone out of me.

I tried to clean up a little. I cut some winter jasmine from the ragged garden and brought it indoors. It looked like a nun in a slum. I bought a hammer and some hardboard and patched up the worst of the neglect. I made it so that I could sit over the fire and not feel the wind at the same time. This was an achievement. Mark Twain built a house for himself with a window over the fireplace so that he could watch the snow falling over the flames. I had a hole that let the rain in, but then I had a life that let the rain in.

A few days after I arrived I heard an uncertain yowling outside. A sound that should have been defiant and swagger-all but that wasn't quite. I put on my boots, took a flashlight and stumbled through the January slutch. The mud was deep and viscous. To keep a path to my house I had to strew it daily with ashes. The ashes were choked with mud, the gutter ran straight off the house down to my doorstep. Any gust brought the tiles off the roof.

Flat up against the wall of the house, if sweating pot-bellied brickwork held together with lichen can be called a wall, was a thin mangy cat. It looked at me with eyes composed of hope and fear. It was soaked and shivering. I didn't hesitate, leant down and took it by the scruff of the neck the way Louise had taken me.

Under the light I saw the cat and I were filthy. When had I last taken a bath? My clothes were stale, my skin was grey. My hair fell in defeated flashes. The cat had oil down one flank and mud punking up the fur of its belly.

'It's bathnight in Yorkshire,' I said and took the cat to the tired old enamel tub on three claw feet. The fourth end rested on a copy of the Bible. 'Rock of ages cleft for me. Let me hide myself in thee.' I bullied the ancient boiler into life with a series of screams, pleas, matches and lighter fuel. It finally rumbled and spat, billowing evil-smelling clouds of steam into the peeling bathroom. I could see the cat's eyes, aghast, watching me.

We did get clean, the pair of us, him wrapped in a handtowel, me in my only luxury, a fleecy bathsheet. His head was tiny with the fur plastered against the skull. He had a notch out of one ear and a bad scar over one eye. He trembled in my arms though I spoke to him softly about a bowl of milk. Later, in the collapsing bed, burrowed under an eiderdown so misused that the feathers didn't move when I shook it, a milk-full cat learned to purr. He slept on my chest all night. I didn't sleep much. I tried to keep awake at night until utterly exhausted so that I could miss the early dreaming sleep of one who has much to hide. There are people who starve themselves by day only to find that in the night their denied bodies have savaged the fridge, taken carcasses raw, eaten cat food, toilet paper, anything to satisfy the need.

Sleeping beside Louise had been a pleasure that often led to sex but which was separate from it. The delicious temperate warmth of her body, skin temperature perfect with mine. Moving away from her only to turn over again hours later and mould myself into the curve of her back. Her smell. Specific Louise smell. Her hair. A red blanket to cover us both. Her legs. She never shaved them enough to keep them absolutely smooth. There was a residual roughness that I liked, the very beginning of the hairs growing back. They were not allowed to appear so I didn't discover their colour but I felt them with my feet, pushing my foot down her shin-bone, the long bones of her legs rich in marrow. Marrow where the blood cells are formed red and white. Red and white, the colours of Louise.

In bereavement books they tell you to sleep with a pillow pulled down beside you. Not quite a Dutch wife, that is a bolster held between the legs in the tropics to soak up the sweat, not quite a Dutch wife. 'The pillow will comfort you in the long unbroken hours. If you sleep you will unconsciously benefit from its presence. If you wake the bed will seem less large and lonely.' Who writes these books? Do they really think, those quiet concerned counsellors, that two feet of linen-bound stuffing will assuage a broken heart? I don't want a pillow I want your moving breathing flesh. I want you to hold my hand in the dark, I want to roll on to you and push myself into you. When

I turn in the night the bed is continent-broad. There is endless white space where you won't be. I travel it inch by inch but you're not there. It's not a game, you're not going to leap out and surprise me. The bed is empty. I'm in it but the bed is empty.

I named the cat Hopeful because on the first day he brought me a rabbit and we ate it with lentils. I was able to do some translating work that day and when I got back from the wine bar Hopeful was waiting by the door with an ear cocked and such a look of anticipation that for a moment, a single clear moment, I forgot what I had done. The next day I cycled to the library but instead of going to the Russian section as I had intended I went to the medical books. I became obsessed with anatomy. If I could not put Louise out of my mind I would drown myself in her. Within the clinical language, through the dispassionate view of the sucking, sweating, greedy, defecating self, I found a love-poem to Louise. I would go on knowing her, more intimately than the skin, hair and voice that I craved. I would have her plasma, her spleen, her synovial fluid. I would recognise her even when her body had long since fallen away.

The Cells, Tissues,
Systems and Cavities
of the Body

THE MULTIPLICATION OF CELLS BY MITOSIS OCCURS THROUGH-OUT THE LIFE OF THE INDIVIDUAL. IT OCCURS AT A MORE RAPID RATE UNTIL GROWTH IS COMPLETE. THEREAFTER NEW CELLS ARE FORMED TO REPLACE THOSE WHICH HAVE DIED. NERVE CELLS ARE A NOTABLE EXCEPTION. WHEN THEY DIE THEY ARE NOT REPLACED.

In the secret places of her thymus gland Louise is making too much of herself. Her faithful biology depends on regulation but the white T-cells have turned bandit. They don't obey the rules. They are swarming into the bloodstream, overturning the quiet order of spleen and intestine. In the lymph nodes they are swelling with pride. It used to be their job to keep her body safe from enemies on the outside. They were her immunity, her certainty against infection. Now they are the enemies on the inside. The security forces have rebelled. Louise is the victim of a coup.

Will you let me crawl inside you, stand guard over you, trap them as they come at you? Why can't I dam their blind tide that filthies your blood? Why are there no lock gates on the portal vein? The inside of your body is innocent, nothing has taught it fear. Your artery canals trust their cargo, they don't check the shipments in the blood. You are full to overflowing but the keeper is asleep and there's murder going on inside. Who comes here? Let me hold up my lantern. It's only the blood; red cells carrying oxygen to the heart, thrombocytes making sure of proper clotting. The white cells, B and T types, just a few of them as always whistling as they go.

The faithful body has made a mistake. This is no time to stamp the passports and look at the sky. Coming up behind are hundreds of them. Hundreds too many, armed to the teeth for a job that doesn't need doing. Not needed? With all that weaponry?

Here they come, hurtling through the bloodstream trying to pick a fight. There's no-one to fight but you Louise. You're the foreign body now.

TISSUES, SUCH AS THE LINING OF THE MOUTH, CAN BE SEEN
WITH THE NAKED EYE, BUT THE MILLIONS OF CELLS WHICH
MAKE UP THE TISSUES ARE SO SMALL THAT THEY CAN ONLY
BE SEEN WITH THE AID OF A MICROSCOPE.

The naked eye. How many times have I enjoyed you
with my lascivious naked eye. I have seen you unclothed,
bent to wash, the curve of your back, the concurve of your
belly. I have had you beneath me for examination, seen the
scars between your thighs where you fell on barbed wire.
You look as if an animal has clawed you, run its steel nails
through your skin, leaving harsh marks of ownership.

My eyes are brown, they have fluttered across your
body like butterflies. I have flown the distance of your
body from side to side of your ivory coast. I know the
forests where I can rest and feed. I have mapped you with
my naked eye and stored you out of sight. The millions of
cells that make up your tissues are plotted on my retina.
Night flying I know exactly where I am. Your body is
my landing strip.

The lining of your mouth I know through tongue and
spit. Its ridges, valleys, the corrugated roof, the fortress of
teeth. The glossy smoothness of the inside of your upper
lip is interrupted by a rough swirl where you were hurt
once. The tissues of the mouth and anus heal faster than
any others but they leave signs for those who care to look.
I care to look. There's a story trapped inside your mouth.
A crashed car and a smashed windscreen. The only witness

is the scar, jagged like a duelling scar where the skin still shows the stitches.

My naked eye counts your teeth including the fillings. The incisors, canines, the molars and premolars. Thirty-two in all. Thirty-one in your case. After sex you tiger-tear your food, let your mouth run over with grease. Sometimes it's me you bite, leaving shallow wounds in my shoulders. Do you want to stripe me to match your own? I wear the wounds as a badge of honour. The moulds of your teeth are easy to see under my shirt but the L that tattoos me on the inside is not visible to the naked eye.

FOR DESCRIPTIVE PURPOSES THE HUMAN BODY IS SEPARATED INTO CAVITIES. THE CRANIAL CAVITY CONTAINS THE BRAIN. ITS BOUNDARIES ARE FORMED BY THE BONES OF THE SKULL.

Let me penetrate you. I am the archaeologist of tombs. I would devote my life to marking your passageways, the entrances and exits of that impressive mausoleum, your body. How tight and secret are the funnels and wells of youth and health. A wriggling finger can hardly detect the start of an ante-chamber, much less push through to the wide aqueous halls that hide womb, gut and brain.

In the old or ill, the nostrils flare, the eye sockets make deep pools of request. The mouth slackens, the teeth fall from their first line of defence. Even the ears enlarge like trumpets. The body is making way for worms.

As I embalm you in my memory, the first thing I shall do is to hook out your brain through your accommodating orifices. Now that I have lost you I cannot allow you to develop, you must be a photograph not a poem. You must be rid of life as I am rid of life. We shall sink together you and I, down, down into the dark voids where once the vital organs were.

I have always admired your head. The strong front of your forehead and the long crown. Your skull is slightly bulbous at the back, giving way to a deep drop at the nape of the neck. I have abseiled your head without fear. I have held your head in my hands, taken it, soothed the resistance, and held back my desire to probe under the skin to the seat of you. In that hollow is where you exist. There the world is made and identified according to your omnivorous taxonomy. It's a strange combination of mortality and swank, the all-seeing, all-knowing brain, mistress of so much, capable of tricks and feats. Spoon-bending and higher mathematics. The hard-bounded space hides the vulnerable self.

I can't enter you in clothes that won't show the stains, my hands full of tools to record and analyse. If I come to you with a torch and a notebook, a medical diagram and a cloth to mop up the mess, I'll have you bagged neat and tidy. I'll store you in plastic like chicken livers. Womb, gut, brain, neatly labelled and returned. Is that how to know another human being?

I know how your hair tumbles from its chignon and washes your shoulders in light. I know the calcium of your cheekbones. I know the weapon of your jaw. I have held your head in my hands but I have never held you. Not you in your spaces, spirit, electrons of life.

'Explore me,' you said and I collected my ropes, flasks and maps, expecting to be back home soon. I dropped into the mass of you and I cannot find the way out. Sometimes I think I'm free, coughed up like Jonah from the whale, but then I turn a corner and recognise myself again. Myself in your skin, myself lodged in your bones, myself floating in the cavities that decorate every surgeon's wall. That is how I know you. You are what I know.

The Skin

THE SKIN IS COMPOSED OF TWO MAIN PARTS: THE DERMIS
AND THE EPIDERMIS.

Odd to think that the piece of you I know best is already
dead. The cells on the surface of your skin are thin and
flat without blood vessels or nerve endings. Dead cells,
thickest on the palms of your hands and the soles of
your feet. Your sepulchral body, offered to me in the
past tense, protects your soft centre from the intrusions
of the outside world. I am one such intrusion, stroking
you with necrophiliac obsession, loving the shell laid out
before me.

The dead you is constantly being rubbed away by the
dead me. Your cells fall and flake away, fodder to dust
mites and bed bugs. Your droppings support colonies of
life that graze on skin and hair no longer wanted. You
don't feel a thing. How could you? All your sensation
comes from deeper down, the live places where the dermis
is renewing itself, making another armadillo layer. You are
a knight in shining armour.

Rescue me. Swing me up beside you, let me hold on to
you, arms around your waist, head nodding against your
back. Your smell soothes me to sleep, I can bury myself
in the warm goosedown of your body. Your skin tastes
salty and slightly citrus. When I run my tongue in a long
wet line across your breasts I can feel the tiny hairs, the
puckering of the aureole, the cone of your nipple. Your
breasts are beehives pouring honey.

I am a creature who feeds at your hand. I would be the squire rendering excellent service. Rest now, let me unlace your boots, massage your feet where the skin is calloused and sore. There is nothing distasteful about you to me; not sweat nor grime, not disease and its dull markings. Put your foot in my lap and I will cut your nails and ease the tightness of a long day. It has been a long day for you to find me. You are bruised all over. Burst figs are the livid purple of your skin.

The leukaemic body hurts easily. I could not be rough with you now, making you cry out with pleasure close to pain. We've bruised each other, broken the capillaries shot with blood. Tubes hair-thin intervening between arteries and veins, those ramified blood vessels that write the body's longing. You used to flush with desire. That was when we were in control, our bodies conspirators in our pleasure.

My nerve endings became sensitive to minute changes in your skin temperature. No longer the crude lever of Hot or Cold, I tried to find the second when your skin thickened. The beginning of passion, heat coming through, heartbeat deepening, quickening. I knew your blood vessels were swelling and your pores expanding. The physiological effects of lust are easy to read. Sometimes you sneezed four or five times like a cat. It's such an ordinary thing, happening millions of times a day all over the world. An ordinary miracle, your body changing under my hands. And yet, how to believe in the obvious surprise? Extraordinary, unlikely that you should want me.

I'm living on my memories like a cheap has-been. I've been sitting in this chair by the fire, my hand on the cat, talking aloud, fool-ramblings. There's a doctor's text-book fallen open on the floor. To me it's a book of spells. Skin, it says. Skin.

You were milk-white and fresh to drink. Will your skin discolour, its brightness blurring? Will your neck and spleen distend? Will the rigorous contours of your stomach swell under an infertile load? It may be so and the private drawing I keep of you will be a poor reproduction then. It may be so but if you are broken then so am I.

The Skeleton

THE CLAVICLE OR COLLAR BONE: THE CLAVICLE IS A LONG BONE WHICH HAS A DOUBLE CURVE. THE SHAFT OF THE BONE IS ROUGHENED FOR THE ATTACHMENT OF THE MUSCLES. THE CLAVICLE PROVIDES THE ONLY BONY LINK BETWEEN THE UPPER EXTREMITY AND THE AXIAL SKELETON.

I cannot think of the double curve lithe and flowing with movement as a bony ridge, I think of it as the musical instrument that bears the same root. Clavis. Key. Clavichord. The first stringed instrument with a keyboard. Your clavicle is both keyboard and key. If I push my fingers into the recesses behind the bone I find you like a soft shell crab. I find the openings between the springs of muscle where I can press myself into the chords of your neck. The bone runs in perfect scale from sternum to scapula. It feels lathe-turned. Why should a bone be balletic?

You have a dress with a décolletage to emphasise your breasts. I suppose the cleavage is the proper focus but what I wanted to do was to fasten my index finger and thumb at the bolts of your collar bone, push out, spreading the web of my hand until it caught against your throat. You asked me if I wanted to strangle you. No, I wanted to fit you, not just in the obvious ways but in so many indentations.

It was a game, fitting bone on bone. I thought difference was rated to be the largest part of sexual attraction but there are so many things about us that are the same.

Bone of my bone. Flesh of my flesh. To remember

you it's my own body I touch. Thus she was, here and here. The physical memory blunders through the doors the mind has tried to seal. A skeleton key to Bluebeard's chamber. The bloody key that unlocks pain. Wisdom says forget, the body howls. The bolts of your collar bone undo me. Thus she was, here and here.

THE SCAPULA OR SHOULDER BLADE: THE SCAPULA IS A FLAT TRIANGULAR SHAPED BONE WHICH LIES ON THE POSTERIOR WALL SUPERFICIAL TO THE RIBS AND SEPARATED FROM THEM BY MUSCLE.

Shuttered like a fan no-one suspects your shoulder blades of wings. While you lay on your belly I kneaded the hard edges of your flight. You are a fallen angel but still as the angels are; body light as a dragonfly, great gold wings cut across the sun.

If I'm not careful you'll cut me. If I slip my hand too casually down the sharp side of your scapula I will lift away a bleeding palm. I know the stigmata of presumption. The wound that will not heal if I take you for granted.

Nail me to you. I will ride you like a nightmare. You are the winged horse Pegasus who would not be saddled. Strain under me. I want to see your muscle skein flex and stretch. Such innocent triangles holding hidden strength. Don't rear at me with unfolding power. I fear you in our bed when I put out my hand to touch you and feel the twin razors turned towards me. You sleep with your back towards me so that I will know the full extent of you. It is sufficient.

THE FACE: THERE ARE THIRTEEN BONES THAT FORM THE SKEL-
ETON OF THE FACE. FOR COMPLETENESS THE FRONTAL BONE
SHOULD BE ADDED.

Of the visions that come to me waking and sleeping the
most insistent is your face. Your face, mirror-smooth and
mirror-clear. Your face under the moon, silvered with cool
reflection, your face in its mystery, revealing me.

I cut out your face where it had caught in the ice on the
pond, your face bigger than my body, your mouth filled
with water. I held you against my chest on that snowy day,
the outline of you jagged into my jacket. When I put my
lips to your frozen cheek you burned me. The skin tore at
the corner of my mouth, my mouth filled with blood. The
closer I held you to me, the faster you melted away. I held
you as Death will hold you. Death that slowly pulls down
the skin's heavy curtain to expose the bony cage behind.

The skin loosens, yellows like limestone, like limestone worn by time, shows up the marbling of veins.
The pale translucency hardens and grows cold. The bones
themselves yellow into tusks.

Your face gores me. I am run through. Into the holes I
pack splinters of hope but hope does not heal me. Should
I pad my eyes with forgetfulness, eyes grown thin through
looking? Frontal bone, palatine bones, nasal bones, lacri-
mal bones, cheek bones, maxilla, vomer, inferior conchae,
mandible.

Those are my shields, those are my blankets, those
words don't remind me of your face.

The Special Senses

HEARING AND THE EAR: THE AURICLE IS THE EXPANDED POR-
TION WHICH PROJECTS FROM THE SIDE OF THE HEAD. IT IS
COMPOSED OF FIBRO-ELASTIC CARTILAGE COVERED WITH SKIN
AND FINE HAIRS. IT IS DEEPLY GROOVED AND RIDGED. THE
PROMINENT OUTER RIDGE IS KNOWN AS THE HELIX. THE LOB-
ULE IS THE SOFT PLIABLE PART AT THE LOWER EXTREMITY.

Sound waves travel at about 335 metres a second. That's
about a fifth of a mile and Louise is perhaps two hundred
miles away. If I shout now, she'll hear me in seventeen
minutes or so. I have to leave a margin of error for the
unexpected. She may be swimming under water.

I call Louise from the doorstep because I know she
can't hear me. I keen in the fields to the moon. Animals
in the zoo do the same, hoping that another of their kind
will call back. The zoo at night is the saddest place. Behind
the bars, at rest from vivisecting eyes, the animals cry out,
species separated from one another, knowing instinctively the map of belonging. They would choose predator
and prey against this outlandish safety. Their ears, more
powerful than those of their keepers, pick up sounds of
cars and last-hour take-aways. They hear all the human
noises of distress. What they don't hear is the hum of the
undergrowth or the crack of fire. The noises of kill. The
river-roar booming against brief screams. They prick their
ears till their ears are sharp points but the noises they seek
are too far away.

I wish I could hear your voice again.

THE NOSE: THE SENSE OF SMELL IN HUMAN BEINGS IS GEN-
ERALLY LESS ACUTE THAN IN OTHER ANIMALS.

The smells of my lover's body are still strong in my
nostrils. The yeast smell of her sex. The rich ferment-
ing undertow of rising bread. My lover is a kitchen cooking partridge. I shall visit her gamey low-roofed den and
feed from her. Three days without washing and she is
well-hung and high. Her skirts reel back from her body,
her scent is a hoop about her thighs.

From beyond the front door my nose is twitching, I
can smell her coming down the hall towards me. She is
a perfumier of sandalwood and hops. I want to uncork
her. I want to push my head against the open wall of her
loins. She is firm and ripe, a dark compound of sweet cattle
straw and Madonna of the Incense. She is frankincense and
myrrh, bitter cousin smells of death and faith.

When she bleeds the smells I know change colour.
There is iron in her soul on those days. She smells like a
gun.

My lover is cocked and ready to fire. She has the
scent of her prey on her. She consumes me when she
comes in thin white smoke smelling of saltpetre. Shot
against her all I want are the last wreaths of her desire
that carry from the base of her to what doctors like to
call the olfactory nerves.

TASTE: THERE ARE FOUR FUNDAMENTAL SENSATIONS OF
TASTE: SWEET SOUR BITTER AND SALT.

My lover is an olive tree whose roots grow by the sea.
Her fruit is pungent and green. It is my joy to get at the
stone of her. The little stone of her hard by the tongue.
Her thick-fleshed salt-veined swaddle stone.

Who eats an olive without first puncturing the swaddle? The waited moment when the teeth shoot a strong
burst of clear juice that has in it the weight of the land,
the vicissitudes of the weather, even the first name of the
olive keeper.

The sun is in your mouth. The burst of an olive is
breaking of a bright sky. The hot days when the rains
come. Eat the day where the sand burned the soles of
your feet before the thunderstorm brought up your skin
in bubbles of rain.

Our private grove is heavy with fruit. I shall worm
you to the stone, the rough swaddle stone.

THE EYE: THE EYE IS SITUATED IN THE ORBITAL CAVITY. IT IS ALMOST SPHERICAL IN SHAPE AND ABOUT ONE INCH IN DIAMETER.

Light travels at 186,000 miles per second. Light is reflected into the eyes by whatever comes within the field of vision. I see colour when a wavelength of light is reflected by an object and all other wavelengths are absorbed. Every colour has a different wavelength; red light has the longest.

Is that why I seem to see it everywhere? I am living in a red bubble made up of Louise's hair. It's the sunset time of year but it's not the dropping disc of light that holds me in the shadows of the yard. It's the colour I crave, floodings of you running down the edges of the sky on to the brown earth on to the grey stone. On to me.

Sometimes I run into the sunset arms wide like a scarecrow, thinking I can jump off the side of the world into the fiery furnace and be burned up in you. I would like to wrap my body in the blazing streaks of bloodshot sky.

All other colours are absorbed. The dull tinges of the day never penetrate my blackened skull. I live in four blank walls like an anchorite. You were a brightly lit room and I shut the door. You were a coat of many colours wrestled into the dirt.

Do you see me in my blood-soaked world? Green-eyed girl, eyes wide apart like almonds, come in tongues of flame and restore my sight.

March. Elgin had promised to write to me in March. I counted the days like someone under house arrest. It was bitter cold and the woods were filled with wild white daffodils. I tried to take comfort from the flowers, from the steady budding of the trees. This was new life, surely some of it would rub off on me?

The wine bar, otherwise known as 'A Touch of Southern Comfort', was staging a spring festival to attract back customers whose overdrafts still hadn't recovered from the Christmas festival. For us who worked there, this meant dressing in lime-green body stockings with a simple crown of artificial crocuses about our heads. The drinks had a spring theme: March Hare Punch, Wild Oat Sling, Blue Tit. It didn't matter what you ordered, the ingredients were the same apart from the liquor base. I mixed cheap cooking brandy, Japanese whisky, something that called itself gin and the occasional filthy sherry with pulp orange juice, thin cream, cubes of white sugar and various kitchen colourings. Soda water to top up and at £5.00 a couple (we only served couples at Southern Comfort) cheap at the price during Happy Hour.

The management ordered a March pianist and told him to make his way at his own speed through the Simon and Garfunkel songbook. For some reason he became autistically stuck at 'Bridge Over Troubled Water'. Whenever I arrived for work at 5 o'clock the silver girl was sailing by on words supplied by a tearful crowd of already tipsy punters. Against the lush chords and the aching tremeloes of our guests, we Spring Greens leapt from table to table, dropping food parcels of pizza and jugs of consolation. I began to despise my fellow man.

Still no word from Elgin. Work harder, mix more cocktails, stay up late, don't sleep, don't think. I might have taken to the bottle had there been anything fit to drink.

'I'd like to see where you live.'

I was behind the bar grimly jigging a few pints of Lethal Extra when Gail Right made it clear that she was coming home with me. At two in the morning when the last of our night birds had been tipped from their sodden nest, she locked up and put my push bike in the hatch of her car. She had a Tammy Wynette tape on the cassette.

'You're very reserved,' she said. 'I like that. I don't get a lot of it at work.'

'Why do you run that place?'

'I have to do something for a living. Can't depend on Prince Charming at my age.' She laughed. 'Or with my tastes.'

Stand by your man, said Tammy, and show the world you love him.

'I'm thinking of having a Country and Western Festival in the summer, what about it?' Gail was taking the corners too fast.

'What will we have to wear?'

She laughed again, more shrilly this time. 'Don't you like your little body stocking? I think you look gorgeous.' She pronounced the word with an accented 'O' so that it sounded less like a compliment and more like the gaping chasm.

'It's very good of you to drop me off,' I said. 'I can offer you something if you like.'

'Ooh yes,' she said. 'Ooh yes.'

We got out of her car under the frozen sky. I unlocked my door with frozen fingers and invited her in with a frozen heart.

'Lovely and warm in here,' she said snuggling herself

in front of the stove. She had a vast bottom. It reminded me of a pair of shorts a boyfriend of mine had once worn which said (GL)ASS. HANDLE WITH CARE. She wiggled and knocked over a Toby jug.

'Don't worry,' I said. 'It was too fat for the fireplace.'

She eased herself into the trembling armchair and accepted my offering of cocoa with a leer about Casanova. I had thought that was an esoteric fact.

'It's not true,' I said. 'Chocolate is a wonderful sedative.' Which isn't true either but I thought Gail Right might be susceptible to a bit of Mind over Matter. I yawned pointedly.

'Busy day,' she said. 'Busy day. Makes me think of other things. Dark exciting things.'

I thought of treacle. What would it be like to be caught in the wallow of Gail Right?

I had a boyfriend once, his name was Carlo, he was a dark exciting thing. He made me shave off all my body hair and did the same to himself. He claimed it would increase sensation but it made me feel like a prisoner in a beehive. I wanted to please him, he smelled of fir cones and port, his long body passion-damp. We lasted six months and then Carlo met Robert who was taller, broader and thinner than me. They exchanged razorblades and cut me out.

'What are you dreaming about?' asked Gail.

'An old love.'

'You like 'em old do you? That's good. Mind you, I'm not as old as I look, not when you get down to the upholstery.'

She gave the armchair a mighty thwack and a cloud of dust settled over her exhausted make-up.

'I have to tell you now Gail that there's someone else.'

'There always is,' she sighed and stared into the murky lumps of her cocoa like a fortune teller on a fix. 'Tall, dark, and handsome?'

'Tall, red and beautiful.'

'Give us a bedtime story then,' said Gail. 'What's she like?'

Louise, dipterous girl born in flames, 35. 34 22 36. 10 years married. 5 months with me. Doctorate in Art History. First class mind. 1 miscarriage (or 2?) 0 children. 2 arms, 2 legs, too many white T-cells. 97 months to live.

'Don't cry,' said Gail, kneeling in front of my chair, her plump ringed hand on my thin empty ones. 'Don't cry. You did the right thing. She would have died, how could you have forgiven yourself that? You've given her a chance.'

'It's incurable.'

'That's not what her doctor says. She can trust him, can't she?'

I hadn't told Gail everything.

She touched my face very softly. 'You'll be happy again. We could be happy together couldn't we?'

Six in the morning and I was lying in my saggy rented double bed with Gail Right sagging beside me. She smelled of face powder and dry rot. She was snoring heavily and would be for some time to come, so I got up, borrowed her car, and drove to the phone box.

We hadn't made love. I'd run my hands over her padded flesh with all the enthusiasm of a second-hand sofa dealer. She'd patted my head and fallen asleep, which was as well since my body had all the sensitivity of a wet-suit.

I put the money in the slot and listened to the ringing tones while my breath steamed up the barren phone box.

My heart was over-beating. Someone answered, sleepy, grumpy.

'HELLO? HELLO?'

'Hello Elgin.'

'What time do you call this?'

'Early morning after another sleepless night.'

'What do you want?'

'Our agreement. How is she?'

'Louise is in Switzerland. She's been quite ill but she's much better now. We have had good results. She won't be back in England for some time if at all. You can't see her.'

'I don't want to see her.' (LIAR LIAR.)

'That's good because she certainly doesn't want to see you.'

The phone went dead. I held on to the receiver for a moment, staring stupidly into the mouthpiece. Louise was OK, that was all that mattered.

I got into the car and drove the deserted miles home. Sunday morning and no-one around. The upstairs rooms were tightly curtained, the houses on the road were still asleep. A fox ran across my path, a chicken hanging limply from its mouth. I would have to deal with Gail.

At home there were only two sounds: the metallic ticking of the clock and Gail's snores. I closed the door on the stairs and left myself alone with the clock. In the very early morning the hours have a different quality, they stretch and promise. I took out my books and tried to work. Russian is the only language I'm good at, which is a help since there aren't that many of us competing for the same jobs. The Francophiles have a terrible time, everybody wants to sit outside a Paris café and translate the new edition of Proust. Not me. I used to think that a tour de force was a school trip.

'You idiot,' said Louise cuffing me gently.

She got up to make coffee and brought it in fresh with the smell of plantations and sun. The aromatic steam warmed our faces and clouded my glasses. She drew a heart on each lens. 'So that you won't see anybody but me,' she said. Her hair cinnabar red, her body all the treasures of Egypt. There won't be another find like you Louise. I won't see anybody else.

I worked until the clock chimed twelve and there was a horrible heaving from upstairs. Gail Right had woken up.

I moved quickly to the kettle, sensing that some appeasement would be necessary. Would a mug of tea protect me? I put out my hand to Earl Grey and settled on Empire Blend. The Stand Up And Be Counted of teas. A man-sized tea. A tea with so much tannin that designers use it as pigment.

She was in the bathroom. I heard the judder judder of the water pipes then the assault against the enamel. Unwillingly the tank was forced to part with every drop of hot water, it wheezed to the very end then came to a stop with a dreadful clank. I hoped she hadn't disturbed the sediment.

'Never disturb the Sediment,' the farmer had said when he'd showed me round the place. He said it as though the Sediment were some fearful creature who lived under the hot water.

'What will happen if I do?'

He shook his head doomfully. 'Can't say.'

I'm sure he meant he didn't know but did he have to make it sound like an ancient curse?

I took Gail her tea and knocked at the door.

'Don't be shy,' she called.

I prised open the door from its stiff catch and plonked the tea on the bathside. The water was brown. Gail was streaky. She looked like a prime cut of streaky bacon. Her eyes were small and red from the night before. Her hair stuck out like a straw rick. I shuddered.

'Cold isn't it?' she said. 'Scrub my back honey will you?'

'Must stoke up the fire, Gail. Can't let you get cold.'

I fled down the stairs and did indeed stoke up the fire. I would gladly have stoked the whole house and left it roasting Gail inside. This isn't polite, I told myself. Why are you so horror-struck by a woman whose only fault is to like you and whose only quality is to be larger than life?

Bam, Bam, Bam, Bam, Bam, Bam, Bam. Gail Right was at the bottom of the stairs. I straightened up and made a quick smile.

'Hello love,' she said kissing me with a suckering sound. 'Got any bacon sandwiches?'

While Gail made her way through what was left of Autumn Effie, the farmer's yearly pig to the slaughter, she told me she was going to change my shifts at the wine bar so that we could work together. 'I'll give you more money as well.' She licked the grease from her lower lip and where it had dripped on to her arm.

'I'd rather not. I like things the way they are.'

'You're in shock. Try it my way for a bit.' She leered at me over the crusts of her breakfast. 'Didn't you enjoy a bit of home company last night? Those hands of yours got everywhere.'

Her own hands were wedging Effie between her jaws as though she feared the pig might still have the guts to make a break for it. She had fried the bacon herself then soaked the bread in the fat before shutting the sandwich. Her fingernails were not quite free of red polish and some of this had found its way on to the bread.

'I love a bacon sandwich,' she said. 'The way you touched me. So light and nimble, do you play the piano?'

'Yes,' I said in an unnaturally high voice. 'Excuse me please.'

I got to the toilet just ahead of my vomit. On your knees, seat up head down, stucco the bowl with porridge. I wiped my mouth and rinsed out with water, spitting away the burning in the back of my throat. If Louise had had chemotherapy she might be suffering this every morning. And I wasn't with her. 'Remember that's the point, that's the point,' I said to myself in the mirror. 'That's the route she won't have to take so long as she's with Elgin.'

'How do you know?' said the piping doubting voice I had come so much to fear.

I crept back into the sitting room and took a swig of whisky from the bottle. Gail was doing her make-up in a pocket mirror. 'Not a vice I hope?' she said squinting under her eyeliner.

'I'm not feeling well.'

'You don't get enough sleep, that's your trouble. I heard you at six o'clock this morning. Where did you go?'

'I had to telephone someone.'

Gail put down her wand of mascara. It said wand on the side of the tube but it looked more like a cowprod.

'You've got to forget her.'

'I may as well forget myself.'

'What shall we do today?'

'I've got to work.'

Gail considered me for a moment then bundled her

tools in their vinyl bag. 'You're not interested in me honey are you?'

'It's not that I . . . '

'I know, you think I'm a fat old slag who just wants a piece of something firm and juicy. Well you're right. But I'd do my share of the work. I'd care for you and be a good friend to you and see you right. I'm not a sponger, I'm not a tart. I'm a good-time girl whose body has blown. Shall I tell you something honey? You don't lose your lust at the rate you lose your looks. It's a cruel fact of nature. You go on fancying it just the same. And that's hard but I've got a few things left. I don't come to the table empty handed.'

She got up and took her keys. 'Think about it. You know where to find me.'

I watched her drive off in her car and I felt depressed and ashamed. I went back to bed, gave up the fight and dreamed of Louise.

April. May. I continued my training as a cancer specialist. They got to call me the Hospital Ghoul down at the Terminal Ward. I didn't care. I visited patients, listened to their stories, found ones who'd got well and sat by ones who died. I thought all cancer patients would have strong loving families. The research hype is about going through it together. It's almost a family disease. The truth is that many cancer patients die alone.

'What do you want?' one of the junior doctors finally asked me.

'I want to know what it's like. I want to know what it is.'

She shrugged. 'You're wasting your time. Most days I think we're all wasting our time.'

'Then why bother? Why do you bother?'

'Why bother? That's a question for the whole human

race isn't it?'

She turned to go and then turned back to me worried.

'You haven't got cancer have you?'

'No!'

She nodded. 'You see, sometimes people who have been newly diagnosed want the inside story on the treatment. Doctors are very patronising, even to highly intelligent patients. Some of those patients like to find out for themselves.'

'What do they find out?'

'How little we know. It's the late twentieth century and what are the tools of our trade? Knives, saws, needles and chemicals. I've no time for alternative medicine but I can see why it's attractive.'

'Shouldn't you have time for any possibility?'

'On an eighty-hour shift?'

She left. I took my book, *The Modern Management of Cancer*, and went home.

June. The driest June on record. The earth that should have been in summer glory was thin for lack of water. The buds held promise but they didn't swell. The beating sun was a fake. The sun that should have brought life was carrying death in every relentless morning.

I decided to go to church. Not because I wanted to be saved, nor because I wanted solace from the cross. Rather, I wanted the comfort of other people's faith. I like to be anonymous among the hymn-singing crowd, the stranger at the door who doesn't have to worry about the fund for the roof or the harvest festival display. It used to be that everybody believed and faith was found in thousands of tiny churches up and down the British Isles. I miss the Sunday morning bells ringing from village to village.

God's jungle telegraph bearing the good news. And it was good news insomuch as the church was a centre and a means. The Church of England in its unexcited benevolent concern was emphatically to do with village life. The slow moving of the seasons, the corresponding echo in the *Book of Common Prayer*. Ritual and silence. Rough stone and rough soil. Now, it's hard to find one church in four that still runs a full calendar and is something more than a bit of communion every other Sunday and the odd parish event.

The church not far from me was a working model not a museum so I chose evensong and polished my shoes. I should have known there'd be a catch.

The building was thirteenth-century in parts with Georgian and Victorian repairs. It was of the solid stone that seems to rise organically from the land itself. Grown not made. The colour and substance of battle. The battle to hew it out and shape it for God. It was massy, soil-black and defiant. Across the architrave of the low front door was a plastic banner which said JESUS LOVES YOU.

'Move with the times,' I said to myself, slightly uneasy.

I walked inside across the cool flagged floor, the particular church cold that no amount of gas fires and overcoats can penetrate. After the heat of the day it felt like the hand of God. I slid into a dark pew with a tree on the door and looked for my prayer book. There wasn't one. Then the tambourines started. These were serious tambourines the size of bass drums, flaunting ribbons like a Maypole and studded round the side like the collar of a pitbull. One came down the aisle towards me and flashed at my ear. 'Praise the Lord,' said its owner, desperately trying to keep it under control. 'A stranger in our midst.'

The entire congregation except for me then broke

into a melody of Bible texts and scattered shouts liberally set to music. The magnificent pipe organ stood shuttered and dusty, we had an accordion and two guitars. I really wanted to get out but there was a burly beaming farmer standing across the main door who looked as though he might get nasty if I ran for it before the collection.

'Jesus will overcome you,' cried the minister. (God the wrestler?)

'Jesus will have his way with you!' (God the rapist?)

'Jesus is going from strength to strength!' (God the body builder?)

'Hand yourself over to Jesus and you will be returned with interest.'

I am prepared to accept the many-sidedness of God but I am sure that if God exists He is not a Building Society.

I had a boyfriend once, his name was Bruno. After forty years of dissolution and Mammon he found Jesus under a wardrobe. In fairness, the wardrobe had been slowly crushing the resistance from his lungs for about four hours. He did house clearances and had fallen foul of a double-doored Victorian loomer. The sort of wardrobe poor people lived in. He was eventually rescued by the fire brigade though he always maintained it was the Lord himself who had levitated the oak ever upwards. He took me to church with him soon after and gave a graphic account of how Jesus had come out of the closet to save him. 'Out of the closet and up into your heart,' raved the Pastor.

I never saw Bruno after that, he gave me his motorbike as a gesture of renouncement and prayed that it might lead me to the Lord. Sadly it blew up on the outskirts of Brighton.

Ripping through this harmless reverie, a pair of hands seized mine and started banging them together as if they were cymbals. I realised I was meant to be clapping in time to the beat and I remembered another piece of advice from my grandmother. 'When in the jungle you howl with the wolves.' I slapped a plastic grin on my face like a server at McDonald's and pretended to be having a good time. I wasn't having a bad time, I wasn't having any time at all. No wonder they talk about Jesus filling a vacuum as though human beings were thermos flasks. This was the most vacuous place I'd ever been. God may be compassionate but he must have some taste.

As I suspected, the sumo farmer was in charge of the collection, so as soon as he had joyfully collected my bent twenty pence piece, I fled. I fled into the raw fields where the sheep continued their grazing as they had done for ten centuries. I fled to the pond where the dragonflies fed. I fled till the church was a hard knot against the sky. If prayer is appropriate it was appropriate here, my back against a dry stone wall, my feet on the slabbed earth. I had prayed for Louise every day since December. I did not know entirely to whom I prayed or even why. But I wanted someone to have care of her. To visit her and comfort her. To be the cool wind and the deep stream. I wanted her to be protected and I would have boiled cauldrons of stuffed newts if I'd been convinced it would have done any good. As to prayer, it helped me to concentrate my mind. To think of Louise in her own right, not as my lover, not as my grief. It helped me to forget myself and that was a great blessing. 'You made a mistake,' said the voice. The voice wasn't a piping sly voice now it was a strong gentle voice and I heard it quite clearly more and more. I did hear it out loud and I was not sure that my wits were still mine to command. What kind of people hear voices? Joan of Arc yes but what about all the others, the sad or sinister ones who want to change the world by tambourine power.

I hadn't been able to reach Elgin this month although I had written to him three times and telephoned him at every hour proper and improper. I supposed him to be in Switzerland but what if Louise were dying? Would he tell me? Would he let me see her again? I shook my head. That would be wrong. That would make a nonsense of all of this. Louise wasn't dying, she was safe in Switzerland. She was standing in a long green skirt by the drop of a torrent. The waterfall ran down from her hair over her breasts, her skirt was transparent. I looked more closely. Her body was transparent. I saw the course of her blood, the ventricles of her heart, her legs' long bones like tusks. Her blood was clean and red like summer roses. She was fragrant and in bud. No drought. No pain. If Louise is well then I am well.

I found one of her hairs on a coat of mine today. The gold streak caught the light. I bound it around my forefingers and pulled it straight. It was nearly two feet long that way. Is this the thread that binds me to you?

No-one tells you in grief-counselling or books on loss what it will be like when you find part of the beloved unexpectedly. The wisdom is to make sure your house is not a mausoleum, only to keep those things that bring you happy positive memories. I had been reading books that dealt with death partly because my separation from Louise was final and partly because I knew she would die and that I would have to cope with this second loss, perhaps just as the first was less inflamed. I wanted to cope.

Although I felt that my life had been struck in two I still wanted life. I have never thought of suicide as a solution to unhappiness.

Some years ago a friend of mine was killed in a road accident. She was crushed to death on her bicycle under the sixteen wheels of a juggernaut.

When I recovered from her death in the crudest sense I started to see her in the streets, always fleetingly, ahead of me, her back to me, disappearing into the crowd. I am told this is common. I see her still, though less often, and still for a second I believe it is her. I have from time to time found something of hers among my possessions. Always something trivial. Once I opened an old notebook and a slip of paper fell out, pristine, the ink firm not faded. She had left it at my seat in the British Library five years earlier. It was an invitation to coffee at four o'clock. I'll get my coat and a handful of small change and meet you in the crowded cafe and you'll be there today won't you, won't you?

'You'll get over it . . . ' It's the clichés that cause the trouble. To lose someone you love is to alter your life for ever. You don't get over it because 'it' is the person you loved. The pain stops, there are new people, but the gap never closes. How could it? The particularness of someone who mattered enough to grieve over is not made anodyne by death. This hole in my heart is in the shape of you and no-one else can fit it. Why would I want them to?

I've thought a lot about death recently, the finality of it, the argument ending in mid-air. One of us hadn't finished, why did the other one go? And why without warning? Even death after long illness is without warning. The moment you had prepared for so carefully took you by storm. The troops broke through the window and snatched the body and the body is gone. The day before the Wednesday last, this time a year ago, you were here and now you're not. Why not? Death reduces us to the baffled logic of a small child. If yesterday why not today? And where are you?

Fragile creatures of a small blue planet, surrounded by light years of silent space. Do the dead find peace beyond the rattle of the world? What peace is there for us whose best love cannot return them even for a day? I raise my head to the door and think I will see you in the frame. I know it is your voice in the corridor but when I run outside the corridor is empty. There is nothing I can do that will make any difference. The last word was yours.

The fluttering in the stomach goes away and the dull waking pain. Sometimes I think of you and I feel giddy. Memory makes me lightheaded, drunk on champagne. All the things we did. And if anyone had said this was the price I would have agreed to pay it. That surprises me; that with the hurt and the mess comes a shaft of recognition. It was worth it. Love is worth it.

August. Nothing to report. For the first time since leaving Louise I was depressed. The previous months had been wild with despair and cushioned by shock. I had been half mad, if madness is to be on the fringes of the real world. In August I felt blank and sick. I had sobered up, come round to the facts of what I had done. I was no longer drunk on grief. Body and mind know how to hide from what is too sore to handle. Just as the burns victim reaches a plateau of pain, so do the emotionally wretched find grief is a high ground from which they may survey themselves for a time. Such detachment was no longer mine. I was drained of my manic energy and also of my tears. I fell into dead sleeps and woke unrested. When my heart hurt I could no longer cry. There was only the weight of wrong-doing. I had failed Louise and it was too late.

What right had I to decide how she should live? What right had I to decide how she should die?

At A Touch of Southern Comfort it was Country and Western Month. It was also Gail Right's birthday. Not surprisingly she was a Leo. On the night in question, hot beyond hell and loud beyond decibels, we were celebrating at the feet of Howlin' Dog House Don. HD² as he liked to be called. The fringes on his jacket would have made a whole head of hair had he needed it. He did need it but he believed his Invisible Toupee was just that. His trousers were tight enough to choke a weasel. When he wasn't singing into his microphone he cradled it against his crotch. He wore a NO ENTRY sign over his bum.

'Cheek,' said Gail and roared at her own pun. 'I've seen better colons on a typewriter.'

HD² was a big hit. The women loved the way he threw them red paper hankies from his top pocket and growled into the bass notes like a gravelly Elvis. The men didn't seem too worried by his bum jokes. He sat on their knees and squawked, 'Who's a pretty boy then?' while the women anchored themselves round another gin and lime.

'I'm doin' a Hen Night next week,' said Gail. 'Strip tease.'

'I thought this was Country and Western?'

'It is. He's gonna wear a bandanna.'

'What about the banana? Doesn't look much from here.'

'It's not the size they're after, it's the laugh.'

I looked at the stage. Howlin' Dog House Don was holding his microphone stand at arm's length and crooning, 'Is it really you oo oo?'

'Better get ready,' said Gail. 'When he's finished this one they'll be queueing at the bar faster than an outing of nuns at the true cross.'

She had mixed a washing-up bowl full of Dolly Parton on Ice, this month's special. I began to line up the glasses and the tiny plastic bosoms that were replacing our cocktail umbrellas.

'Come out for a meal after work,' said Gail. 'No strings. I'm finishing at midnight, I'll finish you too if you fancy it.'

That was how I ended up in front of a Spaghetti Carbonara at Magic Pete's.

Gail was drunk. She was so drunk that when her false eyelash fell into her soup she told the waiter it was a centipede.

'I got something to tell you kiddo,' she said leaning down at me the way a zoo keeper drops a fish at a penguin. 'Want it?'

There was nothing else to have. Magic Pete's was an all-night drinking club, low on amenity, high on booze. It was Gail's revelation or find 50p for the juke box. I didn't have 50p.

'You made a mistake.'

In cartoon land this is where a saw comes up through the floor and teeths a neat hole round Bugs Bunny's chair. What does she mean 'I made a mistake'?

'If you mean about us Gail, I couldn't . . .'

She interrupted me. 'I mean about you and Louise.'

She could hardly get the words out. She had her mouth propped on her fists and her elbows propped on the table. She kept trying to reach for my hand and falling sideways into the ice-bucket.

'You shouldn't have run out on her.'

Run out on her? That doesn't sound like the heroics I'd had in mind. Hadn't I sacrificed myself for her? Offered my life for her life?

'She wasn't a child.'

Yes she was. My child. My baby. The tender thing I wanted to protect.

'You didn't give her a chance to say what she wanted. You left.'

I had to leave. She would have died for my sake. Wasn't it better for me to live a half life for her sake?

'What's the matter?' slurred Gail. 'Cat got your tongue?'

Not the cat, the worm of doubt. Who do I think I am? Sir Launcelot? Louise is a Pre-Raphaelite beauty but that doesn't make me a mediaeval knight. Nevertheless I desperately wanted to be right.

We staggered out of Magic Pete's towards Gail's car. I wasn't drunk but supporting Gail was a staggering sort of business. She was like a left-over jelly at a children's party. She decided she was coming home with me even if I had to sleep in the armchair. Mile by mile she reviewed my mistakes. I began to wish that I'd done as I first intended and kept back some of my story. There was no stopping her now. She was a three-ton truck on a slope.

'Honey, if there's one thing I can't stand it's a hero without a cause. People like that just make trouble so that they can solve it.'

'Is that what you think of me?'

'I think you're a crazy fool. Maybe you didn't love her.'

This caused me to swing the wheel so violently that Gail's gift-box collection of Tammy Wynette tapes skidded over the back and decapitated her nodding dog. Gail was sick down her blouse.

'The trouble with you,' she said wiping herself, 'is that you want to live in a novel.'

'Rubbish. I never read novels. Except Russian ones.'

'They're the worst. This isn't War and Peace honey, it's Yorkshire.'

'You're drunk.'

'That's right I am. I'm fifty-three and I'm as wild as a Welshman with a leek up his arse. Fifty-three. Old slag Gail. What right has she to poke her nose into your shining armour? That's what you're thinking isn't it honey? I may not look much like a messenger from the gods but your girl isn't the only one who's got wings. I've got a pair of my own under here.' (She patted her armpits.) 'I've flown about a bit and picked up a few things and I'll give one of them to you for nothing. You don't run out on the woman you love. Especially you don't when you think it's for her own good.' She hiccuped violently and covered her skirt with half-digested clams. I gave her my handkerchief. Finally she said, 'You'd better go and find her.'

'I can't.'

'Who said?'

'I said. I gave my word. Even if I am wrong it's too late now. Would you want to see me if I'd left you in the lurch with a man you despise?'

'Yes,' said Gail and passed out.

The following morning I caught the train to London. The heat through the carriage window made me sleepy and I slid into a light doze where Louise's voice came to me as if under water. She was under water. We were in Oxford and she was swimming in the river, green on the sheen of her, pearl sheen of her body. We had lain down on the grass sun-scorched, grass turning hay, grass brittle on the baked clay, spear grass marking us in red weals. The sky was blue as in blue-eyed boy, not a wink of cloud, steady gaze, what a smile. A pre-war sky. Before the first world war there were days and days like this; long English meadows, insect hum, innocence and blue sky. Farm workers pitching the hay, women in waist aprons carrying pitchers of lemonade. Summers were hot, winters were snowy. It's a pretty story.

Now here am I making up my own memories of good times. When we were together the weather was better, the days were longer. Even the rain was warm. That's right, isn't it? Do you remember when . . . I can see Louise sitting cross-legged under the plum tree in the Oxford garden. The plums have the look of asps' heads in her hair. Her hair is still drying from the river, curling up round the plums. Against her copper hair the green leaves look like tarnish. My Lady of the Verdigris. Louise is one of the few women who might still be beautiful if she went mouldy.

On that day she was asking me whether I would be true to her and I replied, 'With all my heart.' Had I been true to her?

Let me not to the marriage of true minds
Admit impediments; love is not love
Which alters when it alteration finds
Or bends with the remover to remove.
Oh no it is an ever fixed mark
That looks on tempests and is never shaken
It is the star to every wandering bark
Whose worth's unknown altho' his highth be taken.

When I was young I loved this sonnet. I thought a
wandering bark was a young dog, rather as in Dylan
Thomas's *Portrait of the Artist as a Young Dog*.

I have been a wandering bark of unknown worth but I
thought I was a safe ship for Louise. Then I threw her
overboard.
    'Will you be true to me?'
    'With all my heart.'
    I took her hand and put it underneath my T-shirt.
She took my nipple and squeezed it between finger and
thumb.
    'And with all your flesh?'
    'You're hurting me Louise.'
    Passion is not well bred. Her fingers bit their spot. She
would have bound me to her with ropes and had us lie face
to face unable to move but move on each other, unable to
feel but feel each other. She would have deprived us of all
senses bar the sense of touch and smell. In a blind, deaf and
dumb world we could conclude our passion infinitely. To
end would be to begin again. Only she, only me. She was
jealous but so was I. She was brute with love but so was I.
We were patient enough to count the hairs on each other's
heads, too impatient to get undressed. Neither of us had

the upper hand, we wore matching wounds. She was my twin and I lost her. Skin is waterproof but my skin was not waterproof against Louise. She flooded me and she has not drained away. I am still wading through her, she beats upon my doors and threatens my innermost safety. I have no gondola at the gate and the tide is still rising. Swim for it, don't be afraid. I am afraid.

Is this her revenge? 'I will never let you go.'

I went straight to my flat. I didn't expect to find Louise there and yet there were signs of her occupation, some clothes, books, the coffee she liked. Sniffing the coffee told me that she hadn't been there for some time, the beans had gone stale and she would never permit that. I picked up a sweater of hers and buried my face in it. Very faintly, her perfume.

I was strangely elated to be in my own home. Why are human beings so contradictory? This was the site of sorrow and separation, a place of mourning, but with the sun coming through the windows and the garden full of roses I felt hopeful again. We had been happy here too and some of that happiness had soaked the walls and patterned the furniture.

I decided to dust. I've found before that ceaseless menial work calms the rat-cage of the mind. I had to stop worrying and speculating for long enough to make a sensible plan. I needed peace and peace was not a quality I had come to know.

It was while I was scrubbing away the last of Miss Havisham that I found some letters to Louise from the hospital where she had gone for a second opinion. The letters were of the mind that since Louise was still asymptomatic no treatment should be considered. There was some swelling of the lymphatic nodes but this had remained stable for six months. The consultant advised regular checks and a normal life. The three letters were dated after I had left. There was also a very impressive document from Elgin reminding Louise that he had been studying her case for two years and that in his humble opinion ('May I remind you Louise that it is I and not Mr Rand who is best qualified to make decisions in this uncertain field') she needed treatment. The address of his Swiss clinic was on the letterhead.

I telephoned. The receptionist didn't want to talk to me. There were no patients at the clinic. No, I couldn't speak to Mr Rosenthal.

I began to wonder if the receptionist was one of Inge's.

'May I speak to Mrs Rosenthal?' (how I hated having to say that).

'Mrs Rosenthal is not here any longer.'

'Then may I speak to the doctor?'

'*Mr* Rosenthal' (she underlined my faux pas) 'is not here either.'

'Do you expect him?'

She couldn't say. I slammed down the phone and sat on the floor.

All right. Nothing else for it. Louise's mother.

Louise's mother and grandmother lived together in Chelsea. They considered themselves to be Australian aristocracy, that is, they were descended from convicts. They had a small mews house from whose upper floors they could see the Buckingham Palace flagpole. Grandmother spent all of her time on the upper floors, noting when and when not, the Queen was in residence. Occasionally she broke off to spill food down her front. She had a steady hand but she liked to spill. It made work for her daughter.

Louise was rather fond of her grandmother. With a little twist to Dickens, she called her The Aged Pea, peas were what grandmother spilled the most. Her only comment on Louise's separation from Elgin had been 'Get the money.'

Mother was more complicated and in a very unaristo-cratic fashion worried about what people would say. When I announced myself at the entryphone she refused to let me in.

'I don't know where she is and it's no business of yours.'

'Mrs Fox, please open the door, please.'

There was silence. An Englishman's home is his castle, but an Australian's mews house is fair game. I banged on the door with both fists and shouted Mrs Fox's name as loudly as I could. Immediately opposite, two coiffured heads popped into the window like Punch and Judy in their box. The front door flew open. It wasn't Mrs Fox but The Aged Pea herself.

'Think you're on a kangaroo shoot or somethin'?'

'I'm looking for Louise.'

'Don't you come through these doors.' Mrs Fox appeared.

'Kitty, if we don't let this digger in, neighbours'll think we got either the bugs or the bailiffs.' The Pea eyed me suspiciously. 'You have the look of a thing from the Disinfectant Department.'

'Mother, we don't have a Disinfectant Department in England.'

'We don't? That explains a whole lot of smells.'

'Please, Mrs Fox, I won't be long.'

Reluctantly Mrs Fox stood back and I stepped on to the mat.

When there was a centimetre gap between me and the

door, Mrs Fox shut it and barred my further passage. I could feel the plastic letter-box cover on my spine.

'Get it over with then.'

'I'm looking for Louise. When did you last see her?'

'Ho ho,' said the Pea banging her stick. 'Don't play the Waltzing Matilda with me. What do you care? You walked out on her, now get lost.'

Mrs Fox said, 'I'm glad you're having nothing more to do with my daughter. You broke up her marriage.'

'I've no quarrel with that,' said Grandma.

'Mother, will you be quiet? Elgin is a great man.'

'Since when? You always said he was a little rat.'

'I did not say he was a little rat. I said he was rather small and that unfortunately he had the look of a, well, I said a . . . '

'Rat!' screamed the Pea banging her stick on the door just by my head. She should have been a knife thrower in the circus.

'Mrs Fox. I made a mistake. I should never have left Louise. I thought it was for her own good. I thought Elgin could make her well. I want to find her and take care of her.'

'It's too late,' said Mrs Fox. 'She told me she never wanted to see you again.'

'She's had a worse time than a toad on a runway,' said the Pea.

'Mother, go and sit down, you're getting tired,' said Mrs Fox supporting herself on the banister rail. 'I can deal with this.'

'Prettiest thing this side of Brisbane and look how she's been treated. You know, Louise is the spitting image of myself when younger. I had quite a figure then.'

It was hard to imagine Pea having any figure. She

was like a child's drawing of a snowman, just two circles plonked one on top of the other. For the first time I noticed her hair: it was serpentine in its rising twists, a living moving mass that escaped from its tight bands just as Louise's did. Louise had told me that Pea had been the undisputed Beauty Queen of Western Australia. She had had over one hundred proposals of marriage in the 1920s from bankers, prospectors, city men who unrolled maps of the new Australia they were going to build and said, 'Sweet darling all this is yours when you are mine.' Pea had married a sheep farmer and had six children. Her nearest neighbour had been a day's ride away. I saw her suddenly, dress to the floor, hands on her hips, the dirt track disappearing into the flat of the horizon. Nothing but flat and the bar of the sky measuring the distance. Miss Helen Louise, a burning bush in the dry land.

'What you starin' at digger?'

I shook my head. 'Mrs Fox, have you any idea where Louise has gone?'

'I know she's not in London, that's all. She may be abroad.'

'Got a packet out of the doctor. She left him as lean as a woodlouse in a plastics factory. Heh heh heh.'

'Mother, will you stop it?' Mrs Fox turned to me, 'I think you'd better leave now. I can't help you.'

Mrs Fox opened the door as her neighbours closed theirs.

'What did I tell you all?' said Pea. 'We're in disrepute.'

She turned in disgust and pegged down the hall on her stick.

'You know, don't you, that Elgin was to be in the civil list this year? Louise cost him that.'

'Don't be ridiculous,' I said. 'A happy marriage has

nothing to do with it.'

'Then why wasn't he?' She slammed the door and I heard her crying in the hall. Was it for her lost connection with the great and the good or was it for her daughter?

Evening. Couples out on the sweating streets hand in hand. From an upper window a reggae band with a long way to go. Restaurants were pushing the alfresco style, but a wicker chair on a dirty street with the buses grinding by isn't Venice. I watched the litter blow among the pizzas and raffia carafes. A vulpine waiter fixed his dicky bow in the cashier's mirror, slapped her bottom, put a peppermint on his red tongue and swaggered over to a group of under-age girls drinking Campari and soda. 'Would madams like a something to a eat?'

I caught the first bus regardless of its destination. What did it matter since I was no nearer to Louise? The city was suppurating. The bus driver wouldn't open the doors while the bus was moving. The air in there smelt of burger and chips. There was a fat woman in a sleeveless nylon frock sitting with her legs apart fanning herself with her shoe. Her make-up had slipped into ledges of grime.

'OPEN THE DOORS FUCKFACE,' she shouted.

'Fuck off,' said the driver without looking round.

'Can't you read the notice? Can't you read?'

The notice said DO NOT DISTRACT DRIVER WHILE BUS IS IN MOTION. We were stock still in a traffic jam at the time.

As the temperature mounted the man in front of me resorted to his mobile phone. Like all mobile phone users he had nothing urgent to say, he simply wanted to say it. He looked at us all to see if we were looking at him. When he finally said, 'Goo nye then my mate Kev,' I asked him very politely if I might borrow it for a moment and offered him a pound coin. He was reluctant to separate himself from such an essential part of his machismo but he agreed to punch in the number for me and hold the phone to my ear. After it had rung pointlessly a few times he said, 'That's out then,' pocketed my pound and hung his treasure back round his neck on a bulldog chain. There had been no answer at Louise's house. I decided to go and see for myself.

I found a cab to take me through the thick heat of the dying day and we turned into the square at the same moment as Elgin's BMW pulled up at the kerb. He got out and opened the passenger door for a woman. She was a little business suit number, serious make-up and the sort of hairdo that looks on tempests and is never shaken. She had a small travel bag, Elgin a suitcase, they were laughing together. He kissed her and fumbled for his keys.

'You gettin' out or not?' asked my driver.

I was trying to control myself. On the doorstep breathing deeply I rang the bell. Keep calm Keep calm Keep calm.

The hot date answered the door. I smiled brightly and walked around her into the wide hall. Elgin had his back to me.

'Darling . . . ' she began.

'Hello Elgin.'

He spun round. I didn't think people did that in real life, only in kooky crime thrillers. Elgin moved like Fred Astaire and placed himself between me and the hot date. I don't know why.

'Go and make some tea, darling, will you,' he said and off she went.

'Do you have to pay her to be so obedient or is it love?'

'I told you never to come here again.'

'You told me a great many things I should have ignored. Where's Louise?'

For a split second Elgin looked genuinely surprised. He thought I should know. I looked at the hall. There was a new table with curved legs, a hideous thing in maple inlaid with brass strips. No doubt it had come from the kind of shop where there are no prices but it had its price painted all over it. It was the sort of hall table interior designers buy for Arab clients. Next to it was a radiator. Louise hadn't been here for some time.

'Let me show you out,' said Elgin.

I grabbed him by his tie and jammed him against the door. I've never had any boxing lessons so I had to fight on instinct and cram his windpipe into his larynx. It seemed to work. Unfortunately he couldn't speak. 'Are you going to tell me what's happened, are you?' Pull the tie a bit tighter and watch his eyes pop out.

The hot date came tripping back up the stairs with two mugs. Two mugs. How rude. She stopped dead still like a ham actor then screamed, 'LET GO OF MY FIANCE.' I was so shocked I did. Elgin punched me in the stomach and winded me against the wall. I slipped on to the floor honking like a seal. Elgin kicked me in the shins but I didn't feel that until later. All I could see were his shiny shoes and her patent leather peep-toes. I threw up. While I was crouched over the black and white diamond tiles of the marble floor like an extra in a Vermeer, Elgin said as pompously as a half-strangled man can, 'That's right, Louise and I are divorced.' I was still coughing up egg and tomato sandwich but I struggled to my feet with the grace of an old wino, wiped my hand across my mouth and dragged its stippled backside down Elgin's blazer.

'God you're disgusting,' said the hot date. 'God.'

'Would you like me to tell you a bedtime story?' I asked her. 'All about Elgin and his wife Louise? Oh and about me too?'

'Darling, go out to the car and telephone for the police will you?' Elgin opened the door and the hot date scuttled out. Even in my decrepit state I was taken aback. 'Why does she have to phone from the car, or are you showing off?'

'My fiancée is telephoning from the car for her own safety.'

'Not because there's something you don't want her to hear?'

Elgin smiled pityingly, he had never been very good at smiling, mostly his mouth just moved around his face. 'I think it's time you left.'

I looked down the road to the car. The hot date had the phone in one hand and the instruction manual on her knee.

'I think we've got a few minutes, Elgin. Where's Louise?'

'I don't know and I don't care.'

'That's not what you said at Christmas.'

'Last year I thought I could make Louise see sense. I was mistaken.'

'It didn't have anything to do with the Civil List did it?'

I didn't expect him to react but his pale cheeks turned clown-red. He pushed me roughly down the steps. 'That's enough, get out.' My mind cleared and for a brief Samson moment my strength returned. I stood below him on the steps, below the water-line of his envy. I remembered the morning when he had challenged us in the kitchen. He had wanted us to be guilty, to creep away, our pleasure ruined by adult propriety. Instead Louise had left him. The ultimate act of selfishness; a woman who puts herself first.

I was colt-mad. Mad with pleasure at Louise's escape. I thought of her packing her things, closing the door, leaving him for ever. She was free. Is that you flying over the fields with the wind under your wing? Why didn't I trust you? Am I any better than Elgin? Now you've made fools of us both and sprung away. The snare didn't close on you. It closed on us.

Colt-mad. Break Elgin. This is where my feelings will spill, not over Louise in fountains of thankfulness but here down on him in sulphurous streams.

He started motioning to the hot date, his arms in extravagant semaphore, a silly puppet boy with the keys to a fancy car.

'Elgin, you're a doctor, aren't you? Then you'll recall that a doctor can guess the size of someone's heart by the size of their fist. Here's mine.'

I saw Elgin's look of complete astonishment as my fists, locked together in unholy prayer, came up in a line of offering under his jaw. Impact. Head snapped back, sick crunch like a meat grinder. Elgin at my feet in foetus position bleeding. He's making noises like a pig at the trough. He's not dead. Why not? If it's so easy for Louise to die why is it so hard for Elgin to do the same?

The anger went out of me. I moved his head to a more comfortable position, fetching a cushion from the hall. As I propped his crushed face a tooth fell out. Gold. I put his glasses on the hall table and walked slowly down the steps towards the car. The hot date was half in half out, her mouth fluttering like a moth. 'God. God, oh my God, God.' As though repetition might achieve what faith could not.

The phone dangled uselessly from its strap around her wrist. I could hear the crackly voice of the operator 'Fire Police Ambulance. Which service do you require? Fire Police Ambulance. Which . . .' I took the phone gently. 'Ambulance. 52 Nightingale Square, NW3.'

When I got back to my flat it was dark. My right wrist was badly swollen and I was limping. I put ice into a couple of carrier bags and Sellotaped them around my gammy limbs. I wanted nothing but sleep and I did sleep on the dusty unchanged sheets. I slept for twenty hours then got a cab to the hospital and spent almost as long in the Outpatients Department. I had cracked a bone in my wrist.

In plaster up to my elbow I made a list of every hospital that had a cancer unit. None of them had heard of Louise Rosenthal or Louise Fox. She was not undergoing treatment anywhere. I spoke to her consultant who refused to tell me anything except that he was not advising her at that time. Those friends of hers I had met had not seen her since May when she had suddenly disappeared. I tried her solicitor for the divorce. She no longer had a contact address. After a great deal of difficulty I persuaded her to give me the address she had been using during the case.

'You know this is unethical?'

'You know who I am?'

'I do. And that is why I am making an exception.'

She disappeared to rustle among her files. My lips were dry.

'Here we are: 41a Dragon St NW1.'

It was the address of my flat.

I stayed in London for six weeks until the beginning of October. I had resigned myself to charges being brought against me for whatever damage I had done to Elgin. None came. I walked over to the house to find it shuttered. For reasons of his own I wouldn't be hearing from Elgin again. What reasons when he could avenge himself on me, possibly with a prison sentence? It horrifies me to think about that madness, I've always had a wild streak, it starts with a throbbing in the temple and then a slide into craziness I can recognise but can't control. Can control. Had controlled for years until I met Louise. She opened up the dark places as well as the light. That's the risk you take. I couldn't apologise to Elgin because I wasn't sorry. Not sorry but ashamed, does that sound strange?

In the night, the blackest part of the night, when the moon is low and the sun hasn't risen, I woke up convinced that Louise had gone away alone to die. My hands shook. I didn't want that. I preferred my other reality; Louise safe somewhere, forgetting about Elgin and about me. Perhaps with somebody else. That was the part of the dream I tried to wake out of. None the less it was better than the pain of her death. My equilibrium, such as it was, depended on her happiness. I had to have that story. I told it to myself every day and held it against my chest every night. It was my comforter. I built different houses for her, planted out her gardens. She was in the sun abroad. She was in Italy eating mussels by the sea. She had a white villa that reflected in the lake. She wasn't sick and deserted in some rented room with thin curtains. She was well. Louise was well.

Characteristic of the leukaemic body is a rapid decline after remission. Remission can be induced by radiotherapy or chemotherapy or simply it can happen, no-one is sure why. No doctor can accurately predict whether the disease will stabilise or for how long. This is true of all cancers. The body dances with itself.

The progeny of the stem cell stop dividing, or the rate radically slows, tumour growth is halted. The patient may no longer be in pain. If remission comes early in the prognosis, before the toxic effects of the treatment have battered the body into a wholly new submission, the patient may feel well. Unfortunately, hair loss, skin discoloration, chronic constipation, fever and neurological disturbances are likely to be the price for a few months more life. Or a few years. That's the gamble.

Metastasis is the problem. Cancer has a unique property; it can travel from the site of origin to distant tissues. It is usually metastasis which kills the patient and the biology of metastasis is what doctors don't understand. They are not conditioned to understand it. In doctor-think the body is a series of bits to be isolated and treated as necessary, that the body in its very disease may act as a whole is an upsetting concept. Holistic medicine is for faith healers and crackpots, isn't it? Never mind. Wheel round the drugs trolley, bomb the battlefield, try radiation right on the tumour. No good? Get out the levers, saws, knives and needles. Spleen the size of a football? Desperate measures for desperate diseases. Especially so since metastasis has often developed before the patient sees a doctor. They don't like to tell you this but if the cancer is already on the move, treating the obvious problem, lung, breast, skin, gut, blood, will not alter the prognosis.

I went to the cemetery today and walked amongst the catacombs thinking of the dead. On the older graves the familiar skull and crossbones bore on me with uncomfortable gaiety. Why do they look so pleased, those grinning heads robbed of any human touch? That skulls should grin is repellent to us who come with dark flowers and mournful sober faces. This is a mourning ground, a place of silence and regret. For us, overcoats against the rain, the grey sky and the grey tombs together oppress. Here is the end of us all, but let's not look that way. While our bodies are solid and resist the slicing of the wind, let's not think of the deep mud or the patient ivy whose roots will find us out.

Six bearers in long coats and white scarves carried the body to the grave. To call it a grave at this stage would be to dignify it. In a garden it might be a trench for a new asparagus bed. Fill it with manure and plant it out. An optimistic hole. But this is not an asparagus bed, it is the last resting place of the deceased.

Observe the coffin. This is full oak not veneer. The handles are solid brass not lacquered steel. The lining of the coffin is raw silk padded with seabed sponge. Raw silk rots so gracefully. It makes an elegant tattering around the corpse. The acrylic linings, cheap and popular, don't decompose. You may as well be buried in a nylon sock.

DIY has never caught on. There's something macabre about making your own coffin. You can buy boat kits, house kits, garden furniture kits, but not coffin kits. Providing the holes were pre-drilled and properly lined up I foresee no disasters. Wouldn't it be the tenderest thing to do for the beloved?

The funeral here today is banked with flowers; pale lilies, white roses and branches of weeping willow. It always starts well and then gives way to apathy and plastic tulips in a milkbottle. The alternative is a fake Wedgwood vase jammed up against the headstone rain or shine with a wild Woolworth's spray to topple it over.

I wonder if I'm missing something. Perhaps like calls unto like which is why the flowers are dead. Perhaps they're dead when they're put out. Maybe people think that in a cemetery things should be dead. There's a certain logic in that. Perhaps it's rude to litter the place with thriving summer beauty and autumn splendour. For myself I would prefer a red berberis against a creamy marble slab.

To return to the hole, as we all will. Six feet long, six feet deep and two wide is the standard although this can be varied on request. It's a great leveller the hole, for no matter what fanciness goes in it, rich and poor occupy the same home at last. Air bounded by mud. Your basic Gallipoli, as they call it in the trade.

A hole is hard work. I'm told this is something the public don't appreciate. It's an old-fashioned time-consuming job and it has to be done frost or hail. Dig while the ooze soaks through your boots. Lean on the side for a breather and get wet to the bone. Very often in the nineteenth century a grave-digger would die of the damp. Digging your own grave wasn't a figure of speech then.

For the bereaved, the hole is a frightful place. A dizzy chasm of loss. This is the last time you'll be by the side of the one you love and you must leave her, must leave him, in a dark pit where the worms shall begin their duty.

For most the look before the lid is screwed down lasts a lifetime, eclipses other friendlier pictures. Before sinkage, as they call it at the mortuary, a body must be washed, disinfected, drained, plugged and made-up. These chores were regularly done at home not so many years ago but they weren't chores then, they were acts of love.

What would you do? Pass the body into the hands of strangers? The body that has lain beside you in sickness and in health. The body your arms still long for dead or not. You were intimate with every muscle, privy to the eyelids moving in sleep. This is the body where your name is written, passing into the hands of strangers.

Your beloved has gone down to a foreign land. You call but your beloved does not hear. You call in the fields and in the valleys but your beloved does not answer. The sky is closed and silent, there is no-one there. The ground is hard and dry. Your beloved will not return that way. Perhaps only a veil divides you. Your beloved is waiting on the hills. Be patient and go with nimble feet dropping your body like a scroll.

I walked away from the funeral up through the private part of the cemetery. It had been allowed to run wild. Angels and open bibles were girdled with ivy. The undergrowth was alive. The squirrels that hopped across the tombs and the blackbird singing in the tree were uninterested in mortality. For them worm, nut and sunrise were enough.

'Beloved wife of John.' 'Only daughter of Andrew and Kate.' 'Here lies one who loved not wisely but too well.' Ashes to ashes, dust to dust.

Beneath the holly trees two men were digging a grave with rhythmic determination. One touched his cap as I passed and I felt a fraud for taking sympathy not mine to have. In the dying day the ring of the spade and the low voices of the men were cheerful to me. They would be going home for tea and a wash. Absurd that the round of life should be so reassuring even here.

I looked at my watch. Locking up time soon. I should go, not out of fear but out of respect. The sun setting behind the rows of birch long-shadowed the path. The unyielding flatstones caught the light, it gilded the deep lettering, burst along the trumpets of the angels. The ground was alive with light. Not the yellow ochre of spring but heavy autumn carmine. The blood season. Already they were shooting in the wood.

I hurried my steps. Perversely, I wanted to stay. What do the dead do at night? Do they come forth grinning at the wind whistling through their ribs. What do they care that it is cold? I blew on my hands and reached the gate as the night security guard was clanking the heavy chain and padlock. Was he locking me out or locking them in? He winked conspiratorially and patted his crotch where hung an eighteen-inch length of flashlight. 'Nothin' escapes me,' he said.

I ran over the road to the café, a fancy place on the European model but with higher prices and shorter opening hours. I used to meet you here before you left Elgin. We used to come here together after sex. You were always hungry after we had made love. You said it was me you wanted to eat so it was decent of you to settle for a toasted sandwich. Sorry, Croque Monsieur, according to the menu.

I had scrupulously avoided our old haunts – that's the advice in the grief books – until today. Until today I had hoped to find you or more modestly to find out how you are. I never thought to be Cassandra plagued by dreams. I am plagued. The worm of doubt has long since found a home in my intestines. I no longer know what to trust or what is right. I get a macabre comfort from my worm.

The worms that will eat you are first eating me. You won't feel the blunt head burrowing into your collapsing tissue. You won't know the blind persistence that mocks sinew, muscle, cartilage, until it finds bone. Until the bone itself gives way. A dog in the street could gnaw on me, so little of substance have I become.

The gate from the cemetery leads here, to this café. There's a subconscious reassurance in slipping scalding coffee down an active throat. Let the bogeys and bloody-bones, raw-heads and ghouls bother us if they can. This is light and warmth and smoke and solidity. I decided to try the café, out of masochism, out of habit, out of hope. I thought it might comfort me, although I noticed how little comfort was to be got from familiar things. How dare they stay the same when so much that mattered had changed? Why does your sweater senselessly smell of you, keep your shape when you are not there to wear it? I don't want to be reminded of you, I want you. I've been thinking of leaving London, going back to the ridiculous rented cottage for a while. Why not? Make a fresh start, isn't that one of those useful clichés?

October. Why stay? There's nothing worse than being in a crowded place when you are alone. The city is always crowded. Since I've been in this café with a calvados and an espresso the door has opened eleven times bringing in a boy or a girl to meet a boy or a girl with a calvados and an espresso. Behind the high brass and glass counter the staff in long aprons are joking. There's music on, soul stuff, everyone's busy, happy or, it seems, purposefully unhappy. Those two over there, he pensive she agitated. Things aren't going well but at least they're talking. I'm the only person alone in this café and I used to love being alone. That was when I had the luxury of knowing that soon someone would push open the heavy door and look for me. I remember those times, getting to the assignation an hour early to have a drink by myself and read a book. I was almost regretful when the hour came and the door opened and it was time to stand up and kiss you on the cheek and rub your cold hands. It was the pleasure of walking in the snow in a warm coat, that choosing to be alone. Who wants to walk in the snow naked?

I paid and left. Out here in the street, striding purposefully, I can give the impression that I've got somewhere to go. There's a light on in my flat and you'll be there as arranged with your own key. I don't have to hurry, I'm enjoying the night and the cold on my cheeks. Summer's gone, the cold's welcome. I did the shopping today and you said you'd cook. I'll call and get the wine. It gives me a loose-limbed confidence to know you'll be there. I'm expected. There's a continuum. There's freedom. We can be kites and hold each other's string. No need to worry the wind will be too strong.

Here I am outside my flat. The lights are out. The rooms are cold. You won't come back. Nevertheless, sitting on the floor by the door, I'm going to write you a letter with my address and leave it in the morning when I go. If you get this please answer, I'll meet you in the café and you'll be there won't you. Won't you?

After the roar of the Intercity train, the slow sway of the branch-line carriage. Nowadays British Rail call me 'You the Customer' but I prefer my old-fashioned appellant, 'Passenger'. Don't you think 'I glanced at my fellow passengers' has a more romantic and promising air to it than 'I glanced at the other customers on the train'? Customers buy cheese, loofahs and condoms. Passengers may have all these in their luggage but it is not the thought of their purchases that makes them interesting. A fellow passenger might be an adventure. All I have in common with a fellow customer is my wallet.

At the mainline station I ran beyond the booming intercom and the 'Delayed' board. Behind the parcels depot was a little track that used to be the only track at this station. Years ago the buildings were painted burgundy and the waiting-room had a real fire and a copy of the morning newspaper. If you asked the Stationmaster the time he would pull an enormous gold Hunter from his waistcoat pocket and consult it like a Greek at Delphi. The answer would be presented to you as an eternal truth even though it was already in the past. I was very young when such things happened, young enough to shelter under the Stationmaster's paunch while my father looked him in the eye. Too young to be expected to tell the truth myself.

Now the little track is under sentence of death and may be executed next year. There's no waiting room, nowhere to hide from the squalling wind or beating rain. This is a modern platform.

The wheezing train shuddered to a halt and belched. It was dirty, four carriages long, no sign of guard or conductor. No sign of a driver except for a folded copy of the *Sun* at the engine window. Inside, the hot smell of brakes and the rich smell of oil colluded with the unswept floor into familiar railway nausea. I felt at home at once and settled to watch the scenery through an evocative film of dust.

In a vacuum all photons travel at the same speed. They slow down when travelling through air or water or glass. Photons of different energies are slowed down at different rates. If Tolstoy had known this, would he have recognised the terrible untruth at the beginning of *Anna Karenina*? 'All happy families are alike; every unhappy family is unhappy in its own particular way.' In fact it's the other way around. Happiness is a specific. Misery is a generalisation. People usually know exactly why they are happy. They very rarely know why they are miserable.

Misery is a vacuum. A space without air, a suffocated dead place, the abode of the miserable. Misery is a tenement block, rooms like battery cages, sit over your own droppings, lie on your own filth. Misery is a no U-turns, no stopping road. Travel down it pushed by those behind, tripped by those in front. Travel down it at furious speed though the days are mummified in lead. It happens so fast once you get started, there's no anchor from the real world to slow you down, nothing to hold on to. Misery pulls away the brackets of life leaving you to free fall. Whatever your private hell, you'll find millions like it in Misery. This is the town where everyone's nightmares come true.

In the train carriage, shut behind the thick glass, I feel comfortably locked away from responsibility. I know I'm running away but my heart has become a sterile zone where nothing can grow. I don't want to face facts, shape up, snap out of it. In the pumped-out, dry bed of my heart, I'm learning to live without oxygen. I might get to like it in a masochistic way. I've sunk too low to make decisions and that brings with it a certain lightheaded freedom. Walking on the moon there's no gravity. There are dead souls in uniform ranks, spacesuits too bulky for touch, helmets too heavy for speech. The miserable millions moving in time without hope. There are no clocks in Misery, just an endless ticking.

The train has been delayed and we are sitting in

a cutting with nothing but the rustle of an evening paper and the tired stirrings of the engine. Nothing will intrude upon this passive derelict scene. I've got my feet up on the stained upholstery. The man two seats away is snoring in sleep. We can't get out and we can't get on. What does it matter? Why not relax in the overheated stagnant air? IN THE EVENT OF AN EMERGENCY BREAK GLASS. This is an emergency but I can't lift my arm high enough to smash my way out. I haven't got the strength to sound the alarm. I want to stand up strong and tall, leap through the window, brush the shards from my sleeve and say, 'That was yesterday, this is today.' I want to accept what I've done and let go. I can't let go because Louise might still be on the other end of the rope.

The station at the village is a small one and leads directly on to a lane and through fields spread with winter wheat. There's never a ticket collector, only a 40-watt bulb and a sign that says 'THIS WAY'. I'm thankful for a little guidance.

The path is bulked with cinders that give a high-pitched clink under your shoes. Your shoes will have charcoal patches and flakes of white ash but it's better than mud on a rainy night. It's not raining tonight. The sky is clear and hard, not a cloud, only stars and a drunken moon swinging on her back. There's a line of ash trees by the picket fence that takes you out of man-made things into the deep country where the land's not good for anything but sheep. I can hear the sheep munching invisibly over tussocks of grass thick as a pelt. Be careful to keep on the right, there's a ditch.

I could have got a taxi that late night, not chosen to walk six miles without a torch. It was the slap of the cold, the shock in my lungs that sent me up the cinder path and away from the pub and the telephone. I slung my bag on my back and made for the outline of the hill. Up and over. Three miles up, three miles down. We walked all night once, Louise and I, walked out of darkness as though it were a tunnel. We walked into the morning, the morning was waiting for us, it was already perfect, high sun over a level plain. Looking back I thought I saw the darkness where we had left it. I didn't think it could come after us.

I barged my way through a herd of cattle, hooves braceleted with mud. My own feet were clod-fettered. I hadn't anticipated the run-off, the slow slopes of the hill served as a drain bath for engorged springs. The rain on the dry land from a dry summer hadn't penetrated through the soil to the aquifers, only as far as the springs that fed them. They burst out in froth torrents to end in paddy pools where the cattle waded for long grass. I was lucky that the moon reflected in these waters, picking a path for me, mud-laden but not sodden. My town shoes and flimsy socks put up no resistance. My long coat was soon spattered. The cows reserved for me the incredulous looks that animals give humans in the country. We seem so silly, not a part of nature at all. The interlopers upsetting the rigid economy of hunter and hunted. Animals know what's what until they meet us. Well, tonight the cows have the last laugh. Their peaceful ruminations, their easy bodies, black against the slope of the hill, mock the flapping figure with a heavy bag who stumbles against them. Woa there! Bring that rump back. As a vegetarian I can't even contemplate revenge. Could you kill a cow? It's a game I play with myself sometimes. What could I kill? I get as far as a duck and then I see one on the pond, daft quacking, bum up diving, webbers yellow slashing the brown water. Scoop it out and wring its neck? I've brought them down with a gun and that's easier because it's remote. I won't eat what I can't kill. It seems shoddy, hypocritical. You cows have nothing to fear from me. As a body, the cows raise their heads. Like men in johns, cows and sheep do things in unison. I've always found it disturbing. What have gazing, grazing and micturating got in common?

I went to pee behind a bush. Why in the middle of the night, in the middle of nowhere, one still seeks out a bush is another of life's mysteries.

At the top of the hill, on dry ground, a whistling wind and a view. The lights of the village were like war-time coordinates, a secret council of houses and tracks muffled by darkness. I sat down to finish an egg and cress sandwich. A rabbit ran by and gave me that look of incredulity before flashing its scut down a hole.

Lights in ribbons where the road runs. Hard flares far away at the industrial estate. In the sky the red and green landing lights of an aircraft full of sleepy people. Straight below the softer village lights, and in the distance a single light hung above the others like a guiding lantern in a window. A land lighthouse making certain the route. I wished that it was my house. That having climbed to the top I could see where I was going. My way lay through gloomy thicket and a sharp plunge before the long lane home.

I miss you Louise. Many waters cannot quench love, neither can floods drown it. What then kills love? Only this: Neglect. Not to see you when you stand before me. Not to think of you in the little things. Not to make the road wide for you, the table spread for you. To choose you out of habit not desire, to pass the flower seller without a thought. To leave the dishes unwashed, the bed unmade, to ignore you in the mornings, make use of you at night. To crave another while pecking your cheek. To say your name without hearing it, to assume it is mine to call.

Why didn't I hear you when you told me you wouldn't go back to Elgin? Why didn't I see your serious face? I did think I was doing the right thing and I thought it was for the right reasons. Time has exposed to me a certain stickiness at the centre. What were my heroics and sacrifices really about? Your pig-headedness or my own?

A friend of mine said before I left London, 'At least your relationship with Louise didn't fail. It was the perfect romance.'

Was it? Is that what perfection costs? Operatic heroics and a tragic end? What about a wasteful end? Most opera ends wastefully. The happy endings are compromises. Is that the choice?

Louise, stars in your eyes, my own constellation. I was following you faithfully but I looked down. You took me out beyond the house, over the roofs, way past commonsense and good behaviour. No compromise. I should have trusted you but I lost my nerve.

I scrambled up and judged or guessed my way through the scrubland down to the lane. It was slow going, an hour and a half before I threw my bag over the final ditch and leapt across. Now the moon was high and casting long shadows on the rough road. Silence but for the sudden fox-dart in the trees. Silence but for the early owl. Silence but for my feet scuffing the gravel.

About half a mile away from my cottage I saw it was lit up. Gail Right knew I was coming back, I had telephoned her at the bar. She'd been looking after the cat and had promised to lay me a fire and leave some food. I wanted the food and fire but not Gail Right She would be too big, too present, and I felt I was becoming less present every day. I was tired from walking. My body had a satisfying numbness to it. I wanted my bed, oblivion for a while. I resolved to be firm with Gail.

The moon made the ground look frosty. The ground was silver under my shoes. Where the river ran in a thick line through the trees a low mist hung over the water. The rush of the water was bass and hard, solid deep. I bent and swilled my face, let the cold drops run down my scarf to my thorax. I shook myself and cleaved lungs with air, a hammer of cold that hit from pit to throat. Very cold now and above me a hang of metal stars.

I went into the cottage, the door was unlocked, and there was Gail Right half asleep in the chair. The fire burned like a spell and there were fresh flowers on the table. Fresh flowers and a table-cloth. New curtains in the ragged window. My heart sank. Gail must be moving in.

She woke up and checked her face in the mirror, then she gave me a little kiss and unwound my scarf.

'You're wet through.'

'I stopped at the river.'

'Not thinking of ending it all I hope?'

I shook my head and took off my coat that seemed too big for me.

'Sit down honey. I've got the tea.'

I sat down in the saggy armchair. Is this the proper ending? If not the proper then the inevitable?

Gail returned with a pot steaming like a genie. It was a new pot, not the cracked old thing that had festered on the shelf. New pots for old.

'I couldn't find her Gail.'

She patted me. 'Where did you look?'

'All the places there were to look. She's gone.'

'People don't vanish.'

'Of course they do. She came out of the air and now she's returned to it. Wherever she is I can't go there.'

'And if you could?'

'I would. If I believed in the after-life I'd throw myself in the trout-marked river tonight.'

'Don't do that,' said Gail. 'I can't swim.'

'Do you think she's dead?'

'Do you?'

'I couldn't find her. I couldn't even get near finding her. It's as if Louise never existed, like a character in a book. Did I invent her?'

'No, but you tried to,' said Gail. 'She wasn't yours for the making.'

'Don't you think it's strange that life, described as so rich and full, a camel-trail of adventure, should shrink to this coin-sized world? A head on one side, a story on the other. Someone you loved and what happened. That's all there is when you dig in your pockets. The most significant thing is someone else's face. What else is embossed on your hands but her?'

'You still love her then?'

'With all my heart.'

'What will you do?'

'What can I do? Louise once said, "It's the clichés that cause the trouble." What do you want me to say? That I'll get over it? That's right, isn't it? Time is a great deadener.'

'I'm sorry,' said Gail.
'So am I. I'd like to be able to tell her the truth.'

From the kitchen door Louise's face. Paler, thinner, but her hair still mane-wide and the colour of blood. I put out my hand and felt her fingers, she took my fingers and put them to her mouth. The scar under the lip burned me. Am I stark mad? She's warm.

This is where the story starts, in this threadbare room. The walls are exploding. The windows have turned into telescopes. Moon and stars are magnified in this room. The sun hangs over the mantelpiece. I stretch out my hand and reach the corners of the world. The world is bundled up in this room. Beyond the door, where the river is, where the roads are, we shall be. We can take the world with us when we go and sling the sun under your arm. Hurry now, it's getting late. I don't know if this is a happy ending but here we are let loose in open fields.

ACCLAIM FOR HARUKI MURAKAMI's

SOUTH OF THE BORDER, WEST OF THE SUN

"His most deeply moving novel." —*The Boston Globe*

"Mesmerizing. . . . This is a harrowing, a disturbing, a hauntingly brilliant tale." —*The Baltimore Sun*

"A fine, almost delicate book about what is unfathomable about us." —*The Philadelphia Inquirer*

"Portrayed in a fluid language that veers from the vernacular . . . to the surprisingly poetic." —*San Francisco Examiner & Chronicle*

"Haunting and natural. . . . *South of the Border, West of the Sun* so smoothly shifts the reader from mundane concerns into latent madness as to challenge one's faith in the material world . . . contains passages that are among his finest." —*The New York Observer*

"Haruki Murakami applies his patented Japanese magic realism—minimalist, smooth, and transcendently odd—to a charming tale of childhood love lost." —*New York*

HARUKI MURAKAMI

SOUTH OF THE BORDER, WEST OF THE SUN

Haruki Murakami was born in Kyoto in 1949 and now lives near Tokyo. His work has been translated into more than fifty languages, and the most recent of his many international honors is the Jerusalem Prize, whose previous recipients include J. M. Coetzee, Milan Kundera, and V. S. Naipaul.

www.harukimurakami.com

INTERNATIONAL

BOOKS BY HARUKI MURAKAMI

Fiction

1Q84

After Dark

After the Quake

Blind Willow, Sleeping Woman

Colorless Tsukuru and His Years of Pilgrimage

Dance Dance Dance

The Elephant Vanishes

Hard-Boiled Wonderland and the End of the World

Kafka on the Shore

Killing Commendatore

Men Without Women

Norwegian Wood

South of the Border, West of the Sun

Sputnik Sweetheart

The Strange Library

A Wild Sheep Chase

Wind/Pinball

The Wind-Up Bird Chronicle

Nonfiction

Absolutely on Music: Conversations

Underground: The Tokyo Gas Attack and the Japanese Psyche

What I Talk About When I Talk About Running: A Memoir

SOUTH OF THE BORDER, WEST OF THE SUN

SOUTH OF THE BORDER, WEST OF THE SUN

HARUKI MURAKAMI

TRANSLATED FROM THE JAPANESE BY PHILIP GABRIEL

VINTAGE INTERNATIONAL

Vintage Books

A Division of Penguin Random House LLC

New York

FIRST VINTAGE INTERNATIONAL EDITION, MARCH 2000

The Library of Congress has cataloged the Knopf edition as follows:
Murakami, Haruki
South of the border, west of the sun / Haruki Murakami
p. cm.
Translation of an unpublished work.
I. Title
PL856.U673S68 1998
895.6'35—dc21 97-49459 CIP

**Vintage International Trade Paperback ISBN: 978-0-679-76739-8
eBook ISBN: 978-0-307-76274-0**

www.vintagebooks.com

Printed in the United States of America
34

SOUTH OF THE BORDER, WEST OF THE SUN

1

My birthday's the fourth of January, 1951. The first week of the first month of the first year of the second half of the twentieth century. Something to commemorate, I guess, which is why my parents named me Hajime— "Beginning," in Japanese. Other than that, a 100 percent average birth. My father worked in a large brokerage firm, my mother was a typical housewife. During the war, my father was drafted as a student and sent to fight in Singapore; after the surrender he spent some time in a POW camp. My mother's house was burned down in a B-29 raid during the final year of the war. Their generation suffered most during the long war.

When I was born, though, you'd never have known there'd been a war. No more burned-out ruins, no more

occupation army. We lived in a small, quiet town, in a house my father's company provided. The house was prewar, somewhat old but roomy enough. Pine trees grew in the garden, and we even had a small pond and some stone lanterns.

The town I grew up in was your typical middle-class suburbia. The classmates I was friendly with all lived in neat little row houses; some might have been a bit larger than mine, but you could count on them all having similar entranceways, pine trees in the garden. The works. My friends' fathers were employed in companies or else were professionals of some sort. Hardly anyone's mother worked. And most everyone had a cat or a dog. No one I knew lived in an apartment or a condo. Later on I moved to another part of town, but it was pretty much identical. The upshot of this is that until I moved to Tokyo to go to college, I was convinced everyone in the whole world lived in a single-family home with a garden and a pet, and commuted to work decked out in a suit. I couldn't for the life of me imagine a different lifestyle.

In the world I grew up in, a typical family had two or three children. My childhood friends were all members of such stereotypical families. If not two kids in the family, then three; if not three, then two. Families with six or seven kids were few and far between, but even more unusual were families with only one child.

I happened to be one of the unusual ones, since I was an only child. I had an inferiority complex about it, as if there was something different about me, that what other people all had and took for granted I lacked.

I detested the term *only child*. Every time I heard it, I felt something was missing from me—like I wasn't quite a complete human being. The phrase *only child* stood there, pointing an accusatory finger at me. "Something's not quite all there, pal," it told me.

In the world I lived in, it was an accepted idea that only children were spoiled by their parents, weak, and self-centered. This was a given—like the fact that the barometer goes down the higher up you go and the fact that cows give milk. That's why I hated it whenever someone asked me how many brothers and sisters I had. Just let them hear I didn't have any, and instinctively they thought: An only child, eh? Spoiled, weak, and self-centered, I betcha. That kind of knee-jerk reaction depressed me, and hurt. But what really depressed and hurt me was something else: the fact that everything they thought about me was true. I really *was* spoiled, weak, and self-centered.

In the six years I went to elementary school, I met just one other only child. So I remember her (yes, it was a girl) very well. I got to know her well, and we talked about all sorts of things. We understood each other. You could even say I loved her.

Her last name was Shimamoto. Soon after she was born, she came down with polio, which made her drag her left leg. On top of that, she'd transferred to our school at the end of fifth grade. Compared to me, then, she had a terrible load of psychological baggage to struggle with. This baggage, though, only made her a tougher, more self-possessed only child than I could ever have been. She never whined or complained, never

gave any indication of the annoyance she must have felt at times. No matter what happened, she'd manage a smile. The worse things got, in fact, the broader her smile became. I loved her smile. It soothed me, encouraged me. *It'll be all right,* her smile told me. *Just hang in there, and everything will turn out okay.* Years later, whenever I thought of her, it was her smile that came to mind first.

Shimamoto always got good grades and was kind to everyone. People respected her. We were both only children, but in this sense she and I were different. This doesn't mean, though, that all our classmates liked her. No one teased her or made fun of her, but except for me, she had no real friends.

She was probably too cool, too self-possessed. Some of our classmates must have thought her cold and haughty. But I detected something else—something warm and fragile just below the surface. Something very much like a child playing hide-and-seek, hidden deep within her, yet hoping to be found.

Because her father was transferred a lot, Shimamoto had attended quite a few schools. I can't recall what her father did. Once, she explained to me in detail what he did, but as with most kids, it went in one ear and out the other. I seem to recall some professional job connected with a bank or tax office or something. She lived in company housing, but the house was larger than normal, a Western-style house with a low solid stone wall surrounding it. Above the wall was an evergreen hedge, and through gaps in the hedge you could catch a glimpse of a garden with a lawn.

Shimamoto was a large girl, about as tall as I was, with striking features. I was certain that in a few years she would be gorgeous. But when I first met her, she hadn't developed an outer look to match her inner qualities. Something about her was unbalanced, and not many people felt she was much to look at. There was an adult part of her and a part that was still a child—and they were out of sync. And this out-of-sync quality made people uneasy.

Probably because our houses were so close, literally a stone's throw from each other, the first month after she came to our school she was assigned to the seat next to mine. I brought her up to speed on what texts she'd need, what the weekly tests were like, how much we'd covered in each book, how the cleaning and the dishing-out-lunch assignments were handled. Our school's policy was for the child who lived nearest any transfer student to help him or her out; my teacher took me aside to let me know that he expected me to take special care of Shimamoto, with her lame leg.

As with all kids of eleven or twelve talking with a member of the opposite sex for the first time, for a couple of days our conversations were strained. When we found out we were both only children, though, we relaxed. It was the first time either of us had met a fellow only child. We had so much we'd held inside about being only children. Often we'd walk home together. Slowly, because of her leg, we'd walk the three quarters of a mile home, talking about all kinds of things. The more we talked, the more we realized we had in common: our love of books and music; not to mention cats.

We both had a hard time explaining our feelings to others. We both had a long list of foods we didn't want to eat. When it came to subjects at school, the ones we liked we had no trouble concentrating on; the ones we disliked we hated to death. But there was one major difference between us—more than I did, Shimamoto consciously wrapped herself inside a protective shell. Unlike me, she made an effort to study the subjects she hated, and she got good grades. When the school lunch contained food she hated, she still ate it. In other words, she constructed a much taller defensive wall around herself than I ever built. What remained behind that wall, though, was pretty much what lay behind mine.

Unlike times when I was with other girls, I could relax with Shimamoto. I loved walking home with her. Her left leg limped slightly as she walked. We sometimes took a breather on a park bench halfway home, but I didn't mind. Rather the opposite—I was glad to have the extra time.

Soon we began to spend a lot of time together, but I don't recall anyone kidding us about it. This didn't strike me at the time, though now it seems strange. After all, kids that age naturally tease and make fun of any couple who seem close. It might have been because of the kind of person Shimamoto was. Something about her made other people a bit tense. She had an air about her that made people think: Whoa—better not say anything too stupid in front of *this* girl. Even our teachers were somewhat on edge when dealing with her. Her lameness might have had something to do with it. At any rate, most people thought Shimamoto was not the kind of person you teased, which was just fine by me.

During phys. ed. she sat on the sidelines, and when our class went hiking or mountain climbing, she stayed home. Same with summer swim camp. On our annual sports day, she did seem a little out of sorts. But other than this, her school life was typical. Hardly ever did she mention her leg. If memory serves, not even once. Whenever we walked home from school together, she never once apologized for holding me back or let this thought graze her expression. I knew, though, that it was precisely because her leg bothered her that she refrained from mentioning it. She didn't like to go to other kids' homes much, since she'd have to remove her shoes, Japanese style, at the entrance. The heels of her shoes were different heights, and the shoes themselves were shaped differently—something she wanted at all costs to conceal. Must have been custom-made shoes. When she arrived at her own home, the first thing she did was toss her shoes in the closet as fast as she could.

Shimamoto's house had a brand-new stereo in the living room, and I used to go over to her place to listen to music. It was a pretty nice stereo. Her father's LP collection, though, didn't do it justice. At most he had fifteen records, chiefly collections of light classics. We listened to those fifteen records a thousand times, and even today I can recall the music—every single note.

Shimamoto was in charge of the records. She'd take one from its jacket, place it carefully on the turntable without touching the grooves with her fingers, and, after making sure to brush the cartridge free of any dust with a tiny brush, lower the needle ever so gently onto the record. When the record was finished, she'd spray it and wipe it with a felt cloth. Finally she'd return the

record to its jacket and its proper place on the shelf. Her father had taught her this procedure, and she followed his instructions with a terribly serious look on her face, her eyes narrowed, her breath held in check. Meanwhile, I was on the sofa, watching her every move. Only when the record was safely back on the shelf did she turn to me and give a little smile. And every time, this thought hit me: It wasn't a record she was handling. It was a fragile soul inside a glass bottle.

In my house we didn't have records or a record player. My parents didn't care much for music. So I was always listening to music on a small plastic AM radio. Rock and roll was my favorite, but before long I grew to enjoy Shimamoto's brand of classical music. This was music from another world, which had its appeal, but more than that I loved it because *she* was a part of that world. Once or twice a week, she and I would sit on the sofa, drinking the tea her mother made for us, and spend the afternoon listening to Rossini overtures, Beethoven's *Pastorale*, and the *Peer Gynt* Suite. Her mother was happy to have me over. She was pleased her daughter had a friend so soon after transferring to a new school, and I guess it helped that I was a neat dresser. Honestly, I couldn't bring myself to like her mother very much. No particular reason I felt that way. She was always nice to me. But I could detect a hint of irritation in her voice, and it put me on edge.

Of all her father's records, the one I liked best was a recording of the Liszt piano concertos: one concerto on each side. There were two reasons I liked this record. First of all, the record jacket was beautiful. Second, no

one around me—with the exception of Shimamoto, of course—ever listened to Liszt's piano concertos. The very idea excited me. I'd found a world that no one around me knew—a secret garden only I was allowed to enter. I felt elevated, lifted to another plane of existence.

And the music itself was wonderful. At first it struck me as exaggerated, artificial, even incomprehensible. Little by little, though, with repeated listenings, a vague image formed in my mind—an image that had meaning. When I closed my eyes and concentrated, the music came to me as a series of whirlpools. One whirlpool would form, and out of it another would take shape. And the second whirlpool would connect up with a third. Those whirlpools, I realize now, had a conceptual, abstract quality to them. More than anything, I wanted to tell Shimamoto about them. But they were beyond ordinary language. An entirely different set of words was needed, but I had no idea what these were. What's more, I didn't know if what I was feeling was worth putting into words. Unfortunately, I no longer remember the name of the pianist. All I recall are the colorful, vivid record jacket and the weight of the record itself. The record was hefty and thick in a mysterious way.

The collection in her house included one record each by Nat King Cole and Bing Crosby. We listened to those two a lot. The Crosby disc featured Christmas songs, which we enjoyed regardless of the season. It's funny how we could enjoy something like that over and over.

One December day near Christmas, Shimamoto and I were sitting in her living room. On the sofa, as usual, listening to records. Her mother was out of the house on

some errand, and we were alone. It was a cloudy, dark winter afternoon. The sun's rays, streaked with fine dust, barely shone through the heavy layer of clouds. Everything looked dim and motionless. It was nearing dusk, and the room was as dark as night. A kerosene space heater bathed the room in a faint red glow. Nat King Cole was singing "Pretend." Of course, we had no idea then what the English lyrics meant. To us they were more like a chant. But I loved the song and had heard it so many times I could imitate the opening lines:

> *Pretend you're happy when you're blue*
> *It isn't very hard to do*

The song and the lovely smile that always graced Shimamoto's face were one and the same to me. The lyrics seemed to express a certain way of looking at life, though at times I found it hard to see life in that way.

Shimamoto had on a blue sweater with a round neck. She owned a fair number of blue sweaters; blue must have been her favorite color. Or maybe she wore those sweaters because they went well with the navy-blue coat she always wore to school. The white collar of her blouse peeked out at her throat. A checked skirt and white cotton socks completed her outfit. Her soft, tight sweater revealed the slight swell of her chest. She sat on the sofa with both legs folded underneath her. One elbow resting on the back of the sofa, she stared at some far-off, imaginary scene as she listened to the music.

"Do you think it's true what they say—that parents of only children don't get along very well?" she asked.

I mulled over the idea. But I couldn't figure out the cause and effect of it.

"Where did you hear that?" I asked.

"Somebody said that to me. A long time ago. Parents who don't get along very well end up having only one child. It made me so sad when I heard that."

"Hmm . . . ," I said.

"Do your mother and father get along all right?"

I couldn't answer right away. I'd never thought about it before.

"My mother isn't too strong physically," I said. "I'm not sure, but it was probably too much of a strain for her to have another child after me."

"Have you ever wondered what it would be like to have a brother or sister?"

"No."

"Why not?"

I picked up the record jacket on the table. It was too dark to read what was written on it. I put the jacket down and rubbed my eyes a couple of times with my wrist. My mother had once asked me the same question. The answer I gave then didn't make her happy or sad. It just puzzled her. But for me it was a totally honest, totally sincere answer.

The things I wanted to say got all jumbled up as I talked, and my explanation seemed to go on forever. But what I was trying to get across was just this: The me that's here now has been brought up without any brothers or sisters. If I did have brothers or sisters I wouldn't be the me I am. So it's unnatural for the me that's here before you to think about what it'd be like to have

brothers or sisters.... In other words, I thought my mother's question was pointless.

I gave the same answer to Shimamoto. She gazed at me steadily as I talked. Something about her expression pulled people in. It was as if—this is something I thought of only later, of course—she were gently peeling back one layer after another that covered a person's heart, a very sensual feeling. Her lips changed ever so slightly with each change in her expression, and I could catch a glimpse deep within her eyes of a faint light, like a tiny candle flickering in the dark, narrow room.

"I think I understand what you mean," she said in a mature, quiet voice.

"Really?"

"Um," she answered. "There are some things in this world that can be done over, and some that can't. And time passing is one thing that can't be redone. Come this far, and you can't go back. Don't you think so?"

I nodded.

"After a certain length of time has passed, things harden up. Like cement hardening in a bucket. And we can't go back anymore. What you want to say is that the cement that makes you up has hardened, so the you you are now can't be anyone else."

"I guess that's what I mean," I said uncertainly.

Shimamoto looked at her hands for a time.

"Sometimes, you know, I start thinking. About after I grow up and get married. I think about what kind of house I'll live in, what I'll do. And I think about how many children I'll have."

"Wow," I said.

"Haven't you ever thought about that?"

I shook my head. How could a twelve-year-old boy be expected to think about that? "So how many kids do you want to have?"

Her hand, which up till then had laid on the back of the sofa, she now placed on her knee. I stared vacantly at her fingers tracing the plaid pattern of her skirt. There was something mysterious about it, as if invisible thread emanating from her fingertips spun together an entirely new concept of time. I closed my eyes, and in the darkness, whirlpools flashed before me. Countless whirlpools were born and disappeared without a sound. Off in the distance, Nat King Cole was singing "South of the Border." The song was about Mexico, but at the time I had no idea. The words "south of the border" had a strangely appealing ring to them. I was convinced something utterly wonderful lay south of the border. When I opened my eyes, Shimamoto was still moving her fingers along her skirt. Somewhere deep inside my body I felt an exquisitely sweet ache.

"It's strange," she said, "but when I think about children, I can only imagine having one. I can somehow picture myself having children. I'm a mother, and I have a child. I have no problem with that. But I can't picture that child having any brothers or sisters. It's an only child."

She was, without a doubt, a precocious girl. I feel sure she was attracted to me as a member of the opposite sex—a feeling I reciprocated. But I had no idea how to deal with those feelings. Shimamoto didn't, either, I sus-

pect. We held hands just once. She was leading me somewhere and grabbed my hand as if to say, This way—hurry up. Our hands were clasped together ten seconds at most, but to me it felt more like thirty minutes. When she let go of my hand, I was suddenly lost. It was all very natural, the way she took my hand, but I knew she'd been dying to do so.

The feel of her hand has never left me. It was different from any other hand I'd ever held, different from any touch I've ever known. It was merely the small, warm hand of a twelve-year-old girl, yet those five fingers and that palm were like a display case crammed full of everything I wanted to know—and everything I *had* to know. By taking my hand, she showed me what these things were. That within the real world, a place like this existed. In the space of those ten seconds I became a tiny bird, fluttering into the air, the wind rushing by. From high in the sky I could see a scene far away. It was so far off I couldn't make it out clearly, yet something was there, and I knew that someday I would travel to that place. This revelation made me catch my breath and made my chest tremble.

I returned home, and sitting at my desk, I gazed for a long time at the fingers Shimamoto had clasped. I was ecstatic that she'd held my hand. Her gentle touch warmed my heart for days. At the same time it confused me, made me perplexed, even sad in a way. How could I possibly come to terms with that warmth?

After graduating from elementary school, Shimamoto and I went on to separate junior highs. I left the home I had lived in till then and moved to a new town. I

say a new town, but it was only two train stops from where I grew up, and in the first three months after I moved I went to see her three or four times. But that was it. Finally I stopped going. We were both at a delicate age, when the mere fact that we were attending different schools and living two train stops away was all it took for me to feel our worlds had changed completely. Our friends were different, so were our uniforms and textbooks. My body, my voice, my way of thinking, were undergoing sudden changes, and an unexpected awkwardness threatened the intimate world we had created. Shimamoto, of course, was going through even greater physical and psychological changes. And all of this made me uncomfortable. Her mother began to look at me in a strange way. *Why does this boy keep coming over?* she seemed to be saying. *He no longer lives in the neighborhood, and he goes to a different school.* Maybe I was just being too sensitive.

Shimamoto and I thus grew apart, and I ended up not seeing her anymore. And that was probably (*probably* is the only word I can think of to use here; I don't consider it my job to investigate the expanse of memory called the past and judge what is correct and what isn't) a mistake. I should have stayed as close as I could to her. I needed her, and she needed me. But my self-consciousness was too strong, and I was too afraid of being hurt. I never saw her again. Until many years later, that is.

Even after we stopped seeing each other, I thought of her with great fondness. Memories of her encouraged me, soothed me, as I passed through the confusion and

pain of adolescence. For a long time, she held a special place in my heart. I kept this special place just for her, like a Reserved sign on a quiet corner table in a restaurant. Despite the fact that I was sure I'd never see her again.

When I knew her I was still twelve years old, without any real sexual feelings or desire. Though I'll admit to a vaguely formed interest in the swell of her chest and what lay beneath her skirt. But I had no idea what this meant, or where it might lead.

With ears perked up and eyes closed, I imagined the existence of a certain place. This place I imagined was still incomplete. It was misty, indistinct, its outlines vague. Yet I was sure that something absolutely vital lay waiting for me there. And I knew this: that Shimamoto was gazing at the very same scene.

We were, the two of us, still fragmentary beings, just beginning to sense the presence of an unexpected, to-be-acquired reality that would fill us and make us whole. We stood before a door we'd never seen before. The two of us alone, beneath a faintly flickering light, our hands tightly clasped together for a fleeting ten seconds of time.

2

In high school I was a typical teenager. This was the second stage of my life, a step in my personal evolution—abandoning the idea of being different, and settling for normal. Not that I didn't have my own set of problems. But what sixteen-year-old doesn't? Gradually I drew nearer the world, and the world drew nearer to me.

By the time I was sixteen I wasn't a puny little only child anymore. In junior high I started to go to a swimming school near my house. I mastered the crawl and went twice a week for lap swimming. My shoulders and chest filled out, and my muscles grew strong and taut. I was no longer the kind of sickly kid who got a fever at the drop of a hat and took to his bed. Often I stood

naked in front of the bathroom mirror, scrutinizing every nook and cranny of my body.

I could almost see the rapid physical changes right before my eyes. And I enjoyed these changes. I don't mean I was thrilled about becoming an adult. It was less the maturing process I enjoyed than seeing the transformation in myself. I could be a new me.

I loved to read and to listen to music. I'd always liked books and reading, and my interest in these had been fostered by my friendship with Shimamoto. I started to go to the library, devouring every book I could lay my hands on. Once I began a book, I couldn't put it down. It was like an addiction; I read while I ate, on the train, in bed until late at night, in school, where I'd keep the book hidden so I could read during class. Before long I bought a small stereo and spent my time holed up in my room, listening to jazz records. But I had almost no desire to talk with anyone about the experience I gained through books and music. I felt happy just being me and no one else. In that sense I could be pegged a stuck-up loner. I disliked team sports of any kind. I hated any kind of competition where you had to rack up points against someone else. I much preferred to swim on and on, alone, in silence.

Not that I was a total loner. I managed to make some close friends at school, a few, at least. School itself I hated. I felt as though these friends were trying to crush me all the time and I had to always be prepared to defend myself. This toughened me. If it hadn't been for these friends, I would have emerged from those treacherous teenage years with even more scars.

After I started swimming, I no longer was so picky about the foods I ate, and I could talk with girls without blushing. I might be an only child, but no one gave it a second thought anymore. At least on the outside, it seemed I had freed myself from the curse of the only child.

And I made a girlfriend.

She wasn't particularly pretty, not the type your mother would point out in the class picture as the prettiest girl in school. But the first time I met her, I thought she was rather cute. You couldn't see it in a photo, but she had a straightforward warmth, which attracted people. She wasn't the kind of beauty I could brag about. But I wasn't much of a catch, either.

She and I were in the same class in junior year of high school and went out on dates often. At first double dates, then just the two of us. For whatever reason, I always felt relaxed with her. I could say anything, and she listened intently. I might just be blabbing away about some drivel, but from the expression on her face you'd have imagined I was revealing a magnificent discovery that would change the course of history. It was the first time since Shimamoto that a girl was so engrossed in anything I had to say. And for my part, I wanted to know everything there was to know about her. What she ate every day, what kind of room she lived in. What she could see from her window.

Her name was Izumi. Love your name, I told her the first time we talked. "Mountain spring," it means in Japanese. Throw in an ax, and out would pop a fairy, I said,

thinking of the fairy tale. She laughed. Izumi had a sister, three years younger than her, and a brother, five years younger. Her father was a dentist, and they lived—no surprise—in a single-family home, with a dog. The dog was a German Shepherd named Karl, after Karl Marx, believe it or not. Her father was a member of the Japanese Communist Party. Granted there must be Communist dentists in the world, but the whole lot of them could probably fit in four or five buses. So I thought it was pretty weird that it was *my* girlfriend's father who happened to be one of this rare breed. Izumi's parents were tennis fanatics, and every Sunday would find them, rackets in hand, heading off to the court. A Communist dentist tennis nut what a weird combination! Izumi wasn't interested in politics, but she loved her parents and would join them in a round of tennis every so often. She tried to get me to play, but tennis wasn't my thing.

She envied me because I was an only child. She didn't get along well with her brother or sister. According to her, they were a couple of heartless idiots she wouldn't mind giving the old heave-ho. I always wanted to be an only child, she said, living as I please, with no one bothering me every time I turn around.

On our third date I kissed her. She was over at my place that day. My mother was out shopping, so we had the whole house to ourselves. When I brought my face near and touched my lips to hers, she just closed her eyes and was silent. I'd prepared a full dozen excuses, in case she got mad or turned away, but I didn't need any of them. My lips on hers, I put my arms around her and

drew her close. It was near the end of summer, and she had on a seersucker dress. It was tied at the waist, and the tie hung loosely behind her like a tail. My hand touched the latch of her brassiere. I could feel her breath on my neck. I was so excited my heart felt like it was going to leap right out of my body. My penis was ready to burst; it pushed against her thigh, and she shifted a bit to one side. But that was all. She didn't seem upset.

We sat for some time on the sofa, holding each other tight. A cat was sitting on the chair across from us. It opened its eyes, looked in our direction, stretched, and went back to sleep. I stroked her hair and put my lips to her tiny ears. I thought I had to say something, but nothing came to me. I could barely breathe, let alone speak. I took her hand again, and kissed her once more. For a long time, the two of us were quiet.

After I saw her off at the train station, I couldn't calm down. I went home and lay on the sofa and stared at the ceiling. My mind was in a whirl. Finally my mother came home and said she'd get dinner ready. But food was the last thing I could think about. Without a word, I went out and wandered around the town for a good two hours. It was a strange feeling. I was no longer alone, yet at the same time I felt a deep loneliness I'd never known before. As with wearing glasses for the first time, my sense of perspective was suddenly transformed. Things far away I could touch, and objects that shouldn't have been hazy were now crystal clear.

When Izumi left me that day, she thanked me and told me how happy she was. She wasn't the only happy

one. I couldn't believe a girl had actually let me kiss her. How could I not be ecstatic? Even so, I couldn't be unreservedly happy. I was like a tower that had lost its base. I was up high, and the more I looked off in the distance, the dizzier I became. Why her? I asked myself. What do I know about her anyway? I'd met her a few times, talked a bit, that was it. I was jumpy, fidgety beyond control.

If it were Shimamoto, there would be no confusion. The two of us, with no words spoken, would be totally accepting of the other. No uncomfortable feelings, no unease. But Shimamoto was no longer around. She was in a new world of her own, and so was I. Comparing Izumi and Shimamoto was pointless. The door that led to Shimamoto's world had slammed shut behind me, and I needed to find my bearings in a new and different world.

I was up until the light shone faintly through the eastern sky. I slept for two hours, took a shower, and went to school. I had to find Izumi and talk to her about what had happened between us. I wanted to hear from her lips that her feelings were unchanged. The last thing she'd said was how happy she was, but in the cold light of dawn it seemed more like an illusion I'd dreamed up. School ended without my getting a chance to talk to her. At recess she was with her girlfriends, and when classes were over she went straight home. Just once, when we were in the hallway changing classes, we managed to exchange glances. She beamed when she caught sight of me, and I smiled back. That was all. But in her smile I caught an affirmation of the previous day's

events. *It's all right,* her smile seemed to tell me. *Yesterday really did happen.* By the time I was riding the train home, my confusion was gone. I wanted her, and my desire won out over any doubts.

What I wanted was clear enough. Izumi naked, having sex with me. But that final destination was still a long way down the road. There was a certain order of events one had to follow. To arrive at sex, you first had to undo the fastener of the girl's dress. And between dress fastener and sex lay a process in which twenty—maybe thirty—subtle decisions and judgments had to be made.

First of all I had to get hold of some condoms. Actually, that step was a bit further down the chain of events, but anyhow I had to get my hands on some. Never know when I might need them. But I couldn't just duck into a drugstore, plunk down some money, and waltz out with a box of condoms. I'd never pass as anything other than what I was—a high school junior—not to mention that I was too much of a coward to make the attempt. I could have tried one of the vending machines in the neighborhood, but if anyone caught me red-handed, I'd be up the proverbial creek. For three or four days, I turned this quandary over endlessly in my mind.

In the end, things worked out more easily than expected. I asked a precocious friend of mine, who was sort of our local expert on these matters. See, the thing is, I asked him, I'd like to get some condoms, so what should I do? No sweat, he deadpanned. I can get you a whole box. My brother bought a ton of them through a catalog. I don't know why he bought so many, but his

closet's full of them. One missing box isn't gonna kill him. Fantastic, I enthused. The next day he brought the condoms to school in a paper bag. I treated him to lunch and asked him not to breathe a word. No problem, he said. Of course he spilled the beans, told a couple of people I was in the market for condoms. These people told some others, and it made the rounds of the school until Izumi heard about it. After school, she asked me to come up to the school roof with her.

"Hajime, I heard you got some condoms from Nishida?" she asked. The word *condoms* didn't exactly roll off her tongue. She made it sound like the name of some infectious disease.

"Uh . . . yeah," I admitted. I struggled to find the right words. "It doesn't really mean anything. I just thought, you know, maybe it'd be better to have some."

"You got them because of me?"

"No, not really," I said. "I was just curious about what they were like. But if it bothers you, I'm sorry I'll give them back, or throw them away."

We were sitting on a small stone bench in a corner of the roof. It looked like it might rain at any minute. We were all alone. It was completely still. I'd never known the roof to be so silent.

Our school was on a hilltop, and we had an unbroken view of the town and the sea. Once, my friends and I filched some records from the Broadcast Club room and flung them off the roof—like Frisbees, they sailed away in a beautiful arc. Off toward the harbor they flew, happily, as if life were breathed into them for a fleeting instant. But finally one of them failed to get airborne

and wobbled clumsily straight down onto the tennis court, where some startled freshman girls were practicing their swings. It was detention for us. That had been more than a year before, and now here I was in the same spot, being grilled by my girlfriend about condoms. I looked up at the sky and saw a bird etching a slow circle in the sky. Being a bird, I imagined, must be wonderful. All birds had to do was fly in the sky. No need to worry about contraception.

"Do you really like me?" Izumi asked me in a small voice.

"Sure I do," I replied. "Of course I like you."

Lips pursed, she looked straight into my face. She looked at me so long it made me uneasy.

"I like you too, you know," she said after a while.

But, I thought.

"But," she said, sure enough, "there's no need to rush."

I nodded.

"Don't be too impatient. I have my own pace. I'm not that clever a person. I need lots of time to prepare for things. Can you wait?"

Once again I nodded silently.

"Promise?" she asked.

"I promise."

"You won't hurt me?"

"I won't hurt you."

She looked down at her shoes for a while. Plain black loafers. Compared to mine, lined up next to them, they were as tiny as toys.

"I'm scared," she said. "These days I feel like a snail without a shell."

"I'm scared too," I said. "I feel like a frog without any webs."

She looked up and smiled.

Wordlessly we walked over to a shaded part of the building and held each other and kissed, a shell-less snail and a webless frog. I held her close against me. Our tongues met lightly. I felt her breasts through her blouse. She didn't resist. She just closed her eyes and sighed. Her breasts were small and fit comfortably in the palm of my hand, as if designed solely for that purpose. She placed her palm above my heart, and the feel of her hand and the beat of my heart became one. She's not Shimamoto, I told myself. She can't give me what Shimamoto gave. But here she is, all mine, trying her best to give me all she can. How could I ever hurt her?

But I didn't understand then. That I could hurt somebody so badly she would never recover. That a person can, just by living, damage another human being beyond repair.

Izumi and I went out for more than a year. We dated once a week, went to movies, studied together at the library, or just took long aimless walks. As far as sex goes, though, we never made it all the way. About twice a month I had her over to my house when my parents were out, and we held each other on my bed. But she never took all her clothes off. You never know when someone might come back, she insisted. Overly cautious, you could call her. She wasn't scared; she just hated to be pushed into some potentially embarrassing situation.

So I always had to hold her with her clothes all on and fumble around as best I could beneath her underwear.

"Slow down," she told me whenever my disappointment showed. "I need more time. Please."

Actually, I wasn't in that much of a rush myself. I was just confused, and disappointed by all sorts of things. Of course, I liked her and was grateful that she was my girlfriend. If she hadn't been with me, my teenage years would have been completely stale and colorless. She was basically an honest, pleasant girl, someone people liked. But our interests were worlds apart. She couldn't understand the books I read or the music I listened to, so we couldn't talk as equals on these topics. In this sense, my relationship with her differed dramatically from that with Shimamoto.

But when I sat beside her and touched her fingers, a natural warmth welled up inside me. I could tell her anything. I loved kissing her eyelids and just above her lips. I also liked to push her hair up and kiss those tiny ears of hers, which invariably sent her into a giggling fit. Even now, whenever I think of her, I envision a quiet Sunday morning. A gentle, clear day, just getting under way. No homework to do, just a Sunday when you could do what you wanted. She always gave me this kick-back-and-relax, Sunday-morning kind of feeling.

She had her faults, for sure. She was pretty hardheaded and could have done with a bit more in the imagination department. She wasn't about to take even one step outside the comfortable world she was raised in. She never got so involved in something that she'd totally forget about eating and sleeping. And she loved and respected her parents. The opinions she did put forth—the standard opinions of a sixteen-, seventeen-

year-old girl—were, not surprisingly, pretty insipid. On the plus side, I never once heard her bad-mouth another person. And she never bored me with conceited talk. She liked me and was good to me. She listened carefully to what I had to say and cheered me up. I talked a lot about myself and my future, what I wanted to become, the kind of person I hoped to be. A young boy's narcissistic fairy tales. But she listened intently. "I know you'll be a wonderful person when you grow up. There is something special about you," Izumi told me. And she was serious. No one had ever told me that before.

And holding her—even with her clothes on—was fantastic. What confused and disappointed me, though, was that I could never discover within her something special that existed just for me. A list of her good qualities far outstripped a list of her faults, and certainly far outshone my own, yet there was something missing, something absolutely vital. If only I'd been able to pin down what that was, I know we would have ended up sleeping together. I wouldn't have held back forever. Even if it had taken a long time, I would have persuaded her that it was absolutely necessary for her to sleep with me. But I lacked the confidence to see this through. I was just a rash seventeen-year-old whose head was crammed full of lust and curiosity. But in that head of mine I still knew that if she didn't want to have sex, I shouldn't try to force the issue. I had to wait patiently for the right time.

I did, though, hold Izumi naked in my arms one time. I can't stand holding you with your clothes on, I

pleaded. If you don't want to have sex, that's okay. But I want to see your body, I want to hold you with nothing on. I *have* to, and I can't bear it any longer.

Izumi thought for a while and then said that if it was what I really wanted, she didn't mind. "But promise me, okay?" She looked at me seriously. "That's all you'll do. Don't do anything I don't want to."

She came over to my house on a beautiful clear Sunday in the beginning of November. A bit chilly, though. My parents had to go to a memorial service for someone on my father's side of the family, and actually I should have attended with them. I told them I had to study for a test, and stayed home alone. They weren't supposed to return until that night. Izumi came over in the afternoon. We held each other in my bed, and I took her clothes off. She closed her eyes and let me undress her. It wasn't easy. I'm all thumbs to begin with, and girls' clothes are a pain. Halfway through, Izumi opened her eyes and took over. She had on light-blue panties and a matching bra. She probably bought these specially for the occasion; up till then her underwear was always the kind mothers bought their high-school-age girls. Finally I undressed myself.

I held her naked body and kissed her neck and breasts. I stroked her smooth skin and breathed in its fragrance. Holding each other, naked like this, was out of this world. I felt if I didn't go inside her I'd go insane. But she pushed me firmly away.

"I'm sorry," she said.

Instead, she took my penis in her mouth and licked it all over. She'd never done that before. Over and over she

drew her tongue over the tip of my penis, until I couldn't think straight, and I came.

Afterward, I held her close, caressing every inch of her body. Her body bathed in the autumn light was beautiful, and I kissed her all over. It was truly a gorgeous afternoon. We held each other tight many times, and I came again and again. Each time I came, she went to the bathroom to rinse her mouth.

"What a weird sensation." She laughed.

I had gone out with Izumi for just over a year, but that was without a doubt the happiest time we ever spent together. Naked, we had nothing to hide. I felt I knew more about her than ever before, and she must have felt the same. What we needed were not words and promises but the steady accumulation of small realities.

Izumi lay still for a long while, her head nestled on my chest as if she were listening to my heartbeat. I stroked her hair. I was seventeen, healthy, on the verge of becoming an adult. Wonderful is the only word for it.

Around four, just as she was getting dressed to leave, the doorbell rang. At first I just ignored it. I had no idea who it was; if I didn't answer it, whoever it was would surely give up and go away. But the doorbell rang on, insistent. Damn, I thought.

"Are your parents back?" Izumi asked, blanching. She was out of bed, hurriedly gathering up her clothes.

"Don't worry. They can't be home this early. And they have a key, so they wouldn't ring the doorbell."

"My shoes!" she said.

"Shoes?"

"My shoes are just inside the entrance."

I threw on my clothes, rushed downstairs, and tossed her shoes inside the entry closet. When I opened the door, my aunt was standing there. My mother's younger sister, who lived about an hour's train ride away and visited every once in a while.

"What in the world were you doing? I've been ringing the bell forever," she said.

"I was listening to music with headphones, so I didn't hear you," I replied. "My parents are out—they went to a memorial service. They won't be back till late tonight. I guess you know that, though."

"They told me. I was running an errand in the neighborhood and I knew you were home studying, so I thought I'd cook dinner for you. I've already shopped."

"I can make dinner myself. I'm not a child, you know," I said.

"But I've bought everything. And you're busy, right? I'll just make dinner while you study."

Oh God, I thought. I wanted to curl up and die. Now how was Izumi going to get home? In my house you had to pass through the living room in order to get to the front door, then pass by the kitchen window to get to the gate. Of course, I could introduce Izumi as a friend who came over to see me, but I was supposed to be studying hard for an exam. If it came out that I had a girl over, there'd be hell to pay. I couldn't very well ask my aunt to keep it a secret from my parents. My aunt wasn't a bad person, but keeping secrets was definitely not one of her strong points.

While my aunt was in the kitchen getting her purchases out of the bags, I took Izumi's shoes upstairs.

She was completely dressed. I explained the situation to her.

She turned pale. "What in the world am I supposed to do? What if I can't get out of here? You know I have to be home every night by dinnertime. If I don't, I'll be in big trouble."

"Don't worry. It'll be okay. We'll figure something out," I said, trying to calm her down. But actually I was just as clueless about the next step.

"And I can't find one of my garter belt clasps. I've looked everywhere."

"Your garter belt clasp?" I asked.

"A little metal thing, about this big."

I scoured the room, from the floor to the top of my bed. But I couldn't find it.

"Sorry. Couldn't you skip wearing your stockings just this once?" I asked.

I went into the kitchen, where my aunt was chopping vegetables. We need some salad oil, she said, and asked me to go out to buy some. I couldn't refuse, so I rode my bike over to a nearby store. It was already growing dark outside. At this rate Izumi might be stuck in my house forever. I had to do something before my parents got home.

"I think our only chance is for you to slip out while my aunt's in the bathroom," I told Izumi.

"You really think it'll work?"

"Let's give it a shot. We can't sit around like this, twiddling our thumbs."

I'd wait downstairs till my aunt went to the bathroom, then clap my hands loudly twice. Izumi would

come downstairs, put on her shoes, and leave. If she'd made her escape okay, she would call me from a nearby pay phone.

My aunt sang happily as she sliced vegetables, made miso soup, and fried up some eggs. But no matter how much time passed, she didn't take a bathroom break. For all I knew, she might be listed in the *Guinness Book*, under World's Biggest Bladder. I was about to give up, when she took off her apron and left the kitchen. As soon as I saw she was in the bathroom, I raced to the living room and clapped twice, hard. Izumi tiptoed downstairs, shoes in hand, quickly slipped them on, and as quietly as she could snuck out the front door. I went to the kitchen to make sure she got out the front gate okay. A second later, my aunt came out of the bathroom. I breathed a sigh of relief.

Five minutes afterward, Izumi called me. Telling my aunt I'd be back in fifteen minutes, I went out. Izumi was standing in front of the pay phone.

"I *hate* this," she said before I could get out a word. "I don't *ever* want to do this again."

I couldn't blame her for being angry and upset. I led her to the park near the station and sat her down on a bench. And gently held her hand. Over her red sweater she had on a beige coat. I fondly recalled what lay beneath.

"But today was beautiful. I mean until my aunt showed up. Don't you think so?" I asked.

"Of course I enjoyed it. Every time I'm with you I have a wonderful time. But every time, afterward, I get confused."

"About what?"

"The future. After I graduate from high school you'll go to college in Tokyo, and I'll stay here. What's going to happen to us?"

I'd already decided to go to a college in Tokyo after I left high school. I was dying to get out of my hometown, to live on my own away from my parents. My GPA wasn't that great, but in the subjects I did like I made pretty good grades without cracking a book, so getting into a private college would be no big deal, seeing as how their exams covered only a couple of subjects. But there was no way Izumi would be joining me in Tokyo. Her parents wanted to keep her close at hand, and she wasn't exactly the rebellious type. So she wanted me to stay put. We have a good college here, she argued. Why do you have to go all the way to Tokyo? If I promised not to go to Tokyo, I'm sure she would have slept with me.

"Come on," I said. "It's not like I'm going off to a foreign country. It's only three hours away. And college vacations are long, so three or four months of the year I'll be here." I'd explained it to her a dozen times.

"But if you leave here you'll forget all about me. And you'll find another girlfriend," she said. I'd heard these lines at least a dozen times too.

I told her that wouldn't happen. I like you a lot, I said, so how can I forget you that easily? But I wasn't so sure. A simple change of scenery can bring about powerful shifts in the flow of time and emotions: exactly what had happened to Shimamoto and me. We might have been very close, but moving down the road a couple of

miles was all it took for us to go our separate ways. I liked her a lot, and she told me to come see her. But in the end I stopped going.

"There's one thing I just can't understand," Izumi said. "You say you like me. And you want to take care of me. But sometimes I can't figure out what's going on inside your head."

Izumi took a handkerchief from her coat pocket and wiped away her tears. With a start, I realized she'd been crying for some time. I had no idea what to say, so I sat waiting for her to continue.

"You prefer to think things over all by yourself, and you don't like people peeking inside your head. Maybe that's because you're an only child. You're used to thinking and acting alone. You figure that as long as *you* understand something, that's enough." She shook her head. "And that makes me afraid. I feel abandoned."

Only child. I hadn't heard those words in a long while. In elementary school the words had hurt me. But Izumi was using them in a different sense. Her "only child" didn't mean a pampered, spoiled kid but spoke to my isolated ego, which kept the world at arm's length. She wasn't blaming me. The situation just made her very sad.

"I can't tell you how happy I was when we held each other. It gave me hope, and I thought, who knows, maybe everything *will* work out," she said as we bade each other goodbye. "But life isn't that easy, is it."

On the way back from the station, I mulled over what she'd said. It made sense. I wasn't used to opening up to others. She was opening up to me, but I couldn't do the

same. I really did like her, yet still something held me back.

I'd walked the road from the train station home a thousand times, but now it was like a foreign town. I couldn't shake the image of Izumi's naked body: her taut nipples, her wisp of pubic hair, her soft thighs. And eventually I couldn't stand it any longer. I bought some cigarettes from a vending machine, went back to the park where we'd talked, and lit a cigarette to calm down.

If only my aunt hadn't barged in on us, things might have worked out better. If nothing had disturbed us, we could have had a pleasanter goodbye. We would have been even happier. But if my aunt hadn't come by, someday something similar was bound to happen. If not today, then tomorrow. The biggest problem was that I couldn't convince her this was inevitable. Because I couldn't convince myself.

As the sun set, the wind grew cold. Winter was fast approaching. And when the new year came, there would be college entrance exams and the beginning of a brand-new life. Uneasy though I was, I yearned for change. My heart and body both craved this unknown land, a blast of fresh air. That was the year Japanese universities were taken over by their students and Tokyo was engulfed in a storm of demonstrations. The world was transforming itself right before my eyes, and I was dying to catch that fever. Even if Izumi wanted me to stay and would have sex with me to ensure that, I knew my days in this sleepy town were numbered. If that meant the end of our relationship, so be it.

If I stayed here, something inside me would be lost forever—something I couldn't afford to lose. It was like a vague dream, a burning, unfulfilled desire. The kind of dream people have only when they're seventeen.

Izumi could never understand my dream. She had her own dreams, a vision of a far different place, a world unlike my own.

But even before my new life began, a crisis came to rip our relationship to shreds.

4

The first girl I ever slept with was an only child. Like Izumi, she wasn't exactly the type to turn any heads; most people would hardly notice her. Still, the first time I laid eyes on her, it was as if I were walking down the road one afternoon and a silent bolt of lightning struck me smack on the head. No ifs, ands, or buts—I was hooked.

With a very few exceptions, your typical beautiful women don't turn me on. Sometimes I'll be walking down the street and a friend will nudge me and say, "Wow! Did you get a load of that girl?" But strangely enough, I can't recall a thing about this supposed knockout. And gorgeous actresses or models don't do a

thing for me. I don't know why, but there it is. For me the boundary dividing the real world and the world of dreams has always been vague, and whenever infatuation raised its almighty head, even during my early teens, a beautiful face wasn't enough to get my engines started.

I was always attracted not by some quantifiable, external beauty, but by something deep down, something absolute. Just as some people have a secret love for rainstorms, earthquakes, or blackouts, I liked that certain undefinable *something* directed my way by members of the opposite sex. For want of a better word, call it magnetism. Like it or not, it's a kind of power that snares people and reels them in.

The closest comparison might be the power of perfume. Perhaps even the master blender himself can't explain how a fragrance that has a special power is created. Science sure can't explain it. Still, the fact remains that a certain combination of fragrances can captivate the opposite sex like the scent of an animal in heat. One kind of fragrance might attract fifty out of a hundred people. And another scent will attract the other fifty. But there also are scents that only one or two people will find wildly exciting. And I have the ability, from far away, to sniff out those special scents. When I do, I want to go up to the girl who radiates this aura and say, *Hey, I picked it up, you know. No one else gets it, but I do.*

From the first time I saw that girl, I knew I wanted to sleep with her. More accurately, I knew I *had* to sleep

with her. And instinctively I knew she felt the same way. When I was with her, my body, as the phrase goes, shook all over. And my penis got so hard I could barely walk. I'd probably felt the stirrings of this kind of magnetism—a prototype of it—with Shimamoto, but I was too young to recognize it as such or even to give it a label. When I met this other girl, I was seventeen, a senior in high school, and she was twenty, a sophomore in college. Of all things, she happened to be Izumi's cousin. She already had a boyfriend, but for the two of us, that was beside the point. She could have been forty-two, with three kids, and with a pair of tails growing out of her butt, and I wouldn't have cared. The magnetism was that strong. I couldn't just let this girl walk on by. If I did, I'd regret it for the rest of my life.

Anyway, that's how the person I lost my virginity with happened to be my girlfriend's cousin. And not just any old cousin, but the one she was closest to. Since they were little, Izumi and she often visited each other. The cousin was attending college in Kyoto and lived in an apartment near the west gate of Gosho, the old Imperial Palace. Izumi and I went to Kyoto once, and we phoned her and had lunch together. That was two weeks after the little farce with my aunt.

While Izumi was away for a few minutes, I asked her cousin for her telephone number, saying I'd like to ask her a few things about the college she was attending. Two days later, I called her and asked if I could see her the following Sunday. After a moment's pause, she said okay. Something in her tone of voice made me confident that she was hoping to sleep with me too. The fol-

lowing Sunday I went alone to Kyoto and met her, and by the afternoon, sure enough, we were in bed.

For the next two months we had such passionate sex I thought our brains were going to melt. No movies, no walks, no small talk about novels, music, life, war, revolution. All we did was bang away. We must have talked a little, but I can't for the life of me recall what about. All I remember are detailed concrete images—the alarm clock near her pillow, the curtains on the windows, the black phone on the table, the photos on the calendar, and her clothes tossed aside on the floor. And the smell of her skin and her voice. I never asked any questions, and she reciprocated. Just once, though, as we lay in bed, I suddenly wondered aloud whether she was, perhaps, an only child.

"That's right," she said, with a quizzical look. "But how did you know?"

"No particular reason. I just sensed it."

She looked at me for a while. "Maybe you're an only child too?"

"You got it," I said.

That's all I remember about our conversations.

Only rarely did we take a break to eat or drink. As soon as we laid eyes on each other, without a word exchanged between us, we'd yank off our clothes, hop into bed, and go at it. We just leaped to the chase. I was greedy for what was right before my eyes, and so was she. Every time we met, we had sex four or five times, literally till my juices dried up and the tip of my cock swelled and ached. Despite the passion, and the violent attraction we each felt, it never occurred to either of us

that we might want to become long-term lovers. We were in the midst of a whirlwind that would, in time, pass. Knowing this, that each time we met might very well be the last, only fanned the flames of desire that much higher.

I wasn't in love with her. And she didn't love me. For me the question of love was irrelevant. What I sought was the sense of being tossed about by some raging, savage force, in the midst of which lay something absolutely crucial. I had no idea what that was. But I wanted to thrust my hand right inside her body and touch it, whatever it was.

I liked Izumi a lot, but not once did I experience that irrational power with her. I knew next to nothing about this other girl, yet her effect on me was profound. We never talked seriously about anything because we didn't see the point. If we'd had enough energy to talk, we'd have used it for another round between the sheets.

In the normal course of events we would have been wrapped up in our relationship, without pausing to come up for air, for a few months, and then one of us would have drifted away. The reason being that what we were doing was a necessary, natural act, one allowing no room for doubt. From the first, there was no possibility that love, guilt, or thoughts of the future would enter in.

So if the relationship hadn't been discovered (not to have been found out seems pretty unrealistic, so totally wrapped up was I in having sex with her), Izumi and I might have continued for some time as we had, boyfriend and girlfriend. Whenever summer vacation

rolled around, we'd have gone on dates. Who knows how long the friendship would have lasted. But after a few years, one of us would have shifted away from the other. We were too different, and time would only have magnified our differences. Looking back on it now, it all seems so obvious. Yet even if we had to go our separate ways, if I hadn't slept with her cousin we might have said goodbye as friends and moved on to the next stage of life in one piece.

As it turned out, we couldn't do this.

In truth, I damaged Izumi beyond repair. It didn't take much to realize how hurt she was. With her grades, she should have breezed into a top university, but she failed the entrance exam and ended up attending a small, third-rate girls' college. After my relationship with her cousin came to light, I saw Izumi only once. We talked for a long time in a coffee shop that had been one of our hangouts. I tried to explain things to her as honestly as I could, selecting my words carefully, straining to convey my feelings. This thing between me and your cousin wasn't planned, I said; it was a physical force that swept us off our feet. It didn't even leave me with the sense of guilt about betraying you that you'd expect me to have. It has nothing to do with *us*.

Of course, Izumi couldn't understand what I meant. And she called me a dirty liar. She was right on target. Without a word, I'd slept with her cousin behind her back. Not just once or twice, but ten, twenty times. I betrayed her from the word go. If my actions had been proper, after all, why the need for deception? I wanted to tell Izumi this: I wanted to sleep with your cousin; I

wanted to screw her till my brains fried—a thousand times, in every position imaginable. It has nothing to do with you, I should have insisted from the start. But in reality I couldn't say these kinds of things. That's why I lied—repeatedly. I'd make up some excuse to break a date with her, then zip on down to Kyoto to ball her cousin. There was no getting around it—I was the one to blame.

Izumi found out about us near the end of January, not long after my eighteenth birthday. In February I sailed through all the college entrance exams and was slated to move to Tokyo at the end of March. Before I left town, I called her, over and over. But she wouldn't come to the phone. I wrote her long letters, waiting in vain for a reply. I can't just leave like this, I thought. I can't just leave her here. But there was nothing I could do. Izumi wanted nothing to do with me.

On the bullet train to Tokyo, I gazed listlessly at the scenery outside and thought about myself—who I was. I looked down at my hands on my lap and at my face reflected in the window. *Who the hell am I?* I wondered. For the first time in my life, a fierce self-hatred welled up in me. How could I have done something like this? But I knew why. Put in the same position, I would do the same thing all over again. Even if I had to lie to Izumi, I would sleep with her cousin again. No matter how much it might hurt her. Recognizing this was painful. But it was the truth.

Izumi wasn't the only one who got hurt. I hurt myself deeply, though at the time I had no idea how deeply. I should have learned many things from that experience,

but when I look back on it, all I gained was one single, undeniable fact. That ultimately I am a person who can do evil. I never consciously tried to hurt anyone, yet good intentions notwithstanding, when necessity demanded, I could become completely self-centered, even cruel. I was the kind of person who could, using some plausible excuse, inflict on a person I cared for a wound that would never heal.

College transported me to a new town, where I tried, one more time, to reinvent myself. Becoming someone new, I could correct the errors of my past. At first I was optimistic: I could pull it off. But in the end, no matter where I went, I could never change. Over and over I made the same mistake, hurt other people, and hurt myself in the bargain.

Just after I turned twenty, this thought hit me: Maybe I've lost the chance to ever be a decent human being. The mistakes I'd committed—maybe they were part of my very makeup, an inescapable part of my being. I'd hit rock bottom, and I knew it.

My four years of college were pretty much a waste.

The first year, I was in a few demonstrations, even battled the police. I was out there with the student strikers and showed up at political rallies. I met some wild characters that way, but my heart was never in politics. Linking arms with strangers at demonstrations made me uneasy, and when we had to hurl rocks at the cops, I asked myself if this was really *me*. Was this what I wanted? I wondered. I couldn't feel the requisite solidarity with the people around me. The scent of violence that hung over the streets, the powerful slogans of the day, soon lost their point. And the time Izumi and I had spent together grew more precious in my mind. But there was no going back. I'd bidden that world farewell.

Most of my classes were a complete bore. Nothing excited me. After a while, I was so busy with my part-time job that I hardly ever showed my face at school; luck alone allowed me to graduate in four years. When I was a junior, I had a girlfriend I lived with for half a year. But it didn't work out. I hadn't the foggiest idea what I wanted out of life.

The next thing I knew, the season of politics was over. Like a drooping flag on a windless day, the gigantic shock waves that had convulsed society for a time were swallowed up by a colorless, mundane workaday world.

Once I was out of college, a friend helped me get a job on the editorial staff of a textbook company. I got a haircut, shined my shoes, and bought a suit. It wasn't much of a company, but jobs for literature majors being few and far between that year, and considering my lousy grades and lack of connections, I had to settle for what I could get.

The job was a total bore. The company itself wasn't such a bad place to work, but editing school textbooks didn't brighten my day one bit. At first I thought: Okay, I'll do my best, try to find something worthwhile in it; and for half a year I worked my butt off. Give it your best shot, and something good's bound to happen, right? But I gave up. No matter how you sliced it, this wasn't the job for me. I felt as if the end of my life was staring me in the face. The months and years would drop away one by one, with me bored out of my skull. I had thirty-three years till retirement, chained day after day to a desk, staring at galley proofs, counting lines, checking spelling. I'd get married to some nice girl, have

some kids, the usual twice-a-year bonus the one bright spot in an otherwise tedious existence. I remembered what Izumi had once told me. "I know you'll be a wonderful person when you grow up. There is something special about you." It pained me every time I remembered. *Something special about me, Izumi? Forget it. But I'm sure you know that now. Ah, what the hell, everyone makes mistakes.*

Mechanically, I did the work assigned me, and I spent my free time reading or listening to music. Work is just a boring obligation, I decided, and when I'm not working, I'm going to use my time the best way I can and enjoy myself. So I never went out drinking with the guys from work. Not that I was a loner who didn't get along with people. I just didn't make the effort to get to know my officemates on a personal level. I was determined that my free time was going to be *mine*.

Four or five years passed in a flash. I had several girlfriends, but nothing lasted. I'd date one for a few months, and then start thinking: This isn't what I want. I couldn't find within these women something that was waiting just for me. I slept with a couple of them, but it was no big deal. I consider this the third stage of my life—the twelve years between my starting college and turning thirty. Years of disappointment and loneliness. And silence. Frozen years, when my feelings were shut up inside me.

I withdrew into myself. I ate alone, took walks alone, went swimming alone, and went to concerts and movies alone. I didn't feel hurt or sad. I often thought of Shimamoto and of Izumi, and wondered where they

were now, what they were doing. For all I knew, they might be married, even have children. I would have given anything to see them, to talk with them, even for an hour. With Shimamoto and Izumi, I could be honest. I racked my brains wondering how to get back together with Izumi, how to see Shimamoto again. How wonderful that would be, I imagined. Not that I actually took steps to see that it came true. The two of them were lost to me forever. The hands of a clock run in only one direction. I started talking to myself, drinking alone at night. I was sure I would never get married.

Two years after I started work, I had a date with a girl who had a bad leg. One of the guys from work set me up on a double date.

"Something's wrong with one of her legs," he told me reluctantly. "But she's cute and has a great personality. I know you'll like her. And you won't really notice the leg. She drags it a bit is all."

"Hey, no problem," I replied. Truth be told, if he hadn't mentioned her bad leg, I would have turned him down. I was sick to death of double dates and blind dates. But when I heard about her leg, I somehow couldn't refuse.

You won't really notice the leg. She drags it a bit is all.

The girl was a friend of the guy's girlfriend. They had been classmates in high school. She was on the small side, with decent looks. Hers was a subdued sort of beauty, reminding me of some small animal deep in the woods who seldom showed its face. The four of us went to a movie one Sunday morning and then had lunch together. She hardly said a word. I tried my best to draw

her out, but it was no go. She just smiled. Afterward, we split from the other couple. She and I went to take a walk in Hibiya Park, where we had some coffee. She dragged her right leg, not the left like Shimamoto. The way she twisted it, too, was different. Whereas Shimamoto rotated her leg slightly as she moved it forward, this girl pointed the tip sideways a bit and dragged it straight ahead. Still, their way of walking was remarkably similar.

She had on a red turtleneck sweater and jeans, and a pair of desert boots. She wore hardly any makeup, and her hair was in a ponytail. Though she said she was a senior in college, she looked younger. I couldn't decide if she was just a quiet person or was nervous meeting someone for the first time. Maybe she just didn't have anything to talk about. Anyway, I wouldn't exactly characterize our initial interaction as conversation. The only fact I was able to drag out of her was that she was at a private college, majoring in pharmacology.

"Pharmacology, huh? Is it interesting?" I asked. We were in the coffee shop in the park, having a cup.

She blushed.

"Hey, it's okay," I said. "Making textbooks isn't exactly the world's most exciting activity. The world's full of boring things. Don't worry about it."

She thought for a while and at long last opened her mouth. "It's not that interesting. But my parents own a drugstore."

"Could you teach me something about pharmacology? I don't know the first thing about it. For the past six years I don't think I've swallowed a single pill."

"You're pretty healthy, then."

"I don't even get hangovers," I said. "When I was a kid, though, I was pretty sickly. Took lots of medicine. I was an only child, so my parents were overprotective."

She nodded, and stared into her coffee cup for a while. It was a long time before she spoke again.

"Pharmacology isn't the most thrilling subject," she began. "There's got to be a million things more fun than memorizing the ingredients of different medicines. It isn't romantic, like astronomy, or dramatic, like being a doctor. But there's something intimate about it, something I can feel close to. Something down-to-earth."

"I see," I said. She could talk, after all. It just took her longer than most to find the right words.

"Do you have any brothers or sisters?" I asked.

"Two older brothers. One's already married."

"So you're studying pharmacology because you'll be taking over the family store?"

She blushed again. And was silent for a good long time. "I don't know. My brothers both have jobs, so maybe I will end up running the place. But nothing's decided. If I don't feel like it, that's okay, my father said. He'll run it as long as he can, then sell it."

I nodded, and waited for her to continue.

"But I'm thinking maybe I should take it over. With this leg, it'd be hard to find another job."

So we talked and passed the afternoon together. With plenty of pauses, and long waits for her to continue. Whenever I asked her a question, she blushed. I actually enjoyed our talk, which for me at the time was a real accomplishment. Sitting there in the coffee shop with her, I felt something close to nostalgia well up in me. She began to feel like someone I'd known all my life.

Not that I was attracted to her. I wasn't. She was nice, all right, and I enjoyed our time together. She was a pretty girl and, like my friend said, quite pleasant. But all these good points aside, when I asked myself if there was something in her that would bowl me over, that would zoom straight to my heart, the answer was no. Nada.

Only Shimamoto ever did that to me. There I was, listening to this girl, all the time thinking of Shimamoto. I knew I shouldn't be, but there it was. Just thinking of Shimamoto made me shiver all over, all these many years later. A slightly fevered excitement, as if I were gently pushing open a door deep within me. Walking with this pretty girl with a bad leg through Hibiya Park, though, that kind of excitement, that all-over shivery feeling, was missing. What I did feel for her was a certain sympathy, and a calmness.

Her home—the pharmacy, that is—was in Kobinata. I took her back on the bus. We sat side by side, and she hardly said a word.

A few days later, my friend from work came over and told me the girl really seemed to like me. Next vacation, he said, why don't the four of us go somewhere together? I made some excuse and bowed out. Not that I minded seeing her again and talking with her. Actually, I really did want to have a chance to talk with her sometime. Under different circumstances we might have ended up good friends. But it started with a double date, and the point of double dates is to find a partner. So if I did ask her out again, I'd be taking on a certain responsibility. And the last thing I wanted was to hurt her. All I could do was refuse.

I never saw her again.

6

During this period, one more woman with a lame leg
figured in a strange incident, whose meaning, even now,
I can't totally understand. I was twenty-eight when it
happened.

I was in Shibuya, walking along in the end-of-year
crowds, when I spied a woman dragging her leg exactly
as Shimamoto used to do. She had on a long red overcoat, and a black patent-leather handbag was tucked
under one arm. On her left wrist she wore a silver
watch, more like a bracelet, really. Everything about her
said money. I was walking along the opposite side of the
street, but when I saw her, I rushed across at the intersection. The streets were so crowded it made me won-

der where all these people could possibly have come from, but it didn't take long for me to catch up with her. With her bad leg, she walked fairly slowly, just like Shimamoto, rotating her left leg as she dragged it along. I couldn't take my eyes off the elegant curve inscribed by her beautiful stockinged legs, the kind of elegance only long years of practice could produce.

I tailed her for a long while, walking a little ways behind her. It wasn't easy keeping pace with her, walking at a speed quite the opposite of the crowd around. I adjusted my pace, stopping sometimes to stare into a store window, or pretending to rummage around in my pockets. She had on black leather gloves and carried a red department store shopping bag. Despite the overcast winter day, she wore a pair of sunglasses. From behind, all I could make out was her beautiful, neatly combed hair curled fashionably outward at shoulder length, and her back tucked away in that soft, warm-looking red coat. Of course, if I really wanted to see if she was Shimamoto, I could have circled around in front and got a good look at her. But what if it was Shimamoto? What should I say to her—and how should I act? She might not even remember me, for one thing. I needed time to pull myself together. I took some deep breaths to clear my head.

Taking care not to overtake her, I followed her for a long time. She never once looked back or stopped. She hardly glanced around her. She looked as if she had a place to get to and was determined to get there as soon as she could. Like Shimamoto, she walked with her back erect and her head held high. Looking at her from

the waist up, no one would ever have suspected that she had something wrong with her leg. She just walked slower than most people. The longer I looked at her, the more I remembered Shimamoto. If this wasn't Shimamoto, it had to be her twin.

The woman cut through the crowds in front of Shibuya Station and started up the slope in the direction of Aoyama. The slope slowed her down more. Still, she covered quite a bit of ground—so much you wondered why she didn't take a cab. Even for someone with good legs, it was a tiring hike. Yet on she walked, dragging her leg, with me following at a discreet distance. Nothing in any of the windows caught her eye. She switched her handbag and her shopping bag from right to left a few times, but other than that she kept on walking, never varying her pace.

Finally she left the crowded main street. She seemed to know the layout of the area well. One step away from the bustling shopping area, you entered a quiet residential street. I followed, taking even greater care not to be spotted in the thinned-out crowd.

I must have followed her for forty minutes. We went down the back street, turned several corners, and once again emerged into the main thoroughfare. But she didn't join the flow of passersby. Instead, as if she'd planned it all along, she headed straight into a coffee shop. A small shop selling cakes and sweets. I killed ten minutes or so sauntering back and forth, then ducked into the shop.

It was stiflingly warm inside, yet she sat there, back to the door, still in her heavy overcoat. Her red overcoat

couldn't be missed. I sat down at the table farthest from the entrance and ordered a cup of coffee. I took up a newspaper that was lying there and, pretending to read, watched what she was doing. A cup of coffee lay on her table, but in all the time I watched her, she didn't touch it. Once, she took a cigarétte out of her handbag and lit it with a gold lighter, but other than that she just sat there, without moving, staring out the window. She could have been just taking a rest, or maybe she was deep in thought about some weighty matter. Sipping my coffee, I read the same article a dozen times.

After a long time, she stood up abruptly and headed right toward me. It happened so suddenly I felt as if my heart had stopped. But she wasn't coming over to me. She passed by my table and went to the phone. Dropping in some coins, she dialed a number.

The phone wasn't far from where I was sitting, but what with all the loud conversations and Christmas carols booming out of the speakers, I couldn't make out what she was saying. She talked for a long time. Her coffee, untouched, grew cold. When she passed by me, I could see her face from the front, but still I couldn't be absolutely sure if she was Shimamoto. She had on thick makeup, and half her face was hidden by those sunglasses. Her eyebrows were distinctly penciled on, and her brightly outlined thin lips were drawn tightly together. Her face did remind me of Shimamoto as a young girl, but if someone had said this wasn't her, I could buy that as well. After all, the last time I'd seen Shimamoto, we were both twelve, and more than fifteen years had passed. All I could say for sure was that this

was an attractive young woman in her twenties who had on an expensive outfit. And she had a bad leg.

Sweat rolled down me. My undershirt was soaked. I took off my coat and ordered another cup of coffee. *Just what do you think you're doing?* I asked myself. I'd lost a pair of gloves and gone out to Shibuya to buy a replacement. But as soon as I caught sight of this woman, I was after her like someone possessed. Most people would have gone right up to her and said, *"Excuse me, aren't you Miss Shimamoto?"* But I didn't. I didn't say a thing and followed her. And had finally come to the point where there was no turning back.

Finished with her call, the woman went straight to her seat. Just as before, she sat with her back to me, gazing at the scene outside. The waitress came up to her and asked if she could take the cold coffee away. I couldn't really hear her, but I think that's what she must have asked. The woman turned around and nodded. And, it appeared, ordered another cup of coffee. When it came, though, again she didn't touch it. I continued to give the paper a once-over. Again and again she brought her wrist up to check the time on her silver watch, as if she was impatiently waiting for someone. This might be my last chance, I told myself. If that other person shows up, I'll never be able to talk with her. But I remained rooted to my chair. It's still okay, I explained to myself. It's still okay, no need to rush.

Nothing happened for fifteen or twenty minutes. She kept gazing at the street scene outside. Suddenly, without warning, she stood up quietly, held her handbag to her side, and picked up the department store shopping

bag in one hand. She'd given up waiting, apparently. Or maybe she wasn't waiting for anyone, after all. I watched as she paid her bill at the register and left the coffee shop, then I quickly stood, paid my own bill, and took off after her. I could catch her red overcoat making its way through the crowds. I followed her, weaving my way through the throng.

She had her hand up, trying to flag down a cab. Finally a cab switched on its turn signal and pulled up to the curb. I have to call out to her, I thought. If she gets in the cab, it's all over. Just as I stepped forward, though, someone grabbed my elbow. The powerful grip took my breath away. It didn't hurt, but the strength of that grip made me choke. I turned around, to find myself face-to-face with a middle-aged man, staring straight at me.

The man was a couple of inches shorter than me but powerfully built. In his mid-forties, I guessed. He had on a dark-gray overcoat and a cashmere muffler, both of which looked awfully expensive. His hair was neatly parted, and he wore a pair of expensive tortoiseshell glasses. Seemingly into sports, he was nicely tanned. Skiing? I wondered. Or maybe tennis? I remembered how Izumi's father, who loved tennis, had the same sort of tan. This man looked very much the executive of a prosperous firm, or maybe more like a high official in the government. His eyes told you that. The eyes of a man who was used to giving orders.

"Would you care for some coffee?" he asked quietly.

I followed the woman with my eyes. Bending down to get into the cab, she glanced through her sunglasses in

our direction. At least it seemed to me she looked our way. The cab door closed, and she disappeared from view, leaving me and this middle-aged stranger behind.

"I won't take much of your time," the man said, his tone of voice placid. He was neither angry nor excited. As though holding open a door for someone, he continued to grasp my arm tightly. "Let's have some coffee and talk."

I could have walked away. *I don't want any coffee, and I have nothing to talk about with you. First of all, I don't know who you are, and I'm in a hurry, so if you'll excuse me,* I could have said. But I clammed up and just stared. Finally I nodded and did as he said, following him back into the coffee shop. Perhaps I was afraid of something in that powerful grip. I could feel a strangely immovable force there. More machinelike than human, his grip on me was perfect, never wavering an ounce in pressure. If I had refused his suggestion, what would he have done to me? I couldn't imagine.

But along with being scared, I was half curious as well. I wanted to find out what he could possibly want to talk with me about. Maybe it would lead to some information about the woman. Now that she'd disappeared, this man might be the only link connecting her and me. Besides, the man wasn't about to beat me up in a coffee shop, was he?

We sat down at a table across from each other. Until the waitress came, we didn't say a word. We sat there, staring at one another. The man ordered two coffees.

"Why, may I ask, were you following her for so long?" he asked me politely.

I couldn't answer.

With expressionless eyes, he looked long and hard at me. "I know you were following her all the way from Shibuya," he said. "Follow someone that far, and they're bound to catch on."

I didn't reply. She realized I was following her, went into this coffee shop, and called this man.

"If you don't want to say anything, that's okay. I know what's going on without your having to tell me." He may have been worked up, but you couldn't tell from the polite, quiet way he spoke.

"There are several options here," the man said. "I'm not joking. Whatever I feel like doing, believe me, I can do."

Then he fell silent and continued to look at me. As if to give me the message that he didn't need any explanation, since he had the situation under control. As before, I said not a word. "But I don't want things to get out of hand. I don't want to cause a scene. Understand me? This time only," he said. He raised his right hand, which was lying on the table, reached into his overcoat pocket, and took out a white envelope. All the while, his left hand remained on the table. The envelope was nothing special, just a plain white business envelope. "Just take this, and don't say a word. I know someone put you up to this, and I'd like to settle the whole matter amicably. Not a word about what's happened. Nothing special happened to you today, and you never met me. Understand? If I ever do find out you've said anything, you can rest assured I will find you and take care of the matter. So I'd like you to forget about following her. Neither one of us wants any trouble. Correct?"

Saying this, the man laid the envelope in front of me

and stood up. Snatching up the check, he paid the cashier and strode out of the coffee shop. I sat there dumbfounded. Finally I picked up the envelope on the table and looked inside. There were ten ten-thousand-yen bills. Crisp, new ten-thousand-yen bills. My mouth was parched. I shoved the envelope in my pocket and left the shop. I looked around, making sure that the man wasn't there, then hailed a cab and went back to Shibuya, where this misadventure all began.

Years later, I still had that envelope with the money. Without ever opening it again, I stuck it in a drawer in my desk. On nights when I couldn't sleep, I could see his face. Like an unlucky premonition of something, his face floated up clearly in my head. Who the hell *was* he anyway? And was that woman Shimamoto?

I came up with several theories. It was a puzzle without a solution. I would think of a hypothesis, only to shoot it down. The most convincing explanation was that this man was the woman's lover, who thought I was a private eye hired by her husband to report on her activities. And the man thought his money would buy my silence. Maybe they thought I'd seen the two of them exiting a hotel where they'd had a rendezvous. It made sense. But even so, my gut feeling said no. Too many questions remained.

He said that if he wanted to, there were several things he could do to me, but what things did he mean? Why was he able to grab me in that unexpected way? If the woman knew I was following her, why didn't she hail a cab? She could have shaken me in a minute. And why did that man, not knowing who I really was, toss me an envelope full of so much cash?

It persisted as a riddle. Sometimes I'd think it must have all been a delusion, from start to finish a fantasy I cooked up in my head. Or maybe a very long, realistic dream that somehow I'd mixed up with reality. But it did happen. Inside the drawer of my desk there was a white envelope with ten ten-thousand-yen bills inside, proof that it wasn't a dream. *It really happened.* Sometimes I put the envelope on top of my desk and stared at it. *It really did happen.*

7

I got married when I was thirty. I met my wife one summer vacation while I was traveling alone. She was five years younger than me. I was walking along a road in the country, when all of a sudden it started raining. I ducked into the nearest place I could find to get out of the rain, and she and a girlfriend were already there. All three of us were soaked to the skin, and we soon fell into conversation while waiting for the rain to let up. If it hadn't rained then, if I had taken an umbrella (which was entirely possible, since I seriously debated doing so before I left the hotel), I would never have met her. And if I hadn't met her, I'd still be plugging away at the textbook company, still leaning against the wall in my apartment at night, alone, drinking, and babbling to

myself. Makes me realize how limited our possibilities ever are.

Yukiko and I were attracted to each other from the start. Her friend was much prettier, but I had eyes for Yukiko only. An irrationally strong attraction pulled us together; I'd nearly forgotten what that kind of magnetism felt like. She lived in Tokyo too, so after our return we went out. The more I saw of her, the more I liked. She was, if anything, on the plain side, at least not the type to attract men wherever she went. But there was something in her face that was meant for me alone. Every time we met, I took a good long look at her. And I loved what I saw.

"Why are you staring at me?" she'd ask.

" 'Cause you're pretty," I'd reply.

"You're the first one who's ever said that."

"I'm the only one who knows," I'd tell her. "And believe me, I know."

At first she didn't believe me. But soon she did.

We'd always go to some quiet place and talk. I could tell her anything, up front, no holds barred. I could feel the weight of all I had lost those past ten years, all those years down the drain, bearing down on me. Before it was too late, I had to get some of it back. Holding Yukiko, I felt a nostalgic, long-gone thrill racing through me. When we said goodbye, I was lost once again. Loneliness pained me, silence had me exasperated. A week before my thirtieth birthday, after we'd been dating for three months, I proposed to her.

Her father was the president of a medium-size construction company, and a real character. He'd hardly been to school, yet was a go-getter—a bit too aggressive

for my tastes. Still, I was impressed by his unique outlook on life. I'd never met anybody like him. He tooled around Tokyo in a chauffeur-driven Mercedes but never acted stuck-up. When I went to see him to ask for his daughter's hand in marriage, he just said, "You're not children anymore, so if you like each other it's up to you." I was not much of a catch, a nothing employee of a nothing company, but that didn't faze him one bit.

Yukiko had an older brother and a younger sister. Her brother was vice president of the construction firm and was going to take over the family business. He wasn't a bad sort but was overshadowed by his father. Of the three children, the younger sister, who was in college, was the most outgoing; she was used to getting her way. Come to think of it, she might have made a better president than her brother.

About half a year after I was married, Yukiko's father asked me to come to see him. He'd heard from my wife that I wasn't too thrilled working at a textbook company, and he wanted to know if I was planning to quit my job.

"I have no problem with quitting," I said. "The problem is what I do after that."

"How about coming to work for me?" he asked. "I'll run you ragged, but the pay can't be beat."

"Well, I know I'm not cut out for editing textbooks, but I don't think working in a construction firm's my thing, either," I said truthfully. "I appreciate the offer, but if I'm not suited for the work, the whole thing will end up being more bother than it's worth."

"You're probably right. Shouldn't force people to do what they don't want to do," he replied. It sounded as if

he'd anticipated this answer. We were having a few drinks. His son hardly touched liquor, so sometimes the two of us would drink together. "By the way, my company has a building in Aoyama. It's under construction, should be finished by next month. The location's good, and it'll be quite a place. It's a little off the beaten path now, but the area's going to grow. I was thinking maybe you could open some kind of store there. It's company property, so I'll have to take the going rate for the down payment and rent, but if you'd like to have a go at it, I can lend you as much as you want."

I thought about it for a while. The possibilities were intriguing.

That's how I came to open an upscale jazz bar in the basement of a brand-new building in Aoyama. I had worked at a bar in college, so I was familiar with the ins and outs of running a drinking establishment—the kind of drinks and food you should serve, the music and atmosphere, the sort of clientele to shoot for, etc. My father-in-law's company handled the interior decorating. He brought over a first-rate interior design firm and had them go to it. Their price was surprisingly reasonable, and when the bar was finished, it was a sight to behold.

The bar was more successful than my wildest dreams, and two years later I opened a second one, also in Aoyama. This was a bigger place, featuring a live jazz trio. It took a lot of time and effort, not to mention a great deal of money, but I ended up with a popular, unique sort of club. I'd done a halfway decent job with the opportunity presented to me, and I finally felt able

to relax for a moment. Not coincidentally, this was when my first child, a girl, was born. At first I used to help out behind the counter, mixing cocktails, but after opening the second place, I was too busy with the business end. I had to make sure everything went smoothly—negotiating prices, hiring, keeping records. What I liked best was seeing ideas that had sprung up in my head materialize into something real. I even threw in my two cents' worth regarding the menu. Surprisingly, I wasn't half bad at this kind of work. I loved the process of starting from scratch, creating something, seeing it through till it was absolutely perfect. It was my bar, my own little world. Think you could find this kind of happiness proofreading school textbooks? No way.

During the day I'd take care of all sorts of chores, then at night I'd make the rounds of my two bars, checking out the cocktails to see that they tasted all right, observing the customers' reactions, making sure my employees were up to snuff. And I listened to the music. Each month, I paid back some of what I owed my father-in-law; still, I was making a pretty decent profit. Yukiko and I bought a four-bedroom condo in Aoyama and a BMW 320. And had a second child. Another girl. Before I knew what hit me, I was the father of two little girls.

When I turned thirty-six, I bought a small cottage in Hakone and a red Jeep Cherokee for Yukiko, to shop and ferry the kids around. With the profit from my bars I could have opened a third place, but I didn't plan to expand. Keeping track of all the details of two places was enough; watching over any more would leave me

wasted. I was sacrificing enough time to work as it was. I discussed this with my wife's father, and he suggested I put any extra money into stocks and real estate. It takes hardly any time or effort, he told me. But I knew absolutely zilch about the stock market or real estate. So he said, "Leave the details to me. If you just do as I say, you'll wind up doing okay. There's a knack to these kinds of things." So I invested as he told me to. And sure enough, in a short time I'd racked up a healthy profit.

"Now you get it, right?" he asked me. "There's a special knack to investing. You could work for a hundred years in a company and never end up doing this well. In order to succeed, you need luck and brains. Those are the basics. But that's not enough. You need capital. Not enough capital, and your hands are tied. But above all, you need the *knack*. Without it, all those other things will get you nowhere."

"Guess you're right," I said. I knew what he was getting at. The "knack" he spoke of was the system he'd created. A tenacious, complex system for generating vast sums of money by creating an immense network of contacts, gathering vital information, and investing accordingly. Slipping through the net of laws and taxes, transfiguring itself in the process, the profit thus generated swelled almost beyond measure.

If I hadn't met my father-in-law, I'd still be editing textbooks. Still living in a crummy little apartment in Nishiogikubo, still driving a used Toyota Corona with an air conditioner on the blink. Now, though, in a short space of time I found myself the owner of two bars in one of the snazziest parts of town, the boss of more

than thirty people, and making more money than I'd ever made in my life—or ever dreamed of making. The business was running so well my accountant was impressed, and the bars had a good reputation. I'm not saying I'm the only one who could have done it. Take away my father-in-law's capital and his "knack," and I'd never have gotten off the ground.

But I wasn't entirely comfortable with this arrangement. I felt I was taking a dishonest shortcut, using unfair means to get to where I was. After all, I was part of the late-sixties–early-seventies generation that spawned the radical student movement. Our generation was the first to yell out a resounding "No!" to the logic of late capitalism, which had devoured any remaining postwar ideals. It was like the outbreak of a fever just as the country stood at a crucial turning point. And here I was, myself swallowed up by the very same capitalist logic, savoring Schubert's *Winterreise* as I lounged in my BMW, waiting for the signal to change at an intersection in ritzy Aoyama. I was living someone else's life, not my own. How much of this person I called myself was really me? And how much was not? These hands clutching the steering wheel—what percentage of them could I really call my own? The scenery outside—how much of it was real? The more I thought about it, the less I seemed to understand.

Not that I was unhappy. I had no complaints. Yukiko was a gentle, considerate woman, and I loved her. When she gained a bit of weight after giving birth, she started dieting and exercising seriously. A little weight didn't bother me, though—I still thought she was beautiful. I loved to be with her, and I loved to sleep with her.

Something about her soothed me. No matter what, I'd be damned if I'd ever return to the kind of life I had in my twenties—days of loneliness and isolation. This was where I belonged. Here was where I was loved and protected. And where I could love and protect others—my wife and my children—back. Being in such a position was an unexpected discovery, a totally new experience.

Every morning, I drove my older daughter to her private nursery school, the two of us singing along to a tape of children's songs on the car stereo. Then, before heading out to the small office I rented nearby, I'd play for a while with my younger daughter. In the summer, we'd spend weekends at our cottage in Hakone, watching the fireworks, boating around the lake, and strolling in the hills.

While my wife was pregnant I'd had a few flings, but nothing serious. I never slept with any one woman more than once or twice. Okay, three times, tops. I never felt I was having an affair with a capital *A*. I just wanted someone to sleep with, the same thing my partners were after. Avoiding entanglements, I chose my bedmates with care. Maybe I was testing something by sleeping with them. Trying to see what I could find in them, and what they could find in me.

Shortly after our first child was born, a postcard came, forwarded to me from my parents' home. It was a notice of a funeral, with a woman's name on it. She'd died when she was thirty-six. But I couldn't place the name. The card was postmarked Nagoya. I didn't know a soul in Nagoya. After a while, though, I realized who the woman was: Izumi's cousin who used to live in Kyoto.

I'd completely forgotten her name. Her parents' home, it turned out, was in Nagoya.

It didn't take much to figure out that Izumi herself had sent the card to me. No one else would have. At first, though, her reason was a mystery. But after reading it over several times, I could sense the unforgiving coldness that had gone into it. Izumi never forgot what I had done, and never forgave me. She must have been living a miserable life—a contented woman would never have sent that card. Or if she did, she would have written a word or two of explanation.

The cousin and everything about her came rushing back to me. Her room, her body, the passionate sex we shared. But the total clarity these memories once had for me was gone, like smoke blown away on the wind. I couldn't imagine why she had died. Thirty-six is such an unnatural age to die. Her last name was the same as before, which meant she never married—or had and divorced.

I found out more about Izumi and her whereabouts from an old high school classmate of mine. He'd read a "Tokyo Bar Guide" feature in the magazine *Brutus*, seen my photo in the spread, and learned that I was running the two bars in Aoyama. One evening he came over to where I was sitting at the counter and said, Hey, man, how's it going? No implication that he'd gone out of his way to see me. He just happened to be drinking with some of his buddies and came over to say hi.

"I've been to this bar many times," he said. "It's near my office. But I had no idea you were the owner. What a small world."

In high school I was sort of the outsider, but he had good grades, played sports, and was the type you'd find in student government. He was a pleasant sort, never pushy. An altogether nice guy. He was on the soccer team and had been big to begin with, but now he'd put on a bit of a spread: a double chin, his three-piece suit straining at the seams. All due to entertaining clients all the time, he explained. Big companies are hell on wheels, he said. You've got overtime, entertaining clients, job transfers; do a bad job and they kick your butt, meet your quota and they'll up and raise it. Not the kind of thing decent people should be into. His office, it turned out, was in Aoyama 1-chome, just down the street.

We talked about things you'd expect classmates to talk about when they hadn't seen each other for eighteen years—our jobs, marriage, how many kids we had, mutual acquaintances we'd run into. That's when he mentioned Izumi.

"There was a girl you were going out with then. You were always together. Something-or-other Ohara."

"Izumi Ohara," I said.

"Right, right," he said. "Izumi Ohara. You know, I ran into her not long ago."

"In Tokyo?" I asked, startled.

"No, not in Tokyo. In Toyohashi."

"Toyohashi?" I said, even more surprised. "You mean Toyohashi in Aichi Prefecture?"

"That's right."

"I don't get it. Why did you meet Izumi in Toyohashi? What in the world would she be doing there?"

It seemed he caught something hard and unyielding in my voice. "I don't know why," he ventured. "I just saw her there. But there's not much to tell. I'm not even completely sure it was her."

He ordered another Wild Turkey on the rocks. I was drinking a vodka gimlet.

"I don't care if there's not much to tell. I want to know."

"Well..." He hesitated. "What I mean is, sometimes I feel like it didn't actually take place. It's a spooky feeling, like I was dreaming but it was real, you know? It's hard to explain."

"But it really did happen, right?" I asked.

"Yes," he said.

"Then tell me."

He gave a nod of resignation and took a sip of his Wild Turkey.

"I went to Toyohashi because my younger sister lives there. I was on a business trip to Nagoya, and it was a Friday, so I decided to go over to her place to spend the night. And that's where I met Izumi. She was in the elevator of my sister's apartment building. I was thinking: Wow, this woman's the spitting image of that Ohara girl. But then I thought: No way, can't be. No way I'd meet her in an elevator in my sister's apartment building, in Toyohashi of all places. Her face looked different from before. I don't understand, myself, why I soon realized it was her. Instinct, I guess."

"But it was Izumi, right?"

He nodded. "She happened to live on the same floor as my sister. We got off together and walked down the

corridor in the same direction. She went into the apartment two doors before my sister's. I was curious and checked out the nameplate on her door. Ohara, it said."

"Did she notice you?"

He shook his head. "We were in the same class, but we never really talked. And besides, I've put on over forty pounds since then. She'd never recognize me."

"But was it really Izumi? I wonder. Ohara's a pretty common name. And there must be other people who look like her."

"Yeah, I was wondering the same thing, so I asked my sister. About what kind of person this Ohara was. My sister showed me the list of tenants' names. You know, those lists they make up when they've got to divide the cost of repainting or something. All the tenants' names were on it. And there it was—Izumi Ohara. With Izumi in katakana, not Chinese characters. There can't be that many with the same combination, right?"

"Which means she's still single."

"My sister didn't know anything about that," he said. "Izumi Ohara is the apartment house's mystery woman, I found out. No one had ever spoken with her. If you say hello to her as you pass in the corridor, she ignores you. She doesn't answer the bell when you ring. Not exactly about to be voted Most Popular on the Block."

"That can't be her." I laughed and shook my head. "Izumi isn't that kind of person. She was always outgoing, always smiling."

"Okay. Maybe you're right. Maybe it was someone else," he said. "Someone with exactly the same name. Let's change the subject."

"But the Izumi Ohara there was living alone?"

"I think so. Nobody's ever seen any men go into her place. Nobody has a clue what she does for a living. It's a complete riddle."

"Well, what do *you* think?"

" 'Bout what?"

"About *her*. About this Izumi Ohara who may or may not be someone with the same name. You saw her face in the elevator. What did you think? Did she look all right?"

He pondered that. "All right, I suppose," he answered.

"How do you mean, all right?"

He shook his whiskey glass; it made a clinking sound. "Naturally, she's aged a bit. She's thirty-six, after all. You and me too. Your metabolism slows down. You put on a few pounds. Can't be a high school student forever."

"Agreed," I said.

"Why don't we change the subject? It must have been somebody else."

I sighed. Resting both arms on the counter, I looked him straight in the face. "Look, I want to know. I *have* to know. Just before we left high school, Izumi and I broke up. It was ugly. I screwed up and hurt her a lot. Since then, I've never had a way of finding out how she is. I had no idea where she was or what she was doing. So just tell me the unvarnished truth. It was Izumi, wasn't it?"

He nodded. "If you put it that way, yes, it was definitely her. I'm sorry to have to tell you, though."

"So, honestly, how was she?"

He was silent for a while. "First of all, I want you to realize something, okay? I was in the same class as her

and thought she was pretty attractive. She was a nice girl. Nice personality, cute. Not a raving beauty but, you know, appealing. Am I right?"

I nodded.

"You really want me to tell the truth?"

"Go ahead," I said.

"You're not going to like this."

"I don't care. Just tell me the truth."

He took another mouthful of whiskey. "I was jealous of you, always together with her. I wanted a girlfriend like that too. Now I can let it all out, I suppose. I never forgot her. Her face was engraved on my memory. That's why, running into her out of the blue in an elevator—even eighteen years later—I knew right away. What I'm getting at is this: I have no reason to want to say anything bad about her. It was a shock for me too, you know. I didn't want to admit it was true. Let me put it this way: She's no longer attractive."

I bit my lip. "What do you mean?"

"Most of the kids who live in that apartment building are afraid of her."

"Afraid?" I repeated. I looked at him, uncomprehending. He must have chosen the wrong words. "What do you mean—afraid of her?"

"Hey, how about we call it a wrap? I didn't really want to get into this anyway."

"Wait a second—what does she do? Does she say things to the kids?"

"She doesn't say anything to anybody. Like I said before."

"So kids are afraid of her face?"

"That's right," he said.

"Does she have a scar or something?"

"No scars."

"Well, then, what are they afraid of?"

He finished his whiskey and placed the glass on the counter. And looked at me for a good long time. He appeared flustered and more than a little confused. But something else was in his expression. I could catch a trace of his face as it was back in high school. He looked up for a while, staring off into the distance as if watching a stream flowing off and away. Finally he spoke. "I can't explain it well; besides, I don't want to. So don't ask me any more, okay? You'd have to see it with your own eyes to understand. Someone who hasn't actually seen it won't understand anyway."

I nodded, saying nothing more, just sipping at my vodka gimlet. His tone was calm, but any further inquiries I knew he would turn down point-blank.

He started to talk about the two years he worked in Brazil. You won't believe it, he said, but I ran across one of my junior high classmates in São Paulo, of all places. Working at Toyota as an engineer.

His words blew right by me. When he left, he clapped me on the shoulder. "Well, the years change people in many ways, right? I have no idea what went on between you and her back then. But whatever it was, it wasn't your fault. To some degree or other, everyone has that kind of experience. Even me. No joke. I went through the same thing. But there's nothing you can do about it. Another person's life is that person's life. You can't take responsibility. It's like we're living in a desert. You just have to get used to it. Did you see that Disney film in elementary school—*The Living Desert*?"

"Yeah," I answered.

"Our world's exactly the same. Rain falls and the flowers bloom. No rain, they wither up. Bugs are eaten by lizards, lizards are eaten by birds. But in the end, every one of them dies. They die and dry up. One generation dies, and the next one takes over. That's how it goes. Lots of different ways to live. And lots of different ways to die. But in the end that doesn't make a bit of difference. *All that remains is a desert.*"

He went home, and I sat alone at the counter, drinking. After the bar was closed for the night, after all the customers had gone, even after the staff had straightened up the place and gone home themselves, I sat there, alone. I didn't want to go home right away. I phoned my wife and told her I had something to take care of at work and would be late. I turned out the lights and sat in the dark, drinking whiskey. Too much trouble to get ice out, so I drank it straight.

Everyone just keeps on disappearing. Some things just vanish, like they were cut away. Others fade slowly into the mist. *And all that remains is a desert.*

When I left the bar, just before dawn, a light rain was falling on the main street in Aoyama. I was exhausted. Soundlessly, the rain soaked the rows of tall buildings, standing there like so many gravestones. I left my car in the bar's parking lot and walked home. On the way, I sat down on a guardrail and watched a large crow that was cawing from the top of a traffic signal. The four a.m. streets looked shabby and filthy. The shadow of decay and disintegration lurked everywhere, and I was part of it. Like a shadow burned into a wall.

8

For ten days or so after the feature article with my name and photo appeared in *Brutus*, old acquaintances dropped by the bar to see me. Junior high and high school classmates. Up till then, I'd always wondered who on earth would possibly read all those magazines piled up at the front of every bookstore. But once I myself was featured in one, I discovered that more people than I'd ever imagined were glued to magazines. In hair salons, banks, coffee shops, trains, every place imaginable, people had magazines open in front of them, as if possessed. Maybe people are afraid they'll have nothing to kill time with, so they just pick up whatever happens to be on hand. Beats me.

Anyway, I can't say it was the most thrilling thing in

the world to see these faces from the past. Not that I didn't like talking with them. It put me in a pleasant, nostalgic mood. And they seemed happy to see me. But frankly I couldn't care less about the subjects they brought up. How our old hometown had changed, what other classmates were up to now. As if I cared. I was too far removed from that place and time. Besides, everything they talked about brought back memories of Izumi. Every mention of my hometown made me picture her alone in that bleak apartment. *She's no longer attractive,* my friend had said. *The kids are afraid of her.* I couldn't get those two lines out of my head. And the fact that Izumi never forgave me.

I'd just wanted to give the bar a little free publicity, but not long after the article came out, I began seriously to regret allowing the magazine to report on it. The last thing I wanted was for Izumi to see the article. How would she feel if she saw me, blithely living a happy life, seemingly unscarred by our past?

A month later, though, the cast of old friends had petered out. Guess that's one point in favor of magazines: You have your moment of fame, then *poof!* you're forgotten. I breathed a sigh of relief. At least Izumi didn't show. She wasn't a *Brutus* subscriber, after all.

But a couple of weeks after that, after all the hubbub of the article had been forgotten, the last friend showed up.

Shimamoto.

It was the evening of the first Monday in November. And there, at the counter of the Robin's Nest (the name of the jazz club, the title of an old tune I liked), she sat,

quietly sipping a daiquiri. I was at the same counter, three seats down, completely oblivious to the fact that it was her. I'd observed that an extremely beautiful woman had come into the bar, but that was all. A new customer; I made a mental note. If I had seen her before, I would have remembered; that's how outstanding she was. Before long, I figured, whoever she was waiting for would show up. Not that women never drank alone in the bar. Some single women seem to expect that men will put the moves on them; others seem more to be hoping for it. I could always tell which was which. But a woman this beautiful would not be out drinking alone. A woman like this wasn't the type to be thrilled by men making advances. She'd just find it a pain.

That's why I wasn't paying much attention to her. Sure, I checked her out when she first came in and gave her a glance every once in a while. She wore just a touch of makeup, and a pricey-looking outfit—a blue silk dress, with a light-beige cashmere cardigan. A cardigan as delicate-looking as an onion skin. And on the counter she'd placed a handbag that matched her dress perfectly. I couldn't guess her age. Just the right age, was all I could say.

Her beauty took your breath away, but I didn't figure her for a movie star or a model. Those types did frequent my bar, but you could always tell they were conscious of being on public display, the unbearable *me*ness of being clinging to the air around them. But this woman was different. She was completely relaxed, totally at ease with her surroundings. She rested her chin in her hands on the counter, absorbed in the piano

trio's music, all the while sipping her cocktail as if lingering over a particularly well-turned phrase. Every few minutes, she glanced in my direction. I could sense it, physically. Though I was positive she wasn't really looking at me.

I had on my usual outfit—Luciano Soprani suit, Armani shirt and tie. Rossetti shoes. Believe it or not, I wasn't the type to worry about clothes. My basic rule was to spend the bare minimum on them. Outside of work, jeans and a sweater did me fine. But I did have my own little philosophy of doing business: I wore the kind of clothes I wanted my customers to wear. Doing so, I found, put the staff just that much more on their toes and created the sort of elevated mood I was aiming for. So every time I came to the bar, I made absolutely sure to wear a nice suit and tie.

There I sat, then, checking to make sure the cocktails were mixed correctly, keeping an eye on the customers, and listening to the piano trio. At first the bar was fairly packed, but after nine it started raining, and the number of customers tailed off. By ten only a handful of the tables were occupied. But the woman at the counter was still there, alone with her daiquiris. I started to wonder about her more. Maybe she wasn't waiting for someone, after all. Not once did she glance at her watch or at the entrance.

Finally she picked up her bag and stepped down from her stool. It was nearly eleven. If you wanted to take the subway home, now was the time to get a move on. Slowly, ever so casually, though, she made her way over to me and sat on the adjacent stool. I caught a faint

whiff of perfume. Settling down on the stool, she took a
pack of Salems from her bag and put one in her mouth.
I caught all this out of the corner of my eye.

"What a lovely bar," she said to me.

I looked up from the book I'd been reading and
looked at her uncomprehendingly. Just then something
hit me—hard. As if the air suddenly lay heavy on my
chest.

"Thanks," I said. She must have known I was the
owner. "I'm happy you like it."

"I do, very much." She looked deep into my eyes and
smiled. A wonderful smile. Her lips spread wide, and
small, fetching lines formed at the corners of her eyes.
Her smile stirred deep memories—but of what?

"I like your music too." She pointed to the piano trio.
"Do you have a light?" she asked.

I had neither matches nor a lighter. I called to the bartender and had him bring over a book of the bar's
matches. And I lit her cigarette for her.

"Thanks," she said.

I looked at her straight on. And I finally understood.

"Shimamoto," I rasped.

"It took you long enough," she said after a while, a
funny look in her eyes. "I thought maybe you'd never
notice."

I sat there speechless, gawking at her as though I
were in the presence of some high-tech precision ma-
chinery I'd only heard rumors of. It was indeed Shimamoto in front of me. But I couldn't yet grasp the
reality of it. I'd been thinking of her for so very, very
long. And I was sure I'd never see her again.

"I love your suit," she said. "It's quite becoming."

I nodded wordlessly. The words just wouldn't flow.

"Know something, Hajime? You're much handsomer than you used to be. And a lot better built."

"I swim a lot," I finally managed to say. "I started in junior high, and I've been swimming ever since."

"Swimming looks like so much fun. I've always thought so."

"It is. But if you practice, anyone can learn, you know," I said. As soon as the words left my mouth, I remembered her leg. *What the hell are you talking about?* I asked myself. I was flustered, fumbling for the right thing to say. But the words eluded me. I rummaged around in my suit pockets for a pack of cigarettes. And then remembered. I'd quit smoking five years before.

Shimamoto watched me silently. She raised her hand and ordered another daiquiri, giving the biggest smile. A truly beautiful smile. The kind of smile that made you want to wrap up the whole picture for safekeeping.

"You still like blue, I see," I said.

"Yes. I always have. You have a good memory."

"I remember almost everything about you: the way you sharpen your pencils, the number of lumps of sugar you put in your tea."

"And how many would that be?"

"Two."

She narrowed her eyes a bit and looked at me.

"Tell me something, Hajime," she began. "That time about eight years ago—why did you follow me?"

I sighed. "I couldn't tell if it was you or not. The way you walked was exactly the same. But there was also

something about it that didn't seem like you. I tailed you because I wasn't sure. Tailed isn't the right word. I was just looking for the right moment to talk with you."

"Then why didn't you? Why didn't you just come right out and see if it was me? That would have been faster."

"I don't know, myself," I answered. "Something held me back. My voice just wouldn't work."

She bit her lip a little. "I didn't notice then that it was you. All I could think was that someone was following me, and I was afraid. Really. I was terrified. But once I got in the cab and had a chance to calm down, it came to me. Could that have been Hajime?"

"Shimamoto-san, I was given something then. I don't know what relationship you have with that person, but he gave me—"

She put her index finger to her lips. And lightly shook her head. *Let's not talk about that, all right?* she seemed to be saying. *Please, don't ever bring it up again.*

"You're married?" she asked, changing the subject.

"With two kids," I replied. "Both girls. They're still little."

"That's great. I think daughters suit you. I can't explain why, but they do."

"I wonder."

"Yes—*somehow.*" She smiled. "But at least you didn't have an only child."

"Not that I planned it. It just turned out that way."

"What does it feel like? I wonder. To have two daughters."

"Frankly, a little strange. More than half the children in my older girl's nursery school are only children. The

world's changed since we were kids. In the city, only children have become more the rule, not the exception."

"You and I were born too soon."

"Maybe so," I said. "Perhaps the world's drawing closer to us. Sometimes when I see the two of them playing together at home, I'm amazed. A whole other way of raising children. When I was a child, I always played alone. I thought that was how all kids played."

The piano trio wound up its version of "Corcovado," and the customers gave them a hand. As always, as the night wore on, the trio's playing grew warmer, more intimate. Between numbers the pianist drank red wine, while the bassist smoked.

Shimamoto sipped her cocktail. "You know, Hajime, I wasn't at all sure at first whether I should come here. I agonized over it for nearly a month. I found out about your bar in some magazine I was leafing through. I thought it must be a mistake. You of all people running a bar! But there was your name, and your photograph. Good old Hajime from the old neighborhood. I was happy I could see you again, even if it was in a photograph. But I wasn't sure if meeting you in person was a good idea. Maybe it was better for both of us if we didn't. Maybe it was enough knowing you were happy and doing well."

I listened to her in silence.

"But since I knew where you were, it seemed like a waste not to at least come see you once, so here I am. I sat down over there and watched you. If he doesn't notice me, I thought, maybe I'll just leave without saying anything. But I couldn't stand it. It brought back so many memories, and I had to say hello."

"Why?" I asked. "I mean, why did you think it was better not to meet me?"

Tracing the rim of her cocktail glass with her finger, she was lost in thought. "I thought if I met you you'd want to know all about me. Whether I was married, where I lived, what I'd been up to, those kinds of things. Am I right?"

"Well, I'm sure those would come up."

"Of course."

"But you'd rather not talk about those?"

She smiled perplexedly and nodded. She had a million different variations on a smile. "That's right. I don't want to talk about those things. Please don't ask me why. I just don't want to talk about myself. I know it's unnatural, that it's like I'm putting on airs, trying to be a mysterious lady of the night or something. That's why I thought maybe I shouldn't see you. I didn't want you to think I was some strange, conceited woman. That's one reason I didn't want to come here."

"And the other?"

"I didn't want to be disappointed."

I looked at the glass in her hand. I looked at her straight shoulder-length hair and at her nicely formed thin lips. And at her endlessly deep dark eyes. A small line just above her eyelids caused her to look thoughtful. That line made me imagine a far-off horizon.

"I used to like you very much, so I didn't want to meet you just to be disappointed."

"Have I disappointed you?"

She shook her head slightly. "I was watching you from over there. At first you looked like somebody else.

You were so much bigger with a suit on. But when I looked closer, I could make out the Hajime I used to know. Do you realize that your movements have hardly changed since you were twelve?"

"I didn't know that." I tried to smile but couldn't.

"The way you move your hands, your eyes, the way you're always tapping something with your fingertips, the way you knit your eyebrows like you're displeased about something—these haven't changed a bit. Underneath the Armani suit it's the same old Hajime."

"Not Armani," I corrected her. "The shirt and tie are, but the suit's not."

She smiled at me.

"Shimamoto-san," I began. "You know, I wanted to see you for the longest time. To talk with you. I had so many things I wanted to tell you."

"I wanted to see you too," she said. "But you never came. You realize that, don't you? After you went off to junior high in another town, I waited for you. Why didn't you come? I was really sad. I thought you'd made new friends in your new place and had forgotten all about me."

Shimamoto crushed out her cigarette in the ashtray. She had clear lacquer on her nails. They were like some exquisitely made handicraft, shiny but understated.

"I was afraid, that's why," I said.

"Afraid?" she asked. "Afraid of what? Of me?"

"No. Not of you. I was afraid of rejection. I was still a child. I couldn't imagine that you were actually waiting for me. I was terrified you would reject me. That I would come to your house to see you and you couldn't

be bothered. So I stopped coming. If I was going to get hurt, I thought it would be better to go on living with the happy memories of when we were together."

She tilted her head slightly and rolled a cashew nut in her hand. "Things don't work out easily, do they?"

"No, they don't."

"But we were meant to be friends for a much longer time. I went all the way through junior high, high school, even college, without making a friend. I was always alone. I imagined how wonderful it would be to have you by my side. If you couldn't actually be there, at least we could write to each other. Things would have been a lot different. I could have stood up to life better." She was silent for a time. "I don't know why, exactly, but after I entered junior high, school life went downhill. And that made me close in on myself even more. A vicious circle, you could call it."

I nodded.

"Up to elementary school I did fine, but after that it was awful. It was like I was stuck inside a well."

I knew the feeling. That was just how I felt about the eight years of my life between college and marrying Yukiko. One thing goes wrong, then the whole house of cards collapses. And there's no way you can extricate yourself. Until someone comes along to drag you out.

"I had this bad leg and couldn't do what other people do. I just read books and kept to myself. And I stand out. My looks, I mean. So most people ended up thinking I'm a twisted, arrogant woman. And maybe that's who I became."

"Well, you *are* a knockout," I said. She put another cigarette between her lips. I struck a match and lit it.

"You really think I'm pretty?" she asked.

"Yes. But you must hear that all the time."

Shimamoto smiled. "Not really. Actually, I'm not that wild about my face. So I'm very happy you said that. Unfortunately, other women don't like me much. Many's the time I thought this: I don't want people to say I'm pretty. I just want to be an ordinary girl and make friends like everyone else."

She reached out a hand and lightly brushed mine on the counter. "But I'm happy that you're enjoying life."

I was silent.

"You are happy, aren't you?" she asked.

"I don't know. At least I'm not unhappy, and I'm not lonely." A moment later, I added, "But sometimes the thought strikes me that the happiest time of my life was when we were together in your living room, listening to music."

"You know, I still have those records. Nat King Cole, Bing Crosby, Rossini, the *Peer Gynt* Suite, and all the others. Every single one. A keepsake from my father when he died. I take good care of them, so even now they don't have a single scratch. And you remember how carefully I took care of records."

"So your father died."

"Five years ago, cancer of the colon. A horrible way to go. And he'd always been so healthy."

I'd met her father a few times. He always struck me as being tough as the oak tree that grew in their garden.

"Is your mother well?" I asked.

"Hmm. I guess so."

Her tone of voice bothered me. "You don't get along with her, then?"

Shimamoto finished her daiquiri, put the glass on the counter, and called the bartender over. "Do you have any special house cocktail you'd recommend?"

"We have several original cocktails," I said. "The most popular one's Robin's Nest, after the bar. A little thing I whipped up myself. You use rum and vodka as a base. It's easy going down, but it packs a wallop."

"Sounds good for wooing women."

"Well, I thought that was the whole point of cocktails."

She smiled. "Okay, I'll try one."

When the cocktail was placed in front of her, she gazed at the color, then took a tentative sip. She closed her eyes and let the flavor take over. "It's a very subtle taste, isn't it," she said. "Not exactly sweet or tart. A light, simple flavor, but with some body. I had no idea you were so talented."

"I can't build a simple shelf. I have no idea how to change an oil filter on a car. I can't even paste on a postage stamp straight. And I'm always dialing the wrong number. But I have come up with a few original cocktails that people seem to like."

She rested her glass on a coaster and looked at it for a while. When she tipped the glass, the reflection of the overhead lights shivered slightly.

"I haven't seen my mother for a long time. There was a blowup about ten years ago, and I've barely seen her since. Of course, we did see each other at my father's funeral."

The piano trio finished an original blues number and began the intro to "Star-Crossed Lovers." When I was in

the bar, the pianist would often strike up that ballad, knowing it was a favorite of mine. It wasn't one of Ellington's best-known tunes, and I had no particular memories associated with it; just happened to hear it once, and it struck some chord within me. From college to those bleak textbook-company years, come evening I'd listen to the *Such Sweet Thunder* album, the "Star-Crossed Lovers" track over and over. Johnny Hodges had this sensitive and elegant solo on it. Whenever I heard that languid, beautiful melody, those days came back to me. It wasn't what I'd characterize as a happy part of my life, living as I was, a balled-up mass of unfulfilled desires. I was much younger, much hungrier, much more alone. But I was myself, pared down to the essentials. I could feel each single note of music, each line I read, seep down deep inside me. My nerves were sharp as a blade, my eyes shining with a piercing light. And every time I heard that music, I recalled my eyes then, glaring back at me from a mirror.

"You know," I said, "once, when I was in the last year of junior high, I did go to see you. I felt so lonely I couldn't stand it any longer. I tried calling you, but there was no answer. I rode the train over to your place, but someone else's name was on the mailbox."

"My father was transferred, and we moved two years after you did. To Fujisawa, near Enoshima. And that's where we remained until I went to college. I sent you a postcard with our new address on it. You never got it?"

I shook my head. "If I had, I would have written back. Strange, though. Must have been some slipup somewhere along the line."

"Or maybe we're just unlucky," she said. "Lots of slipups, and we end up missing each other. But anyway, I want to hear about *you*. What kind of life you've had."

"It'll bore you to tears," I said.

"I don't care. I still want to hear it."

So I gave her a general recap of my life. How I'd had a girlfriend in high school but ended up hurting her badly. I spared her the gory details. I explained how something had happened and I had hurt this girl. And in the process ended up hurting myself. How I went to college in Tokyo and worked at a textbook company. How my twenties were filled with friendless, lonely days. I went out with women but was never happy. How from the time I graduated from high school until I met Yukiko and got married, I never really liked anyone. How I thought of her often then, thought how great it would be if we could see each other, even for an hour, and talk. Shimamoto smiled.

"You thought about me?"

"All the time."

"I thought about you too," she said. "Whenever I felt bad. You were the only friend I've ever had, Hajime." Her chin resting in one hand propped up on the bar, she closed her eyes as if all the strength had been drained from her body. She didn't wear any rings. The down on her arms trembled. At last she slowly opened her eyes and looked at her watch. I looked at it too. It was nearly midnight.

She picked up her handbag and slipped off the stool. "Good night. I'm happy I could see you."

I saw her to the door. "Shall I call you a cab? It's rain-

ing, so it might be hard to grab one. If you're thinking of going home by cab, that is."

Shimamoto shook her head. "It's all right. Don't go to any trouble. I can take care of myself."

"You really weren't disappointed?" I asked.

"In you?"

"Yes."

"No, I wasn't." She smiled. "Rest easy. But that suit—it is an Armani, isn't it?"

She wasn't dragging her leg the way she used to. She didn't move very quickly, and if you looked closely, there was something vaguely artificial about the way she walked. Though overall it looked perfectly natural.

"I had an operation four years ago," she said almost apologetically. "I wouldn't say it's a hundred percent, but it's certainly not as bad as it used to be. It was a big operation, with a lot of scraping of bones, patching them together. But things went well."

"That's great. Your leg looks fine now," I said.

"It is," she said. "Probably it was a good decision. Though maybe I waited too long."

I got her coat from the cloakroom and helped her into it. Standing next to me, she wasn't very tall. It seemed strange. When we were twelve, we were about the same height.

"Shimamoto-san. Will I see you again?"

"Probably," she replied. A smile played around her mouth. A smile like a small wisp of smoke drifting quietly skyward on a windless day. "Probably."

She opened the door and went out. Five minutes later, I went up the stairs to the street. I was worried she'd

had trouble flagging down a cab. It was still raining. And Shimamoto was nowhere to be seen. The street was deserted. The headlights of passing cars blurred the wet pavement.

Maybe I had had an illusion, I thought. I stood there a long time, gazing at the rainswept streets. Once again I was a twelve-year-old boy staring for hours at the rain. Look at the rain long enough, with no thoughts in your head, and you gradually feel your body falling loose, shaking free of the world of reality. Rain has the power to hypnotize.

But this had been no illusion. When I went back into the bar, a glass and an ashtray remained where she had been. A couple of lightly crushed cigarette butts were lined up in the ashtray, a faint trace of lipstick on each. I sat down and closed my eyes. Echoes of music faded away, leaving me alone. In that gentle darkness, the rain continued to fall without a sound.

9

I didn't see Shimamoto for a long time after that. Every evening, I sat at the counter of the Robin's Nest, passing the time. I read books, glancing every once in a while at the front door. But she didn't show up. I was afraid I'd said something wrong, something I shouldn't have, that upset her. One by one, I reviewed every word we'd spoken that night. But I couldn't come up with anything. Maybe Shimamoto *was* disappointed. A distinct possibility. She was so beautiful, and her leg was all fixed. What in the world would a woman like that find in me?

The year drew to a close, Christmas came and went, as did New Year's. My thirty-seventh birthday rolled around. And January was suddenly over. I gave up wait-

ing for her and only rarely made an appearance at the Robin's Nest. Being there reminded me of her, causing me to search the faces of the customers in vain. I sat at the bar of my other place, flipping through the pages of books, lost in aimless musings. For the life of me, I couldn't concentrate.

She'd told me I was the only friend she'd ever had. That made me happy and gave birth to the hope that we might be friends again. I wanted to talk with her about so many things, hear her opinion. If she didn't want to say a thing about herself, fine by me. Just to be able to see her, to talk with her, that was enough.

But she didn't come. Maybe she was too busy to find time to see me, I mused. But three months was way too long a gap. Even supposing she couldn't come to see me, at least she could pick up the phone and call. She'd forgotten all about me, I decided. I wasn't so important to her, after all. That hurt, as if a small hole had opened up in my heart. She never should have said that she might come again. Promises—even vague ones like that—linger in your mind.

But in early February, again on a rainy night, she appeared. It was a quiet, freezing rain. Something had come up, and I was at the Robin's Nest earlier than usual. The customers' umbrellas carried with them the scent of the chilly rain. A tenor saxophonist had joined the usual piano trio to play a few numbers. He was pretty well known, and a stir ran through the crowd. As always, I sat on my corner stool at the bar, reading. Shimamoto sat down quietly beside me.

"Good evening," she said.

I put down my book and looked at her. I couldn't quite believe my eyes.

"I was sure you weren't ever coming here again."

"Forgive me," she said. "Are you angry?"

"I'm not angry. I don't get angry at things like that. This is a bar, after all. People come when they want to, leave when they feel like it. My job's just to wait for them."

"Well, anyway, I'm sorry. I can't explain it, but I just couldn't come."

"Busy?"

"No, not busy," she replied quietly. "I just couldn't come here."

Her hair was wet from the rain. A couple of strands were pasted to her forehead. I had the waiter bring a towel.

"Thanks," she said, and dried her hair. She took out a cigarette and lit it with her lighter. Her fingers, wet and chilled from the rain, trembled slightly.

"It was only sprinkling, and I thought I'd catch a cab, so I just wore a raincoat. But I started walking, and ended up walking a long way."

"How about something hot to drink?" I asked.

She looked deep into my eyes and smiled. "Thanks. I'm okay."

In an instant that smile made me forget the three months.

"What are you reading?" She pointed to my book.

I showed it to her. A history of the Sino-Vietnam border conflict after the Vietnam War. She flipped through it and handed it back.

"You don't read novels anymore?"

"I do. But not as many as I used to. I don't know anything about new novels. I only like old ones, mostly from the nineteenth century. Ones I've read before."

"What's wrong with new novels?"

"I guess I'm afraid of being disappointed. Reading trashy novels makes me feel I'm wasting time. It wasn't always that way. I used to have lots of time, so even though I knew they were junk, I still felt something good would come from reading them. Now it's different. Must be getting old."

"Yes, well, it is true you're getting older," she said, and gave an impish smile.

"What about you? Do you still read a lot?" I asked.

"Yes, all the time. New books, old books. Novels and everything else. Trashy books, good books. I'm probably the opposite of you—I don't mind reading to kill time."

She asked the bartender to make her a Robin's Nest. I ordered the same. She took a sip of her drink, nodded slightly, and returned the glass to the countertop.

"Hajime, why are the cocktails here always so much better than at any other bar?"

" 'Cause we do our best to make them that way," I replied. "No effort, no result."

"What kind of effort do you mean?"

"Take him, for instance," I said, indicating the handsome young bartender, who, all serious concentration, was busy breaking up a chunk of ice with an ice pick. "I pay him a lot of money. Which is a secret as far as the other employees are concerned. The reason for the high salary is his talent at mixing great drinks. Most people

don't realize it, but good cocktails demand talent. Anyone can make passable drinks with a little effort. Spend a few months training, and anyone can make your standard-issue mixed drink—the kind most bars serve. But if you want to take it to the next level, you've got to have a special flair. Same with playing the piano, painting, running the hundred-meter dash. Now take me: I think I can mix up a pretty mean cocktail. I've studied and practiced. But there's no way I can compete with him. I put in exactly the same liquor, shake the shaker for exactly the same amount of time, and guess what—it doesn't taste as good. I have no idea why. All I can call it is talent. It's like art. There's a line only certain people can cross. So once you find someone with talent, you'd best take good care of them and never let them go. Not to mention pay them well." The bartender was gay, so sometimes other gays gathered at the counter. They were a quiet bunch, and it didn't bother me. I really liked the young bartender, and he trusted me and worked hard.

"Maybe you have more talent at running a business than would appear," Shimamoto said.

" 'Fraid I don't," I said. "I don't really consider myself a businessman. I just happen to own two small bars. And I don't plan to open any more, or to earn much more than I do right now. Can't call what I do talent. But you know, sometimes I imagine things, pretending I'm a customer. If I were a customer, what kind of bar I'd go to, what kind of things I'd like to eat and drink. If I were a bachelor in my twenties, what kind of place would I take a girl to? How much could I spend? Where would I live and how late could I stay out? All sorts of scenarios.

The more scenarios I come up with, the more focused my image of the bar becomes."

Shimamoto had on a light-blue turtleneck sweater and a navy-blue skirt. Small earrings glittered at her ears. Her tight-fitting sweater revealed the shape of her breasts. I suddenly found it hard to breathe.

"Go on," she said. Once again that happy smile came to her lips.

"About what?"

"Your business philosophy," she said. "I love to hear you talk that way."

I blushed a little, something I hadn't done in a long while. "I wouldn't call it a business philosophy. You know, this whole process is one I've been doing since I was little: Thinking about all kinds of things, letting my imagination take over. Constructing an imaginary place in my head and little by little adding details to it. Changing this and that to suit me. Like I told you, after college I worked for a long time in a textbook company. The work was a complete bore. Absolutely no room for using your imagination. I was sick of it. I couldn't stand to go to work anymore. I felt like I was choking, like every day I was shrinking and someday I would disappear completely."

I took a sip of my drink and glanced around the bar. A nice crowd, considering the rain. The tenor sax player was putting his instrument away in a case. I called the waiter over and had him take a bottle of whiskey to the saxophonist, ask him if he'd like something to eat.

"But here it's different," I continued. "You have to use your imagination to survive. And you can put your ideas into practice immediately. No meetings, no execu-

tives here. No precedents to worry about or Ministry of Education position papers to contend with. Believe me, it's great. Have you ever worked in a company?"

She smiled and shook her head. "No."

"Consider yourself lucky. Me and companies just don't get along. I don't think you'd find it any different. Eight years working there convinced me. Eight years down the tubes. My twenties—the best years of all. Sometimes I wonder how I put it up with it for so long. I guess that's what I had to go through, though, to wind up where I am today. Now I love my job. You know, sometimes my bars feel like imaginary places I created in my mind. Castles in the air. I plant some flowers here, construct a fountain there, crafting everything with great care. People stop by, have drinks, listen to music, talk, and go home. People are willing to spend a lot of money to come all this way to have some drinks—and do you know why? Because everyone's seeking the same thing: an imaginary place, their own castle in the air, and their very own special corner of it."

Shimamoto extracted a Salem from her small purse. Before she could take out her lighter, I struck a match and lit her cigarette. I liked to light her cigarettes and watch her eyes narrow as she stared at the flickering flame.

"I haven't worked a single day in my life," she said.

"Not even once?"

"Not even once. Not even a part-time job. Labor is totally alien to me. That's why I envy you. I'm always alone, reading books. And any thoughts that happen to occur to me have to do with spending money, not making it." She stretched both arms out in front of me. On

her right arm she wore two thin gold bracelets, on her left arm an expensive-looking gold watch. She kept her arms in front of me for a long while, as if they were displaying goods for sale. I took her right hand in mine and gazed for a time at the gold bracelets. I recalled her holding my hand when I was twelve. I could remember exactly how it felt. And how it had thrilled me.

"I don't know ... maybe thinking about ways to spend money is best, after all," I said. I let go of her hand and felt that I was about to drift away somewhere. "When you're always scheming about ways to make money, it's like a part of you is lost."

"But you don't know how empty it feels not to be able to create anything."

"I'm sure you've created more things than you realize."

"What sort of things?"

"Things you can't see," I replied. I examined my hands, resting on my knees.

She held her glass and looked at me for a long while. "You mean like feelings?"

"Right," I said. "Everything disappears someday. Like this bar—it won't go on forever. People's tastes change, and a minor fluctuation in the economy is all it'd take for it to go under. I've seen it happen; it doesn't take much. Things that have form will all disappear. But certain feelings stay with us forever."

"But you know, Hajime, some feelings cause us pain *because* they remain. Don't you think so?"

The tenor saxophonist came over to thank me for the whiskey. I complimented him on his performance.

"Jazz musicians these days are so polite," I explained to Shimamoto. "When I was in college, that wasn't the case. They all took drugs, and at least half of them were deadbeats. But sometimes you could hear these performances that would blow you away. I was always listening to jazz at the jazz clubs in Shinjuku. Always looking to be blown away."

"You like those kinds of people, don't you."

"Must be," I said. "People want to be bowled over by something special. Nine times out of ten you might strike out, but that tenth time, that peak experience, is what people want. That's what can move the world. That's art."

I looked again at my hands, resting on my knees. Then I looked up at her. She was waiting for me to continue.

"Anyway, things are different now. I'm the manager of a bar, and my job's to invest capital and show a profit. I'm not an artist or someone about to create anything. I'm not a patron of the arts. Like it or not, this isn't the place to look for art. And for the manager, it's a lot easier to have a neatly turned out, polite group than a herd of Charlie Parkers!"

She ordered another cocktail. And lit another cigarette. We were silent for a long while. She seemed lost in thought. I listened to the bassist play a long solo in "Embraceable You." The pianist added the occasional accompanying chord, while the drummer wiped away his sweat and had a drink. A regular at the bar came up to me, and we chatted for a while.

"Hajime," Shimamoto said a long time later. "Do you

know any good rivers? A pretty river in a valley, not too big, one that flows fairly swiftly right into the sea?"

Taken by surprise, I looked at her. "A river?" What was she talking about? Her face was utterly expressionless. She was quiet, as if gazing at some faraway landscape. Maybe it was me who was far away—far from her world, at least, with an unimaginable distance separating us. The thought made me sad. There was something in her eyes that called up sadness.

"What's with this river all of a sudden?" I asked.

"It just suddenly occurred to me," she answered. "*Do you know any river like that?*"

When I was a student, I traveled around the country quite a bit, lugging a sleeping bag. So I'd seen quite a few Japanese rivers. But I couldn't come up with the kind of river she described.

"I think there might be a river like that on the Japan Sea coast," I said after a great deal of thought. "I don't remember what it's called. But I'm sure it's in Ishikawa Prefecture. It wouldn't be hard to find. It's probably the closest to what you're after."

I recalled that river clearly. I went there on fall break when I was a sophomore or a junior in college. The fall foliage was beautiful, the surrounding mountains looking as though they were dyed in blood. The mountains ran down to the sea, the rush of the water was gorgeous, and sometimes you could hear the cry of deer in the forest. The fish I ate were out of this world.

"Do you think you could take me there?" Shimamoto asked.

"It's all the way over in Ishikawa," I said in a dry voice.

"Enoshima I could see, but we'd have to fly, then drive for at least an hour. And stay overnight. I'm sure you understand that's something I can't do at the moment."

Shimamoto shifted slowly on her stool and turned to face me. "Hajime, I know I shouldn't be asking this favor of you. I know that. Believe me, I realize it's a burden to you. But there's no one else I can ask. I have to go there, and I don't want to go alone."

I looked into her eyes. Her eyes were like a deep spring in the shade of cliffs, which no breeze could ever reach. Nothing moved there, everything was still. Look closely, and you could just begin to make out the scene reflected in the water's surface.

"Forgive me." She smiled, as if all the strength had left her. "Please don't think I came here just to ask you that. I wanted only to see you and talk. I didn't plan to bring this up."

I made a quick mental calculation of the time. "If we left really early in the morning and did a round trip by plane, we should be able to make it back by not too late at night. Of course, it depends on how much time we spend there."

"I don't think it'll take too long," she said. "Can you really spare the time? The time to fly over there and back with me?"

I thought a bit. "I think so. I can't say anything definitely yet. But I can probably make the time. Call me here tomorrow night, all right? I'll be here at this time. I'll figure out our plan by then. What's your schedule?"

"I don't have any schedule. Any time that's fine with you is fine with me."

I nodded.

"I'm really sorry," she said. "Maybe I shouldn't have met you again, after all. I know I'll only end up ruining everything."

She left just a little before eleven. I held an umbrella over her and flagged down a cab. The rain was still falling.

"Goodbye. And thank you," she said.

"Goodbye," I said.

I went back into the bar and returned to the same seat at the counter. Her cocktail glass was still there. As was the ashtray, with several crushed-out Salems. I didn't have the waiter take them away. For the longest time, I gazed at the faint color of lipstick on the glass and on the cigarettes.

Yukiko was waiting up for me when I got home. She'd thrown a cardigan over her pajamas and was watching a video of *Lawrence of Arabia*. The scene where Lawrence, after all sorts of trials and tribulations, has finally made it across the desert and reached the Suez Canal. She'd already seen the film three times. It's a great film, she told me. I can watch it over and over. I sat down next to her, and had some wine as we watched the rest of the movie.

Next Sunday there's a get-together at the swimming club, I told her. One of the members owned a large yacht, which we'd been on several times offshore, fishing and drinking. It was a little too cold to go out in a yacht in February, but my wife knew nothing about boats, so she didn't have any objections. I hardly ever went out on Sundays, and she seemed to think it was

good for me to meet people in other fields and be outdoors.

"I'll be leaving really early in the morning. And I'll be
back by eight, I think. I'll have dinner at home," I said.

"All right. My sister's coming over that Sunday anyway," she said. "If it isn't too cold, maybe we could take a
picnic to Shinjuku Gyoen. Just us four girls."

"Sounds good," I said.

The next afternoon I went to a travel agency and
made plane and rental car reservations. There was a
flight arriving back in Tokyo at six-thirty in the evening.
Looked like I would be back in time for a late dinner.
Then I went to the bar and waited for Shimamoto's call.
She phoned at ten. "I'm a little busy, but I think I can
make the time," I told her. "Is next Sunday okay?"

That's fine with me, she replied.

I told her the flight time and where to meet me at
Haneda Airport.

"Thank you so much," she said.

After hanging up, I sat at the counter for a while, with
a book. The bustle of the bar bothered me, though, and
I couldn't concentrate. I went to the rest room and
washed my face and hands with cold water, stared at
my reflection in the mirror. I've lied to Yukiko, I told
myself. Sure, I'd lied to her before, when I slept with
other women. But I never felt I was deceiving her. Those
were just harmless flings. But this time was wrong. Not
that I was planning to sleep with Shimamoto. But even
so, it was wrong. For the first time in a long while, I
looked deep within my own eyes in the mirror. Those
eyes told me nothing of who I was. I laid both hands on
the sink and sighed deeply.

10

The river flowed swiftly past cliffs, in places forming small waterfalls, in others coming to a halt in pools. The surface of these pools faintly reflected the weak sun. An old iron bridge downstream spanned the river. The bridge was so narrow one car could barely squeeze across it. Its darkened, impassive metal frame sank deep into the chilled February silence. The only people who passed over the bridge were the hotel's guests and employees, and the people in charge of caring for the woods. When we walked over it, we passed no one going the other way, and looking back, we saw no one. After arriving at the hotel, we had had a light lunch, then we crossed the bridge and walked along the river.

Shimamoto had on a heavy pea coat, the collar turned up, and a muffler wrapped around her up to her nose. She had on casual clothes, good for walking in the mountains, much different from her usual attire. Her hair was tied in back, and she wore a pair of rugged-looking work boots. A green nylon shoulder bag was slung over one shoulder. Dressed like that, she looked just like a high school girl. On either side of the river, hard patches of snow remained. Two crows squatted on top of the bridge, gazing down at the river below, every once in a while releasing grating, scolding caws. Those shrill calls echoed in the leaf-blanketed woods, crossed the river, and rang unpleasantly in our ears.

A narrow, unpaved path continued along the river, a terribly silent, deserted path leading who knows where. No houses appeared beside the path, only the occasional bare field. Snow-covered furrows inscribed bright white lines across the barren land. Crows were everywhere. As if signaling their comrades down the line of our approach, the crows let out short, sharp caws as we passed. They stood their ground, not trying to fly away. From close proximity I could see their sharp, weapon-like beaks and the vivid coloring of their claws.

"Do we still have time?" Shimamoto asked. "Can we walk a little farther?"

I looked at my watch. "We're okay. We should be able to stay here another hour."

"It's so quiet," she said, looking around slowly. Every time she opened her mouth, her hard white breath drifted into the air.

"Is this river what you were looking for?"

She smiled at me. "It's like you could read my mind," she replied. And reached out with her gloved hand to grasp mine, also in a glove.

"I'm glad," I said. "If we came all this way and you said this wasn't the place, then what'd we do?"

"Hey, have more confidence in yourself. You'd never make that kind of mistake," she said. "But you know, walking like this, just the two of us, I remember the old days. When we used to walk home together from school."

"Your leg isn't like it was, though."

She grinned at me. "You seem almost disappointed."

"Maybe so." I laughed.

"Really?"

"I'm just kidding. I'm very happy your leg's better. Just a bout of nostalgia, I guess."

"Hajime," she said, "I hope you understand how very grateful I am to you for doing this."

"Don't worry about it," I said. "It's like going on a picnic. Except we took a plane."

Shimamoto walked on for a while, looking ahead. "But you had to lie to your wife."

"I guess so," I said.

"And that couldn't have been easy. I'm sure you didn't want to lie to her."

I didn't know how to respond. From the woods nearby, a crow let out another sharp caw.

"I've messed up your life. I know I have," Shimamoto said in a small voice.

"Hey, let's stop talking about it," I said. "We've come all the way here, so let's talk about something more cheerful."

"Like what?"

"Dressed like that, you look just like a high school girl."

"Thanks," she said. "I wish I were."

We walked slowly upstream. For a while we proceeded in silence, concentrating on our walking. She couldn't walk very fast but was able to handle a slow but steady pace. She held my hand tight. The path was frozen solid, and our rubber soles hardly made a sound.

Just as she had implied, if only we could have walked this way when we were teenagers, or even in our twenties, how wonderful that would have been! A Sunday afternoon, just the two of us strolling along a river like this ... I would have been ecstatic. But we were no longer high school kids. I had a wife and children, and a job. And I'd had to lie to my wife in order to be here. I had to drive back to the airport, take the flight that arrived in Tokyo at six-thirty, then hurry back to my home, where my wife would be waiting for me.

Finally Shimamoto stopped, rubbed her gloved hands together, and gazed all around. She looked upstream, then downstream. On the opposite shore there was a range of mountains, on the left-hand side a line of bare trees. We were utterly alone. The hot-springs hotel, where we'd had lunch, and the iron bridge, lay hidden in the shadow of the mountains. Every once in a while, as if remembering its duty, the sun showed its face through a break in the clouds. All we could hear were the screeches of the crows and the rush of water. Someday, somewhere, I will see this scene, I felt. The opposite of déjà vu—not the feeling that I'd already seen what was around me, but the premonition that I would some-

day. This premonition reached out its long hand and grabbed my mind tight. I could feel myself in its grip. There at its fingertips was me. Me in the future, grown old. Of course, I couldn't see what I looked like.

"This spot will be all right," she said.

"To do what?" I asked.

She smiled her usual faint smile. "To do what I'm about to do," she replied.

We went down to the riverbank. There was a small pool of water, covered by a thin sheet of ice. On the bottom of the pool several fallen leaves lay still, like the bodies of flat dead fish. I picked up a round stone and rolled it in my hand. Shimamoto took off her gloves and put them in her coat pocket. She undid her shoulder bag, opened it, and removed a small bag made out of a pretty cloth. Inside the bag was an urn. She undid the fastening on the lid and carefully opened the urn. For a while she gazed at what was inside.

I stood beside her, watching, without a word.

Inside the urn were white ashes. Very carefully, so that none would spill out, she poured the ashes onto her left palm. There was barely enough to cover her hand. Ash left after a cremation, I figured. It was a quiet, windless afternoon, and the ash didn't stir. Shimamoto returned the empty urn to her bag, stuck her index finger into the ash, put the finger to her mouth, and licked it. She looked at me and tried to smile. But she couldn't. Her finger remained near her lips.

As she crouched by the river and scattered the ashes, I stood next to her, watching. In an instant the small amount of ash was carried away. She and I stood on the shore, gazing at the water. She stared at her palm, then

finally brushed off the remaining ash and put on her gloves.

"Will it really reach the sea?" she asked.

"I think so," I said. But I wasn't sure. The ocean was a fair distance away. Perhaps the ash would settle somewhere. But even so, some of it would, eventually, reach the sea.

She took a piece of board that lay nearby and began digging in a soft spot of ground. I helped her. When we'd dug a small hole, she buried the urn wrapped in cloth. Crows cawed in the distance, observing our actions from beginning to end. No matter; look if you want to, I thought. We're not doing anything bad. All we did was scatter some burned ash in the river.

"Do you think it will turn to rain?" Shimamoto asked, tapping the tip of her boot on the ground.

I looked at the sky. "I think it'll hold out for a while," I said.

"No, that's not what I mean. What I mean is, will the child's ashes flow to the sea, mix with the seawater, evaporate, form into clouds, and fall as rain?"

I looked up at the sky one more time. And then at the river flowing.

"You never know," I replied.

We headed in our rental car back to the airport. The weather was deteriorating fast. The sky was covered with heavy clouds, no blue visible. It looked like it would snow at any minute.

"Those were my baby's ashes. The only baby I ever had," Shimamoto said, as if talking to herself.

I looked at her, then looked ahead. Trucks sprayed up

muddy melted snow, and I had to turn on the wipers
every once in a while.

"My baby died the day after it was born," she said. "It
lived just one day. I held it only a couple of times. It was
a beautiful baby. So very soft ... They didn't know the
cause, but it couldn't breathe well. When it died it was
already a different color."

I couldn't say a thing. I reached out my hand and
placed it on hers.

"It was a baby girl. Without a name."

"When was that?"

"This time last year. In February."

"Poor thing," I said.

"I didn't want to bury it anywhere. I couldn't stand the
thought of it in some dark place. I wanted to keep it beside me for a while, then let it flow into the sea and turn
into rain."

She was silent for a long, long time. I kept on driving,
not saying a word. She probably didn't feel like talking,
so I thought it might be best to leave her alone. But
soon I noticed that something was wrong—her breathing sounded strange, a mechanical rasping. At first I
thought it was the car engine, but then I realized the
sound was coming from beside me. It was as if she had
a hole in her windpipe and air was leaking out each
time she took a breath.

Waiting for a signal to change, I looked at her. She
was white as a sheet and strangely stiff. She rested her
head against the headrest and stared straight ahead. She
didn't move a muscle, only from time to time would
blink, as if forced to. I drove on for a little while and

found a place to pull over—the parking lot of a boarded-up bowling alley. On top of the building, which looked like an airplane hangar, stood a billboard with a gigantic bowling pin on it. Alone in the huge parking lot, we seemed to be in some wilderness at the edge of civilization.

"Shimamoto-san." I turned to her. "Are you all right?"

She didn't answer. She just sat back against the seat, making that unearthly sound. I put my hand to her cheek. It was as cold as the scenery that surrounded us. Not a trace of warmth. I touched her forehead, but it showed no signs of fever. I felt like I was choking. Was she dying, right here and now? Her eyes were listless as I looked deep into them. I could see nothing; they were as cold and dark as death.

"Shimamoto-san!" I yelled out, but got no response. Her eyes were unfocused. She might not even be conscious. I had to get her to an emergency room, and fast. We'd definitely miss our plane, but there was no time to worry about that. Shimamoto might die, and there was no way I was going to let that happen.

When I started the car again, though, she was trying to say something. I cut the engine, put my ear to her lips, but couldn't make out her words. They were less like words than wind whistling through a crack in a wall. Straining as hard as she could, she repeated her words again and again. Finally a single word came through. "Medicine."

"You want to take some medicine?" I asked.

She gave a tiny nod. So slight a nod I might not have caught it. But it was all she could manage. I rummaged

around in her coat pocket. Purse, handkerchief, key holder with a lot of keys, but no medicine. I opened her shoulder bag. Inside was a small packet of medicine, with four capsules. I showed her the capsules. "Is this it?"

Without moving her eyes, she nodded.

I pushed her seat back, opened her mouth, and placed one capsule inside. But her mouth was bone dry, and nothing would go down. I searched madly for a vending machine, but there was none. And we didn't have time to go looking. The only source of water around was the snow. Thank God there was enough of that. I leaped out of the car, scooped up some clean snow under the eaves of the building, and put it in Shimamoto's wool cap. Bit by bit, I placed the snow in my mouth and melted it. It took a while to melt enough, and the tip of my tongue turned numb. I opened her mouth and let the water flow from mine into hers. Then I held her nose closed and forced her to swallow. She choked a little, but after I did this a couple of times, she was at last able to swallow the capsule.

I looked at the packet. Nothing was written on it, not the name of the medicine, her name, directions. Strange, I thought, considering that such information is usually provided so you won't take a medicine by mistake, or so others will know what to do. I replaced the packet inside her bag and watched her for a while. I had no idea what kind of medicine it was, or what her symptoms were, but since apparently she carried the medicine around all the time, it must work. For her, at least, this was not a totally unexpected attack.

Ten minutes later, some color began to return to her

cheeks. I gently put my cheek to hers; warmth was flowing back. I sighed in relief and had her sit back in her
seat. She wasn't going to die, after all. I put my arms
around her shoulders and rubbed my cheek against
hers. Slowly, ever so slowly, she was returning to the
land of the living.

"Hajime," she whispered in a dry voice.

"Shouldn't we go to a hospital? Maybe we should find
the nearest emergency room," I asked.

"No, we don't need to," she replied. "I'm fine. If I take
my medicine, I'm okay. I'll be back to normal in a few
minutes. What we should worry about is whether we're
going to make that plane."

"Don't worry about that, for God's sake. We'll stay
here until you feel better."

I wiped her mouth with a handkerchief. She took the
handkerchief in her hand and looked at it. "Are you always this kind to everybody?"

"Not to everybody," I said. "To you I am. I can't be kind
to everyone. There are limits to my kindness; even to
how kind I can be to you. I wish there weren't; then I
could do so much more for you. But I can't."

She turned to look at me.

"Hajime, I didn't do this just so we'd miss the plane,"
she said in a small voice.

Startled, I gazed at her. "Of course you didn't! You
don't need to say that. You were feeling sick. It can't be
helped."

"I'm sorry," she said.

"No need to apologize. You didn't do anything
wrong."

"But I've ruined your plans."

I stroked her hair, leaned over and kissed her cheek. I was dying to hold her whole body close to me and feel its warmth. But I couldn't. All I could do was kiss her cheek. It was warm, soft, and wet. "There's nothing for you to worry about," I said. "Everything will work out fine."

By the time we reached the airport and returned the car, it was way past boarding time. Fortunately, though, our plane was delayed. It was still on the runway; the passengers were waiting in the terminal. We both breathed a sigh of relief. They're servicing the engine, the person at the counter told us. We don't know how long it will take, he said; we don't have any more information. It had started to snow when we reached the airport; now it was really coming down. With all the snow, the flight might very well be canceled.

"What'll you do if you can't get back to Tokyo today?" Shimamoto asked me.

"Not to worry. The plane will take off," I said. Not that I had any proof. The idea that it might very well not take off had me depressed. I'd have to come up with a great excuse. Why the heck was I all the way over in Ishikawa? Enough, I said to myself; let's cross that bridge when we come to it. What I had to worry about now was Shimamoto.

"What about you?" I asked. "What'll you do if we can't get back to Tokyo today?"

She shook her head. "I'm fine," she said. "The problem is you. You'll be in hot water."

"Maybe. But never fear—they haven't said the flight's canceled yet."

"I knew something like this would happen," she said as if to herself. "Whenever I'm around, nothing good ever happens. You can count on it. If I'm involved, then things go bad. Things are going smoothly, then I step in and *wham!* they fall apart."

I sat on the bench in the airport lounge, thinking about the telephone call I'd have to make to Yukiko if the flight was indeed canceled. I mulled over possible excuses, but everything I came up with sounded lame. I'd gone out saying I was spending Sunday with the guys from the swimming club, then ended up being snowed in in Ishikawa. No way I could explain that. "When I left the house I was suddenly overcome by this strong desire to visit the Japan Sea, so I went to Haneda Airport," I could tell her. Give me a break. If that's the best I could manage, I might as well clam up. Or better yet, maybe I could try the truth. Before long, I realized with a start that I was actually hoping we would be snowed in and the flight canceled. Subconsciously, I was hoping my wife would find out about my coming here with Shimamoto. I wanted to put an end to excuses, to lies. More than anything, I wanted to remain right where I was, with Shimamoto beside me, and let things take their course.

The airplane finally took off, an hour and a half late. Inside the cabin, Shimamoto leaned against me and slept. Maybe she just had her eyes closed. I put my arm around her shoulder and held her close. Sometimes it seemed she was crying. She was silent the whole time; the first words we spoke were just before the plane landed.

"Shimamoto-san, are you sure you're all right?"

Nestled next to me, she nodded. "I'm fine. As long as I take the medicine. So don't worry." She leaned her head back against my shoulder. "But don't ask me anything, okay? Why that happened."

"Understood. No questions," I said.

"Thank you very much for today," she said.

"What part of today?"

"For taking me to the river. For giving me water from your mouth. For putting up with me."

I looked at her. Her lips were right in front of me. The lips I had kissed as I gave her water. And once more those lips seemed to be seeking me. Slightly parted, with her beautiful white teeth barely visible. I could still feel her soft tongue, which I'd touched slightly as I gave her water. I found it hard to breathe, and I couldn't think. My body burned. She wants me, I thought. And I want her. But somehow I held myself in check. I had to stop right where I was. One more step, and there would be no turning back.

I called home from Haneda Airport. It was already half-past eight. Sorry I'm so late, I told my wife. I couldn't get in touch with you. I'll be back in an hour.

"I waited for a long time. I went ahead and ate dinner. I made stew," she said.

I gave Shimamoto a ride in my BMW, which I'd parked at the airport. "Where should I take you?" I asked.

"You can let me off in Aoyama. I can get back from there by myself," she said.

"Will you be all right?"

She smiled broadly and nodded.

We rode in silence till I got off the highway at Gaien. I'd put a tape of a Handel organ concerto on, real low. Shimamoto held both hands neatly in her lap and looked out the window. It was Sunday evening, and the cars around us were filled with families returning from a day out. I shifted gears briskly.

"Hajime," Shimamoto said as we approached Aoyama Boulevard. "I was thinking back then how nice it would be if the plane didn't take off."

I was thinking exactly the same thing, I wanted to tell her. But I said nothing. My mouth was dry, and words couldn't come. I merely nodded and reached out for her hand. At the corner of Aoyama 1-chome, she told me to stop the car, and I let her out.

"May I come to see you again?" she asked me softly as she opened the door. "You can still stand being around me?"

"I'll be waiting," I said.

Shimamoto nodded.

As I drove away, I thought this: If I never see her again, I will go insane. Once she was out of the car and gone, my world was suddenly hollow and meaningless.

11

Four days after Shimamoto and I returned from Ishi-kawa, I got an unexpected call from my father-in-law. He said he had a favor to ask and invited me to lunch the next day. I agreed, frankly surprised. Usually his busy schedule allowed only for business lunches.

Six months before, his company had moved from Yoyogi to a new seven-story building in Yotsuya. His of-fices occupied the top two floors, and he rented out the lower five to other companies, restaurants, and shops. It was the first time I'd been there. Everything glittered, brand spanking new. The lobby had a marble floor, a cathedral ceiling, flowers piled high in a huge ceramic vase. When I got off the elevator at the sixth floor, I was met by a young receptionist with hair so gorgeous she

looked like she belonged in a shampoo commercial. She called my father-in-law to tell him I had arrived. Her phone was this dark-gray high-tech number that reminded me of a spatula with a calculator attached. She beamed at me and said, "Please go on in. The president is expecting you." A gorgeous smile, though not in the same class as Shimamoto's.

The presidential office was on the top floor, and a large picture window gave a view of the city. Not the most heartwarming scene, but the room was bright and spacious. An impressionist painting hung on the wall. A picture of a lighthouse and a boat. Looked like a Seurat, very possibly an original.

"Business is booming, I take it?" I said.

"It's not bad," he replied. He walked to the window and pointed outside. "Not bad at all. And it's going to get even better. This is the time to make some money. For people in my line of work, a chance like this doesn't come along but once every twenty or thirty years. If you don't make money now, you never will. Do you know why?"

"I have no idea. The construction business isn't exactly my field."

"Look out at Tokyo here. See all the empty lots around? Like a mouth full of missing teeth. If you look down from above like this, there it is for all the world to see, but walk around town at ground level and you'll miss it. There used to be old houses and buildings on those lots, but they've been torn down. The price of land has shot up so much old buildings aren't profitable anymore. You can't charge high rent, and it's hard to find tenants. That's why they need newer, bigger buildings.

And private homes in the city—well, people can't afford their property taxes or inheritance taxes. So they sell out and move to the suburbs. And professional real estate developers buy up the old houses, put 'em to the wrecking ball, and construct brand-new, more functional buildings. So before long all those empty lots will have new buildings on them. In a couple of years you won't recognize Tokyo. There's no shortage of capital. The Japanese economy's booming, stocks are up. And banks are bursting at the seams with cash. If you have land as collateral, the banks'll lend you as much as you possibly could want. That's why all these buildings are going up one after another. And guess who builds them? Guys like me."

"I see," I said. "But if all those buildings arc built, what will happen to Tokyo?"

"What will happen? Well, it'll get more lively, more beautiful, more functional. Cities reflect the way the economy's going, after all."

"That's all well and good, but Tokyo's already choked with cars. Any more skyscrapers, and the roads will turn into one huge parking lot. And how's the water supply going to keep up if there's a dry spell? In the summer, when people all have their air conditioners on, they won't be able to keep up with the demand for electricity. The power plants are run by fuel from the Middle East, right? What happens if there's another oil crisis? Then what?"

"Let the government figure that out. That's what we're paying high taxes for, right? Let all those Tokyo University grads rack their brains. They're always running around with their snooty noses in the air—like they're

the ones who really run the country. Let them put their pointy heads to work for a change. I don't have the answer. I'm a simple builder. Orders for buildings come in, and I build 'em. That's what you call market forces, am I right?"

I said nothing. I hadn't come all the way here to debate the Japanese economy.

"Anyhow," he said, "let's drop all this complicated stuff and go grab a bite. I'm starving."

Getting in his huge black Mercedes, we drove to his favorite grilled-eel restaurant, in Akasaka. We were shown to a private room in the back, where we settled in for a meal. It was the middle of the day, so I only sipped a bit of the sake, but my father-in-law threw back one cup after another.

"You said you had something you wanted to talk about?" I asked. If it was bad news, I'd rather get it out of the way first.

"I have a favor to ask," he said. "Nothing really big. I just need to use your name for something."

"My name?"

"I'm starting a new company, and I need to use somebody else's name as the founder. You don't need any special qualifications. Just your name. I promise it won't cause you any trouble, and I'll make it worth your while."

"Don't worry about that," I said. "If it will help you, you can use my name as many times as you want. But what kind of company are you talking about? If my name's going to be listed as the founder, I might as well know that much."

"Well, to tell you the truth, it's not an actual com-

pany," my father-in-law answered. "It's a company in name only, I should say. It doesn't really exist."

"A fake company, in other words. A dummy company."

"Guess you could say that."

"What's the point? Is it a tax dodge?"

"Hmm ... not exactly," he said reluctantly.

"Bribes?" I ventured.

"Sort of," he said. "I'll be the first to admit this isn't the greatest thing in the world to be involved in. But in my line of work you have to."

"Well, what if some problem develops?"

"There's nothing illegal about forming a company."

"I'm talking about what that company does."

He took a cigarette out of his pocket and lit it with a match. And exhaled smoke into the air above him.

"There won't be any problems. Even if there were, anybody with half a brain could see that you just lent your name to it. Your wife's father asked you to let him use your name, and you did. No one's going to hold you responsible."

I didn't say anything for a while. "Where are all these bribes going to end up?"

"You're better off not knowing."

"Tell me more about these so-called market forces," I said. "Is it going to end up in some politician's pocket?"

"A little," he said.

"Bureaucrats'?"

My father-in-law stubbed out his cigarette in the ashtray. "That would be graft, wouldn't it. They'd arrest me."

"But everybody in your business does it, right?"

"I suppose," he said. And he made a pained face. "But not to the point where they're arrested."

"What about the yakuza? They're pretty helpful when it comes to buying up land, aren't they?"

"I've never gotten along with them. Anyhow, I'm not trying to corner the market. It's lucrative, but I don't do it. As I said, I'm just a simple builder."

I sighed deeply.

"I knew you wouldn't like this," he said.

"It doesn't matter if I like it or not, since you've already included me in the equation and gone ahead, right? On the assumption that I'd agree."

"I'm afraid you're right." He laughed weakly.

I sighed again. "Dad, to tell you the truth, I don't like this kind of thing. I don't mean because it's illegal or anything. But I'm just an ordinary guy, living an ordinary life. And I'd rather not get involved in backroom deals."

"I'm well aware of that," he said. "So leave it all to me. I won't leave you hanging out to dry. If I did, then Yukiko and the children would be involved too. And I'm not about to have that happen. You know how much my daughter and grandchildren mean to me."

I nodded. I couldn't very well refuse his request. It depressed me. Little by little, I would get snared by the world out there. This was the first step; first I say yes to this, then later on it'll be something else.

We ate some more. I drank tea, while my father-in-law put away the sake at an even faster clip.

"How old are you now?" he suddenly asked.

"Thirty-seven," I replied.

He looked at me fixedly.

"Thirty-seven's the age when you play around the most," he said. "Work's going well, your confidence is up. So women come to you, right?"

"In my case, not that many, I'm afraid." I laughed, studying his expression. For a second I panicked, positive that he'd found out about me and Shimamoto, and that's why he asked me here today. But he was just making small talk.

"When I was your age I played around quite a bit. So I won't tell you not to have affairs. It's kind of strange for me to be saying this to my daughter's husband, but actually I think a fling or two on the side isn't all bad. It refreshes you. Get it out of your system every once in a while, and your home life will improve; you'll be able to concentrate on work too. So if you were to sleep around with other women, I for one wouldn't say a word. Playing around's okay by me, but be very careful in choosing your partners. Get involved with the wrong person, and your life goes down the toilet. I've seen it happen a million times."

I nodded. And suddenly recalled hearing from Yukiko about how her brother and his wife weren't getting along. Her brother, a year younger than me, had a girlfriend and didn't come home much anymore. I imagined my father-in-law was worried about his oldest son and that's why he brought all this up.

"Anyhow, don't get involved with some worthless bit of tail. Do that, and you'll soon be worthless yourself. Play around with a stupid woman, and you'll turn stu-

pid too. Which isn't to say you should get involved with some high-class woman. That'd make it tough to go back to what's waiting for you at home. Do you get what I'm telling you?"

"I think so," I replied.

"As long as you keep a few things in mind, you'll do okay. First, don't set the woman up with her own place. That's a definite mistake. Second, no matter what, come back home by two a.m. Two a.m. is the point of no return. Finally, don't use your friends as excuses to cover up your affairs. You may be found out. If that happens, well, there's not much you can do about it. But there's no need to lose a friend in the process."

"It sounds like you're speaking from experience."

"You got it. Man learns from experience alone," he said. "There are some people who don't; I know you're not one of them. You have a very discriminating eye, something only experience can teach you. I've been to your bars just a couple of times, but it's plain to see. You know how to hire good people and how to treat them right."

I was silent, waiting for him to go on.

"You also have a good eye for choosing a wife. Yukiko's very happy living with you. And your children are wonderful kids. I'm grateful to you."

He's pretty drunk, I thought. But I didn't say anything.

"You probably don't know this, but Yukiko tried to commit suicide once. Took an overdose of sleeping pills. We rushed her to the hospital, and she didn't regain consciousness for two days. I was sure she wouldn't make it. Her body was cold, and she was hardly breath-

ing. She's a goner, I figured. I felt like the world had collapsed."

I looked up at him. "When did this happen?"

"When she was twenty-two. Right after she graduated from college. It was over a man. A real jerk she'd gotten herself engaged to. Yukiko looks real quiet, but underneath she's a tough cookie. And smart. That's why I can't figure out why she'd ever get herself involved with a guy like that." He leaned against the pillar in the traditional-style room we were in, put a cigarette between his lips, and lit it. "Well, that was her very first man. The very first time, everyone makes mistakes. With Yukiko, though, it was a huge shock. That's why she tried to kill herself. For a long while afterward she wouldn't have anything to do with men. She'd always been pretty outgoing, but she stopped talking to people and stayed holed up in the house. Once she met you, though, she began to cheer up. She did a complete turnaround. I remember you met each other on a trip?"

"That's right. At Yatsugatake."

"I nearly had to shove her out the door to get her to go. I thought travel might do her good."

I nodded. "I knew nothing about the suicide," I said.

"I thought it was better you didn't know, so I never mentioned it. But it's high time you knew. The two of you are going to be together for a long time, so you'd better know everything—the good and the bad. Besides, it happened a long time ago." He closed his eyes and blew a puff of smoke into the air. "It's funny for me as her parent to say this, but she's a good woman. I've played around a lot and have an eye for the ladies.

Whether she's my daughter or not, I'm able to judge women pretty well. My younger daughter's much prettier, but Yukiko's the better person. You're a good judge of people."

I was silent.

"You don't have any brothers and sisters, do you?"

"No, I don't," I said.

"Do you think I love all three of my children equally?"

"I have no idea."

"How about you? Do you love both of your daughters the same?"

"Sure."

"That's 'cause they're both still little," he said. "Wait till they grow up. First you'll like this one, but then you'll start leaning toward the other. Someday you'll see what I mean."

"Really?" I said.

"I'd never say this to them, but of my three kids, I like Yukiko best. I feel bad for the others when I say this, but there you have it. Yukiko and I get along well, and I can trust her."

I nodded.

"You have a good eye for people, and that's a wonderful talent you've got to cherish. I'm a hopeless case myself, but at least I've helped raise something not quite so hopeless."

I assisted my now thoroughly drunk father-in-law into his Mercedes. He sank back into the rear seat, spread his legs apart, and closed his eyes. I hailed a cab and went home. As soon as I arrived, Yukiko wanted to hear the upshot of our luncheon meeting.

"Nothing really important," I said. "Your father just wanted to have someone to drink with. He ended up pretty drunk. I wonder that he can go back to work in that condition."

"He's always like that." Yukiko laughed. "He has some drinks at lunch, then takes an hour's nap on the sofa in his office. The company hasn't gone belly-up yet. Don't you worry about him."

"He doesn't seem to hold his liquor like he used to."

"No, he doesn't. Before Mom died, he could drink like a fish and never show it. He was tough. But it can't be helped. Everybody gets old."

She brewed a pot of coffee, and we sat at the dining table, drinking it. I decided not to say anything about the dummy company and her father's request. She'd only think he was bothering me, and she wouldn't like it. *It's true you borrowed money from Father, but that has nothing to do with this,* Yukiko would no doubt say. *You're paying it back, with interest, right?* But the situation wasn't quite that simple.

My younger daughter was fast asleep in her room. When I finished my coffee, I enticed Yukiko into bed. We stripped naked and held each other tight there in the glare of the sun. I took my time warming her body up, then entered her. But all the time I was inside her, it was Shimamoto I saw. I closed my eyes and felt I was holding Shimamoto. And I came violently.

I took a shower, then went back to bed, to sleep for a while. Yukiko was already dressed, but after I slipped into bed, she got under the covers and put her lips against my back. I lay silent, with eyes closed. I'd had

sex with her, all the while thinking of another woman, and the guilt was getting to me. I lay there, silent, eyes closed.

"You know, I really do love you," Yukiko said.

"We've been married seven years, we have two kids," I said. " 'Bout time for you to get tired of me, don't you think?"

"Perhaps. But I still love you."

I held her close. And began to undress her. I pulled off her sweater and skirt, her underwear.

"Whoa! You're not planning what I think you're planning, are you?" she asked in surprise.

"Of course," I said.

"Special-entry time for my diary today," she said.

This time I tried hard not to think of Shimamoto. I held Yukiko's body, looking at her face and concentrating only on her. I kissed her lips, her neck, her breasts. And I came inside of her. Afterward, I held her for a long time.

"Are you all right?" she asked, her eyes on me. "Did something happen today with you and Father?"

"Nothing happened," I replied. "Not a thing. I just feel like staying like this for a while."

"Be my guest," she said. And she held me tight, with me still inside her. I closed my eyes and pulled her hard against my body, as though, if I didn't, I would fly off into the void.

As I held her, I remembered the attempted suicide her father had told me about. *I was sure she wouldn't make it. She's a goner, I figured.* If things had taken even the slightest of wrong turns, I wouldn't be holding her

body like this. Gently I touched her shoulder, her hair and breasts. They were real—warm and soft. Beneath my palm I could feel her life. No one could say how long that life would last. Whatever has form can disappear in an instant. Yukiko. This room. These walls, this ceiling, this window. They might all be gone before we knew it. Suddenly Izumi came to mind. That man had hurt Yukiko deeply, and I had done the same to Izumi. Yukiko happened to meet me after that, but Izumi was all alone.

I kissed Yukiko's soft neck.

"I'm going to sleep for a while," I said. "And then I'll go to the nursery school to pick her up."

"Sleep well," she told me.

I slept for just a short time. When I opened my eyes, it was past three p.m. From the bedroom window I could see the Aoyama Cemetery. I sat down in a chair by the window and stared at it for a long time. So many things looked different now, now that Shimamoto had shown up in my life again. I could hear Yukiko preparing dinner in the kitchen. The sounds rang hollowly in my ears, like those transmitted down a pipe from a world terribly far away.

I got the BMW out of the underground garage and headed for the nursery school to pick up my daughter. They had some special program at the school that day, so it was almost four when she appeared at the school gate. You could always count on a line of shiny, expensive cars there—Saabs, Jaguars, even the occasional Alfa Romeo. Young mothers in expensive-looking coats got

out of the cars, collected their children, deposited them in the cars, and took off. My daughter was the only child whose father came to pick her up. When I saw her, I called out her name and waved. She waved her tiny hand and came toward me. Then she saw a little girl sitting in a blue Mercedes 260E and ran over to her, yelling out something. The girl had on a red woolen cap and was leaning out the window of the parked car. The girl's mother wore a red cashmere coat and a large pair of sunglasses. When I went over there and took my daughter's hand, the woman turned to me and smiled broadly. I returned the smile. The red coat and the sunglasses made me think of Shimamoto. The Shimamoto I followed from Shibuya to Aoyama.

"Hi," I said.

"Hi," she said.

The woman was stunning. She couldn't have been much more than twenty-five. Her car stereo was playing the Talking Heads' "Burning Down the House." In the back seat were two paper shopping bags from Kinokuniya. She had a beautiful smile. My daughter whispered for a while to her little friend, then said goodbye. Bye, said the girl. Then she pushed the button and closed the window of the car. I took my daughter's hand and walked her over to where the BMW was parked.

"How was your day? Anything fun happen?" I asked.

She shook her head emphatically. "Nothing fun at all. It was terrible," she said.

"Tough time for both of us," I said. I leaned over and kissed her forehead, and she made the same sour face owners of snobby French restaurants produce when

you hand them your American Express card. "I'm sure tomorrow will be much better," I told her.

I wanted to believe that too. When I opened my eyes tomorrow, the world would be new, and every problem would be solved. But I couldn't swallow that scenario. For I had a wife and two daughters. And I was in love with someone else.

"Daddy?" my daughter said. "I wanna ride a horse. Buy me a horse someday?"

"Sure. Someday," I said.

"When's someday?"

"When Daddy's saved up some money. Then he'll buy you a horse."

"Do you have a piggy bank, Daddy?"

"Yes, a very big one. As big as this car. If I don't save up that much money, I won't be able to buy you a horse."

"If we ask Grandpa, do you think he'll buy me a horse? Grandpa's rich."

"That's right," I said. "Grandpa has a piggy bank as big as that building over there. With lots of money inside. But it's so big it's hard to get the money out."

My daughter thought about it for a while.

"But can I ask Grandpa sometime? To buy me a horse?"

"Sure, you can ask him. Who knows, he might even buy one for you."

We talked about horses all the way home. What color horse she liked. What name she'd give it. Where she would like to ride to. Where the horse would sleep. I put her on the apartment elevator and headed for work. What would tomorrow bring? I wondered. Both hands

on the wheel, I closed my eyes. I didn't feel like I was in my own body; my body was just a lonely, temporary container I happened to be borrowing. What would become of me tomorrow I did not know. Buying my daughter a horse—the idea took on an unexpected urgency. I had to buy it for her before things disappeared. Before the world fell to pieces.

12

From then until the spring, Shimamoto and I saw each
other almost every week. She would stop by one of the
bars, more often than not the Robin's Nest, always past
nine. She'd sit at the bar, have a couple of cocktails, and
leave around eleven. I'd sit beside her, and we'd talk. I
don't know what my employees thought of this, but I
didn't care. It was like when we were in grade school
and I didn't let what my classmates thought about the
two of us concern me.

Occasionally she'd call and invite me to have lunch.
Most often we'd arrange to meet at a coffee shop on
Omote Sando. We'd have a light meal and take a walk.
We'd be together two, at most three, hours. When it was

time for her to leave, she'd glance at her watch and then smile at me. "Guess I'd better be going," she'd say. Her usual wonderful smile. I couldn't read any of her emotions behind that smile. Whether she felt sad at leaving, or not so sad, or maybe relieved to be rid of me, I had no idea. I couldn't even tell if she really did have to get home.

Anyhow, during the couple of hours we were together, we hardly stopped talking. Not once, though, did our bodies come in contact. Not once did I put my arm around her shoulder or even so much as hold her hand.

Back on the streets of Tokyo, Shimamoto had her usual cool, attractive smile. No more the rush of violent emotions she displayed on that cold February day in Ishikawa. The warm closeness born on that day was gone. As if by unspoken agreement, we never once mentioned our strange little trip.

As we walked side by side, I wondered what feelings she held in her heart. And where those feelings would lead her. Sometimes I looked deep into her eyes, but all I could detect was a gentle silence. As before, the line of her eyelids brought to mind the horizon, far off in the distance. At long last I could understand Izumi's loneliness when we were going out. Shimamoto had her own little world within her. A world that was for her alone, one I could not enter. Once, the door to that world had begun to open a crack. But now it was closed.

I felt again like a helpless, confused twelve-year-old. I had no idea what I should do, what I should say. I tried my best to stay calm and use my head. But it was hope-

less. Everything I said and did was wrong. Every emotion was swallowed up in that radiant smile. *Don't worry,* her smile told me. *It's all right.*

I was completely in the dark regarding Shimamoto's life. I didn't even know where she lived. Or who she lived with. Whether she was married, or had been. The only thing I knew was that last February she had had a baby, which died the next day. And that she'd never worked. Still, she always wore the most expensive-looking clothes and accessories, which meant that she had a fair amount of money. That's all I knew about her. She was probably married when she had the baby, but I couldn't be sure. Thousands of babies are born out of wedlock every day, right?

As time passed, Shimamoto began to talk bit by bit about her junior high school and high school days. There being no direct connection between those days and her present life, she didn't mind talking about them. I discovered how terribly lonely she had been. As she grew up, she tried her very best to be fair to everyone around her, never to make excuses. "Start making excuses, and there's no end to it," she told me. "I can't live that kind of life." But things didn't work out well. Her attitude only gave rise to stupid misunderstandings, which hurt her deeply. Steadily, she shut herself away. Waking up in the morning, she'd vomit and refuse to go to school.

She showed me a photograph taken when she entered high school. She was sitting on a chair in a garden, with sunflowers in bloom around her. It was summer, and she had on denim shorts and a white T-shirt. She was gorgeous. Facing the camera, she was smiling

broadly. Compared to her smile now, she looked a bit self-conscious. Even so, it was a wonderful smile. The kind of smile that, through its very precariousness, affected people all the more. Certainly not the smile of a lonely girl spending each day in misery.

"Judging by this picture," I told her, "I'd say you were the happiest girl in the world."

She shook her head slowly. Charming lines appeared at the corners of her eyes; she looked as if she were recalling some far-off scene from the past. "Hajime, you can't tell anything from photographs. They're just a shadow. The real me is far away. That won't show up in a picture."

The photograph brought a pain to my chest. It made me realize what an awful amount of time I had lost. Precious years that could never be recovered, no matter how much I struggled to bring them back. Time that existed only then, only in that place. I gazed at the photo for the longest time.

"What's so interesting about the picture?" she asked.

"I'm trying to fill in time," I replied. "It's been twenty-five years since I saw you last. I want to fill in that gap, even a little."

She smiled and looked at me quizzically, as if there was something weird about my face. "It's strange," she said. "You want to fill in that blank space of time, but I want to keep it all blank."

From junior high through high school, she never had a real boyfriend. She was a beautiful girl, so boys paid attention to her, but she barely noticed them. She went out with a few, but never for very long.

"Boys that age are hard to like. You understand.

Teenage boys are uncouth and selfish. And all they can think about is getting their hand up a girl's skirt. I was so disappointed. I wanted what the two of us used to have."

"Yeah, but when I was sixteen I wasn't any different— uncouth, selfish, and trying to get my hand up a girl's skirt. That was me in a nutshell."

"I guess it was better I didn't meet you then," she said, and smiled. "Saying goodbye at twelve, meeting again at thirty-seven . . . maybe this is the best way for us, after all."

"I wonder."

"Now you're able to think of a few things other than what's under a girl's skirt, right?"

"A few," I said. "But if that's got you worried, maybe next time you'd better wear pants!"

Shimamoto gazed at her hands, resting on the table- top, and laughed. She didn't wear a ring. A bracelet, and a new watch every time we met. And earrings. But never a ring.

"I didn't want to be a burden to any boy," she contin- ued. "You know what I mean. There were so many things I couldn't do. Going on picnics, swimming, ski- ing, skating, dancing at a disco. It was hard enough just to walk. All I could do was sit with someone, talk, and listen to music, which boys that age couldn't stand for very long. And I hated that."

She drank Perrier with a twist of lemon. It was a warm afternoon in the middle of March. Some of the young people passing by on the street outside were decked out in short-sleeved shirts.

"If I had gone out with you then, I know I would have ended up being a burden to you. You would soon have been fed up with me. You would have wanted to be more active, to take a running leap into the wide world outside. And I wouldn't have been able to endure it."

"Shimamoto-san," I said, "that's impossible. I never would have been impatient with you. We had something very special. I can't explain it in words, but it's true. A special, precious something."

She looked at me closely, her expression unchanged.

"I'm not some great person," I continued. "I'm not much to brag about. I used to be pretty crude, insensitive, and arrogant. So maybe I wouldn't have been the right person for you. But there is one thing I am certain about: I never, *ever* would have been fed up with you. That, at least, makes me different from other people you knew. In that sense I am indeed a special person for you."

Shimamoto's gaze again shifted to her hands on the table. She lightly spread her fingers, as if checking all ten of them.

"Hajime," she began, "the sad truth is that certain types of things can't go backward. Once they start going forward, no matter what you do, they can't go back the way they were. If even one little thing goes awry, then that's how it will stay forever."

Once, she called to invite me to a concert of Liszt piano concertos. The soloist was a famous South American pianist. I cleared my schedule and went with her to the concert hall at Ueno Park. The performance was

brilliant. The soloist's technique was outstanding, the music both delicate and deep, and the pianist's heated emotions were there for all to feel. Still, even with my eyes closed, the music didn't sweep me away. A thin curtain stood between myself and the pianist, and no matter how much I might try, I couldn't get to the other side. When I told Shimamoto this after the concert, she agreed.

"But what was wrong with the performance?" she asked. "I thought it was wonderful."

"Don't you remember?" I said. "The record we used to listen to, at the end of the second movement there was this tiny scratch you could hear. *Putchi! Putchi!* Somehow, without that scratch, I can't get into the music!"

Shimamoto laughed. "I wouldn't exactly call that art appreciation."

"This has nothing to do with art. Let a bald vulture eat that up, for all I care. I don't care what anybody says; I like that scratch!"

"Maybe you're right," she admitted. "But what's this about a bald vulture? Regular vultures I know about—they eat corpses. But bald vultures?"

In the train on the way home, I explained the difference in great detail. The difference in where they are born, their call, their mating periods. "The bald vulture lives by devouring art. The regular vulture lives by devouring the corpses of unknown people. They're completely different."

"You're a strange one!" She laughed. And there in the train seat, ever so slightly, she moved her shoulder to touch mine. The one and only time in the past two months our bodies touched.

March passed, and so did April. My younger daughter started going to nursery school. With the kids away from home, Yukiko began doing volunteer work in the community, helping out at a home for handicapped children. Most of the time it was my job to take the kids to school and pick them up again. Whenever I was busy, my wife took over. Watching the children grow, day by day, I could feel myself aging. All by themselves, regardless of any plans I might have for them, my children were getting bigger. I loved my daughters, of course. Watching them grow up made me happier than anything. Sometimes, though, seeing them grow bigger by the month made me feel oppressed. It was as if a tree were growing inside my body, laying down roots, spreading its branches, pushing down on my organs, my muscles, bones, and skin, forcing its way outward. It was so stifling at times that I couldn't sleep.

Once a week I met Shimamoto. And daily I shuttled my daughters back and forth to school. And a couple of times a week I made love to my wife. Since starting to see Shimamoto again, I made love to Yukiko more often. Not out of guilt, though. Loving her, and being loved, was the only way I could hold myself together.

"You've changed. What's going on?" Yukiko asked me one afternoon after sex. "Nobody told me that when men reach thirty-seven their sex drive goes into high gear."

"Nothing's going on. Same old same old," I replied.

She looked at me for a while. And shook her head slightly. "My oh my, I wonder what's going on inside that head of yours," she said.

In my free time I listened to classical music and gazed

out at Aoyama Cemetery. I didn't read as much as I used to. My concentration was shot to hell.

Several times I saw the young woman in the Mercedes 260E. Waiting for our daughters to come out the school gate, we stood there, making small talk, the kind of gossip only someone living in Aoyama would comprehend. Advice about which supermarket lot you could find parking space in, and when; the latest on a certain Italian restaurant, which had changed chefs and now couldn't serve decent food; news that the Meiji-ya import store was having a sale on imported wine next month, etc. Damn, I thought. I've become a regular gossipy hausfrau! But these things were all we had in common.

In the middle of April, Shimamoto disappeared again. The last time I saw her, we were sitting in the Robin's Nest. Just before ten, a phone call came from my other bar, something I had to take care of right away. "I'll be back in thirty minutes or so," I told her.

"All right," she said, smiling. "I'll read a book while you're gone."

I rushed to take care of the chore, then hurried back to the bar, but she was no longer there. It was a little past eleven. On the counter, on the back of a match book, she'd left a message: "Probably I won't be able to come here for a while," the note said. "I have to go home now. Goodbye. Take care."

I was at loose ends for days. I paced around my house, wandered the streets aimlessly, and went to pick up my daughters early. And I talked with the Mercedes

260E lady. We went to a nearby coffee shop to have a cup of coffee, gossiping as usual about the state of the vegetables at the Kinokuniya Market, the fertilized eggs at the Natural House food store, the bargain sales at Miki House. The woman was a fan of Inaba Yoshie's designer wear, and before the season arrived she ordered all the clothes she wanted from the catalog. We talked, too, about the wonderful eel restaurant near the police box on Omote Sando, which was no longer in business. We enjoyed talking. The woman was more friendly and open than she had first appeared to be. Not that I was sexually attracted to her. I just needed someone—anyone—to talk to. What I wanted was harmless, meaningless talk, talk that would lead anywhere but back to Shimamoto.

When I ran out of things to do, I'd go shopping. Once, on a whim, I bought six shirts. I bought toys and dolls for my daughters, accessories for Yukiko. I stopped by the BMW showroom a couple of times to check out the M5; I didn't really plan to buy one but let the salesman give me his pitch.

A few unsettled weeks like this, and I found myself again able to concentrate. I'm going nowhere fast here, I decided. So I called a designer and an interior decorator to discuss remodeling the bars. They were overdue for a little remodeling anyway, and it was high time I did some serious thinking about how I ran my business. Just like with people, with bars there's a time to leave them alone and a time for change. Being stuck in the same environment, you grow dull and lethargic. Your energy level takes a nosedive. Even castles in the air can

do with a fresh coat of paint. I started with the other bar, saving the Robin's Nest for later. I began by removing all the hyper-chic aspects of the bar, which, when you came right down to it, were a pain in the butt, the whole point being to come up with an efficient, functional workplace. The audio system and air conditioning were about due for an overhaul too, as was the menu, which I drastically revamped. I interviewed my employees and came up with a hefty list of suggested improvements. In great detail I laid out to the designer my vision of what the bar should be, had him draw up a plan, then sent him back to the drawing board to incorporate features that had popped into my head in the meantime. We repeated this process a number of times. I selected all the materials, had the contractors draw up estimates, readjusted my budget. I spent three weeks scouring shops throughout Tokyo in search of the world's greatest soap dispenser. All of this kept me extremely busy. But that, after all, was precisely what I was after.

May came and went, then it was June. Still no Shimamoto. I was sure she was gone forever. *Probably I won't be able to come here for a while,* she'd written. It was this *probably* and *for a while* and the ambiguity inherent in them that made me suffer. Someday she might show up again. But I couldn't just sit around, resting my hopes and dreams on vague promises. Keep on like this, I thought, and I'll end up a blithering idiot, so I concentrated on keeping myself busy. I started going to the pool every morning, and I'd swim two thousand meters without stopping, then go upstairs to the gym

for weight lifting. A week of that, and my muscles started to rebel. Waiting at a stoplight one day, I felt my left foot go numb, and I couldn't step on the clutch. Finally, though, my muscles got used to the workout. Hard physical effort left no room to think, and keeping my body always in motion helped me concentrate on the trivia of daily life. Daydreaming was forbidden. I tried my best to concentrate on whatever I was doing. Washing my face, I focused on that; listening to music, I was all music. It was the only way I could survive.

In the summer, Yukiko and I often took the kids to our cottage in Hakone. Away from Tokyo, in the great outdoors, Yukiko and the children were relaxed and happy. They picked flowers, watched birds with binoculars, played tag, splashed about in the river. Or else they just lay around in the yard. But they didn't know the truth. That on a certain snowy winter day, if my plane had been grounded, I would have thrown them all away to be with Shimamoto. My job, my family, my money—everything, without flinching. And here I was, my head still full of Shimamoto. The sensation of holding her, of kissing her cheek, wouldn't leave me. I couldn't drive the image of Shimamoto from my mind and replace it with my wife. Just as I could never tell what Shimamoto was thinking, no one had a clue to what was in my mind.

I decided to spend the rest of our summer vacation finishing up the remodeling. While Yukiko and the children were in Hakone, I stayed in Tokyo alone to supervise the work and give last-minute instructions. I'd swim in the pool, work out at the gym. On weekends I'd

go to Hakone, swim in the Fujiya Hotel pool with my kids, and we'd all have dinner together. And at night I'd make love to my wife.

I was fast approaching middle age, yet had no extra fat to speak of, no thinning hair. Not a single white hair, either. Exercise helped keep the inevitable physical decline at bay. Lead a well-regulated life, never overdo anything, and watch your diet: that was my motto. I never got sick, and most people would have guessed I was barely thirty.

My wife loved to touch my body. She'd touch the muscles on my chest and stomach, and fondle my penis and balls. Yukiko, too, was going to the gym to work out regularly. But it didn't seem to slim her down.

"Must be getting old," she sighed. "My weight goes down, but this roll of pudge is still here."

"I like your body just the way it is," I told her. "You're fine the way you are—no need to work out or go on diets. It's not like you're fat or anything." Which wasn't a lie. I really did like the softness of her body with its bit of extra flesh. I loved to rub her naked back.

"You just don't get it," she said, shaking her head. "You say it's okay for me to look the way I am now, but it takes every ounce of energy I have just to stay in the same place."

An outsider would probably have said we had an ideal life. Certainly I was convinced of it at times. I was fired up about my work and was taking in a good deal of money. I owned a four-bedroom condo in Aoyama, a small cottage in the mountains of Hakone, a BMW, a Jeep Cherokee. And I had a happy family. I loved my wife and my two daughters. What more could anyone

ask for? If, say, Yukiko and the kids had begged me to tell them what they should do to be even better to me, to be loved even more, there was nothing I could have said. I could not imagine a happier life.

But since Shimamoto had stopped coming to see me, I was stuck on the airless surface of the moon. If she was gone forever, no one remained to whom I could reveal my true feelings. On sleepless nights I'd lie in bed and replay over and over in my mind that scene at the snowy Komatsu Airport. Recall it enough times, and the memories would start to fade. Or so I thought. The more I remembered, the stronger the memories became. The word "Delayed" flashing on the flight information board; outside the window, the snow coming down hard. You couldn't see more than fifty yards. On the bench, Shimamoto sat still, hugging herself tight. Her navy pea coat and muffler. Her body with its mixed scent of tears and sadness. I could smell that scent. Beside me, in bed, my wife breathed quietly, asleep. She knows nothing. I closed my eyes and shook my head. *She knows nothing.*

The abandoned bowling alley parking lot, my melting snow in my mouth and feeding it to her. Shimamoto in the airplane, in my arms. Her closed eyes, the sigh from her slightly parted lips. Her body, soft and limp. She wanted me then. Her heart was open to me. Yet I held myself back, back on the surface of the moon, stuck in this lifeless world. And in the end she left me, and my life was lost all over again.

Sometimes I'd wake up at two or three in the morning and not be able to fall asleep again. I'd get out of bed, go to the kitchen, and pour myself a whiskey. Glass

in hand, I'd look down at the darkened cemetery across the way and the headlights of the cars on the road. The moments of time linking night and dawn were long and dark. If I could cry, it might make things easier. But what would I cry over? Who would I cry for? I was too self-centered to cry for other people, too old to cry for myself.

Autumn finally arrived. And when it did, I came to a decision. Something had to give: I couldn't keep on living like this.

13

In the morning after dropping off my daughters at nursery school, I went to the pool and swam my usual two thousand meters. I imagined I was a fish. Just a fish, with no need to think, not even about swimming. Next I showered, changed into a T-shirt and shorts, and started pumping iron.

Then I headed to the one-room flat I used as an office and set to checking the account books, figuring my employees' pay, working on the plan for remodeling the Robin's Nest the following February. At one, as usual, I went home and had lunch with my wife.

"Honey, I had a call from my father this morning," Yukiko said. "Busy as always. He said there's this stock that'll go through the roof, and we should buy as much

as we could manage. Not your run-of-the-mill stock tip, he said, but something extra special."

"If it's going to earn that much, he shouldn't tell us about it but should keep it to himself. Wonder why he didn't."

"He said this was his personal way of saying thanks to you. He said you'd understand what he meant. Do you? He's letting us have his share, you see. He said to invest all the money we have and not to worry, because this stock was hot. If somehow it didn't turn a profit, he'd make sure we didn't lose a penny."

I rested my fork on my plate of pasta. "Anything else?"

"Well, he said we had to move quickly, so I called the bank and had them close out our savings accounts and send the money to Mr. Nakayama at the investment firm. So he could buy the stock. I was only able to scrape together about eight million yen. Maybe I should have bought even more?"

I drank some water. And tried to find the right words. "Before you did all that, why didn't you ask me?"

"Ask you?" she said, surprised. "But you always buy the stocks my father tells you to. You've had me do it any number of times, haven't you? You always tell me to just go ahead and do what I think is right. So that's what I did. My father said there wasn't a minute to lose. You were at the pool and I couldn't get in touch with you. So what's the problem?"

"It's all right," I said. "But I want you to sell all the stock."

"*Sell it?*" She screwed up her eyes as if blinded by a glaring light.

"Sell all the stock you bought, and put the money back in our savings accounts."

"But if I do that, we'll have to pay a lot in transaction fees."

"I don't care," I said. "Just pay it. I don't care if we end up losing. Just sell everything you bought today."

Yukiko sighed. "What happened between you and Father? What's going on?"

I didn't answer.

"What happened?"

"Listen, Yukiko," I began, "I'm getting sick of all this. I don't want to earn money in the stock market. I want to earn money by working with my own hands. I've done a good job up till now. You haven't wanted for money, have you?"

"I know you've done a good job, and I haven't complained once. I'm grateful to you, and you know I respect you. But still, my father's doing this to help us out. Don't you understand that?"

"I understand. Yukiko, do you know what insider trading is? Do you know what it means when somebody tells you there's a one hundred percent chance you'll turn a profit?"

"No."

"It's called stock manipulation," I said. "Somebody inside a company manipulates the stock to rack up an artificial profit, then he and his pals split up the proceeds. And that money makes its way into politicians' pockets or ends up as corporate bribes. This isn't like the kind of stock your father urged me to buy before. That kind of stock *probably* was going to make a profit. That was just

welcome information, nothing more. And most of the time the stock did go up, but not every time. This time is different. This stinks. And I don't want to have anything to do with it."

Fork in hand, Yukiko was lost in thought.

"How can you be sure this is a case of stock manipulation?"

"If you really want to know that, ask your father," I said. "But I can tell you this: stock that's guaranteed not to go down can only result from illegal deals. My father worked in an investment firm for forty years. Worked hard from morning to night. But all he left behind was a crummy little house. Maybe he just wasn't good at it. Every night, my mother was hunched over the household account books, worried over a hundred or two hundred yen that didn't balance. That's the kind of family I was raised in. You said you can only come up with eight million yen. Yukiko, we're talking about real money here, not Monopoly money. Most people ride to work every day, smashed together in packed trains, put in overtime, knock themselves out, and still couldn't come near making that much in a year. I lived that kind of life for eight years, so I know. And there was no way I could make eight million yen. But you probably can't picture that kind of life."

Yukiko was silent. She bit her lip and stared hard at her plate. Realizing that I'd begun to raise my voice, I lowered it.

"You can blithely say that in half a month the money we invest will double. Eight million yen will turn into sixteen million. But something's very wrong with that

kind of thinking. I've found myself sucked into that mind-set, and it makes me feel empty."

Yukiko looked at me from across the table. As I resumed eating, I could feel something inside me shaking. Was it irritation or anger? I couldn't tell. Whatever it was, I was helpless before it.

"I'm sorry. I should have minded my own business," Yukiko said quietly, after a long silence.

"It's okay. I'm not blaming you. I'm not blaming anybody."

"I'll call right now and have them sell every single share. Just stop being angry with me."

"I'm not angry."

Silent, I continued to eat.

"Isn't there something you want to tell me?" Yukiko asked, looking straight at me. "If something is bothering you, tell me. Even if it's something that's hard to talk about. If there's anything I can do, just name it. I'm only an ordinary person, and I know I'm completely naive about everything—including running a business. But I can't stand to see you unhappy. I don't want to see that pained look on your face. What is it you hate about our life? Tell me."

I shook my head. "I have no complaints. I like my job, and I love you. All I'm saying is that sometimes I can't keep up with your father's way of doing things. Don't get me wrong, I like him. I know he's trying to help us out, and I appreciate it. So I'm not angry. I just can't understand who I am anymore. I can't tell right from wrong. So I'm confused. But not angry."

"You certainly look angry."

I sighed.

"And you sigh all the time," she said. "Anyhow, something's definitely bothering you. Your mind's a million miles away."

"I don't know."

Yukiko kept her eyes on me. "There's something on your mind," she said. "But I have no idea what that is. I wish there was something I could do to help."

I was struck by a violent desire to confess everything. What a relief that would be! No more hiding, no more need to playact or to lie. *Yukiko, see, there's another woman I love, someone I just can't forget. I've held back, trying to keep our world from crumbling, but I can't hold back anymore. The next time she shows up, I don't care what happens: I'm going to make love to her. I've thought of her while I've masturbated. I've thought of her while I've made love to you, Yukiko....* But I didn't say anything. Confession would serve no purpose. It would only make us miserable.

After lunch, I returned to my office to continue work. But my mind, indeed, was a million miles away. I felt lousy, preaching to Yukiko like that. *What* I said was all right. But the person who said it was all wrong. I'd lied to Yukiko, sneaking around behind her back. I was the last person who should take the moral high ground. Yukiko was trying very hard to think about me. That was quite clear, and consistent with the kind of person she was. But what about my life? Was there any consistency, any conviction to speak of? I felt deflated, utterly lacking the will to move.

I put my feet up on my desk and, pencil in hand, gazed listlessly out the window. From my office you could see a park. The weather was nice, and there were a number of parents with their children. The children played in the sandbox or slid down the slides, while their mothers kept an eye on them and chatted with other mothers. Seeing these little children at play reminded me of my own daughters. I wanted to see them, to once again walk down the street holding the two of them in my arms. I wanted to feel the warmth of their bodies. But thoughts of them led inexorably to memories of Shimamoto. Vivid memories of her slightly parted lips. Thoughts of my daughters were crowded out by the image of Shimamoto. I could think of nothing else.

I left my office and took a walk down the main street in Aoyama. I went in the coffee shop where Shimamoto and I used to rendezvous, and had some coffee. I read a book and, when I tired of reading, thought again of her. I recalled fragments of our conversations, how she'd take a Salem out of her bag and light it, how she'd casually brush back a lock of hair, how she tilted her head slightly as she smiled. Soon I grew tired of sitting there alone and set out for a walk toward Shibuya. I used to like to walk the city streets, gazing at the buildings and shops, watching all the people. I liked the feeling of moving through the city on my own two feet. Now, though, the city was depressing and empty. Buildings were falling apart, all the trees had lost their color, and every passerby was devoid of feelings, and of dreams.

Looking for an unpopular movie, I entered the the-

ater and watched the screen intently. When the movie was over, I walked out into the evening city streets, went into a restaurant I happened to pass, and had a simple meal. Shibuya was packed with office workers on their way home. Like a speeded-up film, trains pulled into the station and swallowed up one crowd after another. It was right around here, I suddenly recalled, that I'd caught sight of Shimamoto, some ten years before, in her red overcoat and sunglasses. It might have been a million years ago.

Everything came back to me. The end-of-year crowds, the way she walked, each corner we turned, the cloudy sky, the department store bag she carried, the coffee cup she didn't touch, the Christmas carols. Once again a pang of regret swept over me for not having called out to her. I had nothing to tie me down then, nothing to lose. I could have held her close, and the two of us could have walked off together. No matter what situation she was stuck in, we could have found a way out. But I'd lost that chance forever. A mysterious middle-aged guy grabbed me by the elbow, and Shimamoto slipped into a taxi and disappeared.

I took a crowded evening train back. The weather had taken a turn for the worse while I was watching the movie, and the sky was covered with heavy, wet-looking clouds. It looked like it was going to rain at any minute. I had no umbrella with me and was dressed in the yacht parka, blue jeans, and sneakers I'd set out in that morning when I went to the pool. I should have gone home to change into my usual suit. But I didn't feel like it. No matter, I'd decided. I could skip the necktie for once—no harm done.

By seven it was raining. A gentle rain, the kind of autumn drizzle that looked like it would last. As I usually did, I stopped by the remodeled bar first to check out how business was. The place had ended up pretty much as I had envisioned it. The bar was a much more relaxed, efficient place to work. The lighting was more subdued, and the music enhanced this mood. I had designed a small separate kitchen, hired a professional chef, and made up a new menu of simple yet elegant dishes. The kind of dishes that had no extra ingredients or flourishes but which an amateur could never master. They were intended, after all, as snacks to accompany drinks, so they had to be easy to eat. Every month, we changed the menu completely. It had been no easy task to find the kind of chef I had in mind. I finally did locate one, though it cost me, much more than I'd bargained for. But he earned his pay, and I was satisfied. My customers seemed pleased too.

Around nine, I borrowed an umbrella from the bar and headed over to the Robin's Nest. And at nine-thirty, Shimamoto showed up. Strangely enough, she always appeared on quiet, rainy evenings.

14

She wore a white dress and an oversize navy-blue jacket. A small fish-shaped silver brooch graced the collar of her jacket. The dress was simple in design, with no decorations of any kind, yet on her, you'd swear it was the world's most expensive dress. She was more tanned than the last time I'd seen her.

"I thought you'd never come here again," I said.

"Every time I see you, you say the same thing," she said, laughing. As always, she sat down next to me at the bar and rested both hands on the counter. "But I did write you a note saying I wouldn't be back for a while, didn't I?"

"*For a while* is a phrase whose length can't be measured. At least by the person who's waiting," I said.

"But there must be times when that word's necessary. Situations when that's the only possible word you can use," she said.

"And *probably* is a word whose weight is incalculable."

"You're right," she said, her face lit up by her usual smile, a gentle breeze blowing from somewhere far away. "I apologize. I'm not trying to excuse myself, but there was nothing I could do about it. Those were the only words I could have used."

"No need to apologize. As I told you once, this is a bar, and you're a customer. You come here when you want to. I'm used to it. I'm just mouthing off to myself. Pay no attention."

She called the bartender over and ordered a cocktail. She looked closely at me, as if inspecting me. "You're dressed pretty casually for a change."

"I went swimming this morning and haven't changed. I haven't had time," I said. "But I kind of like it. I feel this is the real me again."

"You look younger. No one would guess you're thirty-seven."

"You don't look thirty-seven, either."

"But I don't look twelve."

"True enough," I said.

Her cocktail arrived, and she took a sip. And gently closed her eyes as if listening to some far-off sound. With her eyes closed, I could once more make out the small line just above her eyelids.

"Hajime," she said, "I've been thinking about your bar's cocktails. I really wanted to have one. No matter where you go, you can never find drinks like the ones here."

"Did you go somewhere far away?"

"Why do you say that?" she asked.

"Something about you," I replied. "A certain air. Like you've been gone for some time far away."

She looked up at me. And nodded. "Hajime, for a long time I've . . . ," she began, but fell suddenly silent, as if reminded of something. I could tell she was searching inside herself for the right words. Which she couldn't find. She bit her lip and smiled once more. "Anyhow, I'm sorry. I should have got in touch with you. But I wanted to leave certain things as they are. Preserved, so to speak. Either I come here or I don't. When I do come here, I do. When I don't . . . I'm somewhere else."

"There's no middle ground?"

"No middle ground," she said. "Why? Because no middle-ground things exist there."

"In a place where there are no middle-ground objects, no middle ground exists," I said.

"Exactly."

"In a place where no dogs exist, there are no doghouses, in other words."

"Yes; no dogs, no doghouses," Shimamoto said. And she looked at me in a funny way. "You have a strange sense of humor, do you know that?"

As it often did, the piano trio began playing "Star-Crossed Lovers." For a while the two of us sat there, listening silently.

"Mind if I ask you one question?"

"Not at all," I said.

"What's the deal with you and this song?" she asked. "Every time you're here, it seems, they play that number. A house rule of some sort?"

"No. They just know I like it."

"It is a beautiful song."

I nodded. "It took me a long time to figure out how complex it is, how there's so much more to it than just a pretty melody. It takes a special kind of musician to play it right," I said. "Duke Ellington and Billy Strayhorn wrote it a long time ago. Fifty-seven, I believe."

"When they say 'star-crossed,' what do they mean?"

"You know—lovers born under an unlucky star. Unlucky lovers. Here it's referring to Romeo and Juliet. Ellington and Strayhorn wrote it for a performance at the Ontario Shakespeare Festival. In the original recording, Johnny Hodges' alto sax was Juliet, and Paul Gonsalves played the Romeo part on tenor sax."

"Lovers born under an unlucky star," she said. "Sounds like it was written for the two of us."

"You mean we're lovers?"

"You think we're not?"

I looked at her. She wasn't smiling anymore. I could make out a faint glimmer deep within her eyes.

"Shimamoto-san, I don't know anything about you," I said. "Every time I look in your eyes, I feel that. The most I can say about you is how you were at age twelve. The Shimamoto-san who lived in the neighborhood and was in my class. But that was twenty-five years ago. The Twist was in, and people still rode in streetcars. No cassette tapes, no tampons, no bullet train, no diet food. I'm talking long ago. Other than what I know about you then, I'm in the dark."

"Is that what you see in my eyes? That you know nothing about me?"

"Nothing's written in your eyes," I replied. "It's written in *my* eyes. I just see the reflection in yours."

"Hajime," she said, "I know I should be telling you more. I do. There's nothing I can do about it. So please don't say anything further."

"Like I said, I'm just mouthing off to myself. Don't give it a second thought."

She raised a hand to her collar and fingered the fish brooch. And quietly listened to the piano trio. When their performance ended, she clapped and took a sip of her cocktail. Finally she let out a long sigh and turned to me. "Six months is a long time," she said. "But most likely, probably, I'll be able to come here for a while."

"The old magic words," I said.

"Magic words?"

"*Probably* and *for a while.*"

She smiled and looked at me. She took a cigarette out of her small bag and lit it with a lighter.

"Sometimes when I look at you, I feel I'm gazing at a distant star," I said. "It's dazzling, but the light is from tens of thousands of years ago. Maybe the star doesn't even exist anymore. Yet sometimes that light seems more real to me than anything."

Shimamoto said nothing.

"You're here," I continued. "At least you look as if you're here. But maybe you aren't. Maybe it's just your shadow. The real you may be someplace else. Or maybe you already disappeared, a long, long time ago. I reach out my hand to see, but you've hidden yourself behind a cloud of *probablys*. Do you think we can go on like this forever?"

"Possibly. For the time being," she answered.

"I see I'm not the only one with a strange sense of humor," I said. And smiled.

She smiled too. The rain has stopped, without a sound there's a break in the clouds, and the very first rays of sunlight shine through—that kind of smile. Small, warm lines at the corners of her eyes, holding out the promise of something wonderful.

"Hajime," she said, "I brought you a present."

She passed me a beautifully wrapped package with a red bow.

"Looks like a record," I said, gauging its size and shape.

"It's a Nat King Cole record. The one we used to listen to together. Remember? I'm giving it to you."

"Thanks. But don't you want it? As a keepsake from your father?"

"I have more. This one's for you."

I gazed at the record, wrapped and beribboned. Before long, all the sounds around me—the clamor of the people at the bar, the piano trio's music—all faded in the distance, as if the tide had gone out. Only she and I remained. Everything else was an illusion, papier-mâché props on a stage. What existed, what was *real*, was the two of us.

"Shimamoto-san," I said, "what do you say we go somewhere and listen to this together?"

"That would be wonderful," she said.

"I have a small cottage in Hakone. It's empty now, and there's a stereo there. This time of night, we could drive there in an hour and a half."

She looked at her watch. And then at me. "You want to go there now?"

"Yes," I said.

She narrowed her eyes. "But it's already past ten. If we went to Hakone now, it would be very late when we came back. Don't you mind?"

"No. Do you?"

Once more she looked at her watch. And closed her eyes for a good ten seconds. When she reopened them, her face was filled with an entirely new expression, as if she'd gone far away, left something there, and returned. "All right," she said. "Let's go."

I called to the acting manager and asked him to take care of things in my absence—lock up the register, organize the receipts, and deposit the profits in the bank's night deposit box. I walked over to my condo and drove the BMW out of the underground garage. And called my wife from a nearby telephone booth, telling her I was off to Hakone.

"At this hour?" she said, surprised. "Why do you have to go all the way to Hakone at this hour?"

"There's something I need to think over," I said.

"So you won't be back tonight?"

"Probably not."

"Honey, I've been thinking over what happened, and I'm really sorry. You were right. I got rid of all the stock. So why don't you come on home?"

"Yukiko, I'm not angry at you. Not at all. Forget about that. I just want some time to think. Give me one night, okay?"

She said nothing for a while. Then: "All right." She sounded exhausted. "Go ahead to Hakone. But be careful driving. It's raining."

"I will."

"There's so much I don't understand," my wife said. "Tell me one thing: am I in your way?"

"Not at all," I replied. "It has nothing to do with you. If anything, the problem's with me. So don't worry about it, okay? I just want some time to think."

I hung up and drove to the bar. I could tell from Yukiko's voice that she'd been mulling over our lunchtime conversation. She was tired, confused. It saddened me. The rain was still falling hard. I let Shimamoto into the car.

"Isn't there someplace you need to call before we go?" I asked.

Silently she shook her head. And, as she did on the way back from Haneda Airport, she pressed her face against the glass and stared at the scenery.

There was little traffic on the way to Hakone. I got off the Tomei Highway at Atsugi and headed straight to Odawara on the expressway. I kept our speed between eighty and ninety miles per hour. The rain came down in sheets from time to time, but I knew every curve and hill along the way. After we got on the highway, Shimamoto and I said hardly a word. I played a Mozart quartet quietly and kept my eyes on the road. Shimamoto was lost in thought as she looked out the window. Occasionally she'd glance over at me. Whenever she did, my throat went dry. Forcing myself to relax, I swallowed a couple of times.

"Hajime," she said. We were near Kouzu. "You don't listen to jazz much outside the bar?"

"No, I don't. Mostly classical music."

"How come?"

"I guess because jazz is part of my job. Outside the club, I like to listen to something different. Sometimes rock too, but hardly ever jazz."

"What type of music does your wife listen to?"

"Usually whatever I'm listening to. She hardly ever plays any records on her own. I'm not even sure if she knows how to use the turntable."

Shimamoto reached over to the cassette case and pulled out a couple of tapes. One of them contained the children's songs my daughters and I sang together in the car. "The Doggy Policeman," "Tulip"—the Japanese equivalent of Barney's Greatest Hits. From her expression as she gazed at the cassette and its picture of Snoopy on the cover, you'd think she'd discovered a relic from outer space.

Again she turned to gaze at me. "Hajime," she said after a while. "When I look at you driving, sometimes I want to grab the steering wheel and give it a yank. It'd kill us, wouldn't it."

"We'd die, all right. We're going eighty miles an hour."

"You'd rather not die with me?"

"I can think of more pleasant ways to go." I laughed. "And besides, we haven't listened to the record yet. That's the reason we're here, right?"

"Don't worry," she said. "I won't do anything like that. The thought just crosses my mind from time to time."

It was only the beginning of October, but nights in Hakone were chilly. We arrived at the cottage, and I turned on the lights and lit the gas stove in the living room. And took down a bottle of brandy and two

snifters from the shelf. We sat next to each other on the sofa, as we used to do so many years before, and I put the Nat King Cole record on the turntable. The red glow from the stove was reflected in our brandy glasses. Shimamoto sat with her legs folded underneath her. She rested one arm on the back of the sofa, the other in her lap. The same as in the old days. Back then she probably wanted to hide her leg, and the habit remained even now. Nat King Cole was singing "South of the Border." How many years had it been since I heard that tune?

"When I was a kid and listened to this record, I used to wonder what it was that lay south of the border," I said.

"Me too," she said. "When I grew up and could read the English lyrics, I was disappointed. It was just a song about Mexico. I'd always thought something great lay south of the border."

"Like what?"

Shimamoto brushed her hair back and lightly gathered it behind. "I'm not sure. Something beautiful, big, and soft."

"Something beautiful, big, and soft," I repeated. "Was it edible?"

She laughed. Her white teeth showed faintly. "I doubt it."

"Something you can touch?"

"Probably."

"Again with the *probablys*."

"A world full of *probablys*," she said.

I stretched out my hand and laid it on top of her fingers on the back of the sofa. I hadn't touched her body

for so very long, not since the plane ride back from Ishikawa. As my fingers grazed hers, she looked up at me briefly, then down again.

"South of the border, west of the sun," she said.

"West of the sun?"

"Have you heard of the illness hysteria siberiana?"

"No."

"I read this somewhere a long time ago. Might have been in junior high. I can't for the life of me recall what book I read it in. Anyway, it affects farmers living in Siberia. Try to imagine this. You're a farmer, living all alone on the Siberian tundra. Day after day you plow your fields. As far as the eye can see, nothing. To the north, the horizon, to the east, the horizon, to the south, to the west, more of the same. Every morning, when the sun rises in the east, you go out to work in your fields. When it's directly overhead, you take a break for lunch. When it sinks in the west, you go home to sleep."

"Not exactly the lifestyle of an Aoyama bar owner."

"Hardly." She smiled and inclined her head ever so slightly. "Anyway, that cycle continues, year after year."

"But in Siberia they don't work in the fields in winter."

"They rest in the winter," she said. "In the winter they stay home and do indoor work. When spring comes, they head out to the fields again. You're that farmer. Imagine it."

"Okay," I said.

"And then one day, something inside you dies."

"What do you mean?"

She shook her head. "I don't know. Something. Day after day you watch the sun rise in the east, pass across

the sky, then sink in the west, and something breaks inside you and dies. You toss your plow aside and, your head completely empty of thought, begin walking toward the west. Heading toward a land that lies west of the sun. Like someone possessed, you walk on, day after day, not eating or drinking, until you collapse on the ground and die. That's hysteria siberiana."

I tried to conjure up the picture of a Siberian farmer lying dead on the ground.

"But what is there, west of the sun?" I asked.

She again shook her head. "I don't know. Maybe nothing. Or maybe *something*. At any rate, it's different from south of the border."

When Nat King Cole began singing "Pretend," Shimamoto, as she had done so very long before, sang along in a small voice.

> *Pretend you're happy when you're blue*
> *It isn't very hard to do*

"Shimamoto-san," I said, "after you left, I thought about you for a long time. Every day for six months, from morning to night. I tried to stop, but I couldn't. And I came to this conclusion. I can't make it without you. I don't ever want to lose you again. I don't want to hear the words *for a while* anymore. Or *probably*. You'll say we can't see each other for a while, and then you'll disappear. And no one can say when you'll be back. You might never be back, and I might spend the rest of my life never seeing you again. And I couldn't stand that. Life would be meaningless."

Shimamoto looked at me silently, still faintly smiling.

A quiet smile that nothing could ever touch, revealing nothing to me of what lay beyond. Confronted with that smile, I felt as if my own emotions were about to be lost to me. For an instant I lost my bearings, my sense of who and where I was. After a while, though, words returned.

"I love you," I told her. "Nothing can change it. Special feelings like that should never, ever be taken away. I've lost you many times. But I should never have let you go. These last several months have taught me that. I love you, and I don't want you ever to leave me."

After I finished, she closed her eyes. The fire from the stove burned, and Nat King Cole kept on singing his old songs. I should say something more, I thought, but I could think of nothing.

"Hajime," she began, "this is very important, so listen carefully. As I told you before, there is no middle ground with me. You take either all of me or nothing. That's the way it works. If you don't mind continuing the way we are now, I don't see why we can't do that. I don't know how long we'd be able to, but I'll do everything in my power to see that it happens. When I'm able to come see you, I will. But when I can't, I can't. I can't just come to see you whenever I feel like it. You may not be satisfied with that arrangement, but if you don't want me to go away again, you have to take all of me. Everything. All the baggage I carry, everything that clings to me. And I will take all of you. Do you understand that? *Do you understand what that means?*"

"Yes," I said.

"And you still want to be with me?"

"I've already decided, Shimamoto-san," I said. "I thought about it when you were gone, and I made my decision."

"But, Hajime, you have a wife and two children. And you love them. You want to do what's right for them."

"Of course I love them. Very much. And I want to take care of them. But something's missing. I have a family, a job, and no complaints about either. You could say I'm happy. Yet I've known ever since I met you again that something is missing. The important question is *what* is missing. Something's lacking. In me and my life. And that part of me is always hungry, always thirsting. Neither my wife nor my children can fill that gap. In the whole world, there's only one person who can do that. You. Only now, when that thirst is satisfied, do I realize how empty I was. And how I've been hungering, thirsting, for so many years. I can't go back to that kind of world."

Shimamoto wrapped both her arms around me and rested her head on my shoulder. I could feel the softness of her body. It pushed against me warmly, insistently.

"I love you too, Hajime. You're the only person I've ever loved. I don't think you realize how very much I love you. I've loved you ever since I was twelve. Whenever anyone else held me, I thought of you. And that's the reason why I didn't want to see you again. If I saw you once, I knew I couldn't stand it anymore. But I couldn't keep myself away. At first I thought I'd just make sure it was really you, then head home. But once I saw you, I had to talk to you." She kept her head on my

shoulder. "Ever since I was twelve, I wanted you to hold me. You never knew that, did you?"

"No, I didn't," I admitted.

"Since I was twelve, I wanted to hold you, naked. You had no idea, I suppose."

I held her close and kissed her. She closed her eyes, not moving. Our tongues wound round each other, and I could feel her heartbeat just below her breasts. A passionate, warm heartbeat. I closed my eyes and thought of the red blood coursing through her veins. I stroked her soft hair and drank in its fragrance. Her hands wandered over my back. The record finished, and the arm moved back to its base. Once again we were wrapped only in the sound of the rain. After a while, she opened her eyes. "Hajime," she whispered, "are you sure this is all right? Are you sure you want to throw away everything for my sake?"

I nodded. "Yes. I've already made up my mind."

"But if you'd never met me, you could have had a peaceful life. With no doubts or dissatisfactions. Don't you think so?"

"Maybe. But I *did* meet you. And we can't undo that," I said. "Just as you told me once, there are certain things you can't undo. You can only go forward. Shimamoto-san, I don't care where we end up; I just know I want to go there with you. And begin again."

"Hajime," she said, "would you take off your clothes and let me see your body?"

"You want just me to take off my clothes?"

"Yes. First you take all your clothes off. I want to look at your body. You don't want to?"

"I don't mind. If you want me to," I said. I undressed

in front of the stove. I took off my yacht parka, polo shirt, blue jeans, socks, T-shirt, underpants. Shimamoto had me get down on both knees on the floor. My penis was already hard, which embarrassed me a little. She moved back slightly to take in the whole scene. She still wore her jacket.

"It seems strange to be the only naked one." I laughed.

"It's lovely, Hajime," she said. She came close to me, gently cradled my penis in her hand, and kissed me on the lips. She put her hands on my chest, and for the longest time licked my nipples and stroked my pubic hair. She put her ear to my navel and took my balls in her mouth. She kissed me all over. Even the soles of my feet. It was as if she were treasuring time itself. Stroking time, caressing it, licking it.

"Aren't you going to undress?" I asked.

"Later on," she replied. "I want to enjoy looking at your body first, touching and licking it as much as I want to. If I got undressed now, you'd want to touch me, right? Even if I told you no, you wouldn't be able to restrain yourself."

"You're right about that."

"I don't want to do it that way. It took us long enough to get here, and I want to take it nice and slow. I want to look at you, touch you with these hands, lick you with my tongue. I want to try everything—*slowly*. If I don't, I can't go on to the next stage. Hajime, if what I do seems a little odd, don't let it bother you, okay? I have to. Don't say anything, just let me do it."

"I don't mind. Do whatever you like. But I do feel a bit weird being stared at like this."

"But you are mine, right?"

"Yes."

"So there's nothing to be embarrassed about, is there."

"Guess you're right," I said. "I've just got to get used to it."

"Just be patient a little bit longer. This has been my dream for such a very long time."

"Looking at my body has been your dream? Touching me all over, with all your clothes still on?"

"Yes," she answered. "I've been imagining your body for ages. What your penis looked like, how hard it would get, how big."

"Why did you think of that?"

"Why?" she asked incredulously. "I told you I love you. What's wrong with thinking about the body of the man you love? Haven't you thought about my body?"

"I have," I said.

"I'll bet you've thought about my body while you're masturbating."

"Yes. In junior high and high school," I said, then corrected myself. "Well, actually, not too long ago."

"It's the same with me. I've thought about your body. Women do too, you know," she said.

I pulled her close to me again and slowly kissed her. Her tongue slid languidly inside my mouth. "I love you, Shimamoto-san," I said.

"I love you, Hajime," she said. "There's no one else I love but you. May I see your body a little more?"

"Go ahead," I replied.

She gently wrapped her palm around my penis and balls. "It's wonderful," she said. "I'd like to eat it all up."

"Then what would I do?"

"But I do want to eat it up," she said. As if gently weighing them, she kept my balls in her palm for the longest time. And licked and sucked my penis very slowly, very carefully. She looked at me. "The first time, can I do it the way I want to? You'll let me?"

"I don't mind. Do whatever you want," I said. "Except for eating me up, of course."

"I'm a little embarrassed, so don't say anything, okay?"

"I won't," I promised.

As I knelt on the floor, she put her left hand around my waist. She kept her dress on but with her other hand peeled off her stockings and panties. Then she took my penis and balls in her right hand and licked them. Her other hand she slid under her dress. Sucking on my penis, she began to move her other hand around slowly.

I didn't say a thing. I figured this was her way. I watched the movements of her lips and tongue, and the languid motion of her hand beneath her skirt. Suddenly I recalled the Shimamoto I'd seen in the parking lot of the bowling lanes—stiff and white as a sheet. I recalled clearly what I'd seen deep within her eyes. A dark space, frozen hard like a subterranean glacier. A silence so profound it sucked up every sound, never allowing it to resurface. Absolute, total silence.

It was the first time I'd been face-to-face with death. So I'd had no distinct image of what death really was. But there it was then, right before my eyes, spread out just inches from my face. So this is the face of death, I'd thought. And death spoke to me, saying that my time, too, would one day come. Eventually everyone would

fall into those endlessly lonely depths, the source of all darkness, a silence bereft of any resonance. I felt a choking, stifling fear as I stared into this bottomless dark pit.

Facing those black, frozen depths, I had called out her name. *Shimamoto-san,* I had called out again and again. But my voice was lost in that infinite nothingness. Cry out as I might, nothing within the depths of her eyes changed. Her breathing remained strange, like the sound of wind whipping through cracks. Her regular breaths told me she was still on this side of the world. But her eyes told me she was already given up to death.

As I had looked deep into her eyes and called out her name, my own body was dragged down into those depths. As if a vacuum had sucked out all the air around me, that other world was steadily pulling me closer. Even now I could feel its power. It wanted *me.*

I closed my eyes tight. And drove those memories from my mind.

I reached out and stroked her hair. I touched her ears, rested my hand on her forehead. Her body was warm and soft. She sucked on my penis as if trying to suck out life itself. Her hand, communicating in some secret sign language, continued to move between her legs, under her skirt. A short time later, I came in her mouth; her hand under her skirt ceased moving, and she closed her eyes. She swallowed down the very last drop of my semen.

"I'm sorry," Shimamoto said.

"There's nothing to apologize for," I said.

"The first time, I wanted to do it this way," she said. "It's embarrassing, but somehow I needed to. It's a rite

of passage for the two of us, I guess. Do you know what I mean?"

I pulled her to me and rubbed my cheek against hers. Her cheek felt warm. I lifted up her hair and kissed her ear. And looked into her eyes. I could see my face reflected in them. Deep within her eyes, in the always bottomless depths, there was a spring. And, ever so faintly, a light. The light of life, I thought. Someday it will be extinguished, but for now the light is there. She smiled at me. The usual small creases formed at the corners of her eyes. I kissed those tiny lines.

"Now it's your turn to take off my clothes," she told me. "And do whatever you want."

"Maybe I'm a little short on imagination, but I just like the regular way. Okay?" I said.

"That's all right," she said. "I like it too."

I took off her dress and her bra, set her down on the bed, and kissed her all over. I looked at every inch of her body, touching everywhere, kissing everywhere. Trying to find out everything and store it in my memory. It was a leisurely exploration. We had taken so very long to arrive at this point, and like her, the last thing I wanted to do was hurry. I held off as long as I could, until I couldn't stand it anymore. Then I slowly slid inside her.

We fell asleep just before dawn. I don't know how many times we made love, sometimes gently, sometimes passionately. Once, in the midst of it, when I was inside her, she became possessed, crying violently and pounding on my back with her fists. All the while, I held her tightly to me. If I didn't hold her tight, I felt, she would

fly off into pieces. I stroked her back over and over to calm her. I kissed her neck and brushed her hair with my fingers. She was no longer the cool, self-controlled Shimamoto I knew. The frozen hardness within her was, bit by bit, melting and floating to the surface. I could feel its breath, far-off signs of its presence. I held her tight and let her trembling seep inside me. Little by little, this is how she would become mine.

"I want to know everything there is to know about you," I said to her. "What kind of life you've had till now, where you live. Whether you're married or not. Everything. No more secrets, 'cause I can't take any more."

"Tomorrow," she said. "Tomorrow I'll tell you everything. So don't ask any more till then. Stay the way you are today. If I did tell you now, you'd never be able to go back to the way you were."

"I'm not going back anyway. And who knows, tomorrow might never come. If it doesn't, I'll end up never knowing."

"I wish tomorrow would never come," she said. "Then you'll never know."

I was about to speak, but she hushed me up with a kiss.

"I wish a bald vulture would gobble up tomorrow," she said. "Would it make sense for a bald vulture to do that?"

"That makes sense. Bald vultures eat up art, and tomorrows as well."

"And regular vultures eat—"

"—the bodies of nameless people," I said. "Very different from bald vultures."

"Bald vultures eat up art and tomorrows, then?"

"Right."

"A nice combination."

"And for dessert they take a bite out of *Books in Print.*"

Shimamoto laughed. "Anyhow, until tomorrow," she said.

And tomorrow came. When I woke up, I was alone. The rain had stopped, and bright, transparent morning light shone in through the bedroom window. The clock showed it was past nine. Shimamoto wasn't in bed, though a slight depression in the pillow beside me hinted at where she had lain. She was nowhere to be seen. I got out of bed and went to the living room to look for her. I looked in the kitchen, the children's room, and the bathroom. Nothing. Her clothes were gone, her shoes as well. I took a deep breath, trying to pull myself back to reality. But that reality was like nothing I'd ever seen before: a reality that didn't seem to fit.

I dressed and went outside. The BMW was parked where I left it the night before. Maybe she'd wakened early and gone out for a walk. I searched for her all around the house, then got in the car and drove as far as the nearest town. But no Shimamoto. I went back to the cottage, but she was not there. Thinking maybe she'd left a note, I scoured the house. But there was nothing. Not a trace that she had ever been there.

Without her, the house was empty and stifling. The air was filled with a gritty layer of dust, which stuck in my throat with each breath. I remembered the record,

the old Nat King Cole record she gave me. But search as I might, it was nowhere to be found. She must have taken it with her.

Once again Shimamoto had disappeared from my life. This time, though, leaving nothing to pin my hopes on. No more *probably*s. No more *for a while*s.

I got back to Tokyo a little before four. Hoping against hope that Shimamoto would return, I had stayed at the cottage in Hakone until past noon. Waiting was torture, so I killed time by cleaning the kitchen and rearranging all the clothes in the house. The silence was oppressive; the occasional sounds of birds and cars struck me as unnatural, out of sync. Every sound was twisted and crushed beneath the weight of some unstoppable force. And in the midst of this, I waited for something to happen. *Something's* got to happen, I felt sure. It can't end like this.

But nothing happened. Once she made up her mind, Shimamoto wasn't the type of woman to change it. I had to get back to Tokyo. It seemed farfetched, but if she

did try to get in touch with me, she'd do it through the club. At any rate, staying in the cottage any longer made no sense.

Driving back, I had to force myself to concentrate. I missed curves, nearly ran red lights, and swerved into the wrong lane. When I arrived at the club parking lot, I called home from a phone booth. I told Yukiko I was back and that I was going straight to work.

"You had me worried. At least you could have called." Her voice sounded hard and dry.

"I'm fine. Not to worry," I said. I had no idea how my voice sounded to her. "I don't have much time, so I'm going to the office to check over accounts, then directly on to the club."

At the office, I sat at my desk and somehow managed to pass the time until evening. I went over the previous night's events. Shimamoto must have gotten up while I was asleep and, without sleeping a wink herself, left before dawn. How she got back to the city I had no idea. The main road was far off, and at that hour of the morning it would have been next to impossible to get a bus or taxi in the hills around Hakone. And besides, she had on high heels.

Why did Shimamoto have to leave me like that? The entire time I drove back to Tokyo, the question had tormented me. I told her I would be hers, and she said she'd be mine. And dropping all defenses, we made love. Still, she left me alone, without so much as a word of explanation. She'd even taken the record she'd said was a present. There had to be some rhyme or reason to her actions, but logical thinking was beyond me. All

trains of thought were sidetracked. Forcing myself to think, I ended up with a dully throbbing head. I realized how worn out I was. I sat down on the bed in my office, leaned against the wall, and closed my eyes. Once they were closed, I couldn't pry them open. All I could do was remember. Like an endless tape loop, memories of the night before replayed themselves, over and over. Shimamoto's body. Her naked body as she lay by the stove with eyes closed, and every detail—her neck, her breasts, her sides, her pubic hair, her genitals, her back, her waist, her legs. They were all too close, too clear. Clearer and closer than if they were real.

Alone in that tiny room, I was soon driven to distraction by these graphic illusions. I fled the building and wandered aimlessly. Finally I went over to the club and shaved in the men's room. I hadn't washed my face the entire day. And I still wore the same clothes as the day before. My employees said nothing, though I could feel them glancing at me strangely. If I went home now and stood before Yukiko, I knew I would confess it all. How I loved Shimamoto, had spent the night with her, and was about to throw away everything—my home, my daughters, my work.

I know I should have told Yukiko everything. But I couldn't. Not then. I no longer had the power to distinguish right from wrong, or even grasp what had happened to me. So I didn't go home. I went to the club and waited for Shimamoto, knowing full well my wait would be in vain. First I checked at the other bar to see if she was there, then I waited at the counter of the Robin's Nest until the place closed. I talked with a few

of the regulars, but it was just so much background static. I made the appropriate listening noises, my head filled all the while with Shimamoto's body. How her vagina welcomed me ever so gently. And how she called out my name. Every time the phone rang, my heart pounded.

After the bar closed and everyone had headed home, I stayed there at the counter, drinking. No matter how much I drank, I couldn't get drunk. In fact, the more I drank, the clearer my head became. It was two a.m. when I arrived home, and Yukiko was up and waiting for me. Unable to sleep, I sat drinking whiskey alone at the kitchen table. She came in with her glass to join me.

"Put on some music," she said. I picked up a nearby cassette, flipped it into the deck, and turned down the volume so as not to wake the kids. We sat in silence for a while across the table from each other, drinking whiskey.

"You have somebody else you like, right?" Yukiko asked, staring straight at me.

I nodded. Her words had a decided outline and gravity. How many times had she gone over these words in her mind in preparation for this moment?

"And you really like that person. You're not just playing around."

"That's right," I said. "It's not just some fling. But it's not exactly what you're imagining."

"How do *you* know what I'm thinking?" she asked. "You actually believe you know what I'm thinking?"

I couldn't say a thing. Yukiko was silent too. The music played on softly. Vivaldi or Telemann. One of those. I couldn't recall the melody.

"I think it's likely you have no idea what I'm thinking," she said. She spoke slowly, enunciating each word distinctly, as if explaining something to the children. "I don't think you have any idea."

Seeing I wasn't going to respond, she lifted her glass and drank. And very slowly, she shook her head. "I'm not that stupid, I hope you know. I live with you, sleep with you. I've known for some time you like someone else."

I looked at her in silence.

"I'm not blaming you," she continued. "If you love someone else, there's not much anyone can do about it. You love who you love. I'm not enough for you. I know that. We've gotten along well, and you've taken good care of me. I've been very happy living with you. I think you still love me, but we can't escape the fact that I'm not enough for you. I knew this was going to happen. So I'm not blaming you for falling in love with another woman. I'm not angry, either. I should be, but I'm not. I just feel pain. A lot of pain. I thought I could imagine how much this would hurt, but I was wrong."

"I'm sorry," I said.

"There's no need to apologize," she said. "If you want to leave me, that's okay. I won't say a thing. Do you want to leave me?"

"I don't know," I replied. "Can I explain what's happened?"

"You mean about you and that woman?"

"Yes," I said.

She shook her head emphatically. "I don't want to hear anything about her. Don't make me suffer any more than I already have. I don't care what kind of rela-

tionship the two of you have, or what plans you've made. I don't want to hear about it. What I do want to know is whether or not you want to leave me. I don't need the house, or money—or anything. If you want the children, take them. I'm serious. If you want to leave me, just say the word. That's all I want to know. I don't want to hear anything else. Just yes or no."

"I don't know," I said.

"You mean you don't know if you want to leave me or not?"

"No. I don't know if I'm even capable of giving you an answer."

"When will you know?"

I shook my head.

"Well, then, take your time and think about it." She sighed. "I don't mind waiting. Take as long as you like."

Starting that night, I slept on the sofa in the living room. Sometimes the kids would get up in the middle of the night and ask me why I was sleeping there. I explained that my snoring was so loud these days that their mother and I decided to sleep in separate rooms. Otherwise Mom wouldn't get any sleep. One of the kids would snuggle up next to me on the sofa. And I would hug her tight. Sometimes I could hear Yukiko in the bedroom, crying.

For the next two weeks I spent every day endlessly reliving memories. I'd recall ever single detail of the night I spent with Shimamoto, trying to tease out some meaning. Trying to find a message. I remembered the warmth of her in my arms. Her arms sticking out of

the sleeves of her white dress. The Nat King Cole songs. The fire in the stove. I called up each and every word we spoke that night.

From out of those words, these of hers: *There is no middle ground with me. No middle-ground objects exist, and where there are no such objects, there is no middle ground.*

And these words of mine: *I've already decided, Shimamoto-san. I thought about it when you were gone, and I made my decision.*

I remembered her eyes, looking over at me in the car. That intense gaze burned into my cheeks. It was more than a mere glance. The smell of death hovered over her. She really was planning to die. That's why she came to Hakone—to die, together with me.

"And I will take all of you. Do you understand that? *Do you understand what that means?*"

When she said that, Shimamoto wanted my life. Only now did I understand.

I had come to a final conclusion, and so had she. Why was I so blind? After a night of making love, she planned to grab the steering wheel of the BMW as we drove back to Tokyo and kill us both. No other options remained for her. But something stopped her. And holding everything inside, she disappeared.

What desperate dead end had she reached? Why? And more important, who had driven her to such desperation? Why, finally, was death the only possible escape? I was grasping for clues, playing the detective, but I came up empty-handed. She just vanished, along with her secrets. No *probably*s or *in a while*s this time—she

just silently slipped away. Our bodies had become one, yet in the end she refused to open up her heart to me.

Some kinds of things, once they go forward, can never go back to where they began, Hajime, she would no doubt tell me. In the middle of the night, lying on my sofa, I could hear her voice spinning out these words. *Like you said, how wonderful it would be if the two of us could go off somewhere and begin life again. Unfortunately, I can't get out of where I am. It's a physical impossibility.*

And then Shimamoto was a sixteen-year-old girl again, standing in front of sunflowers in a garden, smiling shyly. *I really shouldn't have gone to see you. I knew that from the beginning. I could predict that it would turn out like this. But I couldn't stand not to. I just had to see you, and when I did, I had to speak with you. Hajime— that's me. I don't plan to, but everything I touch gets ruined in the end.*

I would never see her again, except in memory. She was here, and now she's gone. There is no middle ground. *Probably* is a word you may find south of the border. But never, ever west of the sun.

Every day, I scanned the papers from top to bottom for articles about women suicides. Lots of people kill themselves, I discovered, but it was always someone else. As far as I knew, this beautiful thirty-seven-year-old woman with the loveliest of smiles was still alive. Though she was gone from me forever.

On the surface, my days were the same as ever. I'd drive the kids back and forth to the nursery school, the three of us singing songs as we went. Sometimes in the line of

cars in front of the nursery school I'd see the young woman in the 260E, and we'd talk. Talking with her made me able to forget, at least for a while. Our subjects were limited, as always. We'd exchange the latest news about the Aoyama neighborhood, natural foods, clothes. The usual.

At work, too, I made my usual rounds. I'd put on my suit and go to the bars every night, make small talk with the regulars, listen to the opinions and complaints of the staff, remember little things like giving a birthday present to an employee. Treat musicians who happened to drop by to dinner, check the cocktails to make sure they were up to par, make sure the piano was in tune, keep an eye out for rowdy drunks—I did it all. Any problems, I straightened out in a flash. Everything ran like clockwork, but the thrill was gone. No one suspected, though. On the surface I was the same as always. Actually, I was friendlier, kinder, more talkative than ever. But as I sat on a barstool, looking around my establishment, everything looked monotonous, lusterless. No longer a carefully crafted, colorful castle in the air, what lay before me was a typical noisy bar—artificial, superficial, and shabby. A stage setting, props built for the sole purpose of getting drunks to part with their cash. Any illusions to the contrary had disappeared in a puff of smoke. All because Shimamoto would never grace these places again. Never again would she sit at the bar; never again would I see her smile as she ordered a drink.

My routine at home was unchanged too. I ate dinner with the family and on Sundays took the kids for a walk or to the zoo. Yukiko, at least on the surface, treated me

as she always had. We talked about all kinds of things. We were like childhood friends who happened to be living under the same roof. There were certain words we couldn't speak, certain facts we didn't acknowledge. But there was no unconcealed hostility in the air. We just didn't touch each other. At night we slept separately—I on the sofa, Yukiko in the bedroom. Outwardly, that was the only change in our lives.

Sometimes I couldn't stand how we were just going through the motions, acting out our assigned roles. Something crucial to us was lost, yet still we could carry on as before. I felt awful. This kind of empty, meaningless life was hurting Yukiko deeply. I wanted to give her an answer to her question, but I couldn't. Of course I didn't want to leave her, but who was I to say that? Me— the guy who was going to throw his whole family away. Just because Shimamoto was gone, never to return, didn't mean I could blithely bounce back to the life I'd had and pretend nothing had happened. Life isn't that easy, and I don't think it should be. Besides, lingering images of Shimamoto were still too clear, too real. Every time I closed my eyes, every detail of her body floated before me. My palms remembered the feel of her skin, and her voice whispering in my ear wouldn't leave me. I couldn't make love to Yukiko with those images still implanted so firmly in my brain.

I wanted to be alone, so knowing nothing else, I went swimming every morning at the pool. Then I'd go to my office, stare at the ceiling, and lose myself in daydreams of Shimamoto. With Yukiko's question hanging before me unanswered, I was living in a void. I couldn't go on

forever like that. It just wasn't right. As a human being, as a husband, as a father, I had to live up to my responsibilities. Yet as long as these illusions surrounded me, I was paralyzed. It was even worse whenever it rained, for then I was struck by the delusion that Shimamoto would show up: quietly opening the door, bringing with her the scent of rain. I could picture the smile on her face. When I said something wrong, she would silently shake her head, smiling all the while. All my words lost their strength and, like raindrops glued to the window, slowly parted company with reality. On rainy nights I could barely breathe. The rain twisted time and reality.

When I grew exhausted with these visions, I stared at the scenery outside. I was abandoned in a lifeless, dried-out land. Visions had drained color from the world. Everything, every scene before me, lay flat, mere makeshift. Every object was gritty, the color of sand. The parting words of my old high school classmate haunted me. *Lots of different ways to live. And lots of different ways to die. But in the end ... all that remains is a desert.*

The following week, as if lying in wait, strange events ambushed me one after another. On Monday morning, for no special reason I recalled the envelope with one hundred thousand yen and decided to look for it. Many years before, I'd put it in a drawer in the desk in my office, a locked drawer, second from the top. When I moved into the office, I put some other valuables together with the envelope in that drawer; other than oc-

casionally checking to see that it was there, I never touched it. But now the envelope was gone. This was strange, uncanny even, for I had absolutely no memory of moving it. I was absolutely certain of that. Just to make sure, I pulled open the other drawers and checked them from top to bottom. No envelope.

I tried to remember when I'd last seen it. I couldn't pin down an exact date. It wasn't all that long ago, but not so recently, either. A month ago, maybe two. Three at the most.

Bewildered, I sat down on my chair and stared at the drawer. Maybe someone had broken into the room, unlocked the drawer, and removed the envelope. That wasn't likely, though—the drawer contained more cash and valuables, which were untouched. Yet it *was* within the realm of possibility. Or maybe unconsciously I'd disposed of the envelope and for whatever reason erased the memory from my mind. Okay, I told myself, what does it matter? I was going to get rid of it someday. I just saved myself the trouble, right?

But once I acknowledged that the envelope had disappeared, its existence and nonexistence traded places in my consciousness. A strange feeling, like vertigo, took hold of me. A conviction that the envelope had never actually existed swelled up inside me, violently chipping away at my mind, crushing and greedily devouring the certainty I'd had that the envelope was *real*.

Because memory and sensations are so uncertain, so biased, we always rely on a certain reality—call it an *alternate* reality—to prove the reality of events. To what extent facts we recognize as such really *are* as they seem, and to what extent these are facts merely because we

label them as such, is an impossible distinction to draw. Therefore, in order to pin down reality *as* reality, we need another reality to relativize the first. Yet that other reality requires a third reality to serve as its grounding. An endless chain is created within our consciousness, and it is the very maintenance of this chain that produces the sensation that we are actually here, that we ourselves exist. But something can happen to sever that chain, and we are at a loss. What is real? Is reality on this side of the break in the chain? Or over there, on the other side?

What I felt at that point, then, was this kind of cut-off sensation. I closed the drawer, deciding to forget all about it. I should have thrown that money away when I first got it. Keeping it was a mistake.

On Wednesday afternoon of the same week, I was driving down Gaien Higashidori, when I spied a woman who resembled Shimamoto. She had on blue cotton pants, a beige raincoat, and white deck shoes. And she dragged one leg as she walked. As soon as I saw her, everything around me froze. A lump of air forced its way up from my chest to my throat. *Shimamoto,* I thought. I drove past her to check her out in the rearview mirror, but her face was hidden in the crowd. I slammed on my brakes, getting an earful of horn from the car behind me. The way the woman held herself, and the length of her hair—it was Shimamoto exactly. I wanted to stop the car right then and there, but all the parking spots along the road were full. Two hundred meters or so ahead, I finally found a place and managed to squeeze my car in, then I ran back to find her. But she

was nowhere to be seen. I ran around like a lunatic. She had a bad leg, so she couldn't have gone too far, I told myself. Shoving people aside, jaywalking across streets, I ran up the pedestrian overpass and looked down on all the passersby below. My shirt was soaked with sweat. Soon, though, a revelation dawned on me. She had been dragging the opposite leg. *And Shimamoto's leg was no longer bad.*

I shook my head and sighed deeply. Something must be wrong with me. I felt dizzy, all my strength drained away. Leaning against the crosswalk signal, I stared at my feet for a while. The signal turned from green to red, from red to green again. People crossed the street, waited, crossed, with me immobile, collapsed against the post, gasping for breath.

Suddenly I looked up and saw Izumi's face. Izumi was in a taxi stopped right in front of me. From the rear-seat window, she was staring right at me. The taxi had halted at the red light, and at most, three feet separated her face and mine. She was no longer the seventeen-year-old girl I used to know, but I recognized her at once. The girl I'd held in my arms twenty years before, the first girl I kissed. The girl who, on that fall afternoon so long ago, took off her clothes and lost the clasp to her garter belt. People might change in twenty years' time, but I knew this was her. *Children are afraid of her,* my old classmate said. When I'd heard that, I didn't understand what he meant. I couldn't grasp what those words were attempting to convey. But now, with Izumi right before my eyes, I understood. Her face had nothing you could call an expression. No, that's not an entirely accurate way of putting it. I should put it this

way: Like a room from which every last stick of furniture had been taken, anything you could possibly call an expression had been removed, leaving nothing behind. Not a trace of feeling grazed her face; it was like the bottom of a deep ocean, silent and dead. And with that utterly expressionless face, she was staring at me. At least I think she was looking at me. Her eyes were gazing straight ahead in my direction, yet her face showed me nothing. Or rather, what it showed was this: an infinite blank.

I stood there dumbfounded, speechless. Barely able to support my body, I breathed slowly. For a moment or two, my sense of self really did break down, its very outlines melting away into a thick, syrupy goo. Unconsciously I reached out my hand and touched the window of the cab, stroked the surface of the glass with my fingertips. I had no idea why. A couple of passersby, startled, stopped and stared. But I couldn't help myself. Through the glass, I slowly stroked that faceless face. Izumi didn't move a muscle or so much as blink. Was she dead? No, not dead. She was still alive, in an unblinking world. In a deep, silent world behind that pane of glass, she lived. And her lips, motionless, spoke of an infinite nothingness.

The light finally changed to green, and the taxi took off. Izumi's face was unchanged to the end. I stood rooted to the spot, watching until the taxi was swallowed up in the surge of cars.

I walked back to my car and slumped into the seat. I had to get out of there. As I was about to turn on the engine I was hit by a sudden wave of nausea. Like I was

going to spew my guts out. But I didn't vomit. Resting both hands on the steering wheel, I sat there for a good fifteen minutes. My underarms were drenched in sweat, and an awful smell rose from my body. This wasn't the body that Shimamoto had so gently loved. It was the body of a middle-aged man, giving off an awful acrid stink.

A few minutes later, a patrolman came up to my car and knocked on the window. I rolled it down. "You can't park here, pal," he said, looking around inside. "Get your car out of here." I nodded and started the motor.

"You look terrible. Do you feel sick?" the policeman asked me.

Wordlessly, I shook my head. And started driving.

It took me several hours to recover. I was drained, completely, leaving an empty shell behind. A hollow sound reverberated through my body. I parked my car inside Aoyama Cemetery and stared listlessly through the windshield at the sky beyond. Izumi was waiting for me there. She was always somewhere, waiting for me. On some street corner, beyond some pane of glass, waiting for me to appear. Watching me. I just hadn't noticed.

For several days afterward, I couldn't speak. I'd open my mouth to talk, but the words would disappear, as if the utter nothingness that was Izumi had taken over.

After that strange encounter, though, the afterimages of Shimamoto began, gradually, to fade. Color returned to the world, and I no longer had the helpless feeling that I was walking on the surface of the moon. Vaguely, as if looking through a glass window at changes hap-

pening to someone else, I could detect a minute shift in gravity and a gradual sloughing off of something that had clung to me.

Something inside me was severed, and disappeared. Silently. Forever.

While the trio was on break, I went up to the pianist and told him he no longer needed to play "Star-Crossed Lovers." I mustered up the friendliest smile I could. "You've played it for me enough. It's about time to stop."

He looked at me as if weighing something in his mind. The two of us were friends, had shared a few drinks and gone beyond your usual polite conversation.

"I don't quite understand," he said. "You don't want me to go out of my way to play that song? Or you don't want me to ever play that song again? There's a big difference, and I'd like to be clear about this."

"I don't want you to play it," I said.

"You don't like the way I play it?"

"I have no problems with your playing. It's great. There aren't many people who can handle that tune the way you do."

"So it's the tune itself you don't want to hear anymore?"

"You could say that," I replied.

"Sounds a little like *Casablanca* to me!" he said.

"Guess so," I said.

After that, sometimes when he catches sight of me, the pianist breaks into a few bars of "As Time Goes By."

The reason I didn't want to hear that tune again had nothing to do with memories of Shimamoto. *The song*

just didn't do to me what it used to. Why, I can't say. The special something I'd found ages ago in that melody was no longer there. It was still a beautiful tune, but nothing more. And I had no intention of lingering over the corpse of a beautiful song.

"What are you thinking about?" Yukiko asked me as she came into the room.

It was two-thirty in the morning. I was lying on the sofa, staring at the ceiling.

"I was thinking about a desert," I said.

"A desert?" she asked. She'd sat down next to my feet and was looking at me. "What kind of desert?"

"Just a regular desert. With sand dunes and a few cactuses. Lots of things are there, living there."

"Am I included in this desert too?" she asked.

"Of course you are," I said. "All of us are living there. But actually what's really living is the desert itself. Like in the movie."

"What movie?"

"The Disney film *The Living Desert*. A documentary about the desert. Didn't you see it when you were little?"

"No," she said. I thought that was a bit strange. Everybody in my elementary school had been herded off to the movie theater to watch it. But Yukiko was five years younger than me. She might have been too young to see it when it came out.

"Why don't we rent it next Sunday and watch it together? It's a good movie. The scenery's beautiful, and there're all sorts of animals and flowers. The kids will like it."

Yukiko smiled at me. It had been such a long time since I'd seen her smile.

"Do you want to leave me?" she asked.

"Yukiko, I love you," I said.

"Maybe you do, but I'm asking you whether you want to leave me. The answer is either yes or no. I won't accept any other."

"I don't want to leave you," I said. I shook my head. "I probably don't have the right to say this, but I don't want to leave you. If I left you now, I don't know what would happen to me. I don't want to be lonely ever again. I'd rather die."

She stretched out a hand and placed it on my chest. And looked deep into my eyes. "Forget about rights. I don't think anyone has those kinds of rights," she said.

Feeling the warmth of her hand on my chest, I thought of death. I might very well have died on that day on the highway with Shimamoto. If I had, my body would not exist. I would be gone, lost forever. Like so many other things. But here I am. And here is Yukiko's warm hand on my chest.

"Yukiko," I said, "I love you very much. I loved you from the first day I met you, and I still feel the same. If I hadn't met you, my life would have been unbearable. For that I am grateful beyond words. Yet here I am, hurting you. Because I'm a selfish, hopeless, worthless human being. For no apparent reason, I hurt the people around me and end up hurting myself. Ruining someone else's life and my own. Not because I like to. But that's how it ends up."

"No argument there," Yukiko said quietly. Traces of

her smile remained at the corners of her mouth. "You are definitely a selfish, hopeless person, and yes, you have hurt me."

I looked at her for a while. Nothing in her words seemed to blame me. She was neither angry nor sad. She was merely explaining the obvious.

I took my time, trying to find the right words. "I always feel like I'm struggling to become someone else. Like I'm trying to find a new place, grab hold of a new life, a new personality. I guess it's part of growing up, yet it's also an attempt to reinvent myself. By becoming a different me, I could free myself of everything. I seriously believed I could escape myself—as long as I made the effort. But I always hit a dead end. No matter where I go, I still end up me. What's missing never changes. The scenery may change, but I'm still the same old incomplete person. The same missing elements torture me with a hunger that I can never satisfy. I guess that lack itself is as close as I'll come to defining myself. For your sake, I'd like to become a new person. It may not be easy, but if I give it my best shot, perhaps I *can* manage to change. The truth is, though, if put in the same situation again, I might very well do the same thing all over. I might very well hurt you all over again. I can't promise anything. That's what I meant when I said I had no right. I just don't have the confidence to win over that force in me."

"And you've always been trying to escape that force?"

"I think so," I said.

Her hand still rested on my chest. "You poor man," she said. As if she were reading aloud something writ-

ten large on a wall. Maybe it really was written on the wall, I thought.

"I don't know what to say," I said. "I know I don't want to leave you. But I don't know if that's the correct answer. I don't even know if that's something I myself can choose. Yukiko, you're suffering. I can see that. I can feel your hand here. But there's something beyond what can be seen or felt. Call it feelings. Or possibilities. These well up from somewhere and are mixed together inside me. They're not something I can choose or can give an answer to."

Yukiko was silent for a long time. Every so often, a truck rolled by outside. I looked out the window but could see nothing. Just the unnamed time and space linking night and dawn.

"The last few weeks, I really did think I would die," Yukiko said. "I'm not saying this to threaten you. It's a fact. That's how lonely and sad I was. Dying is not that hard. Like the air being sucked slowly out of a room, the will to live was slowly seeping out of me. When you feel like that, dying doesn't seem like such a big deal. I never even thought of the children. What would happen to them after I died didn't enter my mind. That's how lonely I felt. You didn't know that, did you? You have never seriously given it any thought, have you? What I was feeling, what I was thinking, what I might do."

I didn't say anything. She took her hand away from my chest and laid it in her lap.

"Anyhow, the reason I didn't die, the reason I'm still alive, is that I thought if you were to come back to me, I

would be able to take you back. It's not a question of rights, or right or wrong. Maybe you are a hopeless person. A worthless person. And you might very well hurt me again. But that's not what's important here. You don't understand a thing."

"Most likely I don't," I said.

"And you don't ask anything," she said.

I opened my mouth to say something, but the words wouldn't come out. She was right: I never did ask her anything. Why didn't I? I had no idea.

"Rights are what you build from here on out," Yukiko said. "Or rather, *we* build. We thought we'd constructed a lot together, but actually we hadn't made a thing. Life went too smoothly. We were too happy. Don't you think so?"

I nodded.

Yukiko folded her arms over her chest and looked at me. "I used to have dreams too, you know. But somewhere along the line they disappeared. Before I met you. I killed them. I crushed them and threw them away. Like some internal organ you no longer need and you rip out of your body. I don't know whether that was the right thing to do. But it was the only thing I could do at the time.... Sometimes I have this dream. The same dream over and over. Someone is carrying something in both hands, and comes up to me and says, 'Here, you've forgotten something.' I've been very happy living with you. I've wanted for nothing and never had any complaints. Still, something is chasing me. I wake up in the middle of the night, covered in sweat. I'm being chased by what I threw away. You think you're the only one

being chased, but you're wrong. You're not the only one who's thrown away something, who's lost something. Do you understand what I'm saying?"

"I think so," I said.

"Maybe you will hurt me again. I don't know how I'll react then. Or maybe next time I'll hurt you. No one can promise anything. Neither of us can make any promises. But I do still love you."

I held her and stroked her hair.

"Yukiko," I said, "tomorrow let's begin again. It's too late today. I want to start out the right way, with a brand-new day."

Yukiko looked at me for a while. "I think that you still haven't asked me anything."

"I'd like to start a new life beginning tomorrow. What do you think?" I asked.

"I think that's a good idea," she said, a faint smile on her lips.

After Yukiko went back to the bedroom, I lay for a while on the sofa, staring at the ceiling. It was an ordinary apartment ceiling, nothing special. But still I stared at it closely. Every once in a while, a car's headlights would shine on it. I had no more illusions. The feel of Shimamoto's breasts, her voice, the scent of her skin—all had faded. Izumi's expressionless face floated across my mind. And the feel of the taxi's window separating us. I closed my eyes and thought of Yukiko. Again and again I thought over what she had said. Eyes closed, I listened to the movements within my body. I might very well be changing. And I had to change.

I don't know if I have the strength to care for Yukiko and the children, I thought. No more visions can help me, weaving special dreams just for me. As far as the eye can see, the void is simply that—a void. I've been in that void before and forced myself to adjust. And now, finally, I end up where I began, and I'd better get used to it. No one will weave dreams for me—it is my turn to weave dreams for others. That's what I have to do. Such dreams may have no power, but if my own life is to have any meaning at all, that is what I have to do.

Probably.

As the dawn approached, I gave up trying to sleep. I threw a cardigan over my pajamas, padded out to the kitchen, and made some coffee. I sat at the kitchen table and watched the sky grow lighter by the minute. It had been a long time since I'd seen the dawn. At one end of the sky a line of blue appeared, and like blue ink on a piece of paper, it spread slowly across the horizon. If you gathered together all the shades of blue in the world and picked the bluest, the epitome of blue, this was the color you would choose. I rested my elbows on the table and looked at that scene, my mind blank. When the sun showed itself over the horizon, that blue was swallowed up by ordinary sunlight. A single cloud floated above the cemetery, a pure white cloud, its edges distinct. A cloud so sharply etched you could write on it. A new day had begun. But what this day would bring, I had no idea.

I would take my daughters to nursery school and go swimming. The same as always. I remembered the pool I used to swim in during junior high. The smell of the

place, the way voices echoed off the ceiling. I was in the midst of becoming something new. Standing in front of the mirror, I could see the changes in my body. At night, in the stillness, I swore I could hear the sound of my flesh growing. I was about to be clothed in a new self, about to step into a place where I'd never been.

Sitting at the kitchen table, I watched the single cloud over the cemetery. The cloud didn't move an inch. It was stationary, nailed to the spot. Time to wake my daughters. It was well past dawn, and they had to get up. They were the ones who needed this new day, much more than I ever would. I'd go to their bedroom, pull back the covers, rest my hand on their warm bodies, and announce the beginning of a new day. That's what I had to do. But somehow I couldn't stand up from the kitchen table. All strength was drained from my body, as if someone had snuck up behind me and silently pulled the plug. Both elbows on the table, I covered my face with my palms.

Inside that darkness, I saw rain falling on the sea. Rain softly falling on a vast sea, with no one there to see it. The rain strikes the surface of the sea, yet even the fish don't know it is raining.

Until someone came and lightly rested a hand on my shoulder, my thoughts were of the sea.

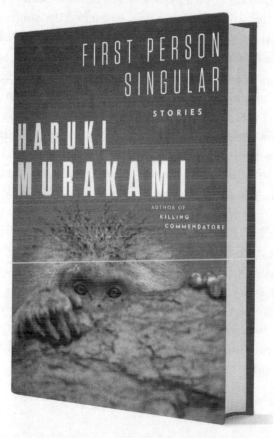